Ivy Pembroke is a law professor who specialises in copyright and trademark law, with a focus on fanfiction. An enthusiastic writer all her life, she loves the backspace button, overuses italics in emails with friends, and thinks there is little better than a story that makes you smile. She splits her time between Mississippi and her home state of Rhode Island.

Also by Ivy Pembroke

Snowflakes on Christmas Street

A Wedding on Christmas Street

Ivy Pembroke

sphere

SPHERE

First published in Great Britain in 2018 in eBook by Sphere
First published in Great Britain in 2019 by Sphere

3 5 7 9 10 8 6 4 2

A CIP catalogue record for this book
is available from the British Library.

ISBN 978-0-7515-7364-0

Typeset in Palatino by M Rules
Printed and bound in Great Britain by
Clays Ltd, Elcograf S.p.A.

Papers used by Sphere are from well-managed forests
and other responsible sources.

MIX
Paper from
responsible sources
FSC
www.fsc.org
FSC® C104740

Sphere
An imprint of
Little, Brown Book Group
Carmelite House
50 Victoria Embankment
London EC4Y 0DZ

An Hachette UK Company
www.hachette.co.uk

www.littlebrown.co.uk

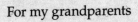
For my grandparents

Prologue

If Jack the Christmas Street dog were to tell you this story, he would tell you that it's about a special group of people who decided that they were better off all together than they were apart.

And Jack's favourite moments on the street were when everyone was indeed all together. The best days were the days when they had parties, and not just because the best quality and amount of food was slipped to him on those days. It was because, on party days, it was the ideal world for a dog: there was nothing but love, everywhere, all around him.

Jack doesn't think very much about the passage of time. He doesn't worry about how the days and weeks and months slip by, turning into years; he doesn't wonder how babies start to crawl and new lovers age into old and children have another year of school to start. Jack doesn't think about those things; they just happen.

And they happen just as much on Christmas Street as they do everywhere. Jack doesn't notice. But Jack isn't telling this story. And to the humans on Christmas Street, the passage of time means new beginnings, new questions, and new neighbours.

Chapter 1

It's already time for another school year! Where did the summer hols go? We here at Turtledove Primary School look forward to welcoming all of our students back for another year filled with fun learning!

'Coo, coo,' said Sam Bishop, and held up the post, where in among the usual junk mail was an actual letter from Turtledove Primary School.

Libby Quinn looked up from where she and Teddy were working on a jigsaw laid out on the coffee table and grinned. 'Oh, look, that means school is around the corner!'

Teddy groaned dramatically and fell backwards onto the floor. Jack, the street dog who happened to be visiting them at the moment, came over to Teddy, tail wagging, to make sure he was okay, and sniffed at him curiously.

'Oh, please!' Libby laughed at Teddy. 'As a teacher, I am mortally offended by your behaviour right now. School is a delightful place you should be happy to return to.'

'I'd be happy if *you* were still my teacher,' Teddy said. 'I don't know about this *new* person.'

Sam was rather glad Libby was no longer Teddy's teacher; it

made the fact that Libby was now Sam's girlfriend much easier to deal with. 'Mrs Dash,' Sam announced, reading from the letter. 'She sounds nice.'

'You're basing that off her *name*,' Teddy said, and Sam thought how Teddy at the ripe old age of nine was exponentially more pitying of his father's hopeless cluelessness than he had been at the age of eight. 'How can you possibly know anything based on her *name*? She *sounds* nice? So did Maleficent.'

'Actually, Maleficent sounds evil, like the word "malevolent",' replied Sam.

Teddy made the epic sound of disgust perfected by sons with regard to fathers.

'Well,' Libby said, 'I know Mrs Dash, so I can say, on more than the basis of just her name, that she's a wonderful teacher and you're going to have a great year.'

Teddy made a face.

'Coo coo,' said Sam, using the traditional Turtledove Primary School method of greeting, and waved the school letter around.

That night, getting ready for bed, Libby groaned dramatically and Sam lifted an eyebrow at her. 'You sound just like Teddy.'

'I can't help it,' said Libby. 'School is right around the corner!'

Sam laughed and crawled onto the bed with her. 'What happened to being mortally offended at the idea that going back to school isn't the best thing to ever happen?'

'Oh, that's just show for the kids,' Libby said. 'The end of summer hols is always *terrible*. New kids to get used to, new morning routines to develop ...'

'I'm sure the new kids will be great,' Sam said. 'And I hear good things about your new morning routine.'

'Oh, do you?' said Libby, grinning up at him.

'I hear your new morning routine makes really excellent breakfasts.'

'You burn, like, *everything*,' said Libby.

'I suppose I do,' Sam replied good-naturedly.

'I mean, the only thing I can really truly trust you with is cereal,' Libby continued.

'I have other advantages,' said Sam, leaning over her.

'Oh, do you? What are they, exactly?'

'Ha,' said Sam. 'You're so hilarious.'

'That's one of *my* advantages.'

'I can't even argue with that,' sighed Sam, settling on his back next to her. 'You win.'

'Do I?'

'I mean, it's true that you're hilarious and I'm bad with everything but cereal.'

'I have every confidence that if there were a way to burn cereal, you would find it.'

'Thank you for your support in the matter,' replied Sam gravely.

There was a moment of companionable silence. From the Pachuta side of the wall came the sound of Emilia on the drums.

Libby remarked, 'I can't believe Teddy sleeps through that.'

'I don't think he does,' Sam responded drily. 'Pretty sure he just stays up as late as he pleases. We're the old folks who are too exhausted to keep up with him.'

'Speak for yourself,' said Libby, and gave Sam a little affectionate nudge.

Sam chuckled. 'Fair enough.'

There was another moment of silence, and then Libby ventured, 'I had a great summer.'

Sam turned his head to look at her next to him on the bed. 'Me, too.'

She smiled at him, laugh lines crinkling along her eyes, and Sam kissed the tip of her nose because he couldn't help it. Sometimes she was too adorable not to be kissed.

'It's been a great year,' said Libby.

'Has it been a whole year?'

'Basically. I mean, definitely since we first met in the supermarket.'

'Ah, yes, and I wooed you over beetroot.'

'It was all very smooth, and stunningly romantic.'

'I'll never forget how you looked standing there holding your carrots,' said Sam, and curled a strand of Libby's auburn hair around his finger. 'And I'll also never forget how you looked when I walked into that school classroom and realised you were my son's teacher.'

Libby laughed. 'Well, imagine my shock in return!'

'I feel like you should have warned me when you met Teddy in the market! You could have said, "I teach little boys around your age, just FYI."'

'I can't just go around saying that to every little boy I encounter! That would be creepy!'

'Well, it would be weirder for me to ask every person I encounter, "Do you think you might be my son's teacher?"'

Libby snorted. 'Well, I'll tell you one thing. I don't think you've ever met Mrs Dash. She is a person you'd remember meeting.'

'Oh, no,' said Sam, stomach sinking a little. 'That doesn't sound like Teddy's going to be in for a good year.'

'Oh, he'll be fine. Mrs Dash is a great teacher, really good with the students, they all adore her. It's just that she's also a *character*.'

'And what does that mean?'

'Hmm.' Libby gazed at him reflectively for a moment, then grinned. 'No, no, I think I'll let you see for yourself. It'll be a delightful surprise for you.'

'Impossible,' Sam said. 'There's no way she could be a more delightful surprise than you.'

Libby, after a moment, leaned forward and kissed him, smiling softly.

The house seemed unbearably quiet without Libby and Teddy in it. Sam wasn't used to that any more. He wandered through the rooms feeling a little sorry for himself in his loneliness and wishing he hadn't let Jack out to visit Bill Hammersley next door.

Which was probably the most selfish thought he'd had in a while. Jack belonged to the entire street and needed to visit everyone, and also Bill, who was older and lived by himself and didn't have any visitors other than Jack and the rest of the street, especially needed the company (even if he liked to pretend that he loved to be alone).

Sam was supposed to be working. He had a million items on his to-do list. But he always had a million items on his to-do list, so that didn't exactly inspire him with ambition. He was never going to finish them all, so he might as well take a few minutes and call his sister Ellen.

She answered with, 'Hello, little brother. How are things?'

'Fine,' he said automatically. 'What are you up to? Are you busy?'

'Between clients at the mo,' she replied. 'So I'm all yours, good timing. I mean to ring you anyway.'

'Oh?'

'Sophie and Evie want to take some photos of the designs they did for your house.'

This gave Sam pause. His teenage nieces had been enthusiastic decorators but their designs hadn't been what anyone would call *practical*. 'I, uh, took the stalactites in the lounge down. They remember that, right?'

'Yes, but you left up that wallpaper they chose.'

'Because wallpaper is an enormous bloody pain to remove,' Sam pointed out.

'Anyway, they want the photos for their portfolio.'

'Their ... portfolio?'

'Their design portfolio.'

'They have a design portfolio?'

'Online,' Ellen said impatiently, as if Sam wasn't making any sense at all.

'Correct me if I'm wrong, but aren't they teenagers? They aren't even in uni yet.'

'Sam, waiting for uni to start your career is so last century, please enter the modern world with the rest of us. Teens have to start driving their online brand as soon as possible, and the photos from your house will really help Sophie and Evie.'

'Wow,' said Sam. 'I'm reconsidering the idea of having a teenager.'

'Too late,' Ellen replied blithely. 'You already have your child well on his way.'

'Damn,' said Sam.

'So anyway, we'll probably be by at some point so the girls can take photos. And I can probably bring some takeaway on whatever night I come, so Libby doesn't have to cook and she doesn't have to eat whatever you try to cook. Bonus all-round for her.'

'Everyone has been so hard on my cooking lately,' said Sam. 'It's been a theme.'

'Easy target,' Ellen explained.

'It is that,' Sam agreed, and let the conversation lapse.

'Sam?' Ellen asked after a moment.

'Still here,' he confirmed.

'You called me,' she told him. 'Was there something you wanted?'

'I . . .' Now that he had rung Ellen and found himself having to say the words out loud, he had a momentary moment of panic. What the hell was he doing? Why had he decided that he could do any of this? It was utter madness and Ellen was going to call him on it immediately.

And then he looked at the photo on his laptop, open so that he could ostensibly work. It was a selfie he'd taken of himself and Teddy and Libby on an outing to the Cotswolds they'd had over the summer. In it, Libby and Teddy were clutching ice creams and balancing on an old stone wall, and they were both laughing at the position he'd had to contort into in order to capture the selfie. It had been a golden, gorgeous afternoon, and in the long, dusky twilight Teddy had ducked into a hedgerow to explore and Sam had kissed Libby back against the branches and neither one of them had protested at the scratchy, unyielding prickliness of their touch. On that day, on the way home, Sam had thought of other moments from his past, of other joyful, oblivious kisses punctuating stolen, secret, insulated days, and how unlikely they had seemed to reoccur. And how now he . . . had them again.

'I'm going to ask Libby to marry me,' he heard himself say to Ellen, his voice steady and matter-of-fact, the statement as unremarkable as a statement about the weather or the grocery list, as undeniable, as inevitable.

Ellen screamed loudly enough that Sam had to hold the phone away from his ear.

Teddy arrived home from school first, walking back as usual with Pari Basak, his best friend who lived two doors down. Sam waited outside for them, and Bill came out to join him, letting Jack loose into the street.

'He's been moping all day about the children being gone,' grumbled Bill, obviously trying to sound like he didn't approve. But Sam, of course, knew by now that Bill's default position of disapproval was just an act.

'He and I should have moped together,' Sam remarked. 'It was bloody lonely in my house all day.'

'Lonely,' harrumphed Bill. 'In my day, we didn't go on about such nonsense. Lonely! We called it peace and quiet and we got stuff done.'

'Yes,' Sam agreed, hiding his fond smile because it would only make Bill grumble more.

Teddy and Pari appeared at the top of the street, and Jack barked as loudly as possible to alert everyone to their presence, circling around them and making little leaps and pirouettes to punctuate his glee. Pari was chattering a mile a minute to Teddy, who was interjecting every so often.

'Hello, kids,' Sam called out when they got close enough.

'Hi, Mr Bishop!' Pari called back happily, and waved enthusiastically.

Teddy waved as well. He didn't look as gleeful as Pari but he didn't look miserable either. He looked like he was doing some deep thinking about everything that had transpired at school.

'Hello, Teddy,' Bill said, with the guff sternness that betrayed his concern. 'How was school?'

'It was good,' Teddy said thoughtfully, and then burst into a smile, so Sam believed him. 'Can I go to Pari's for a bit?' Teddy asked him.

'Can you tell me how school was first?' Sam asked. 'How's your new teacher?'

'OMG,' said Pari.

'What does that mean?' asked Sam.

Pari rolled her eyes.

'*Dad*,' said Teddy, plainly embarrassed beyond words.

'I mean, I know what it *means*,' Sam defended himself indignantly. 'I know what it stands for. I just don't know what it means with regard to your new teacher.'

'She is *something*,' said Teddy emphatically, handing Sam his schoolbag, because apparently Sam's primary occupation these days was His Son's Butler.

'Something bad or something good?'

'She's *amazing*,' Pari said, as she and Teddy went running off.

'Something good!' Teddy called back.

'He's so informative,' remarked Sam to Bill.

'He said it was something good, that's good enough for me,' said Bill, and headed back into his house.

Sam carried Teddy's backpack into his own house.

'Mrs Dash is going to be my *hero*,' Pari announced, with firm finality.

'Who's this?' Emilia Pachuta asked. She dropped a bowl of grapes onto the coffee table for an after-school snack and sat next to Pari's older brother Sai on the floor. Sai was dating Emilia, who also lived next to them on Christmas Street, and so that meant that Emilia was always hanging out with them.

'Our new teacher,' Pari said.

'They have Mrs Dash,' Sai said.

'Ohhhh,' said Emilia. 'Yeah, totally hero material.'

'How was school for you two?' asked Pari.

'Dead pointless,' Sai said, 'because I could stay home all day streaming me playing videogames and making tons of money.'

'Not according to Dad,' Pari reminded him, because that had been a constant fight in the Basak household recently.

'Whatever,' Sai mumbled. 'Dad has no idea.'

'You should listen to your dad,' Emilia said. 'Videogames might be a good hobby but they're probably not going to be your career. I mean, you don't see me quitting school just because I've joined Amazing Spiders.'

'Joined what?' asked Teddy.

'Amazing Spiders. It's my band.'

'Oh,' said Teddy. 'Huh.'

'It's a great name, right?'

'Right,' said Teddy. 'Yeah, absolutely.'

'Teddy and I are going out into the back garden,' Pari announced, taking one final grape and standing, 'because we have a lot of work to do.'

'What sort of work do you lot have to do?' asked Sai, looking surprised.

'*Important* work,' said Pari, very importantly indeed, and then led the way outside confidently, followed by Teddy and Jack.

They all settled in the back garden, even Jack, who, understanding what a momentous occasion this meeting was, ignored the squirrels to sprawl out on the grass with them.

Pari said in a serious Grand Leader voice, 'I think the time has come to take what Mrs Dash said today to heart, and *make a difference*.' She tried to say it with the same impressive grandiosity Mrs Dash had used to say the phrase. She probably couldn't achieve quite Mrs Dash's level but Mrs Dash had had years of practice. Pari was sure she was still rather impressive.

Teddy said, 'Okay. How?'

Pari opened her mouth to inform him exactly how, and then closed it again, and then frowned. After a moment she said, 'Huh.'

Sam actually *was* working when Libby walked in, although he'd taken his laptop downstairs.

'Hello,' he said pleasantly. 'How'd your first day go?'

She smiled at him and dropped onto the couch next to him and disrupted the computer on his lap so she could kiss him. And then she said, 'Good. Really well. I just needed to get back and into the swing of things.'

'Good group of kids?' he asked.

'Yeah. They seem very sweet.'

'What about the parents? Any attractive parents?'

'I've found my attractive parent.'

'I was asking for me.'

'Ha ha,' said Libby. 'Where's Teddy? I was hoping to hear how his day went.'

'Well, naturally he is off with Pari, no doubt rehashing everything that happened. But he seemed to like Mrs Dash. Pari seems to think she's amazing.'

Libby chuckled. 'Yeah, she can have that effect. Well, I can't wait to hear Teddy's adventure of the day over dinner tonight.'

The doorbell rang.

Sam glanced toward the front door curiously. 'Who could that be?'

'Oh!' exclaimed Libby, and leapt to her feet. 'Oh, no! I'm totally running late!'

'Late?' echoed Sam, confused. 'Late for what?'

'Oh, God, did I forget to tell you?' said Libby, even as she rushed out to open the door. 'I told Pen I'd start going running with her after work.' Sam heard Libby open the front door and then say, 'Hi, Pen! I'm so sorry, I just got home and haven't changed yet.'

'That's okay,' Pen responded cheerfully. 'I can wait.'

'Give me two ticks,' said Libby. 'Sam's in here, you can chat with him.'

Libby went jogging up the stairs and Pen Cheever, the freelance writer who lived at the end of the street, came around the front door and into the lounge with Sam. 'Hiya,' she said.

'Hello,' Sam replied.

'You're not going running with us?'

'I am working,' Sam said, gesturing to his closed laptop on the side table. 'Very hard.'

'I am also working very hard. Running is great for writers' block. Plus, it can really clear the brain and give you a bump of energy. It's an endorphin rush. You know? I wrote an article on it once.'

'I am going to take your word on all of this,' said Sam amiably.

Libby came jogging back down the stairs.

'I can't convince Sam to come jogging with us,' said Pen.

'It's okay,' said Libby dismissively. 'He'd only cramp our style.'

'And what style is that?' asked Sam innocently.

'Ha.' Libby finished pulling her hair back in a ponytail. 'We have a lot of style.' She leaned over and pecked a kiss on Sam's lips. 'I'll be back later.'

'See you,' Sam said. 'Have a good run.'

And with that Libby and Pen went off to be healthy runners and Sam sat on his couch like a lump pretending to work.

Maybe, he thought, he should get out of the house.

Chapter 2

The latest trends in interior design will make you wonder why your walls are still the same boring shade they were when you moved in. And isn't it about time you did something about that horrible old carpet?

A few doors down on the street, Max and Arthur Tyler-Moss's house was the same level of base chaos that Sam had come to expect from it, but it was the sort of chaos that felt warm and welcoming and almost irresistible. It was chaos born of love and that was a different sort of chaos altogether.

Their adopted baby Charlie was crawling all over the place grabbing at anything he could, which sometimes was toys and sometimes was decidedly not a toy.

Either way, Max seemed calm about it.

'The house has been baby-proofed,' he said. 'Arthur was insistent. So maybe Charlie is playing with a couple of pots and pans, but it's fine.'

Charlie certainly seemed to agree, banging the pots and pans around with profound enthusiasm.

'So,' Max continued, setting tea down in front of Sam, 'to what do I owe this visit? The usual procrastination?'

'Yeah. Libby's started going running with Pen.'

'They didn't invite you?'

'Not exactly,' Sam hedged.

Max barked laughter. 'You didn't want to go.'

'Well, I mean—' Sam began to defend himself. Then he sighed. 'No, I didn't want to go.'

'I know exactly how you feel, and it's how I feel every time Arthur suggests that we develop a more balanced diet. Must our significant others have so much ambition?'

'I suppose it's part of why we love them,' Sam decided.

'Excellent point.'

And because Max was his friend and because it was the type of decision he kept feeling himself compelled to share with others, Sam raised his voice to be heard over the racket Charlie was making with the pots and pans and said, 'I've decided to ask Libby to marry me.'

Max gasped dramatically enough that Charlie stopped banging his kitchen tools to look at his father in concern. But then Max said, 'Oh, Sam, that's wonderful! Charlie, keep banging away, love, this calls for a celebration!'

'And what a celebration,' Sam said, pleased at the fuss and also vaguely embarrassed by it. He'd felt that way at Ellen's reaction, too.

'For what it's worth, not that you were waiting for my approval – or, I don't know, maybe you were, because I do have fabulous taste – but she's a catch and delightful and the two of you are delightful together so: huzzah, is my final assessment.'

'Huzzah?'

'Yes. It's apt.' Charlie banged particularly enthusiastically on his pot. 'Charlie agrees.'

'Well, good. I'm happy about the huzzah.'

'And also happy to be shortly engaged, I assume.'

'Yes. If she says yes. It's weird, I . . . ' Sam took a deep breath and exhaled into a heavy sigh. 'I keep thinking I should feel more conflicted.'

'You feel conflicted?'

'No, I keep thinking I *should* feel conflicted. And instead I . . . I don't. It doesn't feel like the last time I felt this way, but it shouldn't. And it doesn't feel like a betrayal of Sara, because it isn't. It just feels like . . . I always thought that I'd just *know*, if the right person ever came around again, if lightning struck twice. And . . . I did.'

Max smiled at him softly for a moment as Charlie banged away with his pots and pans. And then he said, 'I am not the right person to talk to about this.'

This surprised Sam, who would have thought Max was the perfect person to talk romance with. 'You're not?'

'I'm sure there are many people you could talk to who would be sensible and tell you that emotions aren't to be trusted and you should make decisions with your head instead of being carried away.'

'Is that what Arthur would say?' guessed Sam.

Max laughed. 'He would have done, when we first met. I don't think he would as much any more. But my point is that I'm never going to be the one to talk you out of this, mate, if that's what you were looking for.'

'No!' protested Sam. 'That's not what I was looking for at all! In fact, I wanted you to validate me!'

'I will absolutely validate you. I knew the moment I met Arthur that I was going to marry him.'

'I assumed,' said Sam, because ... yeah.

'So. How are you going to do it?'

'How am I going to do what?' asked Sam blankly.

'The proposal!' exclaimed Max, and looked down at Charlie. 'Sam is so very silly sometimes.'

'Oh,' said Sam. 'I don't know. I haven't really decided on anything yet.'

'Well, it's imperative,' said Max. 'You have to do it right. You're going to be telling this story the rest of your lives, so you want it to be a good one. It can't just be, "Oh, whilst we were washing the dishes one night, I asked her to marry me."'

'It would be unexpected, though,' Sam ventured.

Max gave him a look. 'Everyone might *say* it was a sweet surprise but they'd all be judging you on the inside.'

'Ah, but that's going to happen anyway,' joked Sam.

'How did you do it the first time? With Sara?'

'Oh, you know, I ...' Sam scratched his nose. 'We were washing the dishes.'

Max burst out laughing. 'Oh, no. Were you really?'

'Yeah,' Sam admitted.

'Well, I didn't mean to belittle you so directly when I came up with the dish-washing example.'

'It's okay.' Sam waved his hand around. 'It was doubtless a questionable tactic. I was young. It can be excused.'

'Yes. You are not excused this time around. You should come up with something spectacular.'

'Hmm,' said Sam. 'No pressure.'

Max shrugged.

'Did you propose to Arthur?' asked Sam.

'I did.'

'What did you do?'

'I bought a new suit.'

'Aww, you wore a dashing suit to propose to him?' said Sam.

Max looked indignant. 'How dull. No. I planted bits and pieces of the suit all along our house. It was a treasure hunt. The suit was designed to make sure Arthur was motivated to play along with the treasure hunt. He isn't always. But also he can seldom resist puzzles and logic games, and I knew that, so all the clues I created were meant to be intriguing little challenges for him. It was glorious, watching him try to work them out.' Max's expression grew soft as he reminisced, gazing into the middle distance. 'He was enjoying himself. He loved the suit and he was tickled I'd given him one. And then the last clue was for him to retrieve the tie, and I'd put it in this crowded jumble of a room that we'd used mainly for storage, and I'd drawn the curtains and disabled the light fixture, so that when he walked in it was dim, and I'd painted a million tiny stars in glow-in-the-dark paint all over the room, so it was basically glowing. They took forever to paint, really, I kept expecting Arthur to ask questions about my secret project but he's so good at just letting me talk about my art at my own pace so he never pressured me. And in the middle of the room I'd looped the tie through the ring I was giving him. And that's how I asked.'

Sam took a moment to envision it: the Arthur-centric treasure hunt, the suit, the glowing room. It was all as convoluted and over-the-top as he'd have expected from Max. He said, 'Was Arthur surprised?'

'I would have said no,' Max said. 'I mean, by the end, he *had* to know that something was up. But instead he seemed to be completely taken aback. I'm not sure it had entered Arthur's calculations of possibilities that someone would ask him to marry him.'

Sam smiled. 'And he said yes, obviously.'

'He did. But he said it was the new suit that sealed the deal. He was more excited about that than the ring.'

Sam laughed.

'I'm thinking of having some work done,' said Pen, because Pen was apparently one of those people who liked to talk while jogging, and also apparently could do the said talking without panting like an idiot because she was so out of breath from being so out of shape.

Libby was not that person.

'You look great,' she panted, like a person who was out of breath from being out of shape.

Pen laughed, and Libby nearly tripped and fell, because not only was Pen wanting to carry on a conversation, she also could *laugh*. Pen was clearly superhuman.

'Not that kind of work,' Pen said. 'House work. I don't know, I just feel like it's time for a change. I was doing this article on interior design trends.'

Of course she was. All of the things that got stuck in Pen's head were the result of articles she was working on.

'And anyway,' Pen continued, 'I found myself looking around my house and thinking, Wow. I do not have a single current

21

interior design trend in this entire house. Everything looks like it was something my grandma decided on. You know?'

Libby did know, because her own apartment had been like that, before she'd moved in with Sam. Sam's house was more updated only because Sam had just moved in and remodelled, and also Sam's nieces had definitely brought some flair into the interior design.

Libby huffed between her heaving breaths, 'So – what are you – thinking of?'

'It's a good question. Have you heard about shiplap? I don't know if I want to add shiplap. But just something with *wood*. I don't know. I think I probably need a carpenter. Do you know any good ones?'

'Not really,' Libby managed.

'Hmm,' mused Pen. 'I'll have to find myself one.'

Sam, helping Teddy set the table for dinner under Jack's watchful supervision, heard Libby call a cheerful farewell to Pen from the front door, saying, 'Same time tomorrow! Sounds good!' And then she dragged her way into the dining room.

'How was the run?' Sam asked, setting the last glass down.

'I'm going to die,' Libby announced dramatically. 'It was horrible. It was the worst thing I've ever done in my life.'

'You just said you'd do it again tomorrow,' Teddy pointed out.

'Oh, well, yeah,' said Libby. 'Obviously.'

22

Arthur tripped on one toy on his way into the house and two more at the entry to Max's studio, which was when he said, 'Something has to be done about the number of toys in this house.'

'We haven't enough storage,' Max said absently, frowning at the canvas in front of him.

'Or possibly we have one very spoiled little boy who has far too many toys,' said Arthur, attempting to be stern but failing entirely, because it was good to see Charlie after an entire day away. He picked him up out of his playpen and smothered him in kisses, listening to his giggles in response, and then he glanced back toward Max, who was now applying paint to the canvas. 'You're working?'

'For a bit more,' Max said. 'Can you take over Charlie duty?'

'With pleasure,' said Arthur, and brought Charlie back downstairs and attempted to organise Charlie's toys so that they would cease littering the entire house. It was slow going, though, since, every time he put a toy in a pile somewhere, Charlie grabbed it and crawled away with it to replace it in some less convenient place where Arthur was going to trip over it. 'You know,' Arthur told Charlie, 'your father and I used to have actual space in this house for *our* things. In the time before we had you. There was such a time.'

Charlie, a fist in his mouth, informed Arthur in very grave and wise babytalk that surely Arthur spoke nonsense, there had never been a time without Charlie and if there had been, it had definitely not had *things* in it. To punctuate this last point, Charlie held up a colourful block and displayed it to Arthur like a salesman, clearly extolling its virtues and why it had to be kept in the very centre of the room, in the direct path from the foot of the staircase.

'Fine,' Arthur sighed. 'You win. It is a lovely block that clearly needs to be displayed for all to see.'

'Listen to you,' Max said, coming down the stairs. 'You're already losing arguments, and he can't even talk yet. We haven't a chance when he's a teenager.'

'By then the entire house will be so full of Charlie's toys that none of us will be able to enter or leave anyway,' said Arthur.

Charlie nodded and babbled his affirmative support for this state of affairs.

Max chuckled and swept Charlie up and said, 'Shall we all have dinner of some sort? What exciting new food shall we try tonight, Charlie?'

'It's probably going to be some sort of pasta again,' Arthur remarked, 'as it's the only thing he's liked so far.'

'He's discerning,' Max said. 'You *would* raise a discerning child, so you can't possibly be heard to complain of it now.'

'I also thought I would raise a *neat* child,' said Arthur, stepping over a few more toys on their way to the kitchen.

'Well, that's my influence,' remarked Max, grinning. 'He had to take after me somehow.'

Max busied himself with poking his head into the fridge, whistling as he did so, and Arthur settled Charlie in his high-chair, and Jack arrived at their back door.

'Right on schedule,' said Max, as he grabbed some treats for the dog.

'You know he does this at every house, right?' said Arthur. 'He literally goes from house to house getting his dinner.'

'Would that we were all so lucky as Jack,' Max said, opening the door for him. 'How goes it, Jack? Is the street quiet tonight?'

'Ja!' exclaimed Charlie upon catching sight of the dog. It was

Charlie's first and so far only word. Arthur had had asked Max what it meant that Charlie had figured out how to say the dog's name before his dads', and Max had just laughed and laughed.

Jack, munching on the treats Max had given him, came up to Charlie's highchair, tail wagging amiably, and sniffed around for any food Charlie had dropped.

'You're too early tonight, Jack,' Arthur told him. 'Prince Charlie hasn't disdained any food by flinging it to the floor yet.'

'Hit the rest of the houses on the street,' Max told Jack, 'and then stop by again. We might have more of a feast for you.'

Jack, tail wagging in what Arthur could imagine was appreciation now, trotted back out into the night.

'Speaking of romantic things,' Max said suddenly, closing their back door.

Arthur looked at him, startled. 'Were we?'

'Well, Jack reminded me.'

'Of romantic things?'

'Of the look on your face when I asked you to marry me.'

Arthur lifted his eyebrows. 'Jack reminded you of that? I'm not sure I find that flattering.'

Max smiled. 'When you were following a complicated treasure hunt created just for you, it truly didn't enter your mind that it must be a prelude to a proposal?'

'I ...' Arthur hesitated before admitting, 'I didn't think we'd been dating each other long enough for you to have a proposal in mind.'

'We'd been dating almost a year,' Max pointed out.

'Yes. And I thought, at our year anniversary, maybe then would be the appropriate time to discuss marriage.'

'You thought in those last few weeks between when I

25

proposed and when we hit our year anniversary, you might reveal yourself to be someone I didn't want to marry?'

'Well.' Arthur shrugged. 'I don't know. Maybe. Anyway, you'd been proposing marriage since the first week, it was hard to know when to take you seriously.'

'When I created an entire treasure hunt just for your benefit, then you could take me seriously.'

'Well, yes, I realised that. What has you thinking of all of this?'

'Sam is going to propose to Libby.'

'Oh,' said Arthur, connecting the dots. 'That's why Jack reminded you of romance.'

'Indeed. And they have been dating even less than we were dating when I proposed, so please don't be too scandalised.'

Arthur smiled and accepted the bowl of pasta Max had put together for Charlie. 'I'm not scandalised. Our marriage has worked out well enough that I'm no longer committed to the idea of a set amount of time going by being necessary.'

'Well, I'm very honoured to have changed your mind on that,' said Max.

'For the time being,' said Arthur, and obediently demonstrated a pasta aeroplane flying around before swooping it towards Charlie's delighted mouth. 'I suppose he decided there was no longer a conflict of interest, now that Teddy has officially started with a new teacher.'

'Oh,' said Max. 'That is a very practical insurance-agent way of thinking about it, I suppose you're right. Anyway, I am delighted for the two of them but I am most distressed because he doesn't seem to have thought terribly hard about *how* he is going to propose.'

'He has time,' said Arthur, amused. 'And not everyone has to draft a whole treasure hunt for a proposal.'

'No,' Max allowed. 'But the best ones will.'

'You won't get any argument from me,' said Arthur gallantly.

Sam and Teddy allowed Libby to take a bath before dinner, because Libby said she desperately needed one and it wasn't like there was any meal being cooked whose timing needed to be adjusted.

'We'll just modify what time we run up to the Chinese,' Teddy assured her cheekily, and Sam said, 'Oi,' good-naturedly and ruffled Teddy's hair.

Eventually Sam and Teddy walked up to the Chinese together, and Jack emerged from his nightly ritual eating at everyone's house to keep them company.

'We really ought to stop everybody feeding Jack,' Sam remarked, 'now that we've caught on to his tricks. He doesn't need to eat six dinners a night.'

'He doesn't really do it for the eating,' Teddy said. 'He just likes to socialise. Is it his fault that people keep offering him food while the socialising is going on?'

'Indeed,' Sam agreed gravely, 'Jack is blameless in this whole affair.'

Teddy grinned.

Sam said, 'School really was all right?'

'Yeah, it was good. It was nice not to be the weird new kid any more. We've *another* weird new kid instead. His name is

Abeo and he's from Nigeria originally, although he's really just moved here from Birmingham.'

'And I hope you are being very nice to the new kid and not saying that he's "weird" just because he's new.'

Teddy gave Sam one of his long-suffering nine-year-old wisdom looks. 'Of *course*, Dad. Abeo's cool and Pari and I have already made friends with him. Pari says he's going to be the honorary member of our venture. She said that means he doesn't have to do anything but he'll still get all the benefits. Right?'

'Basically. What is your venture?'

'We don't know yet, but it's supposed to "Make a Difference."' Teddy put his fingers up into air quotes.

'Is this a homework assignment?' Sam asked.

'No. Just, Mrs Dash encourages all of us to Make a Difference. Just, like, in general. So Pari and I are going to do that somehow. We just haven't figured out how yet.'

Sam smiled. 'Well. Including Abeo as an honorary member in your venture is already making a difference, I think.'

Teddy shrugged, like it was no big deal, but Sam, thinking of how nervous and worried he had been that his son make friends at his new school, fit in, be liked, only just managed to hold himself back from smothering Teddy in an enthusiastic hug.

At their dinner table, over their takeaway, they discussed their adventures for the day, as was still their habit.

Sam said, 'My adventure for the day is getting used to the

two of you not being around any more. It was bonkers, how quiet the house was. *And* I can walk around in my pants all the time now.'

Teddy wrinkled his nose and said, 'Ew, gross,' and Sam grinned at him and said, 'And what was your adventure today?'

'The entire day was an adventure,' Teddy said, in a tone of great complaint. 'School starting up again, new teacher to get used to.'

'It *is* very difficult to break us teachers in,' remarked Libby. She was dressed casually, with her damp hair up in a pony-tail, and she looked cosy and refreshed after her run and its subsequent bath. She no longer looked like she thought death was imminent. Instead, like this, she made running look like the most appealing thing in the world.

'You know,' Sam remarked, 'the point of discussing our adventures is that they're supposed to be *good* things. Challenging things we're looking forward to tackling.'

Teddy looked at him sceptically.

Sam decided the argument wasn't worth it at the moment. 'What about you, Libby? What was your adventure today?'

'Running with Pen,' she answered, digging her chopsticks into her lo mein.

'See?' Teddy said. 'Libby didn't pick a good adventure, either!'

'Yes, I did,' Libby said. 'It was great running with Pen.'

'You said you wanted to die when you got back,' Teddy reminded her.

'Well, that's always what you say after you've done a run,' Libby said dismissively. 'Now I feel great. Anyway. It was

29

interesting, because Pen was telling me she wants to make a change to her house.'

'You were talking while you were running?' Sam asked.

'Well, Pen was. I kind of grunted in response. She's looking to hire a carpenter. Do we know any?'

'We know Bill, who does wooden figures,' said Sam, 'but I don't think he's a carpenter.'

'True. I'm not really sure what she intends to have done. I'm sure I'll hear about it on our next run.'

Chapter 3

Dear Mr Nketia – Thank you so much for your price
quotation for my home renovation project. I'm very excited
to get started! Looking forward to working with you! ☺
   Sincerely, Penelope Cheever

There were enough inhabitants of Christmas Street home
during the day that it wasn't unusual to find them popping
between each other's houses, procrastinating the work they
were supposed to be doing. It *was* unusual for them to all
descend *en masse*, as happened to Sam the next day, when
his doorbell rang and he opened it on Max, Charlie, Pen, and
Pari's mum Diya.

'Hi,' he said. 'Have I forgotten some sort of event?'

'*Sam!*' Pen exclaimed, and then swooped in and hugged
him fiercely.

'Er,' Sam said. 'Okay.' He looked at Max and Diya for clues.

Diya was frowning at him but that was so commonplace at
this point that it told him nothing.

Then she said, 'We *must* have a meeting on this. It's not like
you can be left to your own devices on such a significant matter.'

'What?' Sam said, baffled. 'What is happening right now?'

'Your proposal, of course!' Diya said. 'You know you are very bad at all of the romantic stuff. You need our help on this.'

Sam gave Max an ironic look. 'Really?' he said.

'You didn't exactly say it was a secret,' Max said.

'Well, I definitely don't want Libby knowing about it!'

'I only told Diya because I know that she was very involved in your courtship from the beginning,' Max continued.

'We were all very involved, though,' Pen pointed out.

'Right,' Max agreed. 'Which was why it didn't seem right to tell Diya and not Pen.'

'And then we told Anna as well because we didn't want Anna to feel left out,' concluded Diya, referring to their other neighbour: Anna Pachuta, Emilia's mum. 'Anna's at work now but she said she is happy to share the story of how Marcel proposed to her if it will help you come up with a better proposal idea.'

'I really haven't started thinking about how I'm going to propose,' said Sam.

'And that is exactly what is so alarming to all of us,' announced Diya grimly.

And that was how Sam found himself pouring tea out for a group of his neighbours who were all there to consult on the details of his romantic relationship.

Sam would ask how he'd got himself into this mess, except that he felt like the answer at heart had something to do with Jack, and also, it wasn't really a *mess*. Around the table were a group of people who really cared about Libby and him, and who had worried about how to make them happy, and had come through with supportive advice more times than Sam could count. If they were worried he was going to drop the ball on proposing, well, maybe he couldn't *entirely* blame them.

'Look,' he said patiently, 'I've been doing romantically okay for a while now. Libby and I are doing just fine.'

'You don't want your proposal to just be "romantically okay",' Diya said. 'You want your proposal to be romantically *dramatic*.'

'Yeah, the bar really *should* be higher than "okay",' Max agreed.

'No, I know that. I just ... I just have to give some thought to what I'm going to do. I haven't even got a ring yet.'

'And that is also a choice not to be approached lightly,' Diya said. 'But honestly, the ring is not as important as the moment that goes with it.'

'After all,' Pen added, 'a ring may be a symbol, but the *relationship* is what all of this is really about. And how you choose to ask her should be a reflection of your relationship.'

'Which is why I assume you're not going to put together a treasure hunt for a suit,' said Max. 'That was about Arthur and me.'

'I'm not going to put together a treasure hunt at all,' said Sam. 'I just don't think it's my and Libby's thing.'

'Maybe we should think about what your thing is,' said Diya thoughtfully. 'For instance, Darsh's and my thing was roller-skating.'

There was a moment of silence.

Then Max said, 'Roller-skating? Really?'

'Yes,' said Diya, a little defensively. 'Is that odd?'

'No, no,' said Max heartily. 'I'm just not sure I thought of either one of you as being roller-skaters.'

'We've never seen you roller-skate around the street,' added Sam.

'I'm not going to roller-skate just *anywhere*,' said Diya, as if roller-skating on a street were a shocking proposition. 'It has to be somewhere special. But it's how Darsh and I met. He had just come to this country, and he was looking for good ways to meet people, and I happened to be the only Indian woman at the roller-skating rink.'

'Aw,' said Max. 'It was fate.'

'I taught him how to roller-skate. He was very bad at it. I had learned as a little girl because my father loved it. So I taught Darsh. And when he proposed to me, he did it right in the middle of a roller-skating rink.'

'That sounds so romantic,' said Pen.

'It was,' said Diya, in a dreamy tone of voice unusual for her, since she was usually all brisk pragmatism. It was the tone of voice more than anything that drove it home for Sam: he had to come up with a proposal idea that made Libby sound like *that* when she reminisced about it.

Pen said, 'It also sounds a little bit dangerous.'

'Yeah,' Diya admitted. 'It was that, too. I'm not entirely sure I recommend it. Don't do it, Sam.'

'Duly noted,' said Sam, who didn't know how to roller-skate really, had never been to a roller-skating rink, and had no intention of taking Libby to one for his proposal.

'I could probably write an article on best kinds of wedding proposals,' Pen offered. 'If that sort of research would help.'

'Thanks,' said Sam, 'but I think I just have to take all the inspiration all of you have given me and craft it into my own thing.'

34

'It's a solid plan,' Max agreed.

'And we're here for you, whatever you need,' Diya added.

'After all,' said Pen, 'we're Christmas Street.'

With a second day of school under their belts, the street was starting to settle into the return of routine. Even Sam had to admit the house didn't seem as lonely as it had the day before (even without the impromptu visit from all of his neighbours). Sam stood outside in the light of the waning day waiting for Teddy and Pari and exchanging pleasantries with Bill – by which he meant that he made innocuous comments and listened good-naturedly to all of Bill's grumbles in reply. Emilia and Sai, whose school was slightly closer, came by first, waving to them while never missing a beat in the animated conversation they were having while simultaneously scrolling through their phones.

'Never look up from those phones,' Bill complained. 'In my day we didn't have all of that. If you were talking to someone, you *talked* to them. Face-to-face. Man-to-man.'

'What if you were talking to a woman?' asked Sam blandly.

'That, too,' Bill said, waving his hand around to dismiss the frivolousness of Sam's question.

Sam smiled at the road, watching Jack gambol about as he waited for Teddy and Pari to appear, and that was when his phone sounded with a text message, so he pulled it out of his pocket.

'And see?' said Bill. 'You're on your phone now, too.'

'Just for a second,' said Sam, because the text was from

Ellen, asking if Sam had a plunger she could borrow, which sounded like something she probably needed a fairly speedy response to.

Jack began barking manically a split second before Teddy and Pari appeared at the top of the street, and they waved, and Sam and Bill waved back, and Sam thought, What a lovely, wonderful, amazing street this is.

He was questioning the amazingness of the street after Libby had departed for another run with Pen and his doorbell rang and it was Anna Pachuta.

'Hello?' he said uncertainly. He was friendly with Anna, the way he was friendly with everyone on the street, but Anna was seldom home, and therefore he spent less time interacting with her. Diya was much friendlier with her, as their children were dating. They apparently texted all the time and Diya was always interjecting into conversations, *Well, Anna says so-and-so.* But Sam could count his personal interactions with Anna on one hand.

'Hi,' Anna said.

'Everything okay?' said Sam. 'I hope you don't have a plumbing emergency, because I would be useless in a plumbing emergency.'

'No,' Anna said. 'Marcel is good with plumbing.'

'Of course,' Sam said. 'I just wasn't sure if he was home.'

'Is Libby around?'

Maybe it made marginally more sense that Anna was apparently looking for Libby, although Sam had never seen

36

Libby and Anna talk before. 'No. She's actually started going running with Pen every night.'

'Is Teddy home?'

Sam had no idea why Anna would be asking after Teddy. 'He's at Pari's. He usually is after school. Emilia and Sai watch them while they plot world domination. Actually, you're home early, aren't you?' It suddenly occurred to Sam that part of the reason he never saw Anna was because, well, she was seldom home.

'Early night. It's a date night for Marcel and me. We've been trying to be better about them.' Anna blushed charmingly, and it made Sam smile. It was nice to see someone blushing about a date with their husband a good two decades after the marriage. It gave Sam hope.

'Well,' said Sam, still unsure why Anna was at his door, 'I hope you have a good time, then—'

'Can I come in?'

'Oh,' said Sam. 'Okay.' He stepped aside from the doorway awkwardly to give Anna room to enter before closing the door behind her. It wasn't that he was against having Anna in the house, he just ... didn't know what to say. 'Can I get you something?' he asked politely.

'Diya told me that you're going to propose to Libby,' Anna said, losing all pretence now that she had gained access to the house.

'Yes,' said Sam, resigned to everyone finding it necessary to give him advice. 'Although it's true I haven't decided how yet. I'm still working on it.'

'I wanted to tell you that I'm sure you're going to do just fine,' said Anna firmly.

Sam blinked, taken aback. 'What, really?'

'Yes. I know Diya and Max think you're romantically hopeless—'

Sam sighed in frustration.

'—but I think you've been doing just fine so far, and you'll do just fine with your proposal.'

'*Thank you*,' said Sam, more heartened than he'd realised he would be by such a statement. Maybe the proposal scenario had been weighing on his mind more than he'd been conscious of.

'So. That's my version of a pep talk, I suppose. Emilia's always saying I'm not very good at them and could stand to be a more positive and optimistic person. Which I am striving to do.'

'I think you're doing okay,' Sam smiled. 'If you don't mind my asking, how did Marcel propose to you?'

'Oh,' said Anna. 'I proposed to him. That's how I know you'll be okay. I made up my mind that he was the one I wanted and I didn't want to wait any longer and we were commuting home on the train together – this was when we were still in Poland, before we'd come to the UK – and I said, "Marcel. I think we should get married."' Anna paused, and her eyes got that luminous quality that everyone else's had gained when reminiscing about their proposal stories. 'And I will always remember that moment. It was twilight, and growing dim in the carriage, and Marcel was sitting in the window seat of the train, and beyond him the silhouettes of trees flashed by, blue in the growing darkness, and he looked beautiful when he turned to me and said yes.' After a moment, Anna shook herself out of the recollection and said briskly, as if embarrassed by her display, 'That's how I know you'll be okay. Because my proposal was one of the most beautiful moments I can remember, and it happened on a dingy train we'd taken every day between our dingy jobs and our dingy home. So no matter how it happens, your proposal will be perfect, because it will be a *proposal*.'

'Thank you,' Sam said after a moment. 'That actually is very helpful.'

'Yes,' Anna said, seeming uncertain now. 'Well. Good. I'll tell Diya I helped you out.' She turned and let herself out of his house, and Sam watched her as she walked next door to her own house, and once again re-evaluated this street he lived on: it was *amazing*.

Millie didn't have time to be particular.

She assumed that ordinarily, when looking for housing, one took one's time and saw multiple listings and maybe made pro–con lists to help ease one's decision along. Millie didn't actually *know*, because Millie had never been responsible for looking for housing before. Millie had skipped directly from her parents' house to uni to living with Daniel before she'd even bothered to graduate – because graduating had seemed pointless once she'd met Daniel and Daniel was going to take care of her and she was never going to have to worry about anything ever again.

That had only been a few years ago, but to Millie it seemed several lifetimes ago, and sometimes she sat in the shower and wept about how foolish and naïve and young that Millie seemed to her, so dazzled and so trusting, and Daniel had conducted all of their housing searches without any input from Millie. *I don't want you having to worry about it*, Daniel had told Millie, and Millie had filed that away as just more evidence how much Daniel loved her, of course, he didn't want her to have to worry about anything ever.

But it meant that Millie, having made up her mind to finally, *finally* leave, had no idea how to do it. All Daniel had accomplished, in that sly, stealthy, horrifying way of his, had been to make her as clueless and stupid as he was always telling her she was. *You don't know how to do anything*, Daniel would say, sitting at the kitchen table and patiently writing out a shopping list for her, as if he hadn't just picked up the casserole she'd made and flung it at the wall, leaving bits of food strewn across the plaster and crockery shattered all along the floor. She was on her hands and knees cleaning it, struggling not to cry because Daniel hated that, and saying, *Yes, Daniel*, the way he preferred, and Daniel would say evenly, *It's quite all right. Now you see why I must do everything.*

So Millie, hiding at the library for its public internet access, looked at estate agent listings and felt hopelessly out of her depth and thought of Daniel: *You don't know how to do anything.*

Millie, biting at a nail nervously, happened to catch the eye of a little girl who was skipping through the library wearing a pink superhero cape that fluttered out behind her with every step. She beamed with pride at being the centre of attention, and Millie thought of being so young that you relished every eye on you. The little girl waved sunnily at her and then hurried off toward the children's section.

'Annabeth, *slow down*,' a woman behind her who was clearly

her mother shouted, sounding harried, and then said, 'Sorry, sorry,' to everyone sitting at the bank of public computers.

Millie looked back at her house listings and thought, *You can do this*, and sat up a little straighter, and clicked at the first one she saw that was in her meagre budget. There were no photographs. What there was a bare bones description of the place and the words *centrally located on a charming street*. 'Centrally located' sounded good to Millie; she was, after all, going to have to find herself a job somewhere. The money she'd managed to hide from Daniel by selling baked goods up and down the street would only last so long.

The area of London the house was located in was far away, an area she'd never been to personally and that she also thought it was unlikely Daniel would ever visit. 'Far away' plus 'budget' were Millie's only two requirements.

The fact that it was located on Christmas Street was a bonus. But surely a house located on a street with such a cheerful name boded well.

Millie opened the brand new secret email she'd just signed up for and emailed the contact information for the listing: *I'd like to rent your house*.

It seemed that everyone on Christmas Street knew that Sam was going to propose to Libby, except for Libby herself, and Teddy. And Teddy was a pretty important person to have a conversation with about the proposal.

Sam hadn't spoken to him about it, not because he had mis-givings but because ... once he spoke to Teddy about it there would be no turning back. He would have to have everything in place to move on asking Libby to marry him, both because he didn't trust Teddy to be able to keep such an enormous secret for ever and because once he had Teddy's stamp of approval, he wanted to move forward quickly.

And Bill. Bill also didn't know of all the romantic intrigue on Christmas Street.

So while they waited yet again for Teddy and Pari to return from school, Sam told him. 'I'm going to propose to Libby.'

'It's only right,' said Bill gruffly. 'You should. I'm glad you still believe in the institution of marriage.'

Which was such a typical Bill response that Sam had to suppress laughter. 'Yes,' he said. 'I do.' And then, after he said the words, he realised, well, he *did*. 'I had a good time being married the first time around,' he said. 'I'm looking forward to being married again. And being married to *Libby*. I love her very much.' Which Sam probably would have felt self-conscious about confessing to anybody else but Bill, but Bill took it in the same dismissive stride with which he took everything else.

'Of course you do,' said Bill. 'Presumably that's why you want to marry her.'

'Yes,' Sam agreed. There was another moment of companionable silence, and then Sam said, 'So everyone on the street is concerned that I haven't enough romantic acumen to pull off this proposal properly.'

'Who's "everyone on the street"?' asked Bill.

'Literally *everyone* on the street. I have been subjected to many pieces of advice.'

'How can anyone advise anyone else on their proposal? A

42

proposal's got to be all about the couple. It's personal to the couple. When I proposed to my Agatha I took her to the park we always went to, where she liked to feed the ducks, and I proposed to her there. And that was exactly right and where I should have proposed. None of this big production number la-di-da singing and dancing nonsense you young folk think you have to go through today. Just a good old-fashioned "Agatha, will you marry me?" in a nice setting that you know she likes.'

Sam smiled at Bill's profile, because Bill was steadfastly looking down the street, waiting for Teddy and Pari, in that way he had of avoiding people's eyes while he spoke to them. Sam said, 'That is a lovely proposal story, and sound proposal advice.'

'Well,' grumbled Bill, and then fell silent for a second, clearly searching for what to say. He settled on, 'If you say so.'

Pen continued to want to converse while they were jogging, and Libby was slowly getting better at keeping up her end of the conversation, which meant she'd progressed from periodic grunts to grunts with inflection. But at least it *was* some progress.

'I've hired a carpenter. His name is Jasper. I'm just warning you in case you see a strange man wandering around the street.'

Christmas Street was the sort of street where a stranger stood out, Libby had to admit.

'And speaking of strangers, I've heard a most amazing bit of news. You know the old Blakeley place?'

'No,' huffed Libby.

43

'Yes, you do. It's the abandoned house on the street. The one that no one lives in.'

'Oh, yeah,' panted Libby. 'That one.'

'Well, it's been empty for years. No idea what was going on with it. Some kind of ownership dispute, I think. Siblings feuding about who owned what per cent, you know, that sort of thing.'

'Uh-huh,' grunted Libby, because she thought she ought to indicate that she was listening instead of merely struggling to keep her legs moving.

'Anyway, they've finally settled whatever the dispute was because someone's moving in! Can you imagine? A new neighbour on the street! I can't wait to see who it is!'

The hardest part of Sam's decision to propose to Libby would have been finding time to talk to Teddy without Libby being around, except that Libby had embarked on her new running-with-Pen nightly plan, which meant that it wasn't hard at all for Sam to find an opportunity to talk to Teddy.

And to tell himself that he wasn't nervous about talking to Teddy.

It was true, of course, that Teddy was the only person in the world whose opinion mattered when it came to Libby, and so it was true that a single word from Teddy could bring all of Sam's plans to a screeching halt. But Teddy seemed to like Libby, genuinely like her, maybe even love her. Teddy had been supportive of Sam's relationship with Libby from the very beginning. Teddy hadn't blinked an eye when Libby had moved in with them, and in fact had been enthusiastic about it, seeming to consider it basically an invitation for a never-ending slumber party.

But still, there was a world of difference between Libby moving in and Sam saying that he wanted to marry Libby. Sam had had only one wife, after all: Teddy's mum. Inevitably saying that he wanted a new wife would feel like he was replacing Sara, and he didn't want Teddy to think that Sara occupied any less revered a place in their lives than she had before they'd left America and moved to London and Libby had come into the picture.

In the end, because he was a coward, he started the discussion while they were setting the table for dinner. It was such a prosaic everyday activity that it made the conversation feel low-stakes, much less stressful than if he'd tried to make it special and momentous.

'There's something I wanted to talk to you about,' was how he started, arranging a fork much more carefully than was necessary.

'Uh-huh,' said Teddy, folding napkins studiously and not even bothering to look up. He obviously thought that anything his father could say would probably be dull.

Sam paused to think and wished he'd planned this conversation out. He should have scripted it. That would have been a wise thing to do. 'What would you say,' he decided, 'if I said that I'm thinking of asking Libby to marry me?'

That garnered a reaction. Teddy's head shot up to look at him. 'Seriously?'

Sam, not knowing what else to do, nodded.

'That would be great!' said Teddy, and then, suddenly, 'Oh.'

And Sam understood that reaction, because it was rather how his own reaction had gone. Jubilant delight over wanting to marry Libby, and then the sudden recollection that it would be shadowing a marriage that had come before.

Sam said, feeling his way cautiously, 'What do you think?'

'I think that would be good,' Teddy said, very formally, as if he were telling a butler to bring a guest into the drawing room.

Sam smiled and pulled out a chair and said, 'Let's sit for a minute.'

Teddy sat, and he looked uncertain, torn between faking the casual confidence of a grown-up and letting himself be *young*. 'I mean, it's okay, Dad, I get it that—'

'No. Let's sit and talk about this. Because this isn't just about me marrying someone, this is about our family, and whether we want to bring another person into it. I know Libby's been living here with us, and I think that's been going well.' He paused, waiting for Teddy to agree with this statement.

Teddy nodded.

So Sam went on. 'But I also understand that asking Libby to marry me is another thing entirely. And so, just as I would never have brought Libby into this house without talking to you about it first, I'm not going to ask her to marry me if you would find it upsetting, or if you don't want me to do it, for whatever reason. You don't have to articulate any of what you're feeling.' Sam thought it was only fair to tell Teddy that, since he certainly had done a dismal job lately of articulating himself. Everything in his head was a confused jumble. He just knew that asking Libby to marry him felt right, felt like what he wanted, and felt also like it was what *Sara* would have wanted for them.

Teddy bit his lip and shredded the napkin still in his hands and looked deep in thought.

Sam waited him out. Sam would wait for ever, he thought. In fact, maybe Teddy needed to know that. 'Also, you don't have to come up with some kind of response right now. You can take your time and think about it as long as you want. I want you to know ...' He reached out and put a gentle finger under Teddy's chin to tip his face up so he could see his eyes. 'I want you to know that *you* are the most important person in my life. Your happiness matters a hundred thousand times more to me than anything else happening to me or around me. I maybe haven't said that as much as I could, so I'm saying it now, in case you didn't know. I know that I forced you to move here, and to leave all of your friends, and to start over, and it was rough, and I know that that felt like I ... like I didn't care what you thought. But I did, and I do, and I won't do that to you again with this.'

Teddy swallowed thickly and held Sam's gaze and said, 'I like having Libby around. It's nice, and she's nice. I like that she's funny, and I like that she's ... warm, I guess. That she makes it feel warm in here. And she makes you happy, and you being happy makes *me* happy.'

Sam smiled at him. 'Look at us, both all worried about the other.'

'Yeah,' said Teddy, with a little answering smile, and then he sobered again. 'But then I think ... Then I think, What about Mom?'

It wasn't that they didn't talk about Sara ever, because they did. They talked about her all the time. Sam had never wanted her to be a taboo subject in the house, and Libby was

47

obviously not threatened by her, loved to hear stories about her. But when Sam talked about her, he often called her *your mother*, looking at Teddy. And Teddy had fallen into the same habit somehow: *my mother*, he would say as he told stories. It had been a long time since Sam had heard him say *Mom*, in his American accent, that special name that had belonged to Sara and Sara alone.

So Sam responded in kind. 'If Mom had been given a choice, she would have loved to have been here. Mom would have loved to see who you're growing up to be. Mom would have loved to have met Jack, and Pari, and everyone else on the street. Mom would have loved all of them. And Mom would have wanted more time with you, more time with us. Mom would have wanted all of it.' Sam paused suddenly, his words caught in his throat, unexpectedly feeling the injustice of losing Sara so early all over again. There were lots of ways in which Sam's grieving had happened years ago and he had moved on, but there were lots of other ways in which grieving was an ongoing process that never truly ended, and every time he looked at their little boy and thought how much older he was than the kindergartener who had lost his mum, and how much Sara hadn't got to see, it still felt raw and new.

He took a deep breath and kept going. 'But she didn't get that. For whatever reason, she didn't get that choice. And so I can tell you instead that, given a second choice, Mom would have wanted you to be happy. Us both to be happy. And Libby isn't going to replace her – we could never replace her – but Mom would never want you to feel guilty, or to make a choice you didn't want to make, because you thought you *should*. That wasn't the kind of mum she was.'

'My happiness mattered a hundred thousand times more to her than anything else happening to her or around her,' quoted Teddy.

Sam uttered a laugh that wasn't far off a sob. 'Yeah. Exactly. That's right. I don't know, we both suffered from this inexplicable weakness of loving you a lot.'

Teddy smiled and sniffled and said, 'I think maybe a part of me thought having Libby might mean I wouldn't still miss Mom. But I still do.'

'I know. Me, too.'

'But I still like Libby just as much.'

'I know. Me, too.'

'You *love* Libby,' said Teddy.

'Yes. I do. Quite a lot.'

Teddy grinned suddenly. 'Yeah. I can tell.'

'Oh, can you? Because I said I want to marry her?'

'No, because of the way you look at her. It's nice. It's good. It makes me happy. We're all just being happy together.'

'Yes,' Sam said. 'And that's the best anyone can hope for, really.'

Teddy took a deep breath and then let it out slowly and then said, 'Okay.'

'Okay?'

'Okay. I think it's a good idea, marrying Libby. I'm glad you want to do it.'

'You don't have to make a decision right now,' Sam said. 'Like I said, you can take your time, think it over—'

'I don't need to.' Teddy beamed at him. 'When you first told me, all I could think of was how great that was. It is. It's great. We're all going to be so happy, and that would have made Mom so happy.'

'Yeah,' Sam said, around the lump in his throat. 'Yeah, it really would have.' Then he reached out to tug Teddy in against him for a hug, kissing the top of his head and then resting his chin there. 'How did I get such a great kid?'

'*No* idea,' said Teddy, and Sam could hear the irrepressible smile in his voice. 'You're super lucky.'

'I am,' Sam agreed, because he definitely couldn't argue with that.

'So.' Teddy drew back from Sam and sat up and began setting the table again, completely calm and sedate, and Sam momentarily marvelled. 'It's a secret right now? So it can be a big surprise for Libby?'

'Yeah,' Sam said. 'For now.'

'Tell me how you're thinking of proposing,' Teddy said seriously.

'Well,' said Sam, 'that's the big question that everyone's worrying about.'

'You've got to do it just right. I bet I can help. Actually, I bet Pari and me can help. Oh! This can be how we Make a Difference!'

'You're going to start a proposal consulting venture?' asked Sam.

Teddy shrugged. 'How hard can it be?'

Chapter 4

Water
Fire
Very romantic speech
Would be best if could be done on top of moving train

Jasper Nketia had seen a lot of things in his life. Carpentry took you into a lot of different houses, exposed you to a lot of different decorating styles and a lot of different ways of making decorating decisions. Which was why, when his new client Miss Cheever said, 'Why don't we have some tea first? Ease into the discussion of business,' Jasper just shrugged. People could be funny about their houses, after all. Sometimes they really did need to ease into talking about renovating them. It was a lot to wrap your mind around sometimes.

So Jasper found himself in Miss Cheever's lounge – a cosy room with a single goldfish darting about in a bowl – having a cup of tea.

Miss Cheever said, 'That's my goldfish Chester. Don't mind him. He can be very judgemental.'

'Is Chester going to be helping with the design decisions?'

asked Jasper politely, because one never knew how clients made design decisions.

Miss Cheever laughed. 'No. Goldfish vision is very different from human vision. He and I would probably have very different opinions on what we want.'

'Plus he would probably want you to add more water everywhere,' Jasper suggested.

Miss Cheever laughed again. 'You're right. He probably doesn't understand why the whole house isn't his goldfish bowl. Anyway. Thanks so much for coming out to give me a price and stuff.'

'How much are you looking to spend?' asked Jasper.

'I don't know.' Miss Cheever looked thoughtful. 'I don't want to spend a *lot*, but I want to spend enough to feel like I've made a change. I'm probably going to have to really think about how much is worthwhile.'

There came a scratching from the front door.

Miss Cheever looked at her watch and said, 'Oh, dear, it's time to feed Jack, I almost forgot.'

She got up and went to the door and let in a dog, who trotted in and immediately started barking at Jasper, dancing around in front of him like it was torn between making friends with the intruder and alerting everyone to the intruder's presence.

Miss Cheever spoke to the barking dog. 'It's quite all right, Jack. This is Jasper Nketia. He's our carpenter. He's going to be helping me with some home renovations I have planned.'

Jack was apparently the dog's name, and Jack the dog, having been given permission not to be wary of him, came forward to be scratched behind his ears.

Miss Cheever gave Jack a dog biscuit and sent him on his

way, and then looked frankly at Jasper. 'So here's what I'm thinking.' She lifted her hands in front of her as if painting in the sky. '*Topography*.'

'Topography?' echoed Jasper.

'I've been reading a lot of design blogs,' Miss Cheever explained, 'and houses don't do enough with *levels*. I want my house to have multiple layers. Like *rock*. Like *sedimentary layers*. So one of the things I was thinking was maybe raising my bed a bit. Like, putting it up on a dais. That might be a lot of work for you, but what do you think, Mr Nketia?'

Jasper smiled. 'Jasper is fine.'

Miss Cheever mused about turning her staircase into a slide but then to Jasper's relief vetoed the idea. Otherwise, though, Miss Cheever seemed willing to fully embrace all whimsy. Again, Jasper had definitely had clients request odder things (although the slide on the staircase would have been a new one), so he went along with it genially. Miss Cheever's enthusiastic imagination was infectious. Jasper stood on Miss Cheever's front step as he got ready to leave and felt an odd, buoyant sense of ... possibility. Like this street in its early autumn evening was actually standing on the brink of spring.

Jack the dog was out on the street, sniffing around by two men chatting, one of them pushing a baby in a pram back and forth.

Miss Cheever said, 'Well. I think it's going to be an adventure.'

Jasper laughed. 'At that. A good sort, though. And I think you'll like having a fun house.'

'Me, too.' Miss Cheever looked pleased. 'It'll be more *me*. I actually started this project because I wanted to update my décor, and now I think I'm not so much updating it as *reinventing* it entirely.'

Jasper laughed again.

'Anyway, Jasper, I look forward to working with you.' Miss Cheever stuck her hand out so Jasper could shake it. 'Just let me know what your estimates are and I'll decide which of the projects I can live without and which are definite go-aheads.'

'I should have that to you by the end of the week,' Jasper said. 'Some of it is just going to depend on the type of wood at issue.'

'I understand,' Miss Cheever said. 'Take your time. There's really no rush.'

'Thank you, Miss Cheever. And I'll just—'

'Oh, no, you must call me Pen,' said Miss Cheever. 'And I should introduce you to everyone else.'

'Everyone else?' Jasper echoed, because he'd been under the impression Miss Cheever – Pen – lived alone.

'The rest of the street. They'll want to know if someone new's going to be spending time hanging about. Don't worry, they're all very nice. Max! Marcel!'

The two men talking looked up and waved, and then Jasper found himself with no choice but to follow Pen as she hurried down to talk to them.

'Hello,' she said. 'I wanted to introduce you to Jasper. He's going to be overhauling my house. This is Max and Marcel.'

'Oh,' said the man called Max, shaking Jasper's hand. 'I have a keen interest in this project. I can't wait to hear what astonishing things you have in mind for Pen's house.'

'Topography,' Pen said. 'I want to give my house a sense of depth.'

'I love that,' said Max, sounding as if he really did.

'And how's little Charlie?' Pen said, leaning over the pram.

'Fussy,' said Max. 'New tooth coming in. Hence why we're outside waiting for Arthur, and happened to run into Marcel coming home from work.'

Marcel said to Jasper, 'So what kind of work do you do?'

'Carpentry,' Jasper said. 'Woodwork.'

'Oho,' said Max. 'Bill Hammersley down the street is aces at woodworking. He carves the most cunning little figures.'

'He does,' Pen agreed. 'But Jasper's going to make a dais for my bed. I thought that might be beyond Bill's otherwise considerable talents.'

'A dais for your bed?' Max sounded amused now. 'That *is* topography.'

'Woodworking,' said Marcel thoughtfully. 'I might want to borrow you once Pen's done with you.'

'Me, too, actually,' said Max ruefully. 'We've got some projects around our house that I want to do for Arthur. He's been whingeing about storage for a while now. Charlie's managed to eat up all the wardrobe space we ever had.'

'Babies do that,' said Marcel. 'And then they become teenagers and it's even worse.'

Max laughed. 'Looking forward to it.'

'Hello,' said another man, wandering down to the knot of them. 'Are we having a street meeting?'

'Just introducing everyone to my new carpenter Jasper,' said Pen. 'Jasper, this is Sam.'

Sam said, 'Oh, nice to meet you. I suppose we'll be seeing you around the street.'

'Indefinitely, apparently,' said Jasper, gesturing to Marcel and Max. 'I think I've got two new clients already lined up.'

'Well, in that case, we'll have to invite you to join the little procrastinators' club all of us home-workers have going on.'

'I knew that you lot were just having tea parties all day,' Marcel complained.

Pen laughed and said, 'I'm supposed to be meeting Libby to go for a run, so I think I'll leave before any more of our secret tea party details can be revealed. Jasper, thank you, and I look forward to hearing from you.' And she gave a cheery little wave as she departed.

Pari had been waiting very patiently all day for Libby to go running with Pen, because that was their opportunity to share their proposal ideas with Sam, but Pen was too busy walking some strange man around the street.

'Who's that man Pen's introducing to everybody?' Pari demanded of Teddy.

Teddy glanced out the window, clearly more concerned with the tug of war he was having with Jack than with the strange man, which was definitely misplaced priorities on Teddy's part, thought Pari. 'I don't know.' Teddy shrugged. 'A boyfriend, maybe?'

'No, Pen told me she doesn't want or need a boyfriend to be complete, she likes her life as it is and she offers herself everything she needs,' said Pari wisely, because that speech from Pen had impressed her.

'Then I don't know,' said Teddy, and shrugged again.

'Well, we need to figure it out,' declared Pari, 'because

that man is keeping Pen from taking Libby jogging, and that means that we can't talk to your dad about our proposal ideas – Wait.'

'Wait what?' asked Teddy, succeeding finally in winning the toy from Jack but giving it right back to him. 'Did the guy leave?'

'No. But. I just had an idea.' Pari sat down on the floor with Teddy excitedly. 'About how we can keep Making a Difference after the proposal is over. We can be *spies*.'

'Spies?' Teddy frowned. 'Like James Bond?'

'Like *Harriet*. James Bond is way too dangerous.'

'I was going to say,' agreed Teddy.

'We can be spies. Jack can be our spy dog. The best spies have spy dogs.'

'Jack's going to be an awesome spy dog,' agreed Teddy enthusiastically.

'Our first mission will be to spy on who that man is.'

Teddy glanced out of the window. 'My dad's out there. We could probably just ask him.'

'That would be terrible spying!' Pari chided him.

'A spy uses all methods open to him.'

'To him *or her*,' Pari reminded him.

'Right,' Teddy agreed, and together they got up and went outside.

Everyone said hello to them, because that was how Christmas Street was, and then they didn't even have to *ask*.

'This is Jasper,' Sam said, gesturing to him. 'He's a carpenter who's going to be working to remodel Pen's house.'

They were terrible at keeping secrets, Pari thought. This was the silliest spying ever.

57

'It's going to be an adventure,' said Jasper.

'We are big on adventures on this street,' said Teddy, and everyone laughed.

Pen jogged by them in her jogging clothes, and Pari immediately brightened. Now Operation Proposal could commence.

Pari and Teddy sat very seriously in Sam's lounge, Pari with a notebook on her lap.

'Well,' Sam said. 'This is all very professional. I feel like I ought to be paying you.'

'Making a Difference is payment enough,' Pari said.

'But if you want to buy me *Mass Extinction Event 7*,' Teddy said, 'that'd be cool payment.'

'Uh-huh,' said Sam drily. 'Let's move on.'

Pari cleared her throat. 'On the topic of the proposal, we've conducted some research.'

'What kind of research?' Sam asked curiously, fascinated by how seriously the kids were taking this.

'We watched a bunch of Bollywood films,' Teddy said. 'They were pretty cool.'

'Yes,' said Pari, 'and based on our research, your proposal probably needs a big dance scene. *Lots* of choreography. It should also have water or fire.'

'But it's best if it has both,' added Teddy helpfully.

Sam lifted an eyebrow. 'Well, I don't think ... I mean, that doesn't sound much like a very me proposal. Have you ever seen me dance?'

Teddy looked at Pari. 'It's true, he's a terrible dancer.'

'I guess it's true that I never saw you woo Libby with dancing,' Pari remarked.

'No,' Sam agreed. 'That's not how I wooed her.'

'Hmm.' Pari tapped her pencil against her notebook.

'He wooed her with carrots,' Teddy said helpfully.

'Carrots?' said Pari.

'Well,' said Sam, 'and some beetroot, too.'

'Tell me more,' said Pari.

'You know,' remarked Libby, as she passed the potatoes to Teddy, 'here's an adventure from the other day that I forgot to tell you about.'

'Oh?' said Sam.

'Pen tells me that we're getting a new neighbour.'

'Really? Is someone getting a lodger?' Sam tried to think of who would be the most likely candidate for this. Maybe Pen, but she was redoing her own house. Possibly Bill, although it seemed highly unlikely Bill would let anyone move into his home.

'No,' said Libby, clearly relishing the reveal. 'Someone's moving into that old decrepit empty place.'

'That place is habitable?' said Sam, surprised.

'I thought that place was haunted,' Teddy said.

'No such thing as ghosts,' Sam said automatically.

'I don't know.' Teddy looked doubtful of Sam's authority on the question. 'Have you ever looked at that place?'

Sam had to admit Teddy had a point. The house had been empty for so long that he felt like he and the rest of the street had totally forgotten about it, eyes passing right over the eyesore of it. If any house on the street was going to harbour ghosts, it would definitely be that one.

'Ghosts don't live in any of our houses, so probably they live in that house,' Teddy continued.

'How do you know ghosts don't live in anybody else's house?' asked Libby, sounding genuinely curious.

'We'd hear complaints about it. We hear about everything else on this street all the time.'

Sam had to laugh at that.

Libby laughed as well and said, 'Well, there's a possibility we don't hear about ghosts because there's no such thing as ghosts. But, at any rate, based on the street, I'm guessing any ghosts lingering around here would be friendly ones, so they'd probably welcome a new housemate.'

'Who is it who's moving in?'

'Pen didn't say.'

'I haven't seen any activity around the house,' mused Sam.

'And of course you would know everything going on because your primary activity during the day is to spy on the street,' teased Libby.

'I would have at least noticed people around looking at the place!' Sam pointed out. 'You know that strangers on the street cause everyone here to lock down into red alert.'

'Yes,' said Libby, amused. 'I do know that.'

'Whoever it is, I hope it's someone who'll count as an adventure,' said Teddy. 'Maybe they'll have kids. Or another dog to play with Jack!'

'Two Jacks on the street,' remarked Sam. 'Just imagine.'

Chapter 5

New carpenter????
Pen's new house design?
NEW NEIGHBOUR

'I have something for us to spy on,' announced Teddy as they settled in for Make a Difference planning at the Basak house the next day. It was raining heavily outside, and Jack was sitting gazing sadly out the window, probably thinking of all the squirrels he wasn't able to chase. Sai and Emilia were actually studying for exams for a change at the dining room table, instead of being gross boyfriend and girlfriend.

'Other than Jasper?' asked Pari.

'Who's Jasper?' asked Emilia, who was usually looking to distract herself from study once she actually started it.

'Pen's carpenter,' said Teddy. 'He's redesigning Pen's house.'

'Cool,' said Emilia.

'He's going to put the bed way up high, like kings and queens have it.'

'That sounds awesome,' said Pari. 'Maybe he can do it for my bed, too!'

Teddy shrugged. 'Probably.'

'Good spying, Teddy. We should probably see if we can get all of the plans for Pen's house. That would be a good spy project, right?'

'What's all this about spying?' asked Emilia.

'It's how we're going to Make a Difference,' Pari said.

'A difference in the lives of the people you're spying on?' asked Sai.

Pari hmph'd and turned to Teddy. 'Do you have a spying project other than Jasper?'

'Yes. I found out that someone is moving into the empty house.'

'The empty house?' said Emilia.

'The old, creepy, haunted one?' said Sai.

'Exactly what I said!' Teddy exclaimed.

'That's such great spying, Teddy!' said Pari. 'I wonder who it is! Do you think it'll be another family?'

'I have no idea,' said Teddy.

'That just means we have more spying to do!' said Pari. 'I'm so excited, this will definitely Make a Difference.'

'How will it Make a Difference to spy on someone moving in?' asked Sai.

'We'll be able to share information with the rest of the street. And then that will make it easier to be friends with them. It was much easier to be friends with Teddy once we knew about him.'

This sounded reasonable to Teddy. 'It was easier to be friends with you once I knew about you, too.'

Pari nodded, and Teddy nodded back. Their mission plan

was clear: Get Dad and Libby engaged, and then welcome this new family to the street.

The only problem with having everyone on the street involved with his proposal was knowing that it had to go forward exactly as scheduled. Not that Sam had cold feet or anything. He definitely didn't want to back out. But he did feel like he'd lost some control of the process.

No, he thought, watching his son, his son's friend, his son's friend's mother, and their neighbour go over a literal *checklist* for the proposal: he'd lost possibly *all* control.

'It's going to be tricky,' Diya said. 'You've got to get the timing exactly right.'

'I'm so envious,' Max said, bopping up and down to try to quiet a fussy Charlie. 'I wish I could tag along, too.'

'You know we can't take the risk of Charlie crying and attracting attention,' said Diya brusquely. Diya in Romantic Planning mode took no prisoners and spared no feelings.

'I resent that you think my child wouldn't be perfectly behaved,' said Max, just as Charlie let out a wail.

'It's just going to be a lot of waiting,' Sam assured him.

'Nevertheless, I want to be given a full account. Take notes, kids.'

'Got it covered,' said Pari, brandishing her notebook. It read *Make a Difference* across the front in emphatic letters.

'So you know the plan, right?' said Teddy.

'Do we need to go over it again?' asked Pari. 'We can go over it again.'

'No, I think I'm okay,' Sam promised.

Diya gave him a narrow-eyed look. No one communicated scepticism in Sam's abilities as effectively as Diya.

Except for Teddy, who looked likewise dubious. Teddy was better at it, but that made sense, since Teddy had had nine years of practice.

'We can go over it again,' Diya announced, echoing her daughter.

'Yeah, maybe that's a good idea,' Teddy concurred.

'Go,' said Sam, in good-natured exasperation, herding all of them out of his house. 'You must go or you'll run into Libby coming back with Pen.'

'We'll have everything ready for you,' Pari promised.

'Get her there on time,' Diya urged.

'I will do my best.'

'But don't say that you have to leave because you're planning to propose,' said Pari.

'I will be subtler than that,' Sam promised.

'Subtler?' said Pari.

'He means sneakier,' said Teddy.

'Yes.' Sam smiled. 'Sneakier.' He finally managed to get everyone out of the house, and then Teddy turned back, took a step back into the house. 'Hey,' Sam said, looking down at him.

After a moment, Teddy broke into a wide and beaming smile. 'I'm so excited.'

'Are you?' said Sam, surprised by how relieved he felt. He'd talked this over with Teddy, but it was encouraging to know that Teddy still thought it was a good idea and wasn't having second thoughts. 'Marvellous.'

'Good luck,' Teddy said. 'See you when you're engaged.' He

gave a cheerful wave and skipped down the path to where Pari and Diya were waiting.

Then all three of them waved and moved off down the street. Sam looked after them, and stood for a second waiting to see if Pen and Libby appeared at the top of the street.

And then he thought that might look suspicious, since he didn't usually stand in the doorway waiting for Libby to get back from her run, so he went inside to look as not-suspicious as possible on the sofa.

'We have no food in this house,' Sam announced. He'd rehearsed this whole speech a lot. He'd rehearsed more than he'd rehearsed his actual proposal.

'We never have any food in the house,' Libby said, throwing off his script. Luckily, she was busy pulling her hair into a ponytail and not paying attention to him, so she didn't notice how he probably looked vaguely panicked.

Sam, after taking a moment to collect himself and adjust his plan, said, 'We usually have at least a couple of pieces of fruit. Look at you, jogging almost every day and working hard to get in shape, and we don't even have any apples in the house. We should run to the shops.'

Libby looked at him then, looking amused. 'Apples? That's what you're going to run to the shops for? I think we can survive.'

'And maybe some bananas,' Sam said desperately. His whole plan was going completely awry. He could feel Max and Diya's judgement glowing at him. 'Don't you think we need some bananas?'

'I guess so,' agreed Libby. She had the refrigerator door open and was examining the situation. 'Actually, I think we need some yoghurt, too.'

'Yes,' Sam agreed, pleased that Libby seemed to be coming around.

'And Pen was telling me about watermelon seeds and how good for you they're supposed to be. She apparently wrote some article on the most up-and-coming foods, or something.'

'Leaving aside the idea that foods are up-and-coming ...'

Libby laughed as she straightened away from the refrigerator, sending a grin in Sam's direction, and Sam was struck again by how beautiful she was, and how she'd been beautiful the night he'd met her but she was more beautiful now that she was in his kitchen, laughing at him, there for him to reach out and grab and pull in.

So he did. She came still laughing, and settled against him, and he linked his hands at the small of her back and kissed her smile. Everything inside of him calmed with a happy sigh: he was about to ask this woman to marry him, and it was going to be glorious.

'Do you want to come to the supermarket with me?' he murmured around their kisses.

She chuckled. 'You just made that sound so romantic. How can I resist?'

'We should start in the fruit and veg section,' Sam said, once he got Libby into the supermarket.

'Of course. The home of the apples and the bananas that you're suddenly so obsessed with.'

'The what?' asked Sam blankly, focused on getting Libby into the right position and catching a glimpse of Pari ducking behind a display quickly.

'The apples and the bananas? Isn't that why you wanted to come here?'

'Yes. But. First. We should get carrots.'

'Carrots?' Libby lifted her eyebrows. 'Well, you didn't mention carrots. Is this because you're suddenly going to want to make nutrition shakes?'

'Like Pen?' Sam wrinkled his nose. 'No. Absolutely not.'

Libby laughed. 'I didn't think so.'

'I just like carrots. You like carrots, too.'

'I do like carrots,' Libby agreed. 'This is such a scintillating conversation. I can't believe Teddy preferred to stay at Pari's rather than come to the supermarket to have these conversations with us.'

'Yeah, there's just no accounting for the taste of a nine-year-old,' Sam said, responding absently as his eyes slid over the carrots, until he found exactly the one he wanted. He began nudging Libby toward it, saying, 'Carrots are how we met. Carrots and beetroot.'

'Yes,' Libby said. 'They are . . . '

Libby stopped talking, her eyes on the diamond ring that had been slipped onto one of the carrots.

Sam grinned, as the ring caught the fluorescent lights of the supermarket, reflecting them in alluring winks and flashes.

Libby, her mouth open on an *oh* of surprise, turned to Sam. 'What—'

Sam sank to one knee.

'*Sam,*' said Libby.

Out of the corner of his eye, Sam could see they were attracting attention, as he took Libby's hand in his. 'I thought I'd ask you here,' he said, 'where it all began, before I knew who you were, before I knew how you would change my life, and Teddy's life. Teddy and I love having you in our lives. We love the joy and laughter you've added to our house. And I don't want to speak for Teddy on this point, so I'll just say: I love you. I would like to buy carrots and beetroot with you for the rest of our lives. How does that sound to you?'

Libby stared down at him, looking thoroughly shocked. 'Does that mean . . . Do you mean . . . ?'

'Will you marry me?' Sam finished.

'Yes.' Libby nodded frantically. 'Yes, yes, yes,' she repeated, as Sam slid the ring onto her finger and scattered applause broke out over the fruit and veg. The ring was too big and tipped ruefully to the side and Sam chuckled as he stood to his feet.

'Well, I tried—' he began.

'You *tried*?' interrupted Libby, and took his face in her hands and pulled him in for a fierce kiss. 'You did more than try, that was *beautiful*. Do you really mean it?'

'Of course I really mean it,' said Sam. 'Why else would I have said it?'

'I don't know. I don't know if maybe we happened upon an incongruous diamond ring in the carrot display and you felt obligated to pretend you'd planned this whole elaborate proposal scene.'

'No, I really did plan this whole elaborate proposal scene. Well, with help. Lots and lots of help from the street.'

Libby had pulled back a little bit and was now admiring her ring. 'So everyone on the street knows?'

'Pretty much, yes.'

'Even Mr Hammersley?'

'Yes,' Sam laughed.

'And Bill approves of your intentions.'

'He applauds my commitment to the old-fashioned idea of marriage.'

'Sam, the ring is gorgeous.'

'Do you like it? I wish it fit you. You can always exchange it if you like.'

'No, no, I love it.' Libby swiped at tears that had appeared in her eyes. 'I love it and I love *you*.' She leaned back in for another kiss. 'But how did you know that the ring would be here? You've been with me. Who put the ring here? And how did you know no one would steal it?'

'Well, I said I had help,' Sam said, and nodded beyond Libby.

Libby turned, in time for Pari to barrel into her in enthusiasm.

'Congratulations!' Pari squealed. 'We're so excited to have a street wedding!'

'A street wedding?' said Libby, laughing. 'Is that what we're calling it?'

'Congratulations,' Diya said, coming up to them. 'We weren't sure if Sam could do it.'

Sam rolled his eyes good-naturedly as Libby grinned at him.

'We had to choose just the right carrot to put the ring on, and then we had to stand right by it to make sure no one took it, whilst also keeping an eye out for you,' said Pari. 'It was a *lot*. We had super important jobs. We totally Made a

Difference. We helped come up with the whole scheme in the first place.'

'It's true,' Sam confirmed. 'They did. Pari and Teddy.' Sam located Teddy, hanging back behind Pari and Diya, looking shy and uncertain. He wanted to gesture him forward but he also didn't want to force him to do anything he might not be comfortable with yet.

And then, while Sam was still making up his mind how to approach Teddy, Libby said gently, 'Hello, Teddy.'

'Hi,' Teddy said, with a shy little wave.

'So you helped out with this whole intense operation, huh?'

'Yeah,' Teddy nodded. 'Do you like the ring?'

'I love the ring,' Libby said. 'I loved the proposal. Thanks so much for that. You lot did such a great job.'

'Thanks!' chirped Pari.

'Thanks,' said Teddy, still looking like he was making his mind up about something.

Diya noticed as well, and reached out to grab Pari and pull her back, out of Teddy's way.

And Teddy, after a second, his path clear, walked up to Libby and smiled at her and then hugged her. 'Welcome to the family,' he said.

Libby pressed her face into Teddy's hair and said, 'Thank you, Teddy. It's such a terrific honour. And we're going to have so much fun.'

Teddy backed away from the embrace a little bit and said, 'So many adventures!'

Libby laughed. 'Yes. Every night at dinner.' She looked up at Sam. 'Right?'

And Sam looked at the pair of them, a pair he saw every day

now and had been seeing every day for a while, and smiled. 'Yes. Exactly.'

The next task on Millie's to-do list was to try to find a job. That was actually rather urgent. She had not taken into budgetary account how much her new landlord would demand for security purposes. She was pretty much wiped out. And if she ran out of money . . . If she ran out of money, she *wouldn't* go back to Daniel, she promised herself fiercely.

But she wasn't confident that she would keep that promise to herself if things got really bad. So, she needed a job.

That was the reason she went to the supermarket that evening: to interview for a job. What she did not expect was to run into people getting *engaged*, right there by the carrots. But that was unmistakably what was happening: a man down on one knee in the universal pose of a marriage request.

It gave her pause on her way in. Was that a good omen, or a bad one? She remembered her own marriage proposal, and how everything had seemed like it might be good, from that moment on; there would be nothing left for her to worry about. That had turned out to be laughingly wrong: Millie had never worried so much as she did these days. So did marriage proposals stand for good things or bad? Or maybe things were never so simple as to be one or the other. Maybe they were bad things wrapped up to look like good things.

The happy couple embraced, and Millie thought it was stupid for her to be standing there thinking other people getting engaged was a symbol of anything about *her* life.

Their life choices were their life choices; Millie was making her own, finally, for herself, and that's all she ought to be thinking about.

Millie had never interviewed for a job before. She had thought that had been another one of the luxuries of marriage to Daniel – that she didn't have to work. But instead she now saw it for what so many of those luxuries had been: ways to keep her trapped and helpless and in thrall to him for as long as possible.

So Millie didn't know what to do on a job interview, the way she didn't know what to do for so much of life. But luckily the person interviewing her, a woman who introduced herself as Thea, didn't seem to care much. In fact, she seemed completely disinterested in the entire transaction.

'I just want to double-check,' Millie said at the end of the interview. 'The job wouldn't be customer-facing, right? I mean, I wouldn't have to interact with the customers?'

'You'll mainly be in the back,' said Thea. 'No customers back there.'

That was exactly what Millie wanted to hear.

Pen's remodel design was intense. It was going to keep Jasper busy for a while. Not that Jasper was complaining. It was good money and Pen was pleasant and didn't behave unreasonably toward him about his job, which was a very good thing in Jasper's book. So often clients tried to tell you what to do, or changed their minds a million times and kept making you redo things. Sure, Pen had a barmy plan, but at least she'd settled on it and left him to it, and that made her aces in Jasper's book.

'How's it going?' Pen asked, poking her head in the room.

The only tricky thing about working for Pen, Jasper had discovered, was that she was always looking for a way to procrastinate the latest article she was working on.

He grinned at the piece of wood he was sanding down and said, 'Quite well. How's your article going?'

'Oh, it's dismal. You know, you needn't stay so late. You can go home.'

Jasper shrugged. He didn't want to say he had no one to go home to – although he didn't – because that sounded pathetic and he didn't want to make Pen feel sorry for him.

Pen said, 'Well, I've got to head out.'

'Oh,' Jasper said, and paused. 'Did you want me to leave?' Pen had left him alone in the house before, as she wandered all over the street visiting various neighbours, but maybe this time was different for some reason.

'No,' said Pen. 'You can absolutely stay. Or you can come with me.'

'Come with you?' Jasper asked cautiously, unsure if he was being asked on a date.

It must have showed on his face, because Pen laughed. 'No, no, not like *that*. It's just … if you're going to be spending so much time on the street, you might as well come to street events.'

'Street events?' Jasper echoed. 'Do you have a lot of street events?'

'Indeed,' Pen answered cheerfully. 'Christmas Street is a very special street!'

'I suppose it is,' Jasper agreed affably.

'Anyway, I'm pretty sure Sam down the street just got engaged to his girlfriend. Isn't that nice?'

'Pretty sure?' said Jasper.

'Well, he was supposed to propose tonight. I'm not sure how it went yet, but I'm sure it went well.'

'How do you know he was supposed to propose tonight?'

'Well, we all helped him come up with the proposal.'

Jasper lifted his eyebrows in silent consideration of that, and Pen grinned.

'I told you: this is a very special street. Hang on, though, you're right, I should just text Diya and make sure Libby said yes. It would be dead embarrassing to go down there and have them be in the middle of breaking up or something.'

Jasper refrained from pointing out that he hadn't suggested Pen text anyone, because it seemed easier to just go along with Pen's flow.

Pen's phone dinged with an incoming text. 'Aha!' she exclaimed, holding it up towards Jasper briefly – too briefly for Jasper to register anything about it. 'Victory! She totally said yes! And now we can go and celebrate. And you ought to come. It'll be lovely.'

Jasper looked at the work he was supposed to be doing. 'Well, I mean.'

'No, no,' Pen insisted. 'Come along,' and then she took his hand and dragged him bodily out of the house.

Sam and Libby came home to the entire street standing outside their house, and they erupted into celebratory cheers when they saw them.

'Sam!' Max exclaimed over the din. 'You got it done!'

'He did a beautiful job,' Libby assured Max, letting Anna and Emilia admire her ring.

'Thank you, Libby. See?' Sam said to Max. 'I'm not completely incompetent.'

'Leave him alone,' Arthur said. He had Charlie on one arm and a bottle of champagne in the other.

'Champagne is a smart accompaniment to a baby,' Sam remarked.

'It's for you,' Arthur said, handing it over. 'You and Libby. Congratulations.'

'Thank you,' Sam said.

'Now I want to hear all about the operation,' Max said seriously to Pari and Teddy. 'How did it go?'

'Like *clockwork*,' Pari said proudly. 'Sam did the best job.'

'So much praise,' Sam remarked drily. 'For something so simple.'

'You asked someone to spend the rest of her life with you,' Arthur said. 'It's hardly *simple*.'

'No,' Sam agreed, smiling. 'But in the right circumstances it can *feel* that way.'

'I think I deserve some credit,' said Libby, 'for doing such a good job of being proposed to.'

There was some general laughter and Sam leaned over to give Libby a quick kiss because he couldn't help it.

Bill's door opened, and Jack came dashing outside, barking exuberantly.

'Jack!' shouted Pari. 'Don't worry, the mission went off without a hitch.'

'Pulled it off without Jack, eh?' said Max. 'Poor fellow.'

'Mum said we couldn't bring a dog into the supermarket.'

'You can't!' said Diya.

'Jack's different from other dogs. Jack's *well-behaved*.'

Jack turned in a circle, barking his agreement with that characterisation.

Diya looked less than convinced.

'What is all this hustle and bustle out here?' demanded Bill crankily from his doorway. 'Can't a man even hear his telly? And Jack was sound asleep when all of you woke him up.'

'Libby agreed to marry me,' Sam called to Bill.

'Well, of course she did,' Bill grumbled. 'Is that any reason for all this hullaballoo?' And then he shut his door on them.

Sam looked at Libby and said, 'Bill was basically the only person on the street who truly believed in me. For that reason, he's basically the only person on the street I actually like.'

'Ha ha,' said Max.

'We should go inside,' Sam said. 'Stop bothering all the neighbours.'

'Bill's the only one not here,' Pen pointed out.

Which caused Max to exclaim, 'Jasper the carpenter! Welcome to a typical Christmas Street party!'

Jasper looked partly charmed and partly overwhelmed, which Sam thought was the right reaction for Christmas Street. 'It's quite something.'

This provoked laughter.

'Just wait until the new neighbour arrives and joins in,' said Pen.

'Hey, do you know anything about the new neighbour?' Max asked. 'Because I could have sworn that house was haunted. I am impressed anyone wants to live there.'

'Told you!' Teddy said triumphantly, turning to Sam.

'It's not haunted,' Sam said, and gave Max a hard look.

'Oh,' Max said hastily. 'That's right. It's not haunted.' Max paused. 'Probably.'

'*Max*,' said Sam.

'I mean, I'm just saying, Sam: have you *looked* at the place?'

'It's just an empty house! It doesn't follow that it's *haunted*. Not all empty houses have to be haunted.'

'And anyway, there's no such thing as ghosts,' said Anna.

'Well, I don't know,' said Diya. 'When I was a little girl growing up, my grandmother always used to burn turmeric to frighten the *bhoots*.'

'The *bhoots*?' said Max.

'The ghosts.'

'There's no such thing,' Sam said firmly, because Teddy and Pari were looking more and more alarmed.

Diya seemed to grasp this as well. 'Not here at least,' she said. 'I've never seen any here. Anyway, there's nothing to be frightened of. If they live in that house, they'll bother the new family and not us.'

'That's the spirit,' said Max drily.

Arthur said, 'If we're going to go inside, let's use our house so I can put Charlie to bed.'

'With all this noise?' asked Anna.

'Charlie takes after Max. He'd sleep through a herd of buffalo trampling around him.'

'Buffalo?' said Pari. 'That doesn't seem likely.'

'One never knows,' replied Max wisely.

Chapter 6

Popular wedding dates
Popular wedding venues
Popular wedding flowers
Unique wedding flowers

Sam rang Ellen after Teddy was in bed, while Libby was in the bathroom getting ready for bed, and said when Ellen answered, 'It's done.'

Ellen's shriek was loud and sustained.

Sam shifted the phone away from his ear and shouted toward it, 'If you refuse to behave like a normal person, then I shan't continue this conversation.'

'I am behaving like a normal person!' Ellen shouted back at him. 'This is how a normal person reacts when their little brother says he's getting married!' Then she resumed shrieking.

Sam seemed to remember Ellen behaving this way the first time, too, so at least Ellen stayed consistent. He let her shriek and flipped through the furniture catalogue on the table.

Finally she calmed down enough to call out to Sophie and Evie, 'Girls! Your uncle Sam is getting married!'

Their responses were much more subdued.

'They don't sound that excited,' remarked Sam, amused.

'They're teenagers,' Ellen said dismissively. 'So where's Libby? I want to congratulate her!'

'Upstairs at the moment.'

'Tell me all about it! Was it incredibly romantic?'

'Well. I decided to propose at the supermarket.'

'At the ... supermarket?'

'In the fruit and veg section,' Sam clarified, relishing revealing it to Ellen.

' ... Fruit and veg.'

Sam laughed. 'Yes. It's where Libby and I first met! Remember?'

'Oh, my God,' said Ellen, the recollection clearly striking her.

'Before I knew she was Teddy's teacher or anything.'

'Of course. Potato Lady or something.'

'Carrots,' said Sam. 'I proposed to her with a carrot.'

'Wait, I think there's something wrong with this connection,' said Ellen, 'it sounded like you just said you proposed to Libby with a carrot.'

Sam laughed. 'Yes. That is indeed what it sounded like, because that's what I did. But don't worry: it was better than you're thinking. It was incredibly romantic. Teddy and Pari and the rest of the street approved.'

'The rest of the street?' echoed Ellen.

'Well,' said Sam, 'when you live on Christmas Street, it's inevitable that you will receive lots of helpful suggestions as to exactly how you should propose.'

'Well, that I definitely believe,' remarked Ellen, 'your street is definitely like that. Now I'm offended I wasn't called to any of the street meetings.'

'Got to live on Christmas Street to be part of the Christmas Street meetings. Those are the rules.'

'But there's no room for new inhabitants on Christmas Street!' Ellen protested.

'Actually, you're wrong. We are shortly welcoming a new neighbour onto the street.'

'Where are they moving in? Is the old man getting a lodger?'

Sam laughed. 'I had the same thought, actually. But no. You know that vacant old house that—'

'Wait, that thing? I thought that thing was falling down. Someone's going to move in there?'

'Presumably they'll fix it up.'

'They must be desperate. Or ghost-hunters. Because that thing definitely has ghosts.'

'It doesn't have ghosts.'

'It's haunted.'

'There's no such thing as ghosts.'

'If there's no such thing as ghosts, then what is that unexplained spectre I saw that night in Manchester when we all went out?'

'Wait, all those years ago when we were practically kids? There was no unexplained spectre. You were drunk.'

'Hmm,' said Ellen, in a tone of voice that said that she knew better than Sam and Sam was just wrong. 'Anyway, don't I get any Christmas Street meeting bonus points, seeing as we're family?'

'Well,' said Sam, 'maybe, seeing as Pen's carpenter has started joining the meetings.'

'Right, I expected to be called in next time. There's no way I would have allowed you to propose using *carrots*.'

'It was romantic,' Sam insisted, as Libby came into the room. 'Look, here's Libby, she'll tell you.' He held the phone out to Libby.

'Who is it?' she asked.

'My sister. Tell her how romantic my proposal was.'

Libby smiled and said into the phone, 'It was a very romantic proposal.' And then after a pause, 'No, I'm not just saying that!'

Sam sighed as Libby wandered off with his phone to finish gossiping with Ellen about the proposal.

'So,' said Sam, as they settled into bed that night. 'I'm just checking. I mean, not that I have any doubt in my mind, but . . . I still thought I'd check.'

'Okay,' Libby said. He couldn't see her face in the room's darkness but she sounded a little alarmed by his conversation preface.

He said, '*Did* you think the carrot proposal was romantic?'

Libby laughed.

'No, I'm serious,' Sam said. 'I know you're only going to get proposed to once, and I want to make sure I did it properly, fulfilled all your hopes and dreams, et cetera.'

'How do you know I've never been proposed to before?' Libby asked.

Sam could hear the warm tease in her voice, could envision perfectly what her smile must look like on her face. It was

81

lovely to think of how well he knew Libby and all of her smiles now, well enough to close his eyes and see them in the dark.

He said, 'Oh, right. Sorry. Well, thank you for choosing me out of all of the legions of men who had proposed to you before.'

She said, 'Well, none of them ever proposed to me in a supermarket before. That's really what I was waiting for.'

'I know you're teasing me,' Sam said, 'but I'm just making sure.'

Libby's hand came up to card soothingly through Sam's hair. 'I know. And it was lovely. It was wonderful. It was honestly better than I could have dreamed.'

'Because you could never have dreamed that?' Sam joked.

'Because it was just so perfectly us. And how could I have ever dreamed *us*? I'd never have been able to dream you, and Teddy, or this street, even. In a way it makes it even more perfect that everyone seemed to have a hand in planning it. All of these people are really our family now, and I'm so happy to have all of them in our lives. I'm happy to have you and Teddy in my life most of all, of course, but it was incredible today to be reminded of just how many ways you have changed my life immeasurably for the better.'

Sam shifted so he could press his nose into Libby's hair and breathe deep and murmured, 'Because you have changed my life so immeasurably for the better as well, I am glad to have reminded you of that.'

There was a moment of silence before Libby ventured, 'And Teddy. He seems to really be okay with all of this?'

'I think he's more than okay,' said Sam. 'I talked to him about the whole thing, obviously. A good chat. And I think it was the sort of thing where he suddenly realised the full impact of having you in our lives. Like, we've been happy, and going along, and I don't think he stopped to think all that explicitly about the memory of his mother in the context of all of this.'

'And I would imagine all of this made him think of her,' Libby ventured after another moment of silence.

'Yes. And I feel like it forced him to go through the exercise that I've been going through for months now: that exercise of being really genuinely happy and knowing that would have made Sara happy, and that life really does go on, and that we've been blessed twice now with amazing women. I don't want to make you think – I hope we never make you think – like we're comparing you to Sara, or want you to be a replacement for her.'

'You never do,' said Libby. 'You really never do. And I hope I never make you think like either one of you need to forget Sara, and that I'm *trying* to replace her.'

'You never do,' said Sam, with as much earnestness as Libby had said it. 'You really never do.'

After a moment of a heavy, reflective silence, Sam, so they wouldn't fall asleep on such a weighted note, said, 'When would you like to get married?'

'Oh, blimey, I don't know,' said Libby, exhaling. 'I haven't thought about it. Spring might be nice. Pretty flowers and all that. There's so much planning to do, too, so I'll need some time to get everything in place.'

'Spring sounds lovely,' Sam agreed.

'Do you have a preference?' Libby asked him.

'I really don't. Whatever you like.'

'We'll have to ask Teddy if he has a preference,' said Libby. 'We'll have to ask him if he has a preference for how he'd like to participate in the festivities, too. What role he'd like to play.'

'I don't know if he's thought about it,' Sam admitted. 'We've been pretty focused on getting the proposal right.'

'I can understand that,' said Libby gravely. 'It was quite the operation. You know what we really have to think about?'

'What's that?' asked Sam.

'How are we going to involve Jack in the ceremony?'

Sam laughed.

Libby gave herself a little while to just enjoy her engagement within the confines of Christmas Street. Libby had found that things within the confines of Christmas Street seemed to enjoy a uniquely rosy and comforting warm glow. It was the glow of knowing that everyone around you knew you and liked you and approved of you and was thinking kind thoughts about you. Libby had grown up in a small village, where maybe everyone had been a bit interfering, but where also everyone had known her by name and been keenly interested in her. When she had been young, that had been stifling. She was old enough now to know that everyone on Christmas Street was still a bit interfering in their keen interest in her life, but it was also nice to know that people had your back and you weren't alone in the world. London had been a harsh and difficult transition, and it was nice to feel like she had found a little village in the middle of the city. She knew that lots of people would find it suffocating – lots of the other teachers at school were astonished by Christmas Street stories – but she liked how the people on Christmas Street had reached an understanding amongst themselves of the amount and type of interfering that was expected and accepted. It was a high level but it came from a sweet place of cooperative caring.

She told her colleagues at work about her engagement because it was impossible not to, given that, once it had been properly fitted, she couldn't resist wearing Sam's ring.

The headmaster said pleasantly, 'Oh, a Turtledove wedding! Coo coo!' and Libby emphatically thought that she did not want turtledoves at her wedding.

Cassandra, who taught Year Three, wanted to hear all about the proposal, so Libby told the story.

'Around a carrot?' said Cassandra.

'But how did he know it wouldn't get stolen?' asked George, who taught second grade.

'One of the neighbours was keeping watch,' Libby explained.

The rest of the teachers in the staff room listening to her story all said knowingly some variation of *Oh, yes, the famous Christmas Street neighbours*.

Libby laughed. 'I don't know why you mock. It comes in handy having them all around. Look how handy it came to have someone to watch the carrots for my proposal.'

'Indeed,' agreed George.

'But what would happen if you two broke up?' asked Cassandra.

Libby blinked at her. 'What?'

'Wow,' said Matthew, who taught Reception. 'That's a bit unnecessary, Cass, isn't it?'

'I'm just saying, before you know it the whole street knows your business and is taking sides on rows, and you'd have to think about who gets custody of Christmas Street if you divorce.'

'I don't think I'm going to think about my divorce before I'm even married, ta,' Libby said.

'That's when you should think about it,' said Cassandra wisely.

'Don't mind her,' Matthew said. 'Congratulations, Lib.'

Libby accepted the congratulations and thought again how nice the warm glow of Christmas Street was in comparison to *that*. No one on Christmas Street ever doubted the likely inevitability of a happily-ever-after.

Eventually, Libby found she stopped just gazing at her ring and sighing happily with joy, and she started to get used to the idea that this wedding thing was really going to happen and she probably ought to start thinking seriously about planning it. After all, Libby had been thinking about her wedding in the abstract since she'd been a little girl. So, eventually, she rang the woman who she'd been thinking about her wedding *with* all that time.

In retrospect, Libby thought, maybe it was surprising that she'd waited so long to ring her mother with the happy news. But her mother could – sometimes – not all the time – but sometimes – be the very opposite of the warm Christmas Street glow. And maybe a part of Libby had wanted to get used to the news herself first. Maybe a part of her wanted to make sure it really was all real and she wasn't going to wake up.

Libby sat in the front window of the house and idly watched the new neighbour settling in. She knew that in all the houses up and down Christmas Street, the denizens of the street were watching the activity avidly. Probably Sam's little club of work-from-home procrastinators was hoping to add another member. Jack was one of the Christmas Street neighbours avidly watching the proceedings, but he seemed uncertain about approaching to introduce himself.

As far as Libby could tell, the person moving in was a single woman. She didn't see any kids or other family members running around. And she'd come with only a tiny amount of stuff. Libby had only seen a couple of boxes, at most. Maybe the rest of her belongings were coming later, thought Libby.

Teddy and Pari had been invited to the birthday party of one of the other kids at school, and Sam had volunteered to be the one in charge of bringing them, since Diya had predictably had a million other simultaneous engagements with far-flung acquaintances. Darsh was home, since it was a Saturday, but Sam spent all day every day at home and was happy to get out of the house.

This meant that everything was nice and quiet and Libby had no reason to delay the telephone call.

Her mother picked up warmly with, 'Elizabeth! It's so lovely to hear from you! How is the new school year going?'

And Libby immediately wondered why she had put off calling her, since hearing her mother's voice made her smile and relax into the obvious love and affection. 'Hi,' she responded. 'Going along. Busy.'

'I hope the new students are all settled in?' her mother continued. 'I was so hoping to hear from you. You are much worse at staying in touch once the school year is underway.' It was a gentle chiding, and fairly well deserved, Libby had to admit.

'I know,' she said sheepishly. 'It just gets very busy.'

'And how are Sam and Teddy?' her mother asked. They had been to see Libby's mother over the summer hols, as part of an extended sightseeing jaunt they'd gone on. It had gone exceedingly well. Sam was charming and a wonderful boyfriend, so Libby hadn't thought her mother would object to him in any way, and it was impossible not to love Teddy.

Libby said, 'They're fantastic. I'm actually happy you brought them up because—'

'Olivia Holden,' her mother interrupted, 'has run away with Martin Stamper. What do you think about that?'

Clearly her mother had been anxious to impart this information, and Libby had to admit that it even distracted her from her own news. 'What?' said Libby. 'Really? Run away *where*? Aren't they both eighty?'

'I *know*,' her mother replied, and clucked her tongue. 'I ask you: what even is the point at that age? It's all been very shocking. Olivia's daughter is appalled at her mother. It seems she didn't come down to breakfast one morning, and Joanna went upstairs to check on her, fearing she might be dead.'

'Well, that's dramatic,' remarked Libby.

'Well, as you say, Olivia's no spring chicken. But all Joanna found was a note that she'd run off with Martin, and she's packed up her clothes and brought them all with her, and Olivia finally sent a postcard back, from *Ibiza*. *Imagine*.'

'Wow,' said Libby, and made a note of Ibiza as a possible honeymoon destination. 'Anyway, I wanted to tell you that—'

'Joanna is just beside herself. She's worried Martin might be encouraging her mother to go to a nude beach. That Martin was always talking about nude beaches—'

'I'm getting married,' Libby blurted out, because if she waited to find an opening in the saga of Olivia and Martin, she'd be waiting a very long time.

'What's that, Libby, dear?' her mother said, clearly surprised at being interrupted from her gossip flow.

'I'm getting married,' Libby repeated. 'Sam asked me to marry him.'

After a moment, her mother exclaimed, 'Libby! Oh, my goodness! You should have said earlier! How amazing! How wonderful! How lovely!'

Libby beamed and looked once again down at the engagement ring winking on her finger. 'Thanks.'

'Oh, I simply can't wait. When are you thinking of having the wedding?'

'I haven't done any planning,' Libby said.

'Of course not,' her mother said. 'What was I thinking? How much planning can you do without me there?'

Which was very like her mother to think, Libby thought, smiling. 'I was thinking of spring for the wedding.'

'Oh, yes,' her mother agreed. 'Spring would work well. It really couldn't be a moment sooner than that.'

'No?'

'No. There's so much to do when it comes to a wedding. You've simply no idea. In fact, I ought to come up for a visit, as soon as I can manage it, so that I can help. Have you a spare room?'

At dinner that night, Teddy's adventure of the day was all about the trampoline park where the birthday party had occurred, and how much amazing fun it had been.

Sam's adventure of the day was about how he thought he'd give the trampoline park a whirl, since Teddy had been enjoying it so much, and he was amazing he hadn't broken his leg.

'I don't know what you were worried about, Dad,' Teddy said. 'It's not hard. You just jump around.'

'Someday you're going to be as old as me and I hope I live to see that day so that I can bring you to a trampoline park and tell you to just jump around,' Sam replied.

'I'll still be awesome at it,' Teddy said. 'I think I'm probably just awesome at jumping around.'

'It might be your special talent,' Sam agreed equably. 'Too bad trampolining's not an Olympic sport. Then you could go into it and make us some money and earn your keep in this house.'

Teddy laughed.

'Actually,' Libby said, 'trampolining *is* an Olympic sport.'

'Is it?' Sam said. 'Then, Teddy, I think we know how you're going to be spending the next few years of your life. Constant training.'

Teddy laughed again.

Sam looked at Libby. 'And what about you? What was your adventure for the day?'

'Well, actually, I've had a very adventurous day around here,' Libby said.

Sam and Teddy both looked expectant.

'First, I watched the new neighbour move in.'

'Oh!' Teddy exclaimed. 'That was today? Oh, no! Pari and I were supposed to spy on her.'

'Spy on her?' Sam asked, frowning.

'Don't worry, it's going to Make a Difference in her life.'

'It's going to make a difference in her life to be spied on?' said Sam.

'It'll be like the good sort of spying,' Teddy said. 'Christmas Street spying.'

'I know what you mean,' Libby said supportively. 'There is something really great about Christmas Street spying.'

'I don't know that I want to encourage spying of any sort,' Sam said sceptically.

'Who's the new neighbour?' asked Teddy. 'How many kids do they have?'

'No kids that I could see. It just looked like a single woman. She didn't even have many belongings. Not many boxes at all. But I don't know how effectively I was spying. Probably not as good as you and Pari.'

'No, probably not,' Teddy agreed seriously. 'We're pretty good at spying.'

'You've got quite the resumé of talents,' Sam remarked. 'Trampolining, spying . . . I'm such a proud dad.'

Teddy ignored him. 'Has Jack met the new lady yet?'

'Not that I saw. Possibly he was waiting for you and Pari to go with him to make the introductions.'

'Yeah,' Teddy agreed thoughtfully. 'That would make sense.'

'You didn't go over and say hi?' Sam asked.

'No. I didn't see that anyone did. Moving is super-stressful, I imagine that no one wanted to bother her on the same day she was trying to move in.'

'Move-in day was when I met Bill,' Sam remarked.

'And Jack,' Teddy said. 'Jack came over right away. But it's probably different when there's kids involved.'

'No doubt,' Libby agreed. 'Anyway, I was preoccupied.'

'By what?' asked Sam.

'By my mum,' Libby replied. 'I rang my mum to tell her we were getting married.'

'Oh,' said Sam, sounding surprised. 'I thought you'd rung her before.'

'I should have,' Libby agreed. 'But I think I was waiting to make sure the engagement stuck.'

'Make sure it stuck?' Sam echoed. 'I think I'm offended.'

Libby laughed. 'I just wanted to make sure I hadn't dreamed the whole thing. I mean, a proposal in a supermarket. Could have been some sort of fever-induced hallucination. You never know. But I've still got this ring on my finger, so I'm supposing it's real.' She held up her hand to show off her ring.

'Still real,' Sam assured her drily.

Libby laughed again.

'So what did Rebecca say?' asked Sam.

'She was pleased. Delighted. You know she loves the both of you. She can't wait for the wedding. In fact, she's going to come for a visit soon, so she can help me plan everything.'

'Oh,' said Sam, 'that'll be nice for you. You'll have some help.'

'Pari and Jack and I can help, too, of course,' said Teddy. 'We can Make a Difference.'

'I didn't want to interfere with your busy spying schedule,' Libby said. 'I don't want the demands on your time to get to be too much.'

'We can probably handle it.'

92

'I am especially going to want to know what you would like to do at the wedding,' Libby said. 'And Jack, too, of course.'

'I bet Pari and I could train Jack to be the best ring-bearer dog,' Teddy said confidently. 'He's so smart, he probably barely needs any training at all.'

'When is your mum coming to visit?' Sam asked that night, as they got ready for bed.

Libby finished brushing her teeth and said, 'She didn't say. She had things she wanted to make sure were taken care of at home first. Must make sure the gossip machine will operate without her, et cetera.'

Sam laughed as he turned the blankets down. 'Well, it'll be fun to have her around.'

'So the proposal went very well,' Sam told Bill, as they waited outside together for the kids to come home from school, 'and Libby told her mum and she's going to come for a visit.'

The weather had tipped properly into autumn, and it was grey and misty and cold. Sam felt that he would like nothing more than to collect Teddy and Pari and bring them inside for a nice hot cuppa. It was that kind of day. In fact, Sam should have brought a cuppa outside with him so he could wrap his hands around it and let it warm him in the cool. He found himself glancing at Bill's coat and wondering if it looked as if it was growing threadbare. They would have to find a way

93

to get Bill a new coat, especially if Bill was going to insist on waiting outside for the kids every day.

While Sam was musing over the state of Bill's coat, Bill turned his head and said to him in astonishment, 'Did you say your mother-in-law is coming for a visit?'

Sam was bewildered by the reaction. 'Mother-in-law-to-be, yes.'

'When?' asked Bill with his usual bluntness.

'We don't know yet.'

'For how long is she staying?' Bill continued.

'We haven't discussed it. She didn't mention it. We don't have the details of the visit ironed out yet. Why? Do you know my mother-in-law?' Bill's reaction seemed curiously stern.

'No, but I know *mothers-in-law*,' Bill replied grimly. 'Just . . . in general.'

Sam was amused. 'There's nothing to know about mothers-in-law "in general". Every mother-in-law is different and particular. I've met Libby's mum and she's nice. I'm sure she'll make a very lovely mother-in-law.'

'Meeting *mothers* is one thing,' Bill rejoined gruffly. 'Then the mothers become *mothers-in-law* and all bets are off.'

'Didn't get on with Agatha's mother, eh?' said Sam.

'Oh, I got on with her just fine,' Bill said. 'She didn't get on with *me*.'

Sam laughed.

'Once the realisation hits them that they're stuck with you the rest of their lives as the bloke who stole their daughter away, they change their whole tune.'

'That's a very . . .' Sam tried to think of how to put it delicately, so it didn't sound like he was just proclaiming Bill to be old. 'It's not like that nowadays,' he said, which he wasn't sure achieved his goal of not calling Bill old.

'You're saying I'm old-fashioned,' Bill allowed, 'but just because I'm old-fashioned doesn't mean I'm wrong. I know mothers-in-law.'

Sam said, 'I'm sure it's all going to be fine.'

Sam got Teddy and Pari settled with cups of hot cocoa and a special treat of post-school biscuits. Sam usually tried to be more healthy-snack-orientated after school, but he was feeling in an especially benevolent mood today. He was getting married and all was right with the world. He was actually whistling as he gave a dog biscuit to Jack.

'What's that you're doing?' Teddy demanded, looking at him in alarm.

'Giving Jack a treat,' said Sam, bewildered.

'No, that *noise*.'

'It's whistling.'

'It's dreadful,' said Teddy. 'You should stop.'

'It's not especially good whistling,' added Pari. 'My dad's a really good whistler, you should ask him to give you lessons.'

'Wow,' said Sam. 'What a tough audience.'

The doorbell rang, and Jack went barking to the front of the house, tumbling over his own paws as he did when he got excited.

'Which exciting neighbour has stopped by to visit us with a random request today?' mused Sam aloud, but when he opened the door it was to Libby's mum. Standing right there, in the flesh, with many, many, many bags.

'Oh,' Sam said, surprised. 'Hi.'

'What a greeting,' said Rebecca, lifting her eyebrows at him.

'I mean,' Sam stammered. 'I just mean. Hi.'

'Libby didn't tell you I was coming?'

'No, she did. She absolutely did. I just . . . didn't realise that you were coming *today.*'

'Having made up my mind to come for a visit,' sniffed Rebecca, 'I saw no point in wasting any time. I'm much like you with proposing marriage that way, I suppose.'

Rebecca had swept past him and into the house, which Sam supposed meant that was his cue to gather her luggage. 'Oh,' he said. 'Well, I knew Libby was the one, so . . . ' He smiled winningly.

'Your second one, isn't she?' said Rebecca sweetly. And before Sam could react to that, she said, 'I forgot to say: congratulations,' and then swooped in to kiss his cheek.

'Oh,' he said, nonplussed. 'Right. Yeah.'

'Where's Libby?'

'She's not home from work yet,' said Sam, contemplating the trial of wrestling the luggage up the stairs to the spare bedroom.

'Oh, right, you work from home,' she said vaguely, with an air of scepticism, as if she didn't believe that was a thing that existed.

'Well,' said Sam jocularly. 'Sometimes. I at least give it a try.'

'Hmm,' said Rebecca. 'Do you have any tea in this house?'

Chapter 7

Monday: No sightings. Curtains all closed.
Tuesday: No sightings. Curtains all closed.
Wednesday: Same.
Thursday: Nothing to report.
Friday: SIGH.

'I get the idea,' Sam said slowly, as they were getting ready for bed together, because this was a delicate topic to broach, 'that your mother isn't thrilled with the idea of us getting married.'

'What?' said Libby. 'Don't be silly! Why wouldn't she be happy about that? It's wonderful news.'

'Well, when we all met over the summer she was lovely and charming and nice to us and now she's ... not.'

Libby frowned at him. 'You didn't think she was nice tonight?'

Sam, recognising that he was treading extremely delicate ground, said, 'No, no. I mean, she was very nice.' It felt ridiculous to say, *I just felt like she made a bunch of snide comments to me before you got home*. It made him feel like he was in primary school or something. Also, surely he wasn't going to be one of those people who was going to have issues with his in-laws. Sam had never had any issues with Sara's parents. Libby's dad had died years ago, but Sam had assumed he'd have a good relationship with Rebecca.

Libby, arranging the pillows on their bed with an enthusiasm that wasn't necessary, said, 'Look. My mother can sometimes be difficult to deal with. I understand that. There is, after all, a reason I moved to London.'

'You moved to London because of your mother?' said Sam, because that wasn't something he had ever heard before.

'No,' said Libby. 'I didn't. But it wasn't a drawback to put some distance between us. She can be demanding. But she's also my mum, and she just loves me, and if she's being a little protective right now, well, who can blame her? But she loves you and Teddy. It's going to be fine.' Libby smiled brightly.

'Yeah,' Sam agreed, and hoped he didn't sound hollow. 'Absolutely fine.'

Teddy, Pari, and Jack had discovered that if they took up residence in a certain corner of Max and Arthur's back garden, it gave them a perfect view of the house with the new mysterious inhabitant.

Not that the view had been any benefit at all so far, because the woman kept to herself and was barely ever seen. She had put dark curtains up over the window and kept them tightly drawn, and Teddy, Pari, and Jack, though they looked and looked and looked, never saw a face appear at any of those windows.

Max, amused at having become the central location of this serious undercover spying operation, brought the children out a plate of biscuits whilst Arthur gave Charlie a bath.

'Isn't it late?' he asked, handing the people-biscuits to Teddy and Pari and the dog biscuits to Jack. 'Won't your parents be calling for you?'

'Yeah, probably,' said Teddy glumly.

'They'll want us to have *dinner*,' added Pari.

'And what's wrong with dinner?' asked Max. 'Other than the fact that I just ruined it for you with the biscuits, oops.'

'When we have dinner,' Pari explained wisely, 'it means that the spy house goes unmonitored.'

'Who knows what happens while we're at dinner,' Teddy added.

Max smiled at them. 'Probably not much, I assure you. She's just moved in. She's probably collapsed in the middle of boxes, too exhausted to come to the window.'

'No, Libby said she had almost no boxes *at all*,' said Teddy.

'And that's *super* suspicious,' added Pari. 'Plus, she put all the curtains up and made sure we couldn't see in.'

'Maybe she heard this is a street full of spies,' remarked Max.

Pari brightened. 'Do you think so? I was thinking about advertising.'

'I don't think spies advertise,' Teddy said. 'They have to be stealthy.'

'But how else do they get clients? Maybe she doesn't know we're *nice* spies. Maybe we ought to go and tell her that we'll help her with the unpacking.'

'But we know she doesn't have many boxes to unpack,' Teddy pointed out.

'Right, but it's called *spying*,' said Pari. 'Spies tell *stories*. Right, Max?'

'Sometimes people like to unpack for themselves,' Max said. 'How else do you know where to hide all of your best biscuits from your interfering husband who keeps trying to get you to eat healthy? Now run along home for dinner before I get in trouble for keeping you too late.'

'Bye, Max!' chorused Teddy and Pari, and Jack barked farewell and took off after them.

Which made Max smile, because Jack would be back shortly looking for more food.

Max wandered inside and put the plate of biscuits on the kitchen counter and then went upstairs, where bathtime was done and Arthur was in the middle of storytime. Charlie, drowsy on Arthur's lap, smiled when he saw Max and pointed to the book Arthur was reading to him.

'He says you do better voices,' Arthur said.

'I don't believe that for a second,' Max said gallantly, even though Arthur barely did voices when he read to Charlie.

'You disbelieve the accuracy of my translation of Charlie's babbling?' said Arthur.

'Heaven forbid I disbelieve the accuracy of your anything,' said Max.

Arthur said, 'All right, storytime over, bedtime for little fellows.' He stood and settled Charlie in his crib with his blanket and leaned over and kiss his head. 'Good night, Charlie.'

Max leaned over and kissed the baby as well. 'Have brilliant dreams,' he said, and then waited for Arthur to turn the soothing sailboat-themed nightlight on, and then they headed down the stairs together.

'You know,' Max remarked. 'It's because you don't commit.'

'Don't commit to what?'

'The voices! You have to just really commit to being silly.'

'"Silly" isn't really a word people use to describe me,' said Arthur. 'For good reason.'

'You're silly when you want to be,' Max said, amused. 'Lucky me, I know the real Arthur and see behind your careful non-silly persona.'

'If you spread such vicious rumours about my occasional silliness,' Arthur said as they reached the lounge, 'I shall have to divorce you.'

'Mmm,' said Max absently. 'What shall we watch on telly?'

'You never take my divorce threat seriously,' said Arthur, as he disappeared into the kitchen.

'I never do,' Max agreed, turning the television on and flipping through the stations unhappily.

'What are these biscuits?' asked Arthur, carrying them into the lounge upon his return.

'Oh, I brought them outside to Teddy and Pari. They were in the back garden.'

'Spying on the poor new neighbour again?' said Arthur. He sat on the floor of the lounge and began sorting Charlie's toys into piles.

Max, sprawled on the sofa, watched him. 'You know, when you do that, you make me feel guilty about not helping you.'

'You don't have to help me.'

'You could just leave them. We haven't anywhere to put them.'

'They worry me in the middle of the floor.'

Arthur legitimately did not sound upset, but Max rolled himself off the sofa anyway to help.

'I told you you didn't have to,' Arthur said.

Max ignored him, saying, 'She hung her curtains first.'

'What?'

'The new lady. She put her curtains up before anything else. And she always keeps them tightly closed.'

'She obviously likes her privacy,' said Arthur, and then added drily, 'This street won't know what to do with her.'

'You don't think she's peddling drugs or something in there?'

'Max,' said Arthur, with fond exasperation.

'She could be cooking up methamphetamine or something. I mean, let's face it, the state of that house would suit an illicit drugs operation more than anything else.'

'You are absolutely ridiculous,' Arthur said, still sounding fond, so Max was pleased at being ridiculous.

'Really,' he said, 'that house was vacant for so long, what could it possibly have looked like inside?'

'She may have been desperate,' Arthur conceded.

'Desperate to find a headquarters for her drug-peddling operation.'

Arthur laughed. 'Look, if she *is* a drug dealer, she has chosen literally the worst street in London to try to operate an illicit operation from. Jack and Pari and Teddy'll ferret her out immediately. Nothing goes on in the street that we don't all know about immediately.'

'Wouldn't that be just the feather in their caps?' Max mused. 'Catching an internationally wanted drug dealer?'

'It would certainly be exciting,' Arthur agreed affably.

'Teddy says she didn't have any boxes,' continued Max. 'Isn't that suspicious?'

'Maybe her stuff is coming later,' said Arthur. 'Maybe it got delayed.'

'Hmm. Should we go over and say hello, do you think?' asked Max. 'After all, aren't we that sort of street now?'

Arthur considered. 'Let's wait for Diya. I feel like Diya should definitely be the first one to make an overture.'

'Sensible,' Max allowed.

'Her curtains are always closed,' Teddy said at dinner, 'and we never see her. And she didn't have any boxes.'

'She had a *few* boxes, and I really wish I'd never shared that detail,' sighed Libby.

Sam really wished that they weren't discussing this at dinner. Rebecca was looking especially disapproving and Sam wanted to impress Rebecca with how ordinary and dull their dinners were.

But here they were, discussing one of their usual topics: spying.

'You know,' Sam remarked, 'I really think that your daily adventures should be something other than spying on the poor innocent woman who's moved in. I feel like we're regressing.'

'What's that mean?' asked Teddy.

'It means we're going backwards.'

'How?'

'Well, when we first moved here I used to worry you were spending too much time spying.'

'Spying on who?'

'Everyone on the street. Pari especially. Remember when you were enemies? And then you were always spying on Mr Hammersley to try to figure out his relationship to Jack.'

'It wasn't like that,' Teddy denied breezily.

'Uh-huh,' said Sam ironically, and looked across the table to Libby, who looked amused at the exchange. 'What was your adventure for the day?'

'Today was boring,' said Libby.

'Nope,' said Teddy happily. 'You're not allowed to have a boring day.'

'Fine,' said Libby. 'Well, Pen is talking about possibly building a replica of the Eiffel Tower in her lounge.'

'I see,' said Sam thoughtfully.

'Why?' asked Teddy frankly.

'Yes, what would be the purpose of that?'

Libby shrugged. 'Aesthetic. Pen says she's got a whole aesthetic that she's working toward. She also says Jasper is sceptical about this Eiffel Tower plan, but up to the challenge.'

'Poor Jasper,' said Sam. 'By the end of all this Pen will have paid Jasper enough to build his own mansion somewhere.'

'Well, as we all know, a mansion's not a mansion if it doesn't have a replica Eiffel Tower and a dais for the bed somewhere,' rejoined Libby merrily.

'Who are all these people you're discussing?' asked Rebecca.

'The neighbours,' answered Libby. 'Pen is the neighbour I went jogging with tonight – she always has all the best gossip.'

'I'm surprised Teddy doesn't have the best gossip, since he spends all his time spying.' Rebecca took an innocent bite of her dinner.

Sam lifted his eyebrows at the remark and looked at Libby, who didn't seem to have found it unusual at all.

'So what was your adventure today, Dad?' asked Teddy.

Sam had spent the day trying to avoid Rebecca and her disapproving glances at everything he did. But he said instead, striving for a light casual tone, 'That one's easy. I received a communication from Turtledove Primary School that it's parents' evening next week. So I will finally get to meet the famous Mrs Dash.'

'She's really something,' said Teddy fervently, because his opinion of Mrs Dash had not changed in the six weeks school had been in session.

'I can't wait to see for myself,' said Sam truthfully.

'And what was your adventure for the day, Rebecca?' asked Teddy.

'What's this we're doing?' asked Rebecca, managing to sound disapproving about this as well.

'Every day we talk about an adventure we had that day,' said Teddy. 'It's a thing. Dad makes us do it.'

'Oh, really?' said Rebecca, giving him an arch look. 'You command the dinner table conversation, do you?'

'I don't *command* it,' Sam said, bristling at the choice of word. 'I just, you know, I started it when we first moved back here and Teddy was in a terrible mood all the time and I wanted him to think of it as an adventure instead. And we've just kept it up.'

'Hmm,' said Rebecca. 'Speaking of America.'

'Were we speaking of America?' said Sam.

'I assume you'll be making everyone move back there forthwith?' continued Rebecca.

'I don't "make" anyone do anything,' said Sam.

'Mum,' said Libby, 'you're being ridiculous. No one's moving to America.'

Sam gave Libby a meaningful look.

Libby mouthed across the table to him, *It's fine.*

Diya was indeed the first person on the street to seek to make contact with the new neighbour. It seemed that everyone on the street had had the same idea as Max and Arthur, that Diya ought to serve as the welcoming committee.

Diya just thought it was polite. A new neighbour had moved in who didn't know anybody yet and wasn't part of the crowd.

'It was different before we were all friendly,' Diya told Anna as they worked together on some korma. Diya had offered to teach Anna how to cook, although it was slow going, since Anna worked so much and was frequently tired when she got home. But every once in a while they connected for a lesson, and Diya found that she enjoyed them. She and Anna had spent years mistrusting each other, and often Diya could barely remember why. 'Now that we're all friendly, it seems mean to me.'

'Like we're being exclusive,' Anna said, nodding. 'I could see that.'

'Keep stirring,' Diya prompted, because Anna had a habit of becoming distracted and forgetting. 'Maybe I will take her over some korma when we're done with it. Welcome her properly.'

'It's a bit late tonight,' Anna said, obediently stirring.

'Tomorrow will be better. And who knows? It might not be any good.'

'It will be good,' Diya said. Upstairs came the sound of Emilia playing the drums. Diya said, 'Sai said she's in a band.'

Anna sighed. 'Yes. There's really nothing I can do to convince her not to be in the band. And I don't want to be too harsh about it. She's just a kid. But it's so pointless, you know?'

Diya did know. She clucked her tongue and shook her head sadly. 'They focus so much on the wrong things all the time.'

'Exactly.' Anna sighed. 'Marcel says I should be more patient. He's always reminding me that I was a lot like Emilia when I was her age.'

'You were in a band?'

'No, but I guess he means that I had my head in the clouds. And I guess I did. I had a lot of hopes and dreams that didn't exactly come true. So maybe that means I don't *really* want to stop her from going after hers, if the band is one of them. Maybe the world will just take care of all that for me.'

Diya added coriander to the korma and said thoughtfully, 'Maybe that's true. But it's already a gift we've given them that they can dream in such foolish ways to begin with.'

Diya sent a text to all of the members of the street who were home during the day, apart from Bill Hammersley, who didn't text. Sam didn't respond, which usually meant he was busy working. Max texted that he'd just put Charlie down and didn't want to leave him. Pen texted that yes, *of course* she was looking for an excuse to get out of the house and meet the new neighbour.

Diya met Pen on the pavement in front of her house.

Pen said cheerfully, 'Shall we ask Bill if he wants to come along? We ought at least to bring Jack along as a welcoming committee.'

'I suppose,' said Diya, carrying her korma. 'Bill probably won't want to come.'

Bill definitely did not want to come.

'Just leave the poor woman alone,' was his advice. 'Don't pester her.'

'We're not going to pester her,' Pen insisted. 'We're just going to say hi.'

Jack barked and happily wagged his tail. He'd rushed enthusiastically out of the house to greet Pen and Diya, although luckily he'd focused his greeting on Pen, because Diya still was uncertain around Jack, and Pari always liked to point out that Jack was clever enough to know that.

Diya wondered if they'd get such an enthusiastic welcome from the new neighbour.

'And Diya's bringing her chicken korma because Diya's the best,' Pen continued. 'I should have thought to bake some brownies, too, or something, but I'm terrible. Also, my kitchen is a complete disaster area because we're building tiers on the counters.'

'Tiers?' Diya repeated. 'What does that mean?'

'There are going to be, like, layers.' Pen tried to demonstrate by stacking her hands above each other in the air in front of her. 'Jasper's trying to implement the idea and I think it's going to be great, but in the meantime I really can't cook in my kitchen. It's a mess.' Pen turned back to Bill. 'So, anyway, that means only Diya has something to offer the new neighbour. I'll have to take something later. Sure you don't want to come?'

Bill looked like he could not believe how long they'd been there already. 'Definitely not,' he said flatly, and then closed the door on them.

'Oh, well,' said Pen, and she and Jack headed back down the pavement, Jack's tail wagging again.

Diya followed them over to the new neighbour's house.

Diya had never been to this house before. When she had first moved onto Christmas Street it had been occupied by an old woman who had lived there for ever. And then, upon her death, it had passed into the dispute that had apparently kept it vacant all this time. It had been barely maintained and even now, even though someone had finally moved into it and there were curtains at the windows, it still seemed desolate and empty. Diya thought that it could use some flowers outside or something, although the season for flowers was ending. *Maybe some Halloween decorations*, she mused. Max could help, Max loved decorating.

While Diya was thinking this, Pen had rung the doorbell and received no answer.

'Maybe she's not home,' Pen said, frowning. 'Although I haven't really seen her going out much.'

'She comes and goes sometimes,' Diya said. 'I've seen her every so often. She doesn't just stay in the house all the time.'

'No. I mean, she *could* stay in the house a lot,' said Pen. 'Some people do. The modern era with deliveries and so much internet ordering makes that much easier to accomplish. But no, I've seen her come and go. She just does it at odd hours.

There's no pattern to it like there is to the rest of us.' Pen paused. 'Do we spy a lot on each other on this street?'

'Yes,' Diya answered simply. 'But it all comes from a good place. Try the doorbell again, maybe she just didn't hear it. Are you sure it works? This house has been empty for years, after all.'

'I thought I heard it ring,' Pen said, but she pressed the button again. It was actually unclear whether it rang or not; Diya wasn't sure she'd heard anything. Pen must have had the same thought, because she said, 'Hmm, maybe you're right and this is broken,' as she pressed it a couple more times. 'Never mind, I'll just knock—'

The door opened before Pen could bring her hand down to knock.

The woman who answered at the door was somewhat younger than Diya had expected. In the glimpses Diya had caught of her, hurrying to or from her house, she'd always seemed slightly hunched over, closed in on herself, in a way that had struck Diya as the scurry of an older woman. But this woman was young: younger than Diya herself and possibly a few years younger than Pen. So, while older than Sai and Emilia and clearly an adult finished with her school years, she was young enough that Diya found it even stranger that she would move into such an oddly off-putting house.

The woman had opened the door just a crack, and she peered at them through it uncertainly. 'Hi,' she said. 'Is there something wrong?'

'Not at all,' answered Pen, with her usual good cheer. 'I'm Pen, and this is Diya, and this is Jack' – Jack barked – 'and we just wanted to welcome you to the street.'

The woman looked confused by this. 'Oh,' she said.

'So, welcome!' Pen gestured toward the street, as if presenting it on a game show.

Diya stepped a little past Pen and said, 'Anna and I made some chicken korma last night and wanted to give you some. Anna also lives on the street. She would have come along but she works during the day.' Diya handed her dish of korma to the woman.

The woman reached out to accept it, looking as if she did so automatically, without thinking. And then she looked down at the dish in her hands as if surprised to find it there. And then she looked back up at them. She looked shy, and confused, but not unfriendly, and she said with a small smile, 'I'm Millie.'

'Hi, Millie,' Pen said. 'I hope you're settling in okay.'

'Getting there,' said Millie. 'Still unpacking. You didn't have to bring me anything. This was very nice of you.'

'It's sort of how this street functions,' Pen said. 'We like to help each other out.'

'It's very friendly,' Diya said. 'You'll see our kids running up and down the street together. Don't mind them, by the way, and please let me know if any of them give you any trouble.'

'Oh,' said Millie. 'They really haven't.'

'We also have a street dog,' said Pen, and pointed to Jack, who wagged his tail in greeting. 'You'll also see him wandering all about. He keeps watch over all of us. That's his job.'

Millie stared at Jack. 'Oh,' she said.

'He's a good dog,' Diya offered. 'I don't even like dogs, and he's a good dog.'

'He's the best dog.' Pen looked down at him. 'Huh, Jack?'

Jack barked in agreement.

111

'So, anyway.' Pen turned back to Millie. 'That's Christmas Street, and I hope you'll feel free to come and knock on any of our doors anytime if you ever need a cup of sugar or just want to chat or whatever. And if you see us mingling around out on the pavement, by all means, come and join us. We'll have to make someone throw a party to welcome you properly. I'd do it but my house is being completely remodelled at the moment. Actually, I've an excellent carpenter, if you're in need of one.'

'That's very nice of you,' Millie said, 'but I've been getting along. It's really not—'

'Oh, it's no trouble,' Pen said. 'We really like doing this sort of thing.'

'A party isn't necessary, though,' said Millie. 'I really don't need a lot of fuss.'

'It's not fuss,' said Pen, and smiled broadly. 'It's Christmas Street.'

On the day that his parent–teacher conference with Mrs Dash was scheduled, Sam wasn't sure what to expect.

'How should I dress?' he asked Libby.

Libby laughed. 'Why? You've already pulled one Turtledove teacher, do you need to pull yourself another?'

'No, I just want to make a good impression. And I'm not sure what would make a good impression against someone who is "quite something".'

'Just be yourself. She's a primary school teacher. She's not the Queen.'

'Why are you all dressed up?' Rebecca asked when she saw him. 'Are you actually going to work?'

'I work every day,' Sam said patiently. 'Today I'm going to meet Teddy's teacher.'

'I hope she's not single,' remarked Rebecca. 'I know how that's your type.'

Sam sighed.

Mrs Dash's classroom had been decorated in dramatically glitzy fashion. Every inch of it that could sparkle did. And one corner of the class was dedicated to an enormous papier-mâché dragon that was oozing its way out of the wall, face pulled back in a fierce, sharp-toothed grimace, eyes bulging out with an odd knowing expression, like they knew all of Sam's secrets. Then again, maybe that was an effect of the glitter that had been liberally applied over the dragon's pupils. At any rate, Sam wasn't sure he liked the dragon.

'Oh, I see you've met Clementine,' said a voice behind him. 'Do you like her?'

Sam turned, startled, to find that an older woman had sailed into the classroom. And sailed was the right word for it. She was dressed in clothes that billowed all around her as she moved, so that she gave the impression of soaring instead of moving. Even though she was standing still at the moment, the layers of gauzy fabric were still settling around her from her last movement, quivering expectantly.

Sam stammered, 'Sorry. Who?'

'Clementine. The dragon.' The woman indicated the corner behind Sam, her sleeve floating about her arm as she lifted her hand to point.

Sam barely suppressed the urge to turn around to look at the dragon again, even though he could feel its glittery eyes boring into his back. He said, 'Oh, yeah. She's great,' and hoped he injected enough false bravado into the statement to be convincing.

The woman settled herself on a little stool that was positioned at the head of the classroom, letting all of her layers float languorously down into place around her, and intoned, 'I am Mrs Dash.'

Sam had assumed so, because this woman definitely struck him as 'quite something'. Seated at the head of the classroom in the manner that she was made him think of the caterpillar in *Alice in Wonderland*, perched on his mushroom. Sam managed to say, 'I'm Sam Bishop. I'm Teddy's father.'

'Oh, yes,' said Mrs Dash. '*Teddy.*'

Sam had no idea what that was supposed to mean. He also wasn't sure where he was supposed to sit, or even if he was supposed to sit. Mrs Dash hadn't invited him to sit, and the only seats he saw belonged to the children's desks, and Sam didn't want to squeeze his way into a desk chair. So he stood in front of Mrs Dash and felt like he was waiting for judgement.

'How is Teddy *enjoying* things?' asked Mrs Dash.

Sam had rather thought that he was supposed to ask the question in parent–teacher conferences and be given the information but he wasn't about to raise an objection. 'Well?' he offered.

Mrs Dash tipped her head at him like a bird of prey. 'You sound uncertain.'

'Oh. I mean.' Sam cleared his throat. 'Well. He's enjoying things well.'

Mrs Dash, after a moment, nodded her head, and Sam wondered if he had managed to pass a test. 'Yes. And we are enjoying him. He is delightful. Very bright. A very bright boy. He seems to have adjusted well to his new life here in England. He talks a little about America, but he seems to like it here.'

'Yes,' Sam agreed. 'He has adjusted now. Last year was a little rocky, but he's made friends and I think he's settled in.'

'He has indeed. He has become a classroom leader. It is lovely to see. He has been very vocal in the welcoming of our newest student Abeo.'

'Oh, yes,' Sam said. 'He's mentioned Abeo. I'm glad he's being nice to him. I told him to be.'

'He is a kind and thoughtful boy. He dislikes maths.' Mrs Dash added this in such a non-sequitur way that Sam couldn't tell if Teddy's dislike of maths was another indication of how kind and thoughtful he was or was a more dubious aspect of his personality.

Sam said, 'Like father, like son,' and smiled, but Mrs Dash did not smile in return.

Mrs Dash said, 'I have asked all of the children to consider how they may Make a Difference in the lives of others. Have you yourself considered that, Mr Bishop?'

'Er,' said Sam, caught off-guard. 'Maybe not in so many words, but I'm sure—'

'It is important to Make a Difference, wouldn't you agree? To mark our time upon the planet? And to preferably leave our environment better than we found it?'

'Yes,' Sam agreed fervently. 'It is definitely important to make a difference.'

'Make a Difference,' corrected Mrs Dash.

'That's what I said,' said Sam, confused.

'Is it?' asked Mrs Dash gently.

Sam, after a moment, said, 'So, is everything going okay with Teddy? Is there anything I should be watching out for, or doing more of?'

'That is a question you should ask of yourself. Is there anything you *feel* you should be watching out for as regards to Teddy?'

Sam considered, and found himself saying, because Mrs Dash in her caterpillar-mushroom stance with her bird-of-prey eyes and her gently waving layers of clothing made him powerless to resist saying anything, 'I've just become engaged to be married and so I've been wanting to make sure that Teddy's okay with it. We've been discussing it, of course, and he seems very okay with it, but I suppose, if there's anything in his classwork that might make you think differently, then—'

'I see nothing that concerns me,' said Mrs Dash, with an air of dismissiveness, as if Sam was worrying over nothing. It should have made him feel condescended to, but instead there was something comforting about it, having his misgivings rolled up into such an apparently inconsequential ball. 'Is there anything that you feel you should be watching out for as regards *you*?'

Sam had no idea what to say. He stared at Mrs Dash for a moment, tongue-tied, and then said, 'Well. I don't know if my future mother-in-law likes me very much.'

Mrs Dash shrugged a little, as if to say, *Who can blame her?*

'No words of advice?' asked Sam.

'Combined families are always sources of mysterious currents of emotion. But then again: all other humans are sources of mysterious currents of emotions. We must all find ways to co-exist with each other.'

'Yes,' Sam agreed. 'Do you have any tips as to *how*?'

'Chocolate,' Mrs Dash suggested after a moment.

Chapter 8

You're invited to a Halloween party! to celebrate the engagement of Sam Bishop and Libby Quinn. Fancy dress encouraged!

Sam, as soon as he had escaped from Mrs Dash's classroom, immediately texted Diya with **Have you met Mrs Dash?????** and then texted Libby with **I don't know what just happened.** Libby texted back with **LOL** ☺ and Diya rang him back when he was halfway home.

'I haven't had my conference yet,' Diya said. 'But Pari has me preparing for it like it's an audience with the Prince of Wales.'

'The Queen would probably be more accurate an analogy,' said Sam. 'It was quite something.'

'That's all anyone ever says,' said Diya. 'That she is "something". What does that mean?'

'I really don't know how to describe it,' Sam confessed.

'But did you know that there's a classroom dragon named Clementine?'

Diya was silent for a moment, then said, 'A classroom *dragon*?'

'I mean, it's not a real dragon.'

'Of course it's not a real dragon,' said Diya. 'But then, what is it?'

'Some kind of art project, I guess. I feel like I just went to therapy.'

'Therapy?' echoed Diya.

'Only not terribly productive therapy. She just recommended chocolate as a solution to all of my issues.'

'She's not wrong in pointing out the importance of food,' said Diya.

Diya would think that, thought Sam. But still, Sam popped into a shop on the way home and bought two chocolate bars, and when he got home, he found Rebecca sitting on the couch flipping through a bridal magazine.

'Hey,' Sam said.

'Oh, you're back,' said Rebecca. 'How was the meeting with Teddy's teacher? You seem to have survived.'

'I brought chocolate,' said Sam, and handed her one of the chocolate bars. 'Apparently we need more chocolate.'

'Hmm,' said Rebecca, and looked critically at Sam's body. 'Do you think chocolate is such a good idea for you, at your age and in your condition?'

Sam sighed. So far, he was exceedingly sceptical of Mrs Dash.

119

Diya found Pari outside with Teddy and Jack, in Max and Arthur's back garden.

'What are you doing out here in this back garden?' she demanded. 'Come back into our own back garden.'

'We're trying to spy on the new neighbour,' Pari said.

'You shouldn't be spying on anyone,' Diya said. 'Spying is rude. What are you two drinking?' Because they both had their hands cupped around mugs.

'Hot chocolate,' Teddy said. 'Max made it for us. Because it's cold.'

Diya, frowning, slipped through the break in the fence that led to Max and Arthur's garden, marched Teddy and Pari over to their back door, and knocked on it. Max answered it shortly, with Charlie on his hip.

'Hello there,' he smiled at them.

'These are yours,' Diya said, thrusting Teddy and Pari's mugs at him. 'You don't need to feed them while they're in your back garden spying on the neighbours.'

'It's quite all right,' Max said, as he let down a squirming Charlie so he could crawl over to be kissed by Jack. 'They're no trouble. How is the new neighbour? Is she nice?'

'She's fine,' Diya said.

Pari gasped. 'Do you know the new neighbour, Mum? You never said anything!'

'I brought her some chicken korma that Anna and I made,' Diya said. 'And I didn't say anything because it doesn't really matter, does it?'

'Of *course* it matters! Teddy and I are trying to find out everything about her, so we can Make a Difference in her life!'

'How does finding out everything about her make a difference?' asked Diya, exasperated.

'I don't know. We won't know until we find out everything about her. And then we can help her.'

'Well,' Diya said, 'Pen mentioned having a party of some sort, so you can meet the new neighbour then.'

'Oh, good,' said Max. 'I feel like that relieves me of any obligation to go over there myself, and I can just wait to be social at the party.'

'We are a *friendly* street now,' Pari told Max. 'You should at least say hello.'

'She's trying to unpack,' Max said. 'I didn't want to bother her.'

'She is trying to unpack,' Diya agreed. 'She barely let Pen and me see any of the house, so it must still be a mess of boxes.'

'That's how moving is,' Max said, sweeping Charlie back up into his arms. 'In we go. It's too chilly outside not to have a coat on, Daddy'll have my head if you catch a cold. See you tomorrow, my young double-ohs,' he said to Teddy and Pari, and then closed the door.

'Do you spend *every day* in their back garden?' asked Diya, horrified.

'Since the new neighbour moved in, yes,' said Pari stubbornly.

Diya sighed and began leading the children back to her house.

'What's her name?' asked Pari.

'Her name is Millie. But that's not what I wish to discuss.'

'I should probably go home,' Teddy decided.

'I was just talking to your dad, Teddy, about his meeting

121

with Mrs Dash, and all he had to say was that Mrs Dash is "quite something". What does that mean? I wish one of you would explain what that means.'

'I just want to make sure that you dress as *nicely* as possible, Mum,' Pari said. 'Mrs Dash dresses *so* nicely.'

'Your teacher is like a fashion model?' said Diya.

'Not that kind of dressing nicely,' said Teddy.

It was all very unhelpful and Diya still had no idea what to expect at the parent–teacher conference.

'Well,' said Libby at dinner, sending an arch look across the table to Sam. 'Surely you wish to share with us *your* adventure of the day first. How was Mrs Dash?'

'I am still too dazed to even discuss it,' said Sam.

'What did she have to say?' asked Teddy.

'What did she have to *say*?' echoed Sam. 'I cannot start this story with what she *said*. First let's talk about Clementine.'

'Oh, the dragon,' said Libby and Teddy in unison.

'Why did no one warn me there was going to be a huge glittery dragon in the corner of the room?' demanded Sam. 'That would have been pertinent information.'

'You've got to be surprised by Clementine,' Teddy said.

'She can't exactly be accurately described,' added Libby.

'Well, that one I believe. I found her creepy. Like she was watching everything I did.'

'You must have a guilty conscience,' said Libby, sounding amused.

'Indeed,' murmured Rebecca in agreement.

Sam ignored her. 'And after I managed to get oh-so-delightfully surprised by Clementine, then I got to meet Mrs Dash.'

'And what did she *say*?' asked Teddy impatiently.

'Wait, I'm still not to the point where we're talking about what she said,' said Sam, 'because now I have to discuss what she was wearing. Does she always dress like that?'

'Yes,' said Teddy.

'It was like she was wearing jellyfish,' Sam said. 'They kept pulsing and undulating all around her. They had a life of their own.'

Libby was laughing too hard to respond, almost choking on the pizza they were eating.

Teddy stared at Sam. 'What are you *talking* about? They're clothes. She doesn't wear *jellyfish*.'

'No, I know, they just *looked* like jellyfish. And then she sat on that stool, like the caterpillar in *Alice in Wonderland*.'

Libby started laughing even harder.

Teddy sighed, beleaguered by his difficult father. 'Why can't you just say what she *said*?'

'I just can't believe that this is what class with Mrs Dash is like all the time and you never *told* me,' Sam protested.

'I told you it was something!' Teddy defended himself indignantly.

'Saying it's "something" does not convey what that particular something is. Which was that. Which was ... ' Sam finally shook his head, at a loss for words. 'Which was quite something, you're right.'

'So what did she *say*?' asked Teddy. 'Can we talk about that now?'

'She said you're horrible,' Sam said. 'A terrible little boy who's a nightmare to deal with.'

Teddy grinned, not fooled for a second. 'No, she didn't.'

'No, she didn't. Of course she didn't. You know what she said. She said that you're a delight and very kind and thoughtful and you've been very nice to Abeo, which I very much appreciate.'

Teddy shrugged. 'I mean, yeah. Abeo's nice.'

'You can have him over to play with you and Pari, if you like.'

'I'll have to ask him,' said Teddy.

'I am very glad you got to meet Mrs Dash,' Libby said, finally recovering from her laughter and wiping tears out of her eyes.

'I am, too. Thank you, I suppose, for preserving the surprise.'

'She's really an excellent teacher,' said Libby. 'She's memorable, yes, but she keeps the kids' attention, which is more valuable to a teacher. The students all adore her.'

'She did talk to me about making a difference,' said Sam.

'Making a Difference,' said Teddy.

'Yes,' said Sam. 'That's what I said. Why does everyone keep correcting me?'

'You have to say it with the proper emphasis. Pari keeps telling me.'

'Okay,' said Sam. 'So I see where you're getting the whole idea from. It's rather intimidating, isn't it? She asked me how I was making a difference – sorry, *Making a Difference* – and I couldn't think of anything.'

'Aww,' said Libby. 'That's not true. You make a lot of

difference. You're raising a great little boy, and that's quite an accomplishment.'

'It's true,' said Teddy. 'I'm your difference.'

'Lucky me,' said Sam, and meant it.

Rebecca said, 'Is that why you brought me a chocolate bar? You were trying to make a difference?'

'What did you do?' asked Libby curiously.

'I thought we might need more chocolate around here,' said Sam. 'It seems to me that maybe we don't have enough chocolate in our lives.'

Libby laughed.

Rebecca said, 'I reminded him he has a wedding to get ready for and maybe he should be sparing when it came to chocolate.'

'I'm glad you liked Mrs Dash,' Libby said, putting her book aside as Sam crawled into bed with her.

'Hmm,' said Sam, leaning up to turn the lamp off. '*Did* I like her?'

Libby laughed. 'You did. I could tell that you did.'

'Yeah,' Sam decided, settling next to her. 'I think I did like her. I could see how she makes an impact on the kids. And she did seem like she genuinely cared about the kids, and knew Teddy really well. And I can't fault her for wanting everyone to make a difference.'

'Make a Difference,' Libby corrected him.

'Yes, yes, Make a Difference.' Sam waved his hand around. 'Anyway, it's a good thing to think about. Whether or not we make a difference.'

'You do,' Libby said. 'Like I said, you have Teddy. And I don't mean to make it seem like Teddy is the only meaningful thing in your life, but it's no small feat, raising a child, and doing it alone, and doing the job you've done.'

'It hasn't been alone,' Sam said. 'I mean, it's true, that we lost Sara early, and she was sick for so long before that, but I don't feel like I've been alone in it. Certainly not since moving back here.'

'No. You have your sister, and the entire street. I know. But still. You're his dad, and you've done a great job.'

'Well.' Sam considered. 'Thanks. I guess I've always given that credit to him. I mean, he's amazing.'

'You had a little something to do with it,' Libby assured him, and cuddled close to him.

'Maybe a little,' Sam allowed, and pressed a kiss into her hair.

'But you've also made a difference in my life,' Libby said, her voice muffled against Sam's skin. 'So there's that.'

Sam, after a moment, pressed Libby closer and said, 'You've made a difference in mine, too.'

Libby said, 'I've been thinking. We should plan an engagement party. The street would love it, and it would give us a chance to invite the new neighbour and all get to know her, and my mum could get to know all the neighbours.'

'Oh,' said Sam. 'Yeah. Good idea.' He wasn't entirely sure it was a good idea. Rebecca had so far not displayed any interest in getting to know the neighbours. Sam wanted to ask if Libby still thought Rebecca wasn't making inappropriate digs at him, but he knew it was hopeless: Libby seemed to notice none of the tension that Sam felt like was his constant companion these days.

'It could be Halloween-themed,' said Libby, sounding excited now. 'We could all wear costumes!'

Sam laughed. 'Oh, dear, this street with costumes is going to be, as Teddy would say, quite something.'

Libby laughed. 'You could dress as Mrs Dash.'

'I don't think I could pull off the jellyfish,' Sam said.

'They're not jellyfish. It's just *silk*.'

The following day, while her mother was at the conference with Mrs Dash and her father was still at work, Pari was very bored in her house. Teddy had a dentist appointment and wasn't around. Emilia was at band practice and Sai was upstairs sulking because he couldn't go because he had to watch Pari.

Jack had met her walking home from school, as usual, but he had been soaking wet, so Pari had dried him off thoroughly, and that had killed some time, but now there was literally nothing to do.

Except homework. But that didn't count, of course.

'Everything is so boring,' Pari told Jack. She was sprawled on the floor of the lounge, looking up at the ceiling over her head. Jack was next to her, and he was actually *snoring*. Things were so boring Jack had fallen asleep and was ignoring her.

Then the doorbell rang.

Jack woke with a jerk and a snort and leapt to his feet and immediately began barking.

Pari peered curiously through the window, just as Sai came galloping down the stairs.

'Who is it?' he asked her.

It was a woman holding one of their dishes, and Pari, recognising her, gasped dramatically. 'It's the new neighbour!' And then she almost fell over herself in her eagerness to open the door. 'Hi!' she exclaimed.

The new neighbour was pretty, noted Pari, so she could report later. Brown hair in a messy ponytail, brown eyes, brown coat. Lots of brown.

She said, 'Oh, hi. Is your, er, mum home?'

'No, she's at a school meeting with my teacher. I'm Pari.'

'Oh. Hi. I'm Millie,' she said.

'Millie,' said Pari, and grinned. 'Hi! Welcome to Christmas Street! Have you met Jack? Jack is our street dog. Have you moved in? Do you need any help moving in? Teddy and I could totally help moving in. Teddy's usually here, he's just at the dentist today. But we're great unpackers. We could absolutely help unpack boxes, if you need that.'

'Oh,' said Millie. 'I think I've got it covered, but, er, thanks.'

'Can we do something for you?' asked Sai, who was apparently determined to be as dull as possible and make Millie leave.

Millie looked over at him as he came down the stairs to her. 'I just wanted to bring this dish back to your mother.'

'We can take it,' Sai said, accepting the dish.

'Do you want to come in?' asked Pari. 'We can make you some tea.'

'No, that's okay,' Millie said. 'I just wanted to give you the dish.'

'Great,' Sai said. 'Nice meeting you. We'll see you around.' And then he *closed the door.*

'Sai!' Pari exclaimed in frustration. 'Do you know who that *was*?'

Sai looked at her like she had six heads. 'Yeah. It was the new neighbour. She was returning Mum's dish.' He lifted the dish up. 'This all just happened. Do you not remember it all just happening?'

'I wanted to get her talking! Learn more about her! No one knows anything about her! She's a mystery! How are we supposed to Make a Difference in her life if we don't *know* her?' Pari tagged along behind Sai as he carried the dish into the kitchen.

'I don't think you're going to make a difference in her life by unpacking for her,' Sai remarked. 'You've never unpacked anything. You've never moved.'

Pari scoffed. 'How hard can unpacking be? You take stuff out of boxes and put it into places. Please. I would be excellent at it.'

'Okay,' Sai said. 'Can we be done having this discussion now?' And then he retreated back upstairs.

'So,' Pari said to Jack thoughtfully. 'That's the new neighbour. Millie.'

Sam printed out invitations for their engagement party and hand-delivered them, as was his wont on Christmas Street. He went and joined his fellow procrastinators for tea at Max's house, where Charlie was thinking very hard about the complicated task of taking his first step and Jasper was making an almighty racket upstairs.

'What exactly is he doing?' Sam asked, as Max brought him tea.

'Arthur calls them "storage solutions", but they're just bookcases, in my opinion,' said Max. 'But I think it will help. Charlie's overtaken the entire house and Arthur feels the disarray keenly. I think he would feel better with places to hide the toys away.'

'Storage solutions,' said Sam.

'Yes.' Max nodded and helped Charlie navigate his way around the corner of the coffee table.

Sam looked at Pen, sitting on the other side of him with her own cup of tea. 'Does that mean that your house is all done?'

'Oh, no,' said Pen. 'Actually, the design blogs tell me that maybe I should consider my house to just be a permanent work in progress. They said we should view our houses as art installations. We should always be curating which pieces we wish to see, and rotate them round.'

'Hmm,' remarked Max. 'When I tried to make our house into an art installation, Arthur wanted no part of it.'

'Well, you can come to my house, if you want to feel especially artsy.'

'You know,' said Max, 'I'm offended that you're making your house as artsy as can be and it didn't occur to you to ask for help from your neighbour who *is an artist*. I could have painted you a mural or something.'

'You've got Charlie all day!' Pen protested. 'I didn't want to add stress to your life.'

'Believe me, it wouldn't be stress,' said Max. 'Not that Charlie isn't a delight – because he is – but it would be good to get out of the house every once in a while.'

'You could bring Charlie with you, I suppose,' Pen suggested.

'Perhaps,' said Max.

'He's going to be mobile soon,' Sam pointed out, as Charlie cruised his way around the coffee table again. 'I mean, more mobile than he already is. So that's something to consider.'

'Yeah. He's already a less-than-ideal painting companion,' Max admitted ruefully. 'Painting has been relegated to naptime.'

'Once he's more mobile, though, it'll be easier to do stuff with him, and that'll get you out of the house,' said Sam.

'True,' Max allowed. 'That's a good point.'

'Anyway,' said Sam to Pen. 'Getting back to your in-progress house.'

'Yeah. So we're at the stage now where we're selecting art for the walls.'

'The perfect stage for Max,' Sam pointed out.

'Indeed,' agreed Pen. 'And Jasper's not quite done with all of the carpentry projects the girls came up with. But we're getting so close. The bed dais is in and I *love* it. It makes me feel like a queen climbing into bed every night.'

'Bed daises are going to be the next big thing,' said Max. 'Mark my words. You're a trendsetter. I should invite Jasper down to have tea with us,' said Max. 'This is silly that we would exclude him.' Max stood up and walked to the foot of the stairs, Charlie happily crawling along in his wake, and called up, 'Jasper? Stop working for a mo and come down for a cuppa.'

'So,' Pen said. 'Street news. I went to meet the new neighbour with Diya. She seems nice. A bit shy. Her name is Millie, and I promised we would throw her a party.'

'Oh, speaking of parties,' said Sam, just as Jasper arrived at the foot of the stairs, necessitating conversation pausing so they could greet him. 'How go the storage solutions?' Sam asked him.

'The what?' said Jasper blankly.

'The bookcases,' said Max, and then to Sam, 'Really, only Arthur ever calls them storage solutions.'

'Oh, they're going well,' said Jasper. 'Max picked some wonderful wood out.'

'Because of my impeccable taste,' said Max. 'Come sit with us and have a cuppa.'

'That's okay,' said Jasper. 'You don't have to feel like—'

They all protested, though, including Charlie, who was generally up for joining in general cacophony, and so Jasper eventually relented and sat down with them while Max fetched another cup of tea.

'You were speaking of parties,' Pen prompted Sam, and then, for Jasper's benefit, said, 'We'd like to throw a party for the new woman who just moved on to the street.'

'Oh, yes,' said Jasper. 'I've seen her a few times coming and going.'

'She keeps to herself,' said Pen.

'I think she probably just expects this street to be an ordinary street,' said Jasper.

'You mean, instead of a street where everyone has tea together every day?' said Max, amused.

'We still don't even really know how we got into this state,' said Sam.

'Jack,' said Pen. 'It was Jack.'

'Actually, yes, it was definitely Jack,' Sam agreed.

'So do you already have an idea for what kind of party we should throw for Millie?'

'Well, it's not really a party *for Millie*. Libby and I have decided to have an engagement party.'

Pen gasped with delight.

'We thought the whole street ought to celebrate with us,' Sam continued.

'Considering the whole street was responsible for your engagement?' said Max, sounding amused.

'Your role in the entire operation has been greatly exaggerated,' Sam said. 'But yes. And also the fact that, well, everything that happens on this street involves the entire street, doesn't it? So. Engagement party. Jasper, you should come along as well.'

'Oh,' said Jasper awkwardly. 'It's not necessary to—'

'Nonsense. You're around so much, you should come to any street party. We Christmas Street citizens are not an exclusionary bunch.'

'When are you having the party?' asked Pen.

'Halloween,' said Sam.

'You're celebrating your engagement on a day filled with dastardly tricks and unknown spirits?' asked Max.

'That is a very negative way to characterise Halloween,' said Sam. 'It's also a day of *treats*, isn't it? Anyway, we thought it was a good excuse to make everyone dress up in a costume.'

Max brightened immediately. 'A *costume*. Oh, excellent, Arthur and Charlie and I will definitely be in attendance in a fabulous costume.'

'Arthur in a costume should be worth the price of admission,' remarked Sam.

'It's a great idea,' said Pen, 'and I'll have to think about what my costume should be. In the meantime, have you given any thought to shutting the entire street down?'

'That seems a lot of work,' said Sam warily.

'I'll take care of it!' promised Pen cheerfully.

'Soooo,' said Max, drawing the word out.

'So?' said Sam suspiciously.

'Is this when we're finally going to meet your mother-in-law-to-be? At the party?'

'Yes,' said Sam. 'Libby thinks it's a good idea.'

'That sounds like *you* don't think it's a good idea,' remarked Pen.

'No, no,' Sam protested, and then sighed. 'I don't know what to think, honestly. I met Rebecca over the summer and I thought it went well and now . . . I'm not sure she likes me.'

'Of course she likes you,' Pen said soothingly.

'Who wouldn't like you?' said Max jovially. 'Jasper, don't you think Sam's nice?'

'Sure,' Jasper said. 'I mean, yeah, absolutely, very nice.'

'If only any of you were going to be my mother-in-law,' said Sam.

Max said, 'Look, mothers-in-law are always complicated to deal with. You've got to just grin and bear it. Trust me.'

Chapter 9

Romeo and Juliet
Frankenstein and Bride of Frankenstein
Cleopatra and Antony
Famous lovers who are now dead and ghosts

Sam, on his way out of Max's, paused and looked at the house where the new neighbour lived. Millie, Pen had said her name was. It was true that she kept to herself, and Sam wasn't sure if that was shyness and she wished she had more interaction with everyone on the street, or if Millie just wished they'd all leave her alone.

But he thought that, of course he was going to invite her to the engagement party. She was a Christmas Street inhabitant, and it was a Christmas Street party, and it would be a good opportunity to get to know her a little better so she might feel more integrated and at ease with the rest of the street.

Sam took a chance and knocked on her door. He was just about to give up, assuming that she wasn't home, when the door opened a crack.

'Can I help you?' said the woman who opened it.

'Hi,' he said, and sent her a cheerful little wave. 'I'm Sam. I'm one of your neighbours.'

'Hello,' she said. 'I'm Millie.'

'Welcome to Christmas Street,' Sam said.

'Thank you,' said the woman, and then looked at Sam expectantly, as if she wanted to end the conversation and was waiting for him to cooperate.

'I won't take up too much of your time,' Sam said. 'It's just that I just got engaged.'

'Congratulations,' Millie said politely.

'Thank you. My fiancée and I are planning an engagement party, and now Pen – I think you've met Pen? She came with Diya to drop off the food – anyway, Pen's got it in her head that we ought to shut down the whole street and clearly she wants it to be some epic event and I wanted to be sure to invite you to attend. I didn't want you to feel left out whilst we take up the whole street. It's going to be on Halloween and so we'll all wear some silly costumes and have some silly fun.'

Millie, after a moment, said, 'Thank you for the invitation.'

Which didn't sound especially enthusiastic. Indeed, Sam continued to get the impression that this woman was just waiting for him to finish the conversation and leave her alone.

So Sam obliged her. 'Okay, well, that's all. I just wanted to say hi, and welcome you to the street, and invite you to the party.'

'Thank you,' said Millie, and closed the door on him.

Sam felt like that could definitely have gone better.

When he got home he hid from Rebecca, like a very mature individual, because he couldn't deal with another less-than-stellar interaction.

Sam went outside as usual to wait for Teddy and Pari. And, as usual, Bill was also outside waiting, even though it was a damp, chilly day where Sam felt like the cold was creeping into his bones. Jack was also, as usual, running up and down the street, chasing squirrels whilst he waited for the kids to get back from school. He seemed entirely unaffected by the weather; so did Bill.

Sam said, just for the response he knew he would get from Bill, 'Dismal weather we're having, isn't it?'

'Good British weather,' Bill barked at him, offended on behalf of the good English weather.

Sam suppressed his smile. 'I guess that's true.'

'How's it all going with your mother-in-law over there?' Bill nodded in the direction of Sam's house.

'Oh, great!' said Sam enthusiastically. 'It's going really well!'

And then, unexpectedly, Diya joined them, coming down the street holding a bowl. The bowl turned out to be empty. 'Hi,' she said. 'I'm back early from my cousin's accountant's daughter's house. She's getting settled in nicely.'

'Oh, good,' said Sam vaguely, which he had found tended to be enough of a response when it came to all of Diya's far-flung acquaintances.

'And she managed to give me back my bowl.' Diya held it up. 'That doesn't happen all the time, you know. You'd be amazed how many people just take a bowl and never give it back.'

'Don't any people have any manners any more?' grumbled

Bill, whilst Sam wondered wildly if he had any of Diya's bowls that he'd neglected to return to her.

'The new neighbour gave me my bowl back, too,' said Diya. 'It's always nice when neighbours do that so I can maintain good relations with them.'

Sam tried to determine if Diya said that with a pointed look in his direction. 'Do I have any bowls at my house that belong to you?' he asked uncertainly.

Diya looked genuinely surprised. 'What? No. Everyone on this street is good about returning bowls. It's why we all get along so well.'

'I make it a point never to take a bowl from someone in the first place,' Bill proclaimed. 'You're just asking for trouble when you do that.'

'I never have anything worth putting into bowls to give to people,' said Sam. 'So that's how I deal with that conundrum.'

'I don't understand how either one of you eats,' sighed Diya.

'Whilst I have the two of you here, I would like to formally invite you to my and Libby's engagement party.'

Diya looked charmed. 'Aw, are you having an engagement party? That's lovely!'

'I think Pen is going to try to make it the engagement party of the century. She's shutting the street down and everything.'

'Whatever for?' asked Bill, sounding astonished. 'Will you have a bloody circus at your engagement party or something? Will it need to take up the entire street?'

Sam shrugged. 'Pen is just enthusiastic. She's, like, the anti-Millie.'

'The anti-Millie?' Diya repeated quizzically.

'Millie,' said Sam. 'The new neighbour. She seems nice enough but very ... hesitant. Wouldn't you say?'

'I don't blame her for being hesitant,' said Bill. 'You lot are exhausting.'

'Which was why I thought it was a good idea to not have the party be entirely about *her*. I just think that would have been so awkward.'

'Yes, but I don't understand why she's not enthusiastic, when we have so many people reaching out to her,' Diya frowned.

'That might be the problem,' said Bill. 'You're not leaving the poor woman alone. If she doesn't want to go to your parties, then she doesn't want to go to your parties.'

'What?' asked Diya, blankly, like she could barely comprehend what Bill was saying. 'Why wouldn't she want to go to our parties? We have fantastic parties.'

'*I* don't want to go to your parties,' Bill pointed out.

'Well, you can talk to Millie at the parties,' Diya sniffed. 'The two of you can stand together and not enjoy our parties.'

'I think the street just takes some getting used to,' said Sam. 'None of you wanted to come to my barbecue when I was holding it, remember? Everyone thought that was odd.'

'Well, it *was* odd,' said Diya. 'At the time. Because we didn't know each other yet.'

'And Millie doesn't know us yet,' said Sam. 'She'll ease into us, I'm sure of it. As with you, Bill.' Sam grinned at him, as Bill looked even crankier than usual.

'I'm never easing into you lot,' Bill said gruffly. 'I don't even know what that means.'

'Our engagement party is going to be on Halloween,' said Sam cheerfully, 'and I expect you to wear a costume.'

Christmas Street, Millie had noticed, was almost always abuzz with some sort of activity. London streets often were but Christmas Street activities were different, because they never seemed to happen solo. Everyone on the street seemed to travel in packs. When Millie watched them come and go – which she did an embarrassing amount of the time because she had little else to do – it was always in little clusters. Two of the women went jogging together almost nightly. All the children on the street were almost always together. She'd gleaned that there was a fair number of adults who were home during the day, and they were constantly darting to each other's houses for tea. Even the old man at the end of the street waited every day with one of the other neighbours for the children to come home from school. And always the street dog was trotting around, patrolling up and down the pavement with his tongue lolling out and his tail always wagging.

Millie was bewildered by it. Why were they all constantly together? And why did they keep knocking on her door?

Honestly, all Millie wanted to do was stay in her house, quiet and calm, and live her simple, straightforward life. She had her job on the high street to go to and from, and otherwise she just wanted to be left alone. But nobody on Christmas Street seemed to understand the meaning of that.

If it wasn't the two women showing up on her doorstep with random, unexpected food, it was the man showing up with a random, unexpected invitation. Millie did not want to go to a party with people she didn't know. Actually, she just didn't want to go to a party at all. She wasn't sure why she'd even been invited.

The only person Millie ever really saw consistently alone on Christmas Street was the man who spent a great deal of time at the woman Pen's house. Her boyfriend, Millie assumed. When Millie was hurrying to get to and from work, that man was the only person she encountered in solo form.

There was something arresting about him, Millie admitted, and she thought part of it was just the fact that he was a novelty on this severely social street. But he seemed to radiate a quiet thoughtfulness that drew Millie in. He had a soft, gentle smile that he always gave Millie when they passed on the street, but he never tried to expand it past that one silent greeting, and Millie was relieved by that. The interactions with the nameless man felt like the first interactions in a very long time where she didn't feel crushed by expectations.

She had to start spending more time outside, Millie thought. She had to gain enough confidence to do it. She had to find a way to interact with these people, and make friends, and pull together some semblance of a normal life. If she could just find a way to do that, then . . . Then maybe she would start to feel better about everything. All these people in this street, friendly and cheerful and untroubled – they seemed to think they could just invite her to be part of this, and that she could just step right in.

And maybe she could.

Maybe the only thing holding her back was not believing it herself.

So Millie stepped outside her front door one day with

every intention of just being brave enough to stay outside long enough to change the lightbulb next to her door. It had been burnt out since she'd moved in, and Millie didn't like coming home to a darkened house. She didn't even like going to bed in a darkened house.

The light was just slightly over her head, and she had to stand up on tiptoes to reach it, and she was concentrating very hard on unscrewing the lightbulb, her tongue caught between her teeth in concentration, when a gentle voice behind her said, 'Would you like some help?'

Millie, startled, lost her balance and stumbled and probably would have tumbled entirely off her front step had Pen's boyfriend not been standing right there, close enough to catch her fall.

'Oh,' he said, in that same gentle voice. 'Careful. I didn't mean to startle you. You just looked like you might need some help.'

He was ... so *gentle*. His voice was soft and soothing and his smile was calm and unhurried and his hands, touching her, were so light and unintrusive and Millie honestly didn't know what to do with any of that. How was she supposed to *categorise* him?

She had no idea what to say, which was a thing she had always hated about herself and that Daniel had always mocked about her as well. *Not the most stunning conversationalist*, he would say. *Not known for her wit.*

Millie tried not to think those things, tried to silence the persistent voice in her head all the time, tried to focus instead on finding a way to react to this man. And of course, because she couldn't make up her mind what she ought to do, her body made the decision for her, flinching away from his touch and scrambling back against her door.

'Sorry,' he said again, holding his hands up in an unthreatening gesture, because her level of helpless panic was probably visible.

This, Millie thought desperately, was why she'd been avoiding going outside, and interacting with all these ordinary, untroubled people, as if she were an ordinary, untroubled person herself.

The man's easy, unhurried smile, though, had never faltered, and he kept talking to her in his soothing voice, instead of snapping at her, or looking bewildered by her, or just deciding she wasn't worth his time. He said, 'I'm basically the street handyman at this point, so when I saw a street task to be done, I thought I might offer to help.'

'Oh,' said Millie. *Stunning conversationalist*, she thought.

'I'm Jasper,' he said, and offered his hand for shaking.

Millie managed to accomplish that. And managed to accomplish saying her name in response. 'Millie.'

'It's nice to meet you, Millie. You're new on the street, right?'

'Yes.' Millie nodded. 'And you're Pen's boyfriend?'

Jasper, after a moment, started laughing.

'Sorry,' Millie said hastily. 'I didn't mean to make it sound like I was spying on you, or anything. I just could see you come and go and—'

'No, no,' said Jasper. 'First of all, as far as I can tell, everyone on this street spies on everyone else reflexively. You have been a source of great speculation.'

Millie just wanted the ground to open up so she could sink directly down into it. 'Oh.'

143

'No, no. Not in a bad way,' Jasper said hastily. 'In a good way. I didn't mean to make it sound like – I think we should just start everything again.' He laughed, a laugh as light and easy as the rest of him. Millie wasn't sure but she felt like she might be in danger of dying of envy over how *light* and *easy* everything seemed to be for Jasper. 'What I meant to say is that yes, everyone on this street spies a bit, but it comes from a good place. It's *good* spying, not bad spying. Which maybe sounds like a bit of an oxymoron, but it's a nice street, and they're just looking out for each other, and it's nice. They're not, you know, speculating about you in a bad way. They just want to be friends, and make sure you're not lonely.'

'I'm not lonely,' said Millie automatically, because that was the mantra she had to tell herself to keep herself going forward and not ringing Daniel back. Loneliness was how you made poor choices.

'Right,' Jasper said, with his same soft smile. 'I'm not judging you. I live alone myself, and keep to myself, and all that. It's not the same as being lonely. I get that.'

'You live alone?' said Millie, momentarily confused, and then she supposed that it was true that Jasper seemed to go home every night.

'Yes. That was the other reason I was laughing. I'm not Pen's boyfriend. I'm her carpenter.' Jasper stepped forward and took the new lightbulb out of Millie's hand.

Millie handed it over to him unthinkingly, shifting aside so he could reach the lamp. 'Her carpenter?'

'Yes.' Jasper finished unscrewing the dead lightbulb and began patiently screwing the new one in.

144

'She has a full-time carpenter?'

Jasper laughed. 'She's doing some remodelling. And when I say "some", I mean "a lot". And then the rest of the street has projects, too. So I think I'm going to be here for a while. There you go.' Jasper finished screwing the lightbulb in and then stepped back, looking at Millie. 'It should work now.'

He wasn't crowding her, but the front step was small enough that there was not a lot of space between them. But Millie didn't *feel* crowded. Jasper was large and capable but didn't seem threatening. He made Millie feel relaxed instead of anxious.

She said, 'Thank you.'

He smiled. 'Not at all. Any time. As I say, it's basically my job now. If you've any carpentry jobs you need to have done, you've only to flag me down when you see me walking about the street.'

Millie's house needed an enormous amount of work. She could have kept Jasper busy for the foreseeable future ... if she had any money to pay him with.

Since she didn't have the money, she didn't mention any of her projects. She just said, 'I think I'm okay for now.'

'Now that you've got light again,' said Jasper.

'Now what?' she echoed blankly.

He gestured to her lamp. 'Your light.'

'Yes,' she recalled. 'Yes. My light. I don't like to come home to darkness.'

'Agreed,' Jasper said.

Millie didn't know what else to say. She stood there, stupidly silent and tongue-tied, and hated herself. But what else was there to say? Should she start talking of the weather?

Jasper said, 'Well, I'll see you round the street, then, shall I?'

'Yes,' said Millie, because yes, she would start leaving her house more often, and trying to enter the life of this street, and it wouldn't be terrible, and she would come up with things to talk about with these people, and it was all going to be good. 'Yes, around the street.'

Jasper smiled and moved off, continuing on his way to Pen's house.

Millie stood and watched him and then looked up and down the rest of the street. For the time being, there was no one else out, which was highly unusual, but she wondered how many eyes were watching her from behind closed doors. Maybe not many, she thought. If they were so curious about her, and so eager to make friends with her, they probably would have come outside to talk to her.

As she stood there, one door did open: the old man's door at the end of the street. The street dog came bounding out of it, tail wagging with joy. The old man stood at the door for a second and looked at her where she was standing, now half-way down her front path. After a moment, he lifted his hand in greeting, and she responded. And then he turned and walked back into his house.

Two successful interactions with other people in one day, thought Millie, and felt curiously in danger of feeling giddy over it.

The street dog came trotting up her front path, tail wagging, and stopped a few strides away from her, as if waiting to be invited closer.

Millie looked at the dog and smiled, and then she made a conscious decision to invite the dog in. To move her boundaries aside. To let this dog crowd her a little bit.

She crouched on the path and held her hand out and the dog – had they said his name was Jack? – came up to her, and sniffed at her hand, and wagged his tail, and let her scratch behind his ears. And Millie smiled at him, and looked up and down the street, and smiled some more. Maybe she was *doing* this, and it was all doable, and it would all be okay, against all odds.

And then she went back inside and carefully turned all of the locks she'd had installed on her door and turned the alarm back on. Because, well, she really wasn't as much of an idiot as Daniel had always wanted her to believe.

'If we're having a Halloween party,' Libby remarked, 'it means we have to have costumes.'

'Well, yes,' said Sam. 'I had assumed so.'

'Right,' agreed Libby. 'Except that you are terrible at costumes.'

'I am not terrible at costumes!' protested Sam.

'I respect how hard you tried on Teddy's behalf for his costume last year, but it was fairly last-minute and thrown together.'

'I will have you know that the hallmark of a good Halloween costume is that it's last-minute and thrown together.'

'Well,' said Libby. She was stretching in preparation for Pen arriving for another run. 'If we're going to be the centre of attention of this party, then we shouldn't have a last-minute, thrown-together costume. We should *plan* it.'

'Okay,' Sam agreed. 'So we ought to give thought to what we want to be.'

'Yes,' said Libby.

'I suppose Frankenstein and Frankenstein's Bride is too obvious?'

Libby wrinkled her nose. 'Not very glamorous, is it?'

'Ah, are we meant to have a glamorous costume?'

'Well.' Libby finished tying her shoes and putting her hair back and walked over to Sam. 'We are a very glamorous couple. I feel like we should look the part.'

'We're a glamorous couple?' he said, amused, letting her slot up against him comfortably.

'That's what everyone says about us,' said Libby, grinning.

'Literally no one says that about us,' said Sam, laughing as he leaned down to kiss her.

'Well, let's pretend to be a glamorous couple for the party,' said Libby. 'It's a costume party.'

'I'll think about it.'

'I will, too.'

'I am not wearing a costume,' Rebecca announced staunchly.

'Mum,' Libby said. 'Everyone will have a costume on! It's meant to be fun!'

Rebecca looked dubious.

There was a knock on the door. 'That's Pen,' said Libby. 'See you!' She waved cheerfully and disappeared out the door.

Rebecca said to Sam, 'You should really think about exercising with them.'

Sam didn't bother to respond, because there was nothing he could say. Teddy came running down the stairs and thrust a sheaf of papers into Sam's hands.

'Okay, that's my homework, I'm all done, can I go to Pari's now?'

Sam glanced through it. It did seem to be all done. 'Yes. You can. Hey. One thing first.'

'Uh-huh.' Teddy turned from the door to look back at Sam expectantly.

'So, for this engagement party thing, we have to wear costumes.'

'Yes. I figured you'd just get Aunt Ellen last-minute to show up with some options the way you usually do.'

'Ha ha,' said Sam. 'Very funny. That seriously happened *one time. One time* I forget about Halloween and no one's ever going to let me live it down, apparently.'

'Well, I know what I want to be this year.'

'Okay. Hit me with it.'

'A vampire,' said Teddy. 'I want a dramatic cape.'

'Vampire,' Sam mused. 'Vampires are pretty glamorous, wouldn't you say?'

Teddy shrugged. 'They get to wear dramatic capes.'

Teddy ran out of the house, letting the door slam behind him.

Rebecca said, 'He spends an awful lot of time with the neighbours, doesn't he?'

Emilia was telling a long story about her band rehearsal when Teddy arrived, and Pari was so happy to see him to break up that story.

Jack was happy to see him, too, bouncing all around and barking happily.

Teddy said, 'I'm all done with my homework, so Dad said I could come over.'

'Have you finished your homework, Pari?' Sai asked, frowning. 'I promised Mum I'd make you do it.'

'It's fine,' said Pari. 'It's *mostly* finished.'

'What are you going to be for my dad and Libby's engagement party?' Teddy asked. 'Like, what costume are you going to wear?'

'I want to be a witch,' Pari said. 'And cast spells all night. I already talked to Mum about it and she said I could.'

'Wait, engagement party?' interrupted Emilia. 'Who's having an engagement party?'

'My dad and Libby,' Teddy said. 'You must know that. Everyone's been talking about it. They invited everyone on the street, and Pen found some way to shut the whole street down, or something.'

'We're having a huge party *right on this street*?' clarified Emilia.

Sai gave her a look. 'How do you not know about this? My mum's been planning the menu for days.'

'I rehearse a lot,' Emilia said defensively.

'Yeah, you do,' agreed Sai.

'Are your dad and Libby home now?' asked Emilia.

'Just my dad. Libby went running with Pen.'

'In this weather?' said Pari, wrinkling her nose. It was wet and cold outside, so unpleasant that even Jack hadn't wanted to go out.

'They run in *every* weather,' Teddy said. 'My dad says they're dedicated.'

'Or something,' said Sai.

Emilia said, 'I'll be right back,' and went dashing out the door.

'What's up with her?' said Teddy.

'No idea,' said Pari. 'Let's talk about Millie. Has your dad mentioned if she's coming to the party yet?'

'No,' said Teddy. 'He invited her, but he says it wasn't clear if she was going to come or not.'

'I mean, she *has* to come,' said Pari frankly. 'The entire street is going to be there. She doesn't want to be the one person who doesn't show up on the whole street.'

'I guess.' Teddy shrugged. 'I don't know, it's not like she does a lot of hanging out with us.'

'She wants to. I know she does. I got to look into her eyes.'

Teddy rolled his own eyes. 'You met her one time at the door while she was returning your mum's dish.'

'But we had a *connection*,' said Pari.

'The conversation lasted one minute and she thought you were weird,' said Sai.

'Shh!' Pari said to him. 'I think maybe Millie's just uncertain if she wants to attend the party because she hasn't thought up a cool costume yet. Maybe we could help her. Maybe it would Make a Difference.'

Chapter 10

Old people music
Music that old people will like
Halloween music
Halloween music that old people will like

Sam had literally just sat down behind his desk to finish up the last of his work for the day whilst Libby was running and Teddy was at Pari's when the doorbell rang. Wondering who it could possibly be, he was surprised to open it on Emilia.

'Emilia,' he said. 'Come in out of the rain. You don't even have a coat on.'

Emilia stepped into the house, looking a little damp and very pink-cheeked. 'It's okay. I just wanted to run over here as soon as I heard.'

'As soon as you heard what?' Sam asked, faintly alarmed. 'Is something wrong?'

'Teddy said that you're having an engagement party?'

'Yes,' Sam said. 'On Halloween. Didn't your parents

mention it to you? I ran into Marcel a few days ago and made sure to invite him—'

'We're doing it here on the street, right? That's what Teddy said.'

'Yeah, Pen's managed to get permission from the council to block it all off,' said Sam.

'Great,' said Emilia, smiling broadly. 'That'd be perfect.'

'Perfect for what?'

'How'd you like my band to provide the music?'

'Oh,' said Sam, caught off-guard. 'I don't know, we hadn't thought about—'

'You're going to need music,' Emilia insisted.

'Yes,' Sam agreed. 'I mean, that's probably true. But we just haven't—'

'Do you have anyone else providing the music?'

'Not yet,' said Sam. 'Again, we haven't—'

'My band is *incredible*,' Emilia said. 'I promise. I mean, you've heard me play the drums so you know I'm good, and everyone else is just as good as me.'

'That's great,' said Sam, still trying to figure out how he could get out of having a random teenage band play at his engagement party. 'We just—'

'And we can even learn to play some old music for you.'

This gave Sam pause. 'Old music?'

'Yeah, you know. Music for old people. Old*er* people,' Emilia corrected herself, clearly catching that she had said something wrong if she was trying to get Sam to hire her.

Except that actually, she had just something very right. 'Old music?' Sam echoed. 'You think Libby and I want old music at our engagement party?'

153

'Well, I don't know,' Emilia said. 'Maybe? Probably? I'm just saying my band could do it.'

'Well, I will have you know,' Sam heard himself proclaiming, 'that Libby and I are not as old as you think, and we would be delighted to have your band play at our engagement party.'

Emilia's face lit up. 'That is *aces*! And we're even a reasonable price and everything, I swear! Thanks again! Bye!' Emilia ducked back outside.

Rebecca said, 'Did you just agree to let *teenagers* play at your engagement party?'

'I think so, yes,' said Sam.

'Libby is not going to be happy that you're treating the engagement party like it's a joke,' sniffed Rebecca.

Libby and Teddy's adventures of the day were both about costume ideas. Teddy gave his vampire desire and also said that he wanted a costume that was somewhat better than his aunt's cast-off pieces, which made Libby laugh and laugh and text Ellen to see if she had any 'vampire chic' for Teddy to wear.

Libby divulged Pen's contributions to the costume debate. 'She thinks we should think outside the box,' said Libby. 'Maybe go with something like Romeo and Juliet. But I pointed out that you and I are not teenagers.'

Sam forced a laugh on that front.

'And anyway,' remarked Libby, 'it's not like Romeo and Juliet had the best ending. I'm not sure I want us to emulate Romeo and Juliet. Let's try, you and I, not to have a tragic ending, hmm?' Libby smiled at him across the table.

Sam managed a smile back.

Libby said, 'What's up with you? You're awfully quiet over there.'

'Yeah, Dad,' Teddy said. 'What's your adventure for the day?'

'Yes, Sam, maybe you should talk about the great decisions you made today,' added Rebecca sweetly.

'I may have, kind of accidentally, hired Emilia's band to play at our engagement party,' said Sam.

Libby lifted her eyebrows. 'Emilia's band?'

'Yeah.'

'Have you ever even heard Emilia's band?'

'No.'

'Then how do you know they're any good?'

'I'm sure they're good,' said Sam. 'Emilia's good, after all.'

Libby stared at him. 'We're going to have a random assortment of teenagers provide the music at our engagement party?'

'I'm sure it won't be that bad,' Sam said. 'She offered to have them learn old music for us.'

Libby blinked. 'What?'

'*Exactly*,' said Sam. '*Old music*. When she said that, I think ... I think maybe I began making poor decisions after she assumed that I must like "old music".'

Libby started laughing. 'Oh, Sam, *really*?'

'I mean, *old music*.'

'Our taste *is* probably old music to Emilia.'

'Well, anyway. Now we're going to recapture our youth with Emilia's band at our engagement party.'

'That's fine,' said Libby. 'It'll be a bit of an adventure.'

Rebecca snorted.

'She promised me they would be a reasonable price, too,' Sam continued gamely.

'We're *paying*?' said Libby.

Teddy was a vampire and Pari was a witch but there was much debate as to what Jack ought to be.

Teddy asked Mr Hammersley one day, and Mr Hammersley said, 'Dogs don't need to wear costumes!'

'But the engagement party is a costume party,' Teddy said. 'What costume are you going to wear?'

'I am not wearing any costume,' Mr Hammersley grumbled, and went back inside his house.

Teddy and Pari debated Jack's costume a great deal. Dad suggested he be a devil, but Teddy thought that would send the wrong message about Jack's role on the street.

'And what is Jack's role on the street?' Libby asked, where she was sitting cross-legged on the couch marking papers.

'He's the king of the street,' Dad remarked.

'That would be silly, though,' Teddy said. 'He doesn't want to wear a crown all night. That would be too much for him. We have to have a *good* costume for him.'

'Sorry,' said Dad. 'Clearly this requires an intellect greater than mine.'

'I'll have to ask Pari,' mused Teddy.

Libby snorted laughter from the couch.

In the end, though, he and Pari came up with the *best* costume for Jack. The only costume for Jack.

'He should be a spy,' Pari said. 'Since we're not going as spies, he can represent our spying for us.'

Teddy was delighted by this costume idea, and even more delighted when he asked Dad what a spy costume looked like, and Dad said, 'Probably a tuxedo.'

So Jack wore a smart bow tie the night of the engagement party.

'Doesn't he look dashing?' Libby said when she saw him. She was dressed as a vampire queen, because she said she *did* want to wear a crown on her head all night and they had decided to go as an entire vampire family.

'You look pretty,' Teddy told her.

Libby grinned. 'But I am supposed to look terrifying!'

'You look *glamorous*,' said Dad, and smiled at her and kissed her, and Teddy smiled and thought that this was nice, and that this was going to be their life now, and that was even nicer.

Rebecca wasn't wearing any sort of costume at all, because Rebecca was way less fun, but Teddy was trying to follow Dad's advice to focus on the positive.

Outside, Christmas Street was decorated for Halloween. Mostly that had been Max's doing; he had pushed Charlie about in his pram and supervised the draping of twinkling fairy lights and swooping bats over the street. Charlie hadn't been too happy about being confined to his pram so much, but he had been mollified by the big smiling jack o'lanterns that Max filled their house with.

'It looks like Halloween was sick all over this house,' Arthur remarked, stepping over a few artfully scattered spiders.

'It looks magnificent,' said Max, pleased with the state of the house and the street.

'It does,' said Arthur, as he finished tying his tie in the mirror. He sounded amused and indulgent, which was Max's favourite way for Arthur to sound.

'And,' said Max, catching Arthur up around the waist and resting his chin on Arthur's shoulder, 'now we have *storage solutions.*'

'Yes,' agreed Arthur drily. 'Although you've filled them with severed fingers.'

'Not *actual* severed fingers,' said Max. 'That would be inappropriate. They're decorations.'

'You know you're going to traumatise our son,' Arthur said. 'Twenty years from now Charlie's going to be in therapy talking about the time he knocked a bin of severed fingers over onto his head.'

'If that's what he's in therapy about,' Max remarked, turning from Arthur to put the finishing touch on his own costume, 'then I will consider us to have excelled as parents.'

'Fair enough,' Arthur allowed, watching Charlie, who was sitting in the middle of their room messing up the careful spikes Max had arranged his thick hair into. 'He's ruining your brush.'

'Oh, no,' said Max, and rushed to scoop Charlie up into his arms. 'There's a reason for the funny hair,' he told Charlie.

'You know, most families dress their babies up as pumpkins for Halloween,' remarked Arthur.

'We are not most families,' said Max.

'Don't I know it,' Arthur replied, but he was smiling as he said it.

'I know this is our first real gig,' Emilia was telling her band-mates by way of a pep talk, 'but let's pretend it's not.'

Spike and Malcolm looked a little shell-shocked to find themselves on an actual *stage*.

'There's a stage,' Spike said.

'Yeah,' said Emilia. 'Bands are supposed to play on stages.'

'But where did a stage come from?' asked Spike.

'Does your street just always have a stage in the middle of it?' asked Malcolm.

Emilia rolled her eyes. 'Of course not. One of my neigh-bours set it up and she just goes over the top with everything. It's just how she is. I mean, it's not a *huge* stage.'

And it wasn't. But it was a stage, raised up over the rest of the street, with a proper sound system and everything. And there would be people filing in and dancing. There were already some early arrivals milling about. Non-Street people. None of the Street people had come out yet.

'I hope we're good enough for this,' said Malcolm dubiously.

'Hey,' Emilia said sharply. 'We are definitely good enough for this.'

'And we are making *actual money*,' said Spike. 'So let's just go out there and play whatever these people want us to play, right?'

'Oh, you're not going to talk about artistic integrity?' said Malcolm.

'Not tonight,' said Spike. 'Tonight is about selling out for some cash.'

Emilia sighed dramatically and glanced off to the side of the stage, where Sai was watching. He sent her a wave and a smile of clear support, and she smiled back at him gratefully. If nothing else, Sai believed in her. She had the best boyfriend.

'Okay,' said Emilia. 'We should do, like, a sound check.'

'Do you even know how to do that?' asked Malcolm.

'Sure,' said Emilia, who had no idea how to do that. But she went off behind the drums and counted them in and they played a few bars of their first notes. 'How'd it sound?' she called off to Sai.

'Sounded great!' Sai called back enthusiastically.

Someone started shouting Emilia's name by the edge of the stage.

It turned out to be Sophie and Evie, Teddy's cousins, who had arrived with their mum, and they were dressed as zombies.

'Your make-up looks amazing,' Emilia said admiringly, stopping by the edge of the stage to talk to them.

'Right?' said Sophie, preening a bit.

'Thanks!' said Evie. 'We did each other's make-up, and we think we did a pretty good job.'

'If we do say so ourselves,' said Sophie.

'Whose is better?' asked Evie.

Emilia shook her head. 'Nope. Not getting involved.'

Sophie and Evie both laughed.

'Look how cool you look up here!' Evie said. 'Like a real rock band and everything!'

'We're totally a real rock band!' Emilia said.

'Who are your bandmates?' asked Sophie, twirling one strand of hair around her finger. It had been dyed zombie grey, so it probably wasn't as alluring as Sophie had intended it to be, as she glanced at Spike and Malcolm behind Emilia.

In Emilia's opinion, Spike and Malcolm were no one to start twirling hair around your finger over, but who was she to stand in the way of possible true love, or whatever. 'Spike and Malcolm,' Emilia said, and beckoned them over where they were lingering around looking awkward at the appearance of unknown females. 'These are my friends Sophie and Evie. They've got Christmas Street relatives. This is Spike, and Malcolm.'

Spike and Malcolm said shy hellos and Sophie and Evie said shy hellos and Emilia sat there amused and pleased that she already had a boyfriend and so she didn't have to exchange these shy hellos with strangers.

They all stood together awkwardly for a moment. Emilia decided probably she was supposed to be saying something that would ease the conversation. So she said, 'Pretty nice night, huh?'

Maybe that hadn't been the most brilliant thing to say.

Everyone agreed with her vaguely.

After another few seconds of awkwardness, Emilia said, 'So we should probably keep getting ready for the gig ...'

'Yeah, yeah,' said Sophie, still twirling her hair.

'See you later,' said Evie.

Sophie and Evie moved off into the crowd.

'Clearly she and I had a thing going on,' Spike told Malcolm. 'Clearly.' He paused and looked at Emilia. 'What was her name?'

Emilia rolled her eyes. 'Sophie. And can we move on here?

Sophie'll be around all night, you can flirt with her when our set is done.'

'Her sister was cute, too,' Malcolm said. 'Is it okay if I talk to her sister?'

'As long as you don't cramp my style,' said Spike.

Emilia sighed and shook her head and thought maybe it was going to be a long night.

Chapter 11

Hey – This is Sam's sister Ellen. I know you don't know
me but I wanted to get in touch with you about Sam's
engagement party. He told me that you can't make it,
which I totally understand, but I have an idea . . .

Millie could hear the party getting started on the street outside.
The band, who as far as she could tell was entirely teenagers,
including one of the street teenagers, kept doing sound checks
outside. Or, at least, she assumed they were sound checks,
because they kept starting up and then stopping again, and
she hoped that wasn't supposed to be their music.

Millie stood in her bedroom and looked at herself in the
mirror and gave herself a pep talk. She was dressed as a
scarecrow, because she hadn't wanted to dress as anything
too scary and because that had been a pretty easy and
cheap costume. She hadn't wanted anything too complicated. It was going to be enough effort to make herself leave
the house.

She thought she looked ... frumpy. But well, how else
would she look? She was dressed as a scarecrow. She'd *wanted*

to look frumpy. That had been the point. But now she was second-guessing everything. As usual.

Millie recognised that she was stalling, delaying, because she was nervous. That was all this was.

'You look fine,' she told her reflection. 'You look great. This is going to be a good evening. No,' she corrected herself sternly. 'This is going to be an *amazing* evening.'

Millie was rethinking that when she got down to the street, because she was early, and she didn't recognise anyone, and she was wondering if she should go back inside.

When, from out of nowhere, a voice gruffly said, 'You're the new girl, yeah?'

Millie looked over at a person she recognised, with relief, as the old man from down the street. 'Yes,' she said, smiling. 'Yes, I am. Millie.'

'I'm Bill. And I approve of the fact that you moved in without any fuss. So many of the young people these days, they have to make such a *fuss* about things.'

'Oh,' said Millie. 'Well. I didn't have much stuff, I suppose—'

'Millie!' exclaimed someone Millie recognised as Pen. 'You came! I'm so pleased! Everyone will be so delighted.' Pen was dressed as ... a plant? That was the best Millie could come up with. Lots of green leaves. She said enthusiastically, because it seemed like a thing she should say, 'Your costume looks great!'

'Thanks!' said Pen, and patted at a couple of the fronds of leaves tangled into her hair. 'It makes a statement, right?'

'What are you meant to be?' barked Bill without preamble.

'I'm a *plant*,' said Pen.

'A man-eating plant?' asked Bill.

'Why would I be a man-eating plant?' asked Pen.

'Well, you're a person inside a plant,' said Bill.

'No, no. This is just my plant costume. I'm just a normal plant. It's meant to raise awareness for the environment. The environmental issues facing the planet are too serious for any of us to ignore, Bill.'

Bill didn't look convinced.

Millie, wanting to fill the uncomfortable silence, said, 'Well, I think it looks great.'

'Thanks,' Pen said again, and then, 'And are you a scarecrow?'

Millie nodded.

Pen looked at Bill. 'Where's your costume?'

'Foolishness,' said Bill.

'You have to wear a costume to a Halloween party!' protested Pen.

Which was when Diya walked up without any costume.

'Diya!' Pen complained. 'You are undercutting my argument about having to wear a costume. Where's your costume?'

'I couldn't wear one,' said Diya. 'I can't stay here very long. One of my cousins had a baby, I have to run to her house, we're helping to make some food for her first few days home.'

'That's nice of you,' said Millie.

'Diya spends all of her time bringing food to people,' Pen said. 'As you've experienced.'

'It's a nice thing to do,' said Diya.

'It is,' agreed Millie. 'The food was delicious.'

'I'm glad you enjoyed it,' said Diya. 'And your costume is cute. Has anyone seen Sam and Libby yet? I wanted to congratulate them before I have to run.'

'Not yet,' said Pen, and then let out a high-pitched squeal that made Millie jump.

After a second, Millie realised what had provoked the squeal, because the couple from across the street with the baby were heading toward them, carrying the baby. The baby looked dubious about everything going on, and Millie sympathised with him, but he also looked adorable, dressed in some kind of outfit covered with splashes of colour, with more splashes of colour dotted selectively over his face and in his spiked-up hair. The baby looked bright and festive, especially since the man carrying him was dressed entirely in a pristine white suit, complete with a white fedora. The man's husband was also dressed in a suit, although his was a more usual grey, although it was still a remarkably well-cut suit. Daniel had frequently worn suits but they had never been suits of such quality.

'Look at the three of you!' cooed Pen, and immediately reached for Charlie, who went happily, waving a chubby hand at her in greeting.

'What are you meant to be?' asked Diya.

'What are *you* meant to be?' countered the man in the white suit.

'I'm going to another party,' Diya explained, 'so I couldn't wear a costume.'

'I do not accept your excuse,' the man said, with mock sternness.

'Don't mind him,' said the man in the grey suit to Millie. 'He's very nice, he just makes a terrible first impression on people. You're the new neighbour, right?'

'Yes,' said Millie, shaking the hand the man offered. 'I'm Millie.'

'I'm Arthur, and that's Max, and that's Charlie.'

'Don't tell lies, darling, I make wonderful first impressions,' said Max, smiling broadly at Millie as he also shook her hand. 'You're a scarecrow, yes? It's adorable. You need a little crow on your shoulder. You should have told me, I could have dressed Charlie as a crow and loaned him to you.'

'We don't loan our child out,' Arthur said.

'We could for a good cause. And if the price was right. It's about time he started making us money, he's been hanging about the house for eleven months doing absolutely nothing.'

Arthur said, 'This is what I mean, about the first impression thing.'

Max laughed and said to Millie, 'He loves me a great deal, he just likes to hide it.'

Millie smiled in response. It was a lot, she thought – they were a lot of people – but they were *nice*, and there was a definite ease to their interactions with each other, and that ease didn't make Millie feel excluded, as she had feared, but rather made her feel safe. They had opened up their circle to her with such simplicity, as if it were obvious she should be tugged into their flow, and Millie might have still had her doubts but the more that she met people who didn't have these doubts, the more her doubts started to seem irrelevant. Millie had moved to this street in search of a new life, wanting to start over and erase her past, and all of these people were helping with this, in making assumptions that she was an ordinary person who could just *do* these things.

There was a spooky overdramatic laugh, and then a man dressed as a vampire descended upon them, holding his cape up to cover most of his face except for his eyes. 'I vant to drink your blood,' he proclaimed in a bad Transylvanian accent, and descended upon Diya.

Diya rolled her eyes and laughed at the same time and said, 'Don't be ridiculous.'

'I'm not being ridiculous, I'm being a vampire,' said the man, straightening and looking over the crowd. 'How do you like Diya's costume? She's my innocent victim.'

'I am definitely not your innocent victim,' Diya said.

The man laughed. 'True, no one would mistake you for that.'

Diya said to Millie, 'This is my husband Darsh. Darsh, this is the new neighbour I was telling you about, Millie.'

'Oh,' said Darsh, dropping the cape so that he could shake Millie's hand. 'Yes. Welcome to the street. I hope we haven't over-welcomed you. Sometimes my wife can be over-welcoming.'

'Not really!' exclaimed Diya. 'I just brought her food.'

Darsh smiled with obvious fondness and slipped his arm around his wife's waist.

'Oh, no,' Millie said. 'No one's been "over-welcoming". Everyone's been wonderful. I don't even know what to do, everyone's been so wonderful,' she admitted.

'This street can be like that,' said Arthur.

'That's an understatement,' grumbled Bill.

'What are you supposed to be?' Darsh asked of Max. 'I mean, it's a nice suit, but.'

'Oh, this old thing?' said Max, preening a little in his suit. 'I just pulled it out of my wardrobe.'

'That actually is true,' said Arthur, chagrined. 'He actually did own an entirely white suit.'

'From your wedding?' asked Diya.

'God, no,' said Max. 'Arthur said I wasn't allowed to dress like a cherub at our wedding.'

'It would have been false advertising,' Arthur said.

'I thought it was *ironic*. Anyway, tonight I am . . . ' Max drew himself up a little taller to dramatically make the announcement. 'A blank canvas.' He gestured to his white suit.

Millie laughed along with everyone else.

'Wait,' said Pen. 'Does that make this little bloke a paintbrush?'

'Indeed!' said Max, obviously delighted Pen had made the connection.

'And what are you meant to be, then?' Darsh asked Arthur.

Arthur opened his mouth to reply but Max beat him to it, saying, 'Isn't it obvious? He's the artist's muse,' and leaned over and kissed Arthur's cheek.

Arthur smiled at him and said, 'Yes. That's my role tonight.'

'But there's no artist,' said Pen.

Max and Arthur looked at her.

'You have a paintbrush and a canvas and a muse but no artist,' Pen pointed out.

There was a moment of silence.

Then Max said, 'Minor detail. It's still a fantastic costume idea. And what are you meant to be? A plant of some sort?'

'Yes,' said Pen. 'Just a plant.'

'Like a Venus fly trap?' asked Arthur.

'No,' said Pen. 'Just a plant.'

'A man-eating plant,' clarified Max.

Pen frowned. 'That's what Bill thought, too.'

Max waggled a finger between himself and Bill. 'Great artistic minds think alike.'

'It's just a plant,' Pen said.

'It's to raise environmental awareness,' Millie said, to help her out, and Pen gave her a grateful look.

And then a loud peal of feedback echoed out over the street, causing universal wincing.

The Christmas Street teenager in the band was standing at the microphone, dressed in Renaissance garb, and she winced, too, and then said, 'Sorry. Sorry about that. Anyway, happy Halloween, everyone!' There was scattered applause in reaction to that. 'We are the Amazing Spiders!' she continued, and gestured to encompass herself and the two boys on the stage with her. 'And I just realised that sounds like a Halloween thing, but we're always called that.'

'They should have dressed as spiders,' Max murmured. 'Missed opportunity there.'

'Maybe you can offer to be their stylist,' Arthur replied, taking Charlie from Pen because now he was fussing.

'We're going to be playing some songs for you, but first, we're all here at this party to celebrate Sam and Libby's engagement, so! Here's Sam and Libby!' And then she raced from the microphone to settle herself behind the drum set, where she played an enthusiastic drum roll.

Sam and his fiancée strode out, with their son, and all of them were dressed as vampires, capes billowing out, faces streaked artistically with blood. Next to them trotted Jack the street dog, wearing a smart bow tie. They waved to the crowd, and there were whistles and applause and shouts of congratulations.

Millie heard Darsh murmur, 'Oh, dear. Is it okay that I chose the same costume as them? What are the rules on that?'

Sam wasn't sure what he'd expected the engagement party to be like. He'd decided they ought to have it on a whim, really, Halloween theme and all. But it turned out to be delightful. Exactly what he wanted. It was a little messy and chaotic but it was filled with love, and he felt that was entirely what his life was like and it was exactly what he adored about his life. He didn't even mind the fact that Rebecca spent the entire evening standing sourly to the side looking disapproving, because the rest of his life was just so *perfect*, and if he had to deal with this one little blip, he could definitely get through it.

So he and Libby stood on a stage, the overkill of which was just so very Pen, with Teddy and Jack between them, and waved to the small knot of their gaily dressed friends, and Sam thought, *Perfect. This is perfect. This is everything I want in life.* He couldn't resist catching Libby up as they exited the stage to give her a kiss of dazzled affection.

'I'm happy, too,' she said when he pulled back, and so he knew that she understood exactly what he was trying to say.

As they exited the stage they were caught up in crowds of well-wishers. Sam hadn't had many people to invite. Aside from the street and Ellen, most of his friends were in the States. But Libby had invited her friends from work, and a few friends from childhood who now lived in London. She wasn't terribly close to them but if they were going to have the entire street shut down, Libby had said, they ought to try to make it worthwhile.

The headmaster of the school congratulated them and Sam

felt only slightly awkward at the fact that this was the man who glanced through Teddy's grades every year and probably judged Sam's parenting abilities.

'He doesn't,' Libby told him when Sam confided that fear to her.

'I don't believe you,' Sam said. 'He totally does.'

'Well, now he judges me, too, for whatever Teddy does. Does that make you feel better?'

Sam considered. 'Actually, yes.'

Libby shook her head a little bit at him, smiling.

Mrs Dash was also there. Libby called her Camilla, which was definitely not something Sam felt capable of doing. She had come dressed as a mummy, which made perfect sense, because it allowed the literal gauze she was wearing to float all about her as she moved.

Sam said, after she gave her congratulations and left, 'I think she might be a witch. That might have been a more accurate costume.'

'She's not a witch,' said Libby patiently.

'How does she get her clothes to *do* that?' Sam asked.

'It's all about the fabric,' Libby said. 'It isn't a trick—'

There was another squeal of feedback, causing everyone to look over at the stage. Sam had to admit that the feedback was effective in cutting through the buzz of conversation to get everyone's attention.

Ellen was standing at the front of the stage before the microphone, surprising Sam.

Ellen had, maybe predictably, dressed as a demon, but Sam was pretty sure she was some kind of sex demon. He hadn't asked because that wasn't the sort of thing you wanted to ask your sister. But he couldn't begrudge her, because Ellen had always loved dressing-up and she looked delighted about her costume. And Sam shut off his brother-hearing at the small cluster of wolf whistles that greeted her appearance.

'Settle down, settle down,' Ellen said, grinning so widely that absolutely no one took seriously the idea that she wanted them to settle down. 'For those of you who might not know me, I am Sam's sister Ellen. So I am not a Christmas Street inhabitant, just a Christmas Street in-law.'

'You're an honorary one!' someone shouted. Maybe Max, Sam thought.

'Aww, thank you,' said Ellen. 'That makes me happy.' She cleared her throat and said, 'Okay, but enough of that, let's get down to business. And the business is this. As all of you know, we are here today to celebrate my little brother getting engaged, to a wonderful woman.' Ellen found Sam and Libby in the crowd and smiled at them. 'Some of you are new friends. Actually, almost all of you are new friends. So you don't quite know exactly what my brother has been through over the past few years. To be honest, none of us really know. But what I will tell you is that he has borne it all with a strength and determination and good humour that I could only hope to emulate. I may not say this often enough, Sam, but I would like to be you when I grow up. The way in which you took everything life threw at you – and it was so much more than anyone deserves – and you kept going, and you have raised your amazing little boy, and you have made this life for both of you. There was a time when I worried about you, and maybe I will always worry a little bit about you, but you look less these days like you're waiting for the moment when you can't handle everything. You look more like you know how to handle everything now.'

The crowd was raptly silent, and Sam stared at Ellen and felt a jumble of emotions he couldn't parse through. It was like living all of the recent years all at once, every momentous occasion that had knocked him over the head and all of the pulling himself and Teddy up through the quicksand that had accompanied them. Every single daily adventure, hitting him all at once.

Ellen took a deep breath and said, 'You deserve happiness more than anyone I know. I mean, everyone deserves happiness, but you . . . you just deserved a break. You deserved a moment to get to take a breath. You deserve this moment of feeling like you have everything under control. And that is why I cannot thank Libby enough. Because I know that you have everything inside you to handle everything yourself – I've watched you do it – but I'm happy that she is in your life now so you know that you don't have to. Libby, I can never put into words what it means to watch my brother find this happiness again that I know he thought he'd lost for ever, was for ever in his past, would never be his again. He may never have said that out loud – he may never have said that even to himself – but you are miraculous, Libby. I think he makes you happy. I hope he makes you happy. You tell me he does, and if he ever doesn't you should let me know because I am not above giving him a little clip upside the head.'

The crowd laughed a little. Libby laughed, and took Sam's hand in hers, and squeezed it, and leaned closer against him.

Ellen laughed and swiped at tears up on the stage and said,

'When you said you wanted to move back to London, I was so selfishly overjoyed to have you back, and to have Teddy near, and now there isn't a day that goes by that I don't think how lucky I am to have the two of you, and now Libby, and even all of *you*.' Ellen gestured out to the crowd at large, provoking more laughter and some applause, and she laughed again and swiped at more tears. 'And I know that's all selfish of me, so it also makes me happy that moving back to London seems to have agreed with you. I hope that every day from this point on is filled with the level of happiness that the two of you bring to everyone around you.' Ellen lifted her glass and said, 'To Sam and Libby.'

And the crowd around them said, 'To Sam and Libby,' and Sam smiled at Ellen and tried to pretend he wasn't crying and let Libby kiss him quickly and wipe away some of his tears.

And then Ellen said, 'And, before I forget, that wasn't actually why I was coming up here. I was really coming up here because I got in touch with your friends in the States for you. I know you were sad none of them could be here today to share in your joy, and they wanted to be here as well, so they pitched in and sent along a present, which Max graciously said he would hold for me. Max?'

Max appeared on the stage, in a pristine white suit, with Arthur, also in a lovely suit, helping him carry a large and apparently heavy box.

'And your friends have given all of us a case of very high quality champagne. You've got classy mates, Sam.' Ellen grinned at him. 'And they sent it with a note. "Dear Sam and Libby, Congratulations! Here's some champagne to get your celebration off to a good start. Wish we could be there, Christmas Street."'

Sam laughed. He'd got in touch with all of his friends in the States, of course, and they'd all been amazing in their kind congratulatory notes in response. It had been a bit of a relief, he had to admit, to know that he had the blessing of these friends who had been Sara's friends, too. He'd really only needed Teddy's blessing, but it was still nice to know. And it was extra-nice to know that Ellen hadn't forgot that portion of his life and had managed to get this physical manifestation of their support to him.

'Should we open it?' Ellen called to him.

'Yes!' Sam called back, and that provoked a chorus of shouting and applause.

Chapter 12

Set List Ideas:
Songs about Halloween
Songs about love
Songs about love on Halloween?????

On the stage, Emilia's band was definitely managing to play ...
something.

'But which song is it supposed to be?' asked Max, trying to
sound as polite as possible.

'I have no idea,' said Anna, with a little sigh. 'But they've
practised so very hard.'

'They're sweet,' said Libby. 'I'm glad they're our entertainment.'

'Emilia gave me a hard sell,' said Sam.

'Did she?' Anna actually beamed with pride, pushing a
peacock feather out of her face. She was dressed as a ghost,
but a ghost from the Victorian era, meaning she was dressed
in an old-fashioned dress and wearing a hat whose peacock
feathers had been in her way all night.

'Yes. She came to the house and gave me a whole pitch,' said Sam.

'And just so you know,' said Libby, 'the thing that swayed Sam was the implication that our taste in music might be "old".'

Everyone started laughing, including Millie, who felt as if she hadn't laughed so much in a very long time. A very, very long time, actually, upon reflection. But this street was *lovely*. She was so glad she'd talked herself into leaving the house and going to the party.

'Our taste in music isn't old,' said Max, 'her taste in music is just young.'

'Keep telling yourself that,' Arthur said. He was cradling Charlie, who was clearly exhausted. 'In the meantime, I am putting our son to bed.'

'Do you want me to come along?' asked Max.

Arthur shook his head. 'No. Stay. Have fun. Drink champagne.'

'Should we tell Emilia to play the drums less loudly?' asked Anna.

Arthur laughed. 'No, we'll see if we can get Charlie to sleep through anything. That is our goal. Good night, everyone. Congratulations again, Sam and Libby.'

Everyone chorused goodbyes, and Arthur turned to go and then said, 'Oh! Is that Jasper underneath those bunny ears?'

Millie looked over to where Arthur was gesturing at someone dressed, yes, as a bunny. And yes, that person was Jasper.

'Yes,' he said, sounding sheepish. 'It's meant to be a zombie bunny, though. See?' He pointed to the fake blood he had painted around his mouth. 'It's from eating brains.'

'Don't worry,' said Arthur drily. 'I'll hardly judge your costume. I'm dressed as an artist's muse. Thank you for the storage solutions, by the way. Max is using them to store severed fingers, so they are absolutely being put to good use.'

'To store ... what?' asked Jasper quizzically.

'Long story,' said Arthur, smiling and shaking his head. 'Max can explain. Goodnight!'

Everyone said goodnight again, and then Pen said, 'Jasper! Welcome to the party! I'm so delighted that you came. I was worried you wouldn't.'

'Well,' said Jasper, 'I wasn't going to. I thought, after all, it isn't my street, and I barely know the happy couple. And then I ... ' Jasper's eyes found Millie and he smiled at her, before turning back to the rest of the group. 'And then I thought, What have I better to do?'

There was laughter.

'I mean,' said Max, 'that is about where we should be on your list of desirable things you could do with your evening. If you had something better to do, you ought to do that instead.'

'But what's better than us?' demanded Pen.

'Anyway, congratulations to the happy couple,' Jasper said to Sam and Libby, and then presented them with a bottle of wine. 'Sorry,' he said, 'I tried to think of an appropriate carpentry gift and just ... went for the obvious.'

'No, no, the obvious is good,' said Libby.

'We definitely will not look down on the obvious,' Sam agreed.

'We do have to come up with some sort of carpentry project for you, though,' said Libby. 'Now that we know you're the street carpenter.'

'The street carpenter?' said Bill. 'What sort of street needs a carpenter?'

'Our street, apparently,' said Libby.

'I'm having Jasper do some remodelling for me, and then he's doing some storage solutions for Arthur and Max, and then he's doing a—'

'Top-secret project for me,' Marcel cut Pen off hastily.

Anna lifted her eyebrows at Marcel. 'A top-secret project? What's that?'

'A surprise,' said Marcel.

Anna continued to look suspicious.

'A *good* surprise,' Marcel insisted, and looked to everyone else for help. 'Isn't it a good surprise?'

Everyone nodded and said it was a good surprise. Millie nodded, too, even though she had no idea if it was a good surprise or not.

Anna looked cautiously appeased.

'A live band and everything,' remarked Jasper. 'This is quite the party.'

'That's our daughter's band,' Anna said proudly. 'She's the drummer.'

'Oh, that's lovely.' Jasper peered up toward the stage. 'The drummer dressed as a Renaissance lady.'

'She and her boyfriend decided to come to the party as Romeo and Juliet,' said Anna.

There was a moment of silence.

Libby said, 'Yeah, we thought about that, but then there's the matter of how *Romeo and Juliet* ends.'

'I know,' Anna agreed, with a little sigh. 'She didn't think it through. Or she liked the drama. That's teenagers for you.'

'That was also Romeo and Juliet's teenage problem,' remarked Max. 'Didn't think it through. And rather liked the drama.'

'Well, you know,' said Libby, 'who among us, et cetera.'

'Hang on,' said Sam good-naturedly. 'I think I want to hear more about your teenage transgressions. Do I know about these?'

'I never kiss and tell,' said Libby demurely.

'*Kiss* and tell,' said Sam. '*Really?*'

'Anyway,' Bill said, clearly disinterested in the entire conversation, making the rest of the group laugh. 'What's this about being the street carpenter? I understand you're helping out with some projects.'

'Aww, don't get jealous, Bill,' Pen said, and tried to put a fond arm around Bill, although Bill shrugged it off. 'You're still our favourite street woodworker.'

'Oh, do you work with wood, too?' asked Jasper.

'No. Not really,' said Bill gruffly.

'He's being modest,' said Max. 'Bill is an incredible artist. He does beautiful things with wood. Whittles and such.'

'Do you?' Jasper looked at Bill admiringly. 'I ought to have you add some ornamentation to all the work I've been doing around here.'

Pen gasped with delight. 'Oh, Jasper, what a wonderful idea! That would be fabulous!'

'Now, now,' Bill grumbled, looking pleased nonetheless. 'I'm sure that isn't necessary.'

'Bill was the one who did the woodworking around the shelving unit we made for Jack,' Max said.

'Jack?' said Jasper.

'Our dog!' said Max.

'Oh, right, the street dog,' Jasper said.

'How dare you forget we have a street dog?' said Pen jokingly.

'Oh, I could never forget that,' replied Jasper. 'I simply forgot his name.'

'Anyway,' Max said, 'Bill and I made him a shelving unit for Christmas last year. We store his toys and things on it. Mostly it gets used by the kids.'

'*Sporadically* it gets used by the kids,' Sam corrected Max. 'The kids are pretty terrible at keeping things orderly.'

Max shrugged negligently. 'They're kids. It's how they are.'

'Arthur's going to love that attitude when Charlie gets older,' remarked Libby, amused.

Max laughed. 'Don't I know it. I can't wait. Well, Bill, do you want to show off our handiwork to Jasper?' Max looked at Jasper. 'Want to see it?'

'Sure,' Jasper agreed. Millie thought maybe he glanced her way before moving off, but maybe it was just her imagination.

'*Millie!*' squealed Pen, when they'd left. 'I think Jasper might like you!'

So apparently it wasn't just Millie's imagination.

'That's ridiculous,' said Millie, grateful for the fact that she had covered her face in make-up so her blush was probably obscured. Anyway, the lighting was dim, so that was probably helping, too.

'Leave her alone,' Libby said mildly. 'Poor Millie has just finally decided to join us for a party, and you are horrifying her.'

'I'm not horrifying her!' Pen protested. 'But I will leave you alone.'

'Thank you,' said Libby.

Millie sent Libby a grateful look, and Libby winked at her.

'Speaking of being left alone,' said Pen, 'I feel bad that we haven't really been including your mother. Where is she?'

'Oh,' said Libby. 'Yeah. She's . . . not much of a party person, I guess. I mean, this kind of party person. In fact, you're right, I should go check on her.'

Libby had been in the middle of the most glorious evening. She had actually consciously been thinking that she was the luckiest person in the universe, that her life was amazing, that she couldn't believe that she'd found Sam and fallen for him and he had come complete with this astonishing street with all these odd and fabulous people on it. Libby had been lonely in London, had been longing for a replacement for the village she had lost, and she had found it, and surrounded by the circle of them whilst Emilia's band played earnestly, Libby had been basking in happiness.

She wasn't sure if her mother was having a good time, though. She kept hanging back on the edge of the crowd, barely participating. Libby felt bad about this. Her mum knew no one; Libby should have been paying closer attention to make sure she was having fun.

'Hi, Mum,' Libby said, coming up to her.

'Hello,' her mother said pleasantly, and smiled at her.

'It's a lot, isn't it?' said Libby sympathetically.

'Oh, I'll say,' her mother replied. 'Just a bit. You've been away from home a long time, so I think you've forgotten, but village fêtes are nothing like this.'

'I haven't been away from home that long,' said Libby. 'I haven't *forgotten* home.'

Her mother looked at her mildly. 'Haven't you?'

Libby said, 'Mum. Of course not. Look, why don't you come and let me introduce you to everyone?'

'That's quite all right,' said her mother.

'Mum—' Libby started.

'No, no,' her mother protested. 'I've got a headache coming on. It's . . . a bit loud.'

On stage, Emilia's band was still gamely playing along.

'They haven't been totally terrible,' Libby said. 'I mean, they've definitely been trying.'

'I do hope you're able to have an opinion when it comes to the entertainment for your wedding,' remarked her mother, 'since Sam didn't allow you to have any say here.'

'That's not really what happened,' said Libby.

'So what will you do if Sam engages this delightful band again for the wedding? Again, without consulting you?'

'He wouldn't,' said Libby. 'Look. We'd talk about it. Sam's not going to be unreasonable. It's just . . . Sam's got a soft heart. How could he turn down Emilia's first gig?'

'First gig,' murmured Libby's mother. 'I wonder why.'

Libby, uncertain, opened her mouth to say . . . something.

And that was when suddenly, from the stage, the music crashed to a halt amidst a cacophony of barking.

Teddy and Pari and Jack had been having a truly exceptional time at the party. Given the run of the street, with so many people to spy on, they were spoilt for choice.

They spent some of the time hiding behind the stage, scoping out who would the best people for them to spy on, trying to choose people they thought looked the most interesting, and like they had the most to learn about. They finally eventually settled on Mrs Dash, because it was irresistible to have the opportunity to learn more about Mrs Dash.

So Teddy, Pari, and Jack commenced Operation Mrs Dash. It was more challenging than they had anticipated, and that's what made it fun. Sure, it was easy to get up close to Mrs Dash, hiding in the crowd. With everyone dressed in costumes, there were lots of capes and props and other odd cover to take advantage of. There was a particularly helpful person dressed as a wizard with voluminous robes, and that hid them a lot of the time. The problem, though, was that, while they could get close to her, they couldn't *hear* her, and how were they supposed to learn anything about her if they couldn't hear her conversations?

They retreated to Teddy's back garden for some peace and quiet and to regroup regarding their plan of attack on Mrs Dash.

'Maybe we *don't* have to hear her,' Teddy suggested.

Pari gave him a look. 'How are we going to learn things about her if we can't hear her?'

'We'll watch who she's talking to,' Teddy said. 'And then we can go talk to them. They'll probably tell us about her, because they won't know who we are. We're basically undercover all the time to people we don't know.'

Pari looked thoughtful. 'That's a good point.' Then she looked at Jack. 'What do you think, Jack?'

Jack barked and wagged his tail, so it was unanimous.

Mrs Dash mainly talked to the other teachers, though, and

so they weren't quite as undercover as they had hoped to be. It was okay, though, because it was weirdly interesting to be interacting with teachers outside of school.

'They're just, like, *real people*,' Pari remarked, as they took a break from their exhausting spying efforts with some chocolate biscuits behind the stage.

'Yeah,' Teddy agreed. 'It's cool, right?' He munched happily on a biscuit. 'I mean, I guess we should have realised that because Libby's just a real person.'

'Yeah, but Libby's different. The first time you met Libby she was in a supermarket, so you knew she was a real person. There was more of a question mark with all of these other teachers.'

'That's true,' Teddy allowed. 'So I suppose that means Mrs Dash is really just a regular person, too. She probably, like, cooks herself dinner and stuff.'

'Huh,' said Pari. 'That's really kind of disappointing. I thought there would be something amazing to discover.'

Teddy sighed. 'We'll have to come up with some other excitement.'

Which was exactly when, on the stage, the kid who had been doing the singing announced, 'We are the Amazing Spiders, so here! Have some spiders!'

Pari and Teddy hadn't been paying much attention to the band, but when they said there were going to be spiders, they seemed more interesting. They turned out not to be real spiders but instead a little cascade of fake spiders that were attached to some kind of string that the lead singer flicked around on the stage next to him, like a puppet or something.

Pari sighed and said, 'Another disappointment. Not even real spiders.'

Except that Jack clearly didn't realise that they weren't real spiders, or at least weren't interesting. Jack went dashing out onto the stage, barking furiously at what he obviously thought was a dangerous invasion.

The band stopped playing. The singer tried to get the spiders away from Jack but that just made them twitch more frantically on their strings. The other boy in the band came running over. Emilia, behind the drum set, stood up, shouting, 'Jack! Jack!'

And then the singer, still trying to escape from Jack, got himself all tangled up in the string from the spiders and hit the microphone stand, which caused the microphone stand to go crashing down to the street, and because it was wired it dragged the other speakers precariously to the edge of the stage, and feedback squealed loudly, and then somehow all of the fairy lights strung over the street went out.

'Wow,' said Pari admiringly. 'Now *that* was something interesting.'

Chapter 13

Fourteen enormous white bows
Fourteen enormous red bows
Fourteen enormous wreaths
Garland (measure)
Additional lights?? (check light strands)

Luckily no one was hurt. That was what everyone kept saying, as they untangled the mess that had been created. Bill was saying that this was why you didn't turn streets into concert venues and Libby's mother was saying that this was why you didn't hire teenagers to perform concerts and Anna and Marcel were clearly growing more and more frustrated with that statement. There were questions about whether it was a good idea to bring fake spiders onto the stage, and an assertion that they were called the *Amazing Spiders*, so they had to show off some spiders, and then there was some discussion about whether this was Jack's fault, which Teddy and Pari were very vocally against, since Jack had only been protecting them from the spiders, and Jack hadn't known they were fake, because who expected fake spiders to show up.

Millie hung back, off to the side, uncertain what she could do to help or if her help was even needed. Certainly it looked as if everything was okay, especially since Max began laughing and couldn't stop, and soon most of the crowd began joining in. Millie smiled, as the people around her laughed, and laughed joyfully, without malice, over the silly twists that life could take. It had been a while since Millie had thought of life's twists as being silly, as being something deserving of genuine laughter. She was struck suddenly by the very thought of it, by the idea of life being something this *light*.

'Hello,' Jasper said, startling her out of her reverie. He was still wearing his bunny ears, but they'd begun to droop over the course of the evening, meaning he looked like a floppy-eared bunny now. Who had eaten brains.

'Hi,' Millie said, and tried not to think about criticisms about conversation. She could do this. She had done it so far. She'd had a lovely evening. And life, once again, felt *light*.

'Quite a thrilling party, isn't it?' asked Jasper, smiling, and gestured to the crowd, who were still squabbling a little bit but were mainly laughing at each other.

'I've never seen anything like it,' said Millie.

'Never seen a street dog attack fake spiders during a band performance?' asked Jasper, grinning.

Millie laughed. 'Oddly enough, no.'

They stood for a moment in companionable silence, watching the street resolve the issue. Someone had retrieved a toy for Jack, and the kids were playing tug-of-war with him. The band didn't look inclined to start playing again. In fact, Sam's two nieces had appeared out of the crowd and were now both looking very concerned over the state of the band members. Sai and Emilia stood to the side looking amused.

'The band should probably change its name,' Millie said. 'Are "amazing spiders" a good thing to be?'

'Well, I suppose they are amazing.' Jasper grinned at her. 'They think it's edgy. They're teenagers. Don't you remember being that young?'

'Not really,' Millie said honestly, and then realised that she should have lied about that. Jasper had just meant it as innocent party talk and she had gone and made it heavy and serious. 'I mean,' she tried to correct herself hastily, looking up at Jasper, and then everything she was going to say died in her throat.

Jasper was looking at her, not pityingly, which she always hated and dreaded, but thoughtfully, reflectively. And Millie knew that she had given more away than she had wanted to, and she ordinarily hated when she did that – she wanted so much to be able to control the picture of who these new strangers thought she was, so that she could start over with a whole new life – but the look on Jasper's face wasn't horrifying. It wasn't something she wanted to run from. It felt like ... It felt like something she could maybe settle into.

Which was dangerous for entirely different reasons.

'This is a nice street,' Jasper said eventually, his eyes still steadily on her and his voice a little rough. 'It's the sort of street where maybe you can ... start to remember being a teenager.'

Millie tore her gaze away from Jasper, looked out over the rest of the street, and thought, *Maybe. Maybe.* Aloud she said, 'I should go.' And then hated herself for that cowardly impulse. Running. She was always *running*.

'Oh,' Jasper said. 'Don't feel like you have to—'

'No,' Millie said. 'It's not you, or anything, it's just … been a long evening, and the party's winding down, and I should … go.'

'Right,' Jasper said. 'Right.'

Millie tried not to look back regretfully as she slipped into her house and locked all the locks behind her. And she tried not to be too hard on herself as she divested herself of her costume. She had made herself get out of the house, and she had had a genuinely good time, and that had been her goal.

How was she supposed to know that achieving that goal would carry its own whole new set of terrifying implications?

The clean-up from the party was, like everything else on the street, a huge joint effort. Rebecca seemed not to know what to make of it.

'You're all going to help clean together?' she said.

'Well, we all made the mess together,' Libby said cheerfully. 'It's just like the village, Mum. Works just like the village.'

'But it's London,' Rebecca said.

'A nice little slice of London,' said Libby. 'London is basically a series of little villages linked by the public transport system.'

'Here you are, Rebecca,' said Sam, setting a cup of tea down in front of her. 'You needn't come out cleaning with us, of course.'

'Why would I have to?' asked Rebecca blankly.

'Oh,' said Sam awkwardly. 'Sorry, I thought maybe you

were worried we'd ... Okay, never mind. Let's go out and see how things look.' Sam paused at the bottom of the stairs to shout, 'Teddy!'

It was Jack who responded, bounding down the stairs and immediately to the door.

'Yes,' Sam said to him, 'everyone's outside trying to clean up the rest of the mess you made last night.'

Jack wagged his tail and barked to dispute that characterisation.

Sam opened the door and let Jack streak out onto the street, where Emilia and Sai were already outside, surveying the aftermath. They'd brought in all the food-related items, but the decorations, bedraggled and droopy, were still strewn along the street. 'Did your parents make you come outside to help?' Sam asked, amused.

'Yes,' they both replied sulkily.

Sam laughed and turned back to his own recalcitrant child. 'Theodore! Come and help! Jack's already outside!'

'Coming, coming!' Teddy said, and came dashing out the door to join Jack, at roughly the same time Pari came rushing outside, as if they'd planned it.

Diya stepped outside, too, and waved to Sam, who waved back as he held the door for Libby.

'We shouldn't be long,' Libby said to Rebecca. 'It really doesn't look that bad,' and then they stepped outside.

It was a brisk, grey day, and the teenagers were actually working surprisingly quickly, as if they wanted to get out of the weather as soon as possible.

Libby said to Sam, as they walked toward the scene of the most detritus, 'You wouldn't hire Emilia's band for our wedding, right?'

'Well,' remarked Sam, 'for our wedding, I doubt that this scene would be repeated.'

'No, I mean. I don't think I want Emilia's band to play at our wedding.'

'Okay,' Sam agreed quizzically.

'And you just kind of made the decision to have Emilia's band play here without consulting me.'

Sam stopped walking so he could face Libby, tugging her to a stop next to him. 'Hey. I explained that to you. I was a little ambushed and manipulated.'

'No, I know,' said Libby, her eyes darting toward the clean-up they had to do. 'I just want to make sure you don't let it happen when it comes to planning our actual wedding. I want to do that.'

'Right,' said Sam slowly. 'Of course. I get that. Libby—'

'We should help clean,' said Libby.

'Aw, look,' said Max, coming out with Charlie in a push-chair. 'If it isn't the young lovers.'

'Yeah,' said Libby, with a quick smile, as she headed off to where everyone else was working.

Sam stood and watched her.

Max said, 'Everything okay?'

'Yeah,' said Sam. 'Just a long couple of days.'

Diya said, coming up to them, 'I can't help for very long, I have to run off to—'

'Of course you do,' said Max, amused.

Sam decided to forget about how odd Libby was being about Emilia's band. It had been a silly engagement party, it wasn't supposed to be a solemn, serious event. And he'd made Emilia happy, and he refused to think that was a bad thing. So Sam

193

focused on what had been important about letting Emilia's band play and asked Emilia, 'How did you like playing your first gig?'

Emilia lost the sulky posture she'd had and basically glowed. 'It was *amazing*. Just like the Amazing Spiders! Although we're maybe going to rethink actually bringing the fake spiders out on stage. It's sad, though, because Spike worked so hard making that whole thing, threading the spiders onto the fishing line. They were basically our mascots.'

'Well,' said Sai reasonably, 'as I keep telling you, how often do you think there's going to be a random dog at your gigs running after spiders?'

'I don't know,' said Emilia. 'It might be pretty often. Lots of people have dogs, and we'll probably just be performing in people's back gardens and stuff. It's not like we're going to be playing arenas.'

'Yet,' said Sai loyally. 'But it's a good point. If you play any festivals, there might be dogs about.'

'Exactly.'

The grown-ups all exchanged indulgent looks over the buoyant optimism of the youngest among them.

'And what about you lot?' Max asked Teddy and Pari. 'Did you enjoy all the trouble you got into at the party?'

'We didn't get into trouble!' Pari denied.

'We didn't know Jack would freak out over the spiders,' Teddy said.

'We were really very good,' Pari said.

'No spying?' said Sam.

'Oh, well, no, we spied,' said Teddy.

Diya sighed. 'I really don't think we should be spying on people. I don't want to develop a reputation.'

'What did you learn by spying?' asked Libby.

'The teachers,' Pari announced, sounding dramatically offended, 'are all just *normal people.*'

Libby began laughing, which Sam was relieved to hear. He hadn't realised that he'd been worrying so much until Libby's laughter made the knot in his stomach loosen a bit.

'You sound so outraged to learn that,' Sam remarked, deciding that maybe they could just fall back into easy banter.

'We thought Mrs Dash might have some amazing secret,' Teddy explained. 'But no, she just seems to be a regular person.'

'Oh, well, actually, I'm not sure I agree with you on that. I'm pretty sure Mrs Dash definitely has some amazing secret,' said Sam.

'Yeah,' said Diya. 'I meant to say to you, I could have had a bit more *preparation* for my conference with her.'

Sam laughed. 'Did you enjoy meeting Clementine the dragon?'

'Which one was Mrs Dash?' Max asked.

'She was dressed as a mummy,' Libby said, 'and she's a nice woman. She just has a flair for the dramatic.'

'Ooh,' said Max, 'a woman after my own heart. Speaking of dramatics. It is time to explain to all of you my plan for Christmas decorations.'

There was some general groaning and Diya said, 'Oh, no, is it that time of year again?'

'Don't act as if this time of year isn't the best time of year,' said Max.

'Hiya,' said Pen, happily joining the fray. 'Are we talking about how Bonfire Night is the best time of year?'

'No, *Christmas* is the best time of year,' Max said. 'Here on *Christmas Street.*'

'True. And you know what happens before Christmas: Bonfire Night. Which we should all go to again as a street.'

'Except that you didn't go last year,' Max pointed out.

'Yeah,' said Pen. 'I was thinking about that.'

'You shouldn't have to sit at home again,' Sam said. 'We'll work something out with Jack.'

'Maybe Millie would watch Jack,' Diya suggested. 'She seems to like him, and she seems to spend a lot of time at home.'

'No, Millie should come with us!' Pen protested. 'We shouldn't leave the newest member of the street out of the most fun!'

'I don't know,' said Libby. 'I don't want to force fun onto Millie.'

'Don't you think she had a good time last night?' asked Pen. 'I thought she did!'

'No, I'm sure she did,' Libby agreed. 'I just feel like it might not be her thing to socialise all the time. Which is kind of what this street expects you to do.'

Diya frowned. 'Not *all* the time. We're just being friendly.'

'I don't mean it as a criticism,' Libby said gently. 'I'm very fond of all of you. I just mean that I understand that Millie might just want some time to herself.'

'She really does keep to herself a lot,' Sam agreed.

'She could just be shy,' said Pen.

'Libby's right, though: we don't want to put too much pressure on her,' said Sam.

'Hmm,' said Pen, clearly considering this.

'I will say one thing, though,' remarked Max.

Everyone looked at him expectantly.

Arthur said, 'Go ahead and tell us. You've set it up rather dramatically.'

Max grinned and said, 'I think Jasper likes her. And I think she might like Jasper.'

'Yeah, I *did* think there was something going on there,' Pen agreed.

'Yes, but, again, I didn't want to embarrass her,' Libby said.

'Did Jasper say anything to you about it?' Pen asked Max.

'No. It was just a feeling that I had. I'm very good at spotting romance wherever it occurs.'

'Did you spot it with Libby and me?' asked Sam curiously.

Max smirking at him. 'At Bonfire Night? Yes. But you two were the most obvious ever. Millie and Jasper are far subtler than you.'

'I wasn't trying to be subtle,' Libby said. 'I decided that Sam really needed to be hit over the head with my interest.'

'Ha ha,' Sam said. 'I just was cautious about making a move on my son's teacher. Can you blame me?'

'Not really. This is why I'm so relieved to have the dating bit over with.' Libby flashed the diamond on her finger.

'That is a relief,' Diya agreed.

Emilia said, 'Speaking of people dating, I think we're all going to go on a triple date with Sophie and Evie.'

'Who is?' Sam asked, surprised.

'The other band members,' said Libby.

'Honestly, you didn't notice?' said Max.

'They were flirting all night,' agreed Pen.

'You didn't even have to be a Max-level expert to spot that,' added Arthur.

'Well, Charlie,' Max announced. 'Today is a very important day in your young life.'

Charlie was busy trying to crawl his way down the stairs, so Max had to catch him and drag him back and close the door this time.

'And it is *not* a very important day because it's the day you fall down the stairs and we have to rush you to A&E.'

Charlie, plainly offended by Max's doubts about his ability to get himself down the stairs safely, stuck his fist in his mouth and gnawed on it.

Max said, 'Today, young Charles, is the day that we begin the Christmas decoration. Christmas decorating, you see, is the best time of year, because it's the time of year when your father allows us to turn the *entire house* into a piece of art. Inside and out. We love Christmas.'

Charlie kept gnawing on his fist but at least he looked like he was listening, even if he didn't yet look entirely convinced.

'So.' Max began dragging out the boxes containing all of his Christmas decorations, so he could go through what they had and how it would work for this year's Christmas theme. And, upon seeing a number of boxes that he could empty and make a mess out of, Charlie finally got into the spirit of Christmas.

'Hello?' called Jasper, curiously, venturing to stick his head into Max's house when ringing the doorbell got no response.

He thought he was supposed to be working in the house today, but maybe he got it wrong. But the door being open was suspicious.

'Oh, good!' Max called from upstairs. 'Jasper! You're here!'

'I'm ... here,' said Jasper, confused, as Max came jogging down the stairs with Charlie in one hand and a variety of jumbled things in the other hand.

'I know that you are supposed to be making me storage solutions,' said Max.

'Yes,' said Jasper. 'Hello, Charlie,' he said, because Charlie was waving at him happily.

'But, how would you like a change of plans?'

'Oh,' said Jasper. 'Do you want me to work at Pen's today? Because I'm sure I could—'

'No, no. Totally different sort of project. You see. It is almost Christmas.'

It was the beginning of November. 'Is it?' said Jasper.

'Yes. Right around the corner. Which means Christmas Street is about to become very busy.'

'Ah, you take the name very seriously, do you?' said Jasper.

'Very seriously indeed. Me especially. It's an excuse for an art project. And that is exactly what I have in mind for the day.'

'An art project?' echoed Jasper.

'Yeah. Ordinarily I just do all of this myself, but Charlie's a bit of a handful, and I could use some help this year. I know it's not strictly in your job description but I promise it would be fun.'

Jasper considered. It was unlike him, to just spend a day doing Christmas lights instead of carpentry. But it seemed like the magic of Christmas Street: you did things out of the ordinary. Like go to a costume party full of relative strangers and have a delightful time nonetheless. And that wasn't entirely due to the presence of Millie, either. Although Millie had certainly helped.

'Sure,' Jasper said. Why start detaching now? Might as well get even more intertwined with the life of the street. He was probably past the point of no return.

So that was how Jasper found himself holding a baby and listening to Max explain a complicated design plan that he had for the Christmas decorations. Jack the street dog had wandered up and was also listening to Max. Charlie, having spotted Jack, was busy cooing delightedly at him.

'I've arrived at a marvellous theme for this year,' Max said, as he spread several sets of lights out on the front garden.

'You mean a theme other than festive and Christmasy?' said Jasper.

Max laughed. 'Yes. Think outside the box, Jasper.'

'Yeah,' said Jasper, thinking of the bed on the dais and mini-Eiffel Tower at Pen's house. 'That seems to be a speciality of this street.'

Max laughed again. 'Indeed. So, the theme this year is ...' Max paused so that he could give this pronouncement the proper solemnity, hands in the air. '*Marriage.*'

'Marriage,' repeated Jasper.

'Sam and Libby are getting married, so I thought it would be appropriate.'

'Right,' Jasper agreed slowly. 'I mean, I get the reference, just ... what does it have to do with Christmas?'

'It will involve fairy lights,' Max replied.

'Ah,' said Jasper.

Max smiled. 'Look, last year these kids had a nativity play that involved an insurance agent.'

'An insurance agent?'

'Indeed. Which is what Arthur does for a living, so, as you can imagine, he was beyond delighted to be consulted.'

'He actually got consulted for the nativity play?'

'Well, they wanted insurance-agent verisimilitude.'

'This was a serious nativity play.'

'It was about climate change,' said Max.

Bill tried to ignore the racket outside for as long as he could, focused on a particularly tricky part of the dog he was whittling for Teddy. It was supposed to resemble Jack, and it was tricky to whittle according to a real model. He'd used to try it all the time for Agatha and found it frustrating. But he'd wanted to try it again for Teddy.

It was, however, impossible to concentrate when there were periodic crashing sounds and Jack kept running up and down the street barking. So, eventually, Bill tugged open his door to see what was happening.

What was happening was that Max had a ladder leaned up against the side of his house, and the carpenter was up at the top of it, and Max was at the bottom holding his baby and trying to supervise.

'What the dickens is going on out here?' Bill demanded, as Jack came up to explain what was happening.

'Christmas decorating!' Max said cheerfully.

'Oh, good Lord,' said Bill, sighing in resignation. Max was stubborn as anything about the Christmas decorations.

'I'm sorry,' said the older woman coming out of Sam and Libby's house. 'But aren't those lights on my daughter's house?' She pointed to a string that was arching out between the two houses.

'Yes,' Max said. 'I'm in charge of decorating the whole street.'

'They've *approved* this?' she said.

'Blanket approval,' said Max.

'There's no use arguing,' said Bill, with another sigh. 'He'll have his way with the Christmas decorations.'

'Well, that's just madness,' said the woman. Bill tried to remember her name but couldn't.

Jack came up to her, tail wagging, and the woman immediately recoiled away from him.

'Oh, that's just Jack,' Bill explained. 'He keeps tabs on everyone.'

'He isn't keeping tabs on *me*,' said the woman. 'He's just a stray dog.'

'He belongs to all of us,' said Max.

'He's hardly "stray",' frowned Bill.

'Well, I think it's quite unusual,' the woman said, 'to invite a dog into all of your houses when you've barely any idea where it's been. You have a *baby*,' she sniffed at Max.

Max said stiffly, 'My baby's fine, thanks for your concern.'

'Hmm,' said the woman, turning to go back into the house.

Bill said, 'Will you be staying here a while?'

'I'm helping to plan my daughter's wedding,' she replied loftily.

'Well, then, you'd probably better get used to the way the street works,' remarked Bill.

Chapter 14

Goodgymming is an opportunity for all of us to turn our commitment to exercise into a commitment to others – in short, it's perfect for Making a Difference.

Jasper and Max had a late lunch together in Max's kitchen, whilst Charlie napped upstairs.

Max said, 'Thanks so much for the help.'

'It barely got started,' Jasper pointed out.

'Oh, I know,' said Max. 'But that's okay. It's a long, multi-day affair, the decorating. It's just harder than I anticipated it being, with Charlie. I thought I'd just stick him in his pram and he'd be content to watch me, but I should have known that wouldn't fly. Charlie is seldom content to sit still. Which I appreciate. We wanted to raise an ambitious child, Arthur and I, a child who would want to seize the world in his hands and be proactive and have all this agency. We just didn't think through what that would mean for us in our downtime.'

Jasper laughed. 'I would imagine most parents barely get to think through what having a child means.' And then he realised how that sounded and corrected himself hastily. 'Not that having a child isn't wonderful.'

Max smiled. 'No, it's fine. I understand what you mean. So did you have fun at the party? I hope you did. I'm glad you got to come.'

'I did have fun,' Jasper said. 'Even if I felt like my costume was nothing at all next to yours.'

'Oh, please, Arthur and I just wore suits. We were feeling very lazy.'

'I wore some bunny ears and painted some blood around my lips,' Jasper pointed out.

'But it was clever,' said Max.

'So,' Jasper began, and thought better of it, and shut his mouth, and then reconsidered and inhaled to speak again, and then decided against it again.

Max lifted his eyebrows, amused. 'Yes?'

'I mean. I don't know. Probably I shouldn't say anything.'

'Now, now,' Max said. 'You're so invested in the life of this street you're helping us hang our Christmas decorations. That is surely invested enough to be an honorary Christmas Street citizen, and no citizen of Christmas Street avoids saying things.'

Jasper laughed. 'I've noticed. Millie ... ' Jasper trailed off, unsure what he wanted to say.

Max smiled. 'Yes. Millie. I suspected things about you and Millie.'

'Was I that obvious?' asked Jasper, stricken.

'Well, I have a keen insight when it comes to romantic feelings,' said Max. 'But also yes, sorry to say, you were that obvious.'

'Oh, dear,' sighed Jasper. 'I hope it wasn't alarming to Millie. Do you know much about her?'

Max shook his head. 'She's new, as you know. None of us really know anything about her. She keeps to herself a lot.'

'I think she probably keeps to herself a normal amount,' said Jasper. 'It's just that it seems out of the ordinary on this street.'

'True,' Max allowed. 'So maybe she just needs some time to warm up to us. I could put in a good word for you. I mean, I don't know how much my word will count, but there you go.'

'It can't *hurt*,' said Jasper. 'It's true that she does strike me as being a little shy, and I don't want to do anything to make her feel uncomfortable, or anything like that. So I was wondering if anyone even knew ... how she felt about me, for instance.'

'Well, if I get to talk to her,' said Max, 'I will definitely ask her. Discreetly, of course.'

'I would appreciate that,' said Jasper.

'Also,' said Max, 'traditionally the entire street goes on an outing for Bonfire Night. You should come along.'

'You go to a bonfire together?' said Jasper.

'Yes. We are really quite sickening, on the whole.'

Jasper laughed. 'I've noticed.'

Sam was in the middle of a conference call when he heard Max begin work on the Christmas lights outside. He glanced out the window because he was bored and watched for a little while. Max was up on the ladder and Jasper was holding Charlie. They had literally enlisted the carpenter to be a babysitter now, Sam thought, and shook his head and smiled and tried to focus on the conference call.

And then a commotion began outside and really, he *had* to stay on the conference call, so he watched a little helplessly as his future mother-in-law started to cause some kind of altercation, and even Bill looked like he spoke to her harshly, and bloody hell, Rebecca was taking poorly to street life.

Sam sighed and thought that he was going to have to go downstairs and deal with that. He was glad that his conference call wasn't over yet and so he could hide a little while longer.

He texted Ellen as the conference call droned on. **I don't think Libby's mum is really taking to street life.** He meant *I don't think Libby's mum is really taking to me,* but he thought that sounded too pathetic to put into a text.

Christmas Street life? came Ellen's text back.

Yes, Sam confirmed.

Well, give her some time. That street can take some getting used to, replied Ellen.

Sam sighed and supposed Ellen was right.

And then Ellen texted, **Btw, now Sophie and Evie are dating teen rock stars or something like that?????? I blame you for this.**

Sam suppressed a laugh. He was, after all, still on a conference call.

When the conference call was over he had a brief break so he wandered downstairs. He thought, under the guise of grabbing lunch, he could talk to Rebecca.

He found Rebecca on the sofa reading a novel. She looked up when he appeared and said immediately, 'One of your neighbours is putting fairy lights all over your house.'

'Yes,' Sam agreed. 'It's street-wide decorating. He basically treats it like an art installation.'

'How do you know you'll like what he does?'

Sam shrugged. 'I suppose I don't. But he's an artist, and so far I've never seen him do anything distressing. He's not going to make, like, a penis or something out of fairy lights.'

Rebecca looked appalled.

Sam said, 'Probably I should not have used that as an example. Let's pretend I didn't use that as an example.'

'I just think it's odd how many decisions you allow your neighbours to make for you,' sniffed Rebecca.

'Not really,' Sam said. 'It's collaborative. It's just that we all get along so why not—'

'It's like with the dog,' said Rebecca.

'The dog? You mean Jack?'

'Yes, I suppose that's his name. How do you know the conditions under which that dog is being placed? It seems risky to bring an animal like that, who's so often out of your control, into a house with a child in it?'

'Not really,' said Sam. 'We share him amongst the street. It's a very controlled environment.'

'It just takes some getting used to.'

Sam wanted to point out that Rebecca lived in a village where, as far as Sam could tell, everyone was constantly involved in each other's business. But he refrained for the sake of the harmony of the house.

Arthur came home to Max outside dealing with fairy lights. He'd elaborately twined many strands together and was now draping them into a complicated pattern.

'What's this?' Arthur asked.

'Marriage,' Max said, stepping back and looking pleased at his handiwork.

'Is it?' asked Arthur. 'And here all along I thought marriage was simply the state of our existence, rather than fairy lights.'

Max grinned at him and kissed him and said, 'You know what I mean. It's my theme for this Christmas. See, the many strands of lights twining together are *married*.'

'It's a poly relationship, I see,' remarked Arthur.

Max laughed. 'A bit, maybe. And then they're supposed to look like waves crashing into each other. What do you think?'

'That could use some work,' said Arthur.

'Yeah, I agree,' mused Max.

'Where is our child?'

'Oh!' exclaimed Max. 'A most excellent thing happened.'

'What's that?'

'Charlie is a terrible helper.'

'He's ten months old,' Arthur pointed out.

Max shrugged. 'He was bored and being fussy and I was maybe struggling with him a bit and then Sai arrived.'

'Sai? Sai Basak?'

'Yes. And he offered to watch him for me. And Sai's been watching Pari his whole life so I thought this sounded like a great idea.'

'But Pari is practically grown-up,' Arthur said, a little alarmed.

Max gave him a look. 'Darling. You are always very skittish about leaving Charlie with anyone but us.'

'With good reason,' Arthur defended himself. 'It's terrifying.'

'Yes. And you're always working through little insurance agent horror stories in your head.'

'Probabilities,' Arthur said wryly. 'They're called probabilities.'

'Anyway,' said Max, 'I am literally a few feet away from our door, should Sai find Charlie too difficult to handle. I'm not worried.'

Max wasn't worried but Max never worried; worrying was Arthur's job. Arthur tried not to hurry into their house, tried to make sure his pace was very leisurely, but he knew he wasn't fooling Max.

When Arthur entered the house, though, it was surprisingly calm and comfortable. Charlie was curled up on Sai's lap, listening as Sai read him a book.

'Oh,' Arthur said, halting in the front room and trying not to sound as surprised as he felt.

'Da!' exclaimed Charlie, which was the closest he got to *Daddy*, and then wrestled his way off Sai's lap to crawl to Arthur.

'Hello, little one,' Arthur said, lifting him up into his arms to cover him with kisses. And then he looked at Sai. 'Hi.'

'Hi,' Sai said. 'I hope you don't mind. He wasn't very happy about putting up the Christmas decorations with Max.'

'I don't mind at all,' Arthur said. 'I guess I'm just surprised you were hanging around ready to watch Charlie.'

Sai shrugged. 'I've got kind of used to watching kids. But Teddy and Pari are old enough now that they pretty much just spend all of their time spying around in your back garden. Hope you don't mind, by the way.'

'It's fine,' said Arthur. 'I've grown resigned to my back garden being the central control for the spying operation.'

'And Emilia's been super busy with her band. I mean, her band is great and stuff, well, you got to hear them, they're awesome.'

'Yes,' said Arthur carefully. 'They are indeed something.'

'So I don't want to cramp her dream or anything like that, and I really don't mind, but it means I don't have much to do.' Sai shrugged again.

'What about studying for your exams?' asked Arthur.

Sai grinned. 'Well, I'd much rather watch Charlie than study.'

'Of course you would,' said Arthur. 'But I'd rather not get in trouble with your mum and dad for that.'

'I know,' said Sai ruefully. 'It was only for a couple of minutes.'

'Yes, and thank you,' Arthur said sincerely. 'I appreciate it.'

'No problem. I could see it was frustrating Max,' said Sai. 'I'll head out now. Bye, little Char.' Sai held up his hand for Charlie to execute a high-five, and then he grinned at him and ruffled his hair. 'Bye,' he said to Arthur.

'Bye,' Arthur replied, and looked down at Charlie in his arms, thinking, reflectively, of Max, being frustrated. 'Well, Charlie, shall we think about what we might have in this house worth eating for dinner?'

Arthur hunted up something that could pass as dinner and called Max in from fiddling with his decorations. Max talked enthusiastically about his plans for the street and then asked Arthur about his day and before they knew it was bathtime and then bedtime and it was one of those evenings where they both felt almost too exhausted even for telly.

Arthur crawled his way onto the sofa next to Max, to at least give some TV a try before admitting how old they were and going to bed, and he yawned and said, 'You've had a busy day, you must be exhausted.'

'Mmm,' said Max noncommittally.

Arthur thought about what Sai had said and said, 'Charlie was difficult with the decorations?'

'He was bored. You know how he is when he's bored. It was good, though. I had help virtually all day.'

'All day?'

'Yeah, Jasper helped me.'

'Jasper helped you with your Christmas decorations?' said Arthur. 'I thought Jasper was supposed to be creating storage solutions for us.'

'Well,' said Max. 'Yes. Technically.'

'Technically?' said Arthur drily.

'But he was here and the storage solutions can be dealt with any time, whereas the Christmas decorations must be dealt with now. These were exigent circumstances. Surely you, as an insurance agent, understand when dire things occur that must be dealt with on an emergency basis.'

'Yes,' said Arthur, tone still desert-dry. 'I am indeed familiar with such things. I wasn't aware that our baby son was causing them.'

'Oh, Charlie causes nothing but exigent circumstances,' said Max earnestly.

Arthur, after a moment, laughed. 'Actually, I can't argue with you there. So Jasper helped you with Charlie?'

'Yes. Also he asked me for information about Millie.'

'About Millie?'

'Yes, he's clearly interested in her. And she's clearly inter-ested in him.'

'Is this your romantic radar picking this up?' asked Arthur.

'Of course. Don't sound so sceptical. My romantic radar is what got me you.'

'No, it's not,' said Arthur. 'I promise you.'

Max laughed. 'I told Jasper I'd put in a good word for him.'

'What? With who? Millie?'

'Yes, that's who we're talking about.'

'How are you putting in a good word for him with Millie? We never talk to Millie.'

'We could talk more to Millie.'

Arthur sighed. 'Let's not bother Millie if she doesn't want to be bothered.'

'You sound like Libby,' Max accused. 'Millie came to our party, I think she might want to be friends with us.'

'She might have just done that to be polite.'

'I think she had fun.'

'Does Jasper know how incredibly indiscreet and unsubtle you're going to be about putting in a good word for him?'

'How dare you impugn my reputation by implying I am not the *most* subtle and discreet?'

'Uh-huh,' said Arthur, and for a moment silence descended upon them. And Arthur thought, well, there was probably no better time to broach this subject. 'Max. About Charlie.'

'Yes?'

And then Arthur paused, trying to collect his thoughts. He'd broached the subject but he wasn't entirely sure how to say what he wanted to say. He shifted to make sure he could see Max, because he thought that was vital, being able to read Max's face so that he could truly get a feel for how Max was reacting. Max had a silver tongue and his words could not always be trusted, but his face by now was an open book to Arthur.

'If Charlie is too much for you—'

Max looked immediately offended. 'Who said Charlie is too much for me?'

Arthur paused. 'Okay, that was the wrong way of putting that.'

'Oh, there's a *right* way of putting that?' Max retorted hotly.

'All I mean is . . . if you would like a break from—'

'Our son?' Max cut in swiftly.

'I don't mean this in a bad way,' Arthur said. 'So please take a deep breath and don't take it that way. I get a break. I go to work every day and I get a break. I don't know if I could be the one in the house all the time with the baby. It made sense because you work from home, and so we made you do it, but we never really discussed – not really – what that was going to mean for you and your art, and how much your life was going to change, whilst I still went off to work every day. And, remember, I promised you I wouldn't let you do all the emotional labour, so this is me saying to you that we have to *talk* about this. You can't feel like you can't talk to me about this. It's *important*.'

Max, after a long moment, agreed, 'Yes. Okay. You're right. I can't. We should talk about it.'

'So,' said Arthur, when Max didn't seem inclined to keep going on his own. 'Let's talk about it.'

'I love Charlie, and I even love being home with him. He's

a delightful companion every day. And it's not like I was ever used to being super-productive on this street, there's a whole contingent of people willing and happy to enable procrastination at all times.'

'Yes,' Arthur agreed.

'But the thing is that they're all grown-ups, and when I was in the middle of a fantastic painting, I could just say to them, "No. Wait. Stop. I'm in the middle of something." I can never say that to Charlie.'

'And that must be frustrating.'

'It is a bit,' Max admitted. 'I imagine it'll get better as he gets older, and as he gets better able to understand things, but right now . . . yeah. It's a bit frustrating. Like, the thing with the decorations today was just . . . he wasn't into them. They're a thing I adore and I guess I thought they would translate immediately, and I don't know why I thought that. He's a baby. They were interesting to him for about half a second.'

Max looked so dejected that Arthur felt heartbroken for him. Arthur thought it was fairly obvious that Max had imagined Charlie would love hanging out with his cool artist dad, and hadn't thought through how long it would be before Charlie understood things like *artist* and *coolness*. 'He's still a baby, as you say. I'm sure when he gets older he's going to be all about the Christmas decorations, and he'll be so excited to help you come up with a theme and help you put them up. He is going to love being home with you. You're going to be his best friend.'

'I mean,' said Max glumly, 'it's not that I want to *monopolise* him.'

214

'I know,' Arthur smiled. 'Listen, in the meantime, maybe you need to take more breaks.'

'What do you mean?'

'I talked to Sai, and he's clearly bored with Emilia off rehearsing all the time.'

'Yes,' Max said. 'Doesn't know what to do without her.'

'And Charlie clearly likes him, so, I don't know, if we want to ask Sai if he wants to baby-sit a few evenings a week, until I get home, then that might be a good idea.'

Max brightened immediately, and Arthur was relieved to have hit upon an acceptable solution. 'That would be brilliant! At least until the Christmas decoration project is done.'

'Beyond that, too,' Arthur insisted. 'You deserve to be able to take a break. You deserve to be able to just do whatever you want to do for a while. It doesn't make you a bad father.'

'No, I know,' said Max, although Arthur, watching his face and reading him like a book, doubted it.

'I go to work every day, and you would never call me a bad father.'

Which made Max horrified. 'What? No. What are you talking about? You're a *fantastic* father. You're utterly devoted to Charlie.'

'Right,' Arthur agreed calmly. 'Exactly. So this is me saying to you: you can also go to work every day. Charlie doesn't have to be your job. We never said that he would be.'

Max, after a moment, nodded. 'Okay. I see what you're saying.'

'Do you?' Arthur asked.

'Yes. I do. It's going to take me a bit to internalise it, but ... yes. I do.'

215

Arthur supposed he could not ask for more than that. 'Good,' he said. 'Work on internalising it. I'll help you.' He leaned up to give Max a kiss.

Max said, 'You know, you've got very good at this emotional labour side of things.'

'Have I?'

'You excel at everything you put your mind to, it's bloody annoying about you.' But Max said it whilst smiling, so Arthur merely laughed and kissed him again.

'Hmm,' said Sam, frowning at the latest edition of the *Turtledove Chronicle*, Mrs Dash edition. Which Sam looked somewhat less forward to than he had Libby's edition, primarily because he and Libby used the *Turtledove Chronicle* as an opportunity for flirtation, and Mrs Dash used the *Turtledove Chronicle* to deliver endless dramatic proclamations that Sam always worried were passive-aggressive comments on his ability to parent. There were frequent articles that started with sentences like, *Parents should pay special attention to small details, like lunches and matching shoelaces, as those small details express love*, and Sam had spent some time fretting about whether Teddy's shoelaces matched (because he couldn't tell). Sam had mentioned this to Diya, though, and Diya had said that she thought they were commentaries on *her* ability to parent ('There was one about allowing children access to your "secret grown-up life" that was definitely about taking your children to parties,' she'd said), and after that Sam had tried to take them less personally.

But this particular issue of the *Turtledove Chronicle* Sam was viewing with a special sort of suspicion.

'What's that look for?' asked Libby, coming into the kitchen dressed for a run with Pen.

'Have you ever heard of goodgymming?'

'Is it doing really good things for yourself because you're taking care of yourself?' asked Libby, and poked Sam playfully in the stomach.

'It's doing really good things for the *community* because you're taking care of yourself,' said Sam, and brandished the *Turtledove Chronicle* at Libby. 'It's Mrs Dash's latest entry in the Make a Difference sweepstakes.'

'Aww,' said Libby, glancing at the article. 'It sounds lovely. I should bring it up with Pen.'

'I think it's a commentary on the fact that I don't exercise enough,' said Sam worriedly, since God knew he was getting enough commentary on that from Rebecca that it had started to get into his head.

Libby started laughing.

'That isn't funny!' Sam protested.

'You have a guilty conscience and you allow Mrs Dash to prick at every bit of it,' remarked Libby playfully. 'Don't feel guilty about failing to help yourself *or* your community.'

'That's a very mean way of putting it,' grumbled Sam.

'See you!' Libby called, on her way out the door to being very self-righteous in her exercising habits.

At least, so Sam thought.

Chapter 15

Bonfire & Firework Display!
Gates open at **6.00pm**, Bonfire starts at **7.00pm**,
Firework display starts at **8.00pm**.

Admission:
Adults £4. Children £1. Under fives Free.

Limited parking available – car park £1.

Food available. Children's rides.

For safety reasons – no personal fireworks or
sparklers. No alcohol allowed.

Under fourteens must be
accompanied by an adult.

Hello,' said Pen, knocking on Sam and Libby's door one night, 'we are having an impromptu street meeting.'

'And what's that mean?' asked Libby.

'Just discussing things. Max was outside doing Christmas decorations and a bunch of us gradually just joined so we thought we'd have a meeting.'

'Okay,' Libby agreed, and turned back into the house to grab a coat and the cup of tea she'd just had Sam pour. 'Impromptu street meeting,' she said to Sam.

'I heard,' said Sam.

'You have those here?' asked Rebecca, and Sam suppressed a sigh. Rebecca had still not settled into street life, even though Sam still did not see what was difficult about it. But she still flinched every time Jack walked by her, which Jack could clearly sense, because he'd been spending less time at the house, which had been upsetting Teddy, who basically wanted to just sleep at Bill's with Jack, which definitely told Sam where his place in Teddy's life was. And Rebecca was still obviously suspicious of Max's Christmas decoration project, to a degree that seemed absurd to Sam.

'We've never had them before,' Libby said.

'Not in so many words,' said Sam. 'We do just hang about chatting on the street often enough.'

'Yes,' Libby said. 'True. We never called them "street meetings" before, but I suppose they are.

'Hmph,' said Rebecca. 'Well, I suppose you can collect Teddy from the neighbours' at the street meeting.'

Another thing Rebecca disapproved of was how much time Teddy spent at other people's houses.

219

'We'll be right back, Mum,' Libby said patiently, and Rebecca turned back to her book and Sam and Libby stepped outside together.

Sam didn't say anything about how much Rebecca disliked basically everything about Christmas Street and their life on it, because it didn't seem like that would be productive. Instead, he and Libby walked in silence toward the impromptu street meeting, and Sam tried to pretend it was a comfortable silence instead of a tense one.

'What are we all doing?' Libby asked brightly, as they reached their neighbours. Jack, delighted to have so many people standing around outside – and all his favourite people at that – came trotting up to greet them with tail wags and swipes of his tongue.

'Being impressed by Max's Christmas decorations,' said Diya.

'Aw, cheers,' said Max.

'They are brilliant,' agreed Libby. 'What's the theme this year?'

Max grinned. 'Care to guess?'

'Oh, God,' said Libby, blowing out a breath. 'Not really, that's too stressful. Hmm. Joy and peace?'

'*Marriage*,' said Max. 'You see how the lights are all being married together?'

'Oh,' said Libby, and Sam couldn't read her tone. 'I do see. Huh.'

'So, whilst I have us all together,' said Pen, 'or, well, most of us. Bill refused to come outside because he said I was being daft.'

There was general laughter.

'And Arthur's in with sleeping Charlie,' Pen continued. 'And Millie didn't answer her door, which means she's either avoiding us or working.'

'She's probably working,' Diya said. 'I'm not sure where she works but she comes and goes at odd hours.'

'For the rest of us, we should talk about the Bonfire Night outing,' Pen said.

'The *annual* Bonfire Night outing,' said Max. 'It is, after all, a tradition now.'

'Yes,' agreed Pen, beaming with pride at this.

'Last year I stayed home with Jack, as all of you might remember,' Pen went on.

'It was indeed very memorable,' said Anna, smiling at her.

'But it doesn't seem fair to make Pen do it again this year,' Max said. 'She should get to participate in some of the fun. I'm all right with staying home—'

'Aw, but don't you want to bring Charlie to the bonfire?' said Pen. 'I think he would enjoy it!'

'He'll either enjoy it or hate it. Charlie can be difficult to predict,' said Max.

'But he knows his own mind,' said Anna admiringly. 'Good for him.'

'Next time he announces his own mind by screaming at us loudly, I'll bring him to your house,' said Max ruefully.

Anna laughed.

'Is Bill coming along on the outing again?' Sam asked.

'Oh, yes,' said Pen. 'He wouldn't miss it.'

Sam lifted his eyebrows. 'I doubt that's what Bill said.'

It was Pen's turn to laugh. 'No, of course not, but I'm definitely going to get him to tag along.'

'You should try that trick on Libby's mum,' said Sam without thinking, and Libby gave him a sharp look.

'She doesn't want to come to Bonfire Night?' said Pen.

Libby said, 'It isn't really her thing. All these people around she doesn't know.'

'But she'd know us if she came!' protested Pen.

'If she's staying home,' said Max, 'maybe she could watch Jack.'

'I don't think that's a good idea,' Sam said quickly.

Everyone looked at him expectantly.

'They don't exactly get along,' Sam explained awkwardly, 'Jack and Rebecca.'

'Jack,' Max said to Jack, who bounced around him happily at the attention, 'you haven't won Rebecca over yet? Where's your canine charm?'

Jack barked with glee.

'She's just not that much of a dog person,' Libby said. 'It's not a big thing.'

'Jack was fine last year,' Sam pointed out. 'He doesn't seem to be that alarmed by the fireworks. Do we really have to have anyone watching him?'

Anna said, 'Actually, along those lines, I'm thinking that I can watch Jack. After all, it was really my cats who caused all the excitement last year.'

'You don't want to come along?' Max said. 'You missed last year's outing, too.'

'Yes,' Anna said. 'But I missed last year's outing because of ... very different circumstances. Because I didn't realise what the outing meant, and what was happening around the outing. This year ... I want to miss the outing for very different reasons. I want to miss it *knowingly*. I want to miss it because Jack is our street dog, and I'm part of the life of the street.'

'Plus,' said Marcel, smiling down at Anna, 'I'm going to miss it, too.'

'Well, then,' Pen said, 'that seems like a lovely evening in front of you.'

'You should really come,' Libby told her mother earnestly.

'To Bonfire Night?' she said. 'But I won't know anyone.'

'But you'll *meet* everyone. And I think you'd feel better if you met the people on the street and knew how lovely they are. It's just like the village.'

'No, it's not. I know everyone in the village.'

'Yes. And you would know all these people, too, if you came with us to Bonfire Night.'

Her mum shook her head. 'It still wouldn't be the same. I've known all the people in the village *for ever*. These people are basically strangers.'

'Mum—' Libby began.

'No, no. I know that you feel as if you know them, but in the grand scheme of your life, you've just met them. Of course they're still strangers, compared to everyone who knew you as a little girl. But, of course, you *like* getting to be surrounded by strangers, don't you? After all, you moved here, didn't you?'

'Are we going to have that fight again?' sighed Libby.

'No,' replied her mother simply. 'What would be the point? But I *suppose* that this is one of those things I just have to put up with, isn't it? Bonfire Night with all of your neighbours, your sudden decision to get married – just things I'm expected to go along with.'

'Mum,' said Libby. 'It wasn't sudden, and those things aren't equivalent. It's a *Bonfire Night*. Please don't be so dramatic.'

'Fine,' said Rebecca. 'Then I'll go and I'll try not to be too "dramatic" about it.'

'Good,' said Libby, relieved. 'Thank you.'

Bonfire Night was exactly as it had been the year before: chilly and misty. Teddy again complained about the ridiculousness of scheduling an outdoor holiday for November and Sam privately agreed. But with Rebecca around, Sam didn't want to do anything that might raise her suspicion about him as a future husband choice. For all he knew, his longing for the Fourth of July as an appropriate time for an outdoor celebration would cause Rebecca to brand him too American and lump him in with the rest of the Christmas Street citizens she found undesirable for some reason.

Sam made Teddy bundle up to keep himself warm and as ever Teddy whinged a great deal about this.

'The hat is stupid,' he grumbled. 'It makes me look stupid.'

'It doesn't make you look stupid,' Sam said. 'It's a hat. I'm wearing a hat.'

Teddy lifted his eyebrows at Sam.

Sam said, 'And you think that my hat makes me look stupid, do you?'

'Well,' said Teddy, 'it doesn't make you look *smart*.'

'Since when are you a fashion expert?' Sam asked, grinning, and basically tackled Teddy into an embrace because these days you had to hug Teddy through stealth tactics.

Teddy complained and wriggled out of Sam's grasp but he was also laughing and grinning by the time Sam was done with him.

Teddy said, 'I hope you don't let Rebecca bother you too much.'

Sam blinked, surprised. 'What?'

'I know it makes you nervous that you think she doesn't like the street, or whatever.'

'What makes you think that?' Sam asked.

'When we do our daily adventures at dinner, and hers are always something about having to cope with the street doing some weird thing, your face is pretty classic.'

'Well,' said Sam, 'at least she does the adventures now. I feel like we're making some progress.'

Teddy shrugged, unconcerned. 'You're always impatient with people, you know. You think we ought to like things right away. But it took me a while to come round to the street, too.'

That was true, and Sam had never thought that about himself before, but maybe he *was* impatient with others over that. 'Did I boss you into liking the street?' he asked.

Teddy shook his head. 'Nah, I'm used to you. I came to like it on my own. But I'm just saying. Sometimes new things take a little while.'

Sam wanted to point out that at least Teddy had immediately liked Jack, so that maybe other things on the street had been suspect but there had been *something* for Sam to work with. But Sam decided to leave it.

Instead he said sincerely, 'Thanks for that.'

'No problem,' Teddy said brightly. 'Can I run over to Emilia's to say goodbye to Jack before we leave for the bonfire?'

'Yeah,' Sam agreed, and listened to Teddy go barrelling down the stairs. After a moment he followed, meeting Libby at the bottom, knotting a scarf around her neck.

'Hello, you,' she said, and then tipped her head at him. 'Is it Bonfire Night that puts you in such a good mood?'

'Hmm?' said Sam. 'Not particularly. I've just been thinking about what unpleasant weather it is to stand around outside in.'

'But you look very pleased,' Libby said.

'Just in a good mood,' said Sam. 'Can't I be in a good mood for no reason at all? For the reason that I am marrying a beautiful woman who I love very much?' Sam smiled at her and pulled her in for a kiss.

'Oh,' said Libby, and smiled and kissed him back. 'Well. Yes. You can be in a good mood for that reason. I hope the next thing I say to you isn't going to destroy this good mood.'

'What next thing?' asked Sam.

Rebecca emerged from the kitchen, bundled up for the cold. 'Are we ready?' she asked.

'My mum has decided to come to Bonfire Night,' announced Libby brightly.

'Oh, yay,' said Sam. 'That's so great. How wonderful.'

Rebecca didn't look fooled for a second.

Libby peeked out the window. 'Everyone seems to be assembling, so yes, let's go.'

Rebecca sighed, as if having to go to Bonfire Night with the rest of the street was an enormous burden on her, and Sam suppressed his annoyance and texted Ellen instead.

Am I impatient with people when they don't like things immediately?

Ellen's response was quick. **Yes. You're impatient with YOURSELF when you don't like things immediately. It's just that you're such an incurable optimist.**

Sam was still reading the text message as he met everyone else in the middle of the street. It wasn't normally how he thought of himself, as an optimist, but maybe Ellen had a point. After all, he'd uprooted his son and moved him to London just on the vague hope that it would turn out okay, and that had probably been the move of an optimist.

'What are you looking so thoughtful about?' Libby asked, looping her arm through his.

'Ellen saying I'm an optimist.'

'Oh, you're definitely an optimist,' Libby agreed. 'You've a tendency toward happiness and you want everyone else to share it and you're disappointed when they don't.'

'I've never thought of myself that way,' said Sam thoughtfully.

The walk to the park for the bonfire had a festive atmosphere, the street folk chattering away amongst each other. Emilia had a break from band rehearsal for the evening and she and Sai walked hand-in-hand at the front of the crowd.

'Oh, young love,' said Max approvingly.

Darsh laughed and Diya rolled her eyes a little bit.

227

Max said, 'You know, it's nice that all of our secret couples from last year feel comfortable being out in the open this year. We've made progress.'

'I suppose that's true,' Sam agreed.

'It's absolutely true. Look how far all of us have come. You've got Libby, Emilia and Sai are out in the open and Emilia's got a band, Arthur and I have Charlie, Diya and Darsh have to come to love Jack.'

'I've got a brand new exciting interior design,' added Pen.

'And we've added Jasper to our coterie,' said Max happily, and gestured to Jasper.

'Three cheers for Jasper!' said Pen, and there was general applause for Jasper.

Jasper looked vaguely embarrassed. 'I still don't know entirely how this happened.'

'It's okay,' Sam said. 'There is no explanation. The street just takes you in.'

'That makes it sound vaguely supernatural and scary,' remarked Max.

'Exactly what I was thinking,' Rebecca remarked, which was the first thing she'd said the whole walk.

'Please don't scare the children like you did with your insistence that the empty house was haunted,' said Sam to Max.

'Did you terrify the children?' Arthur asked.

'Only a little bit,' said Max defensively. 'And, really, everyone thought that house was haunted.'

'It's true, in addition to Jasper, we've added Millie to the street,' Pen pointed out. 'Even if she doesn't want to come on our outings with us.'

'She's just shy,' Max said. 'I think it's just shyness.'

'Honestly,' Arthur said, 'you can see how this street can be overwhelming.'

'Yes,' agreed Rebecca fervently.

Then Bill said, 'Rebecca's right,' which startled everyone.

'What?' said Sam.

'You know her name?' said Max.

'Shh,' Arthur said to Max, and gave him a little shove.

Bill frowned and said, 'Of course I know her name. She was introduced to me, wasn't she? And Rebecca's right: you lot are overwhelming. You like chattering about with each other so you assume everyone must. I understand it more now, what your whole . . . ' Bill gestured in the air, apparently at a loss for the proper word to describe the street, and then settled gruffly on, '*package* is. But it takes a while. Just give Millie a bit of time.'

There was a beat of silence.

Rebecca said, 'Well said.'

Pen said, with a frown on her face, 'Are we overwhelming?'

Diya said, 'I thought we were just *bubbly*.'

Max looked at her. 'Bubbly? Who described you as bubbly?'

'It's a good description, no?' said Diya.

Arthur gave Max a look and Max said gallantly, 'Sure!'

'Well,' said Pen to Rebecca happily. 'At least you're here with us now! See, we might be overwhelming but we can win people over in the end!'

'Yes,' agreed Rebecca faintly.

'I just want to say that I agree with Bill,' said Arthur. 'This street can be overwhelming, especially for those of us with more retiring personality types. You're all wonderful, but you're not what we're expecting, and it takes us a second to process it all. Millie probably just needs her processing time after the engagement party. I mean, it was barely a week ago.'

'Good point,' Pen allowed.

'The processing bit is the best bit,' Max advised Jasper. 'They get a little furrow between their brows and you can kiss it away. Not that you're at that point with Millie yet, I'm just advising you.'

'I should never have told you,' said Jasper, long-suffering but smiling.

'Sorry,' said Max, sounding genuinely regretful. 'I'm just the worst.'

'He doesn't get out enough now,' said Arthur. 'We're going to work on it.' And then he took Max's arm in his hand and nudged him toward the opposite line for tickets.

Everyone chorused goodbye to them and Rebecca murmured to Libby, 'Oh, so you're all going to separate?'

It came out loudly enough that Diya glanced over at them narrow-eyed.

Libby said, 'It's impossible to all stay together once we get inside.'

'This was actually how Libby and I happened to go on our first date,' said Sam.

'Your first date was at Bonfire Night?' remarked Rebecca.

'Kind of,' said Libby, and looked at Sam. 'I thought Teddy's school trip was our first date.'

'It wasn't the supermarket?' said Diya.

'I wooed you in so many glamorous locations,' said Sam, 'how can we choose just one?'

Libby couldn't help but laugh, although her mother looked less amused.

'It's only a bonfire,' said Sam. 'Nothing special or different about it. We just enjoy ourselves. Just sometimes with the rest of the street.'

'Dad,' Teddy said, as Sam was paying for their admission, 'can Pari and I go spying?'

'I don't like this word "spy",' Diya complained. 'I keep trying to convince all of you not to spy.'

'Yeah,' Sam said.

'You're just going to let them go spying?' said Libby's mum.

'They're fine,' said Sam dismissively.

Diya called ahead, 'Sai! Pay some attention to your sister, please!'

Sai sent back a little wave of acknowledgement without ever breaking his focus on Emilia.

'Max is right,' Sam remarked. 'Young love.'

Chapter 16

Bridge is usually played between four people but it
can be adapted into Honeymoon Bridge for exciting
play between two people!

Jasper didn't quite understand how he'd come to be going to
Bonfire Night with the rest of Christmas Street. He blamed
Max for it, as he had to blame Max for most things, or
maybe more accurately the lethal combination of Max and
Pen, who fed off each other in their ridiculous visions. Max
had come over to see the progress on Pen's house – 'What
you're doing when you're not building storage solutions
for me,' he'd joked – and had been duly impressed with the
bed dais and the mini-Eiffel Tower and the other features
of whimsy and absurdity that Pen had planned around the
house. So impressed that Jasper half-expected Max to hire
Pen for a consultation, although Max was an artist himself
and his Christmas decorations proved he wasn't afraid to
think outside the box. Jasper assumed it was Arthur who
kept their house from being an explosion of odd decorating

ideas the way Pen's house had become, but Max was clearly slightly envious of the fact that Pen's only housemate was Chester the goldfish, and Chester went along with everything.

At any rate, at one point after the inspection of Pen's house, Jasper found himself accepting the invitation for a cup of tea, and that was when Pen and Max ganged up on him about the subject of Bonfire Night.

'You should totally come with us,' Pen said. 'It is the most fun. It's even more fun than the Halloween engagement party.'

'It's just a bonfire,' Jasper said, amused, with a little shrug.

'Were you already planning to go to a bonfire?' asked Max, juggling Charlie, as he often was when trying to have adult conversations.

'No,' Jasper said.

'What was your plan for the evening?' asked Pen.

'I don't know,' said Jasper, embarrassed, because he didn't want to admit that he had no plans. These people on Christmas Street always had plans; they wouldn't understand if he said he was 'planning' on just sitting alone in his house.

Max surprised him by saying, 'It's a perfectly acceptable plan to just sit alone in your house.'

Jasper blinked. 'Is it?'

'Yes,' said Max. 'Most of the time. Just not on Bonfire Night.'

Jasper laughed because he couldn't help it.

'Come to the bonfire with us,' said Pen. 'You'll have fun.'

'Aaaaaaand,' said Max, sing-song, and then trailed off with a meaningful look.

Jasper could translate that look: *Millie might be there.* And he didn't want that to be a deciding factor for him – he barely

233

knew Millie, after all, it was ridiculous to make plans based on Millie.

But Jasper still found himself at Bonfire Night, notwithstanding. And Millie wasn't there but he found that he wasn't even that disappointed, because, Jasper realised, he just *liked* these people.

As they wandered through the park, he found himself next to Libby, who he had not spent much time talking to.

He said, 'I meant to tell you, I had a lovely time at your engagement party, thanks for inviting me.'

'Not at all! I'm told you're an honorary Christmas Street citizen. As a former honorary Christmas Street citizen, I welcome you.'

'You were a former honorary citizen?' said Jasper.

'Well, I'm marrying into the street,' said Libby. 'When I met Sam he was already living on Christmas Street, and my dating him meant that I got folded into street life, too.'

'So it's like dating an entire street,' said Jasper.

Libby laughed. 'Kind of. But they're all very nice.'

Yes, Jasper thought. He tended to agree.

The park was crowded for Bonfire Night – far more crowded than Rebecca was used to. And worse than all these weird strangers on Sam's street being overly familiar with her were all these weird strangers completely ignoring her. There was too much ability to feel ... pointless in this city, Rebecca thought. She didn't like it. It made her uneasy. Pointlessness was a thing Rebecca did not approve of.

The old man from next door – Bill, his name was – said, 'Too many people.'

Rebecca looked at him in relief. Finally. An *ordinary* person on this street. '*Exactly.*'

'I feel like every time I turn around there's new people. More and more.'

'Oh,' said Rebecca, realising. 'And I suppose I'm one of them.'

'Oh,' said Bill, 'I didn't mean it like *that.*'

'No, no,' said Rebecca thoughtfully. 'I suppose I didn't think about how I am contributing to how many people are around.'

'Well, there's nothing bad about that,' said Bill. 'We're all just people, after all.'

'True,' allowed Rebecca, looking around at all the strangers. 'Although probably some of us are more or less annoying than others.'

'Sam's a good sort,' said Bill, so roughly she had to duck her head to hear him. He wasn't looking at her, his eyes out over the crowd.

'Pardon?'

'Sam,' said Bill, moving his hand in an awkward gesture. 'He's a good sort.'

'Oh,' said Rebecca, unsure how to respond.

'I'm just saying: you don't have to be hard on him. If I had a daughter, Sam would be the sort I'd want to choose for her.'

'Really?' said Rebecca. 'But what if your daughter were Sam's second choice?'

Before Bill could respond, Teddy came running up to them. 'Mr Hammersley, I've had the best idea that we ought to take Jack to this park sometime, when it's not Bonfire Night and he wouldn't be scared.'

'Well, now,' said Bill, 'this park is a long way to go when you can just play with Jack on the street.'

'Yeah, but it would be an *adventure* and my dad totally approves of adventures.'

'That's true,' Rebecca had to agree. 'His dad is obsessed with adventures.'

'Now, now,' said Bill. 'That's a daft thing that's really harmless, isn't it, now?'

That Rebecca found it harder to agree with.

As the bonfire roared, the citizens of Christmas Street meandered through the crowd, coming together and parting again in little casual knots. Sam kept catching sight of Teddy, usually with Pari nearby, and Sai and Emilia near as well. Sai never looked as if he was paying much attention to Teddy and Pari but the fact that Sam always saw him near them meant he had to be paying attention.

Rebecca and Bill caught up to them after a brief time of separation. Sam couldn't even imagine what they'd been discussing but Rebecca didn't look any unhappier than she ordinarily did, so Sam decided to just be pleased that Bill had kept her occupied for a little while.

Eventually they reconnected with Arthur and Max. Charlie was sound asleep in his pram.

'Sleeping in this racket?' Sam asked. Teddy had never been a sleeper. Sam and Sara had basically spent all of Teddy's first couple of years refusing invitations and staying home, because Teddy's rigid bedtime routine could not be disturbed.

'It's performance art,' said Max.

'He's not really sleeping?' said Sam.

'Oh, no, he's really sleeping,' Max said. 'But he is doing it artistically, to show how dull and boring and beneath his notice he finds this entire outing.'

'What will happen when the fireworks start?' asked Libby.

'It's anyone's guess,' said Arthur, yawning.

'We were thinking of leaving early, actually,' said Max. 'No need to ruin everyone else's fireworks-viewing experience with a possibly fussy baby. And all of us could probably do with a good night's sleep.'

As if on cue, Teddy came up to them, whining, 'When do the fireworks start?'

'Yes,' Sam said drily. 'All of us could do with a good night's sleep.'

'What's that mean?' asked Teddy suspiciously.

Pari came up as well, also looking tired but in an excited kind of way, like she was going to crash as soon as the fireworks were over. And behind them came Sai and Emilia, holding hands.

'You,' Sam said to Sai, 'are an excellent babysitter, thank you.'

'Isn't he, though?' said Max, pleased. 'He's been watching Charlie for us.'

Sai shrugged, looking embarrassed. 'It's no work at all. Charlie's no trouble.'

'It's been enormously helpful, though,' Arthur said. 'It's helped Max get enough free time to get the Christmas decorations done.'

'I think it's great,' said Emilia. 'I was worried Sai would be bored whilst I was off doing my band thing. I'm glad he's got a bit of a job.'

'Not that Charlie's work,' teased Max, grinning.

'It's great,' Sai said bashfully. 'I'm having fun.'

'Well,' said Sam, 'we'll watch the kids for you. You and Emilia can go off and enjoy yourselves.'

'Thanks,' Sai said brightly, both he and Emilia visibly perking up at being set free from obligations.

They took off into the crowd, and Sam turned to Teddy and Pari. 'Well? Who wants candy floss?' Both hands went up, so Sam looked at Libby and said, 'I'll be back. Candy floss for you?' Libby shook her head. 'Anyone else?' Max and Arthur shook their heads. Bill didn't but Sam was pretty sure he could guess where Bill stood on the question of candy floss. Rebecca looked as if she'd barely heard the question but Sam also thought he could guess what Rebecca thought of candy floss, too.

So he took off with Teddy and Pari dancing in his wake.

'I mean, there's lot of possibilities,' Pari said to Teddy, apparently resuming a conversation with him as if it had never been interrupted.

'It's true,' Teddy agreed. 'They're practically limitless.'

'What's this now?' Sam asked. If they were going to talk about it in front of him, he thought it wasn't prying to ask for details.

'Who Millie Really Is,' said Pari, and Sam heard all the capital letters that Pari put in the statement.

Sam lifted his eyebrows at her. 'And who do you think she really is?'

'I don't know,' said Pari. 'But you lot are always saying she likes to keep to herself. *Why* would she keep to herself if she didn't have a secret?'

'Lots of people like to keep to themselves,' Sam replied. 'They're not all harbouring secrets.'

'Still. A mysterious woman shows up on Christmas Street and doesn't want to become best friends with the rest of us. Seems suspicious, doesn't it?'

No, thought Sam, he was living with just such a woman. 'You have a lot of confidence that we must be amazing people to be friends with and anyone who doesn't want to be friends with us must be bonkers.'

Pari gave him a you-are-being-silly look and said, 'We *are* amazing people to be friends with.'

Pen, with Darsh and Diya and Jasper in tow, found her people on the edge of the crowd, save Sam and the kids and the teenagers.

'They went to get candy floss,' Libby said to Pen's questioning look.

'You two,' Diya accused, a little out of breath, and poked a finger between Pen and Libby.

Libby lifted her eyebrows. 'What have we done?'

'You've been exercising!' accused Diya. 'You're probably what Mrs Dash was talking about with her goodgymming!'

'You know,' said Libby, 'Mrs Dash really doesn't write the *Turtledove Chronicle* to anyone in particular.'

'What's gymgooding?' asked Pen curiously.

'It was in the *Turtledove Chronicle*,' Libby explained. 'You use running as an opportunity to do greater good for the community. For instance, you could run every day to go visit an older lonely person.'

239

'We don't have to run to do that,' grumbled Diya.

'You can run for big group projects, too,' said Libby. 'Mrs Dash gave examples. Some communities run to parks and then plant trees, or they run to a food bank to sort cans. You know, things like that.'

'I love this idea!' exclaimed Pen. 'And we're running anyway, we should definitely just add it to what we're already doing! *In fact* ...' Pen said this with a special flourish, beaming at all of her fellow street inhabitants.

'What?' asked Diya suspiciously.

'We should make it a street project! We could all pitch in!'

'That sounds like it would delight the kids,' remarked Libby. 'They're always looking for ways to Make a Difference.'

'Mrs Dash put all these ideas in their heads,' complained Diya.

'They're *good* ideas,' said Darsh, sounding amused. 'I think it sounds like a nice thing to do. Except I will just donate some money because I am clearly too busy working to actually train for a run.'

'Everyone can pitch in in different ways,' Pen said.

'Then I suppose,' said Diya thoughtfully, 'I can provide the food.'

Millie, on the evening of Bonfire Night, trudged home from work tiredly. What she wanted to do was get into her house and lock her door and curl up and just be *tired*. It seemed that kind of day and that kind of weather.

But once she was home, she felt overcome with sadness.

She was tired to the point of wanting to weep with it, and the house was quiet and felt cavernous with the silence. She'd tried to make her home cosy, so she wouldn't feel it overwhelming her with cold emptiness the way she had felt her previous home did, and most of the time she thought she'd succeeded, but tonight it just seemed awful.

It wasn't that she missed Daniel. She knew by now to be wise enough and honest enough in her conversations with herself that she didn't miss Daniel. But she missed the *habit* of him, the fact of him. He hadn't been nice or joyful or delightful to have around, not by any means, but what he had been was the ability to have *someone* there. The loneliness creeping up on her was the worst.

And then it dawned on her – she was living on the world's friendliest street. There was no reason to put herself through feeling this way.

It wasn't her natural instinct to seek out strangers for reasons of comfort, but since they had made themselves so open and available to the idea of her approaching them, maybe she should try it. Maybe her natural instincts, after all, weren't terribly trustworthy.

She had nothing to offer for an impromptu visit: no bottle of wine to bring along with her, no homemade pudding. She supposed she would just have to show up on the doorstep and say, *Talk to me so I'm not alone*. She supposed she would just have to swallow her pride that way.

She went to Pen's house. Pen had been the most insistently forthcoming member of the street, and Millie thought she would be the one most excited about an impromptu visit. But Pen didn't answer her door and it wasn't until that moment that Millie remembered what night it was: Bonfire Night. The street had been going on an outing to watch fireworks. Millie had been invited along but she had already volunteered to work that night and anyway, she hadn't been sure about continuing down the path of entwining herself with street life. The party had worked out well, but the party had taken place right outside of her house, and she would have been able to flee back to safety if she'd had to. Which she'd done. Going somewhere else was another question entirely.

But that meant she was all alone on the street. Not even Jack was out and about.

In the distance, fireworks started, and Millie felt as if she could weep.

And that was when Anna's door opened and she called out, 'Hello! Were you looking for Pen?'

Anna's proposal to stay home with Marcel and Jack had been impulsive, but she was very happy with her decision. The cats and Jack were getting along, all of them snoozing in the lounge, and she and Marcel were playing cards, a favourite occupation of theirs from younger days that they were trying to revive. It was a nice, cosy, lovely evening.

'This is how it will be in a couple of years,' Marcel said.

'What do you mean?' said Anna.

'When Emilia goes away to uni. It'll just be you and me, every night, trying to make conversation and not bore each other terribly.'

Anna laughed, and it was a relief to her that she could laugh about these things, that they now felt secure enough in their future to tease each other about it. 'Are you bored?' she asked coquettishly. 'Am I boring you?'

'Not at all,' Marcel grinned. 'Never.'

They played a few more rounds.

Marcel said, 'Anyway, as long as we live on this street, we'll never truly be alone.'

'I think it's nice,' said Anna. 'Don't you think it's nice?'

'Yes,' said Marcel. 'I do. I always have. And I'm glad that we've all become friends. I think Diya is a good friend for you.'

'You're just saying that because now I make excellent Indian food,' said Anna.

'I never said I didn't have selfish reasons for liking Diya,' responded Marcel.

Anna laughed and glanced out the window just as Millie walked by. 'Huh,' she said. 'That's odd.'

'What?' asked Marcel, already distracted by the game again.

'I think Millie just walked down the street.'

'So?'

'So? So she never just walks down the street like that.'

'Never in her life?' Marcel lifted his eyebrows.

'She keeps to herself. Hey, you're the one who was just all thrilled to death over how close the street is.' Anna stood.

'Where are you going?'

'To check to make sure she's all right. Close-knit street, remember?' Anna opened the door and could tell that she startled Millie. 'Hello! Were you looking for Pen?'

'I thought everyone had gone to the bonfire. I mean, I remembered when Pen didn't answer the door, but then I thought everyone had gone.'

'Someone had to stay home with Jack,' Anna said, as Jack, curious, came to the door to peek out. 'We don't like to leave him roaming alone when the fireworks are going on. Although he doesn't seem terribly bothered by them.'

Millie smiled at Jack's appearance. 'I was wondering where he'd gone. The street seemed awfully lonely without him.'

'Was there something you needed?' Anna asked.

Millie hesitated. 'No,' she said finally. 'No, that's okay.'

And Anna remembered being the one who'd stayed behind last year out of caution, or fear, or not knowing if she was really wanted by the group. She said to Millie, 'Why don't you come in for some tea?'

Millie shook her head. 'That's okay. I don't want to bother—'

'It wouldn't be a bother at all. Please come in.'

Millie, after a moment's further hesitation, nodded.

Chapter 17

> Help wanted: Goods-in and other
> typical stockroom activities. Must be available
> to work nights and weekends.

The Pachuta house was warm and cosy and bright. Jack came over and snoozed directly on Millie's feet, which was lovely. There were two cats curled up on the sofa purring. Anna put a steaming cup of tea in a china teacup in Millie's hands, and Anna's husband Marcel smiled at her welcomingly, and it was so nice to be around people, in this safe, brilliant house, that Millie didn't even let herself feel awkward for having crashed their obvious date night. Their date night could resume when she was done with her tea and felt steadier about going back to her house.

'So how are things, Millie?' Marcel asked kindly. 'Settling in?'

Except for when she had irritating panic attacks about being alone in her own house and had to wander the street looking for company, thought Millie. 'Everyone's been really nice,' Millie said. And then, after a moment, 'I hope I haven't seemed ... ' She didn't know how she seemed.

'You don't,' Anna said, even though she couldn't possibly have any idea what she was denying.

'The street I lived on before this one wasn't like this,' Millie tried to explain.

'No street is like this one,' said Marcel drily.

'Right,' Millie agreed. 'So I've just been ... I'm not really used to ... all these people. If that makes sense. All these people ... taking an interest.' Millie laughed a little shrilly. 'I feel like I have to do something interesting to merit all the attention.'

'No,' said Anna, shaking her head. 'That's not what's happening.'

'I mean, it might be happening with the little ones,' said Marcel, 'but they just want everything to be as interesting as possible at all times, do Teddy and Pari.'

'And they often manage to achieve it,' added Anna.

'But the rest of the street just ... cares,' Marcel said.

'We just want to make sure you're okay. It's what we do. We try to be here for each other when we're not okay.'

Millie tried not to feel like bursting into tears over such a simple statement, but it was a near thing. It was just that it had been ... forever ... since someone had said they wanted her to be okay. 'That's so nice,' Millie managed to say, which was not at all what she meant.

Arthur and Max were the first to return from Bonfire Night, pushing a sleeping Charlie in his pram. Charlie later slept through the fireworks as well, which made Arthur and Max lucky parents.

Everyone else came back in fairly high spirits. Emilia and Sai shared a brief kiss and parted ways to go to their separate houses, where each of them had a pair of doting parents who glowed with love and showered them with safety and security. Teddy and Pari were sleepy and triumphant, with slightly queasy tummies from too much food. Their parents stripped them out of cold, smoky clothing and tucked them into bed, thinking about another Bonfire Night already come and gone.

Pen greeted Chester happily and thought of goodgymming and how lucky she was to have such incredible friends. Jack followed Bill home and curled up on the foot of his bed familiarly, and Bill thought how foolish his neighbours were and how silly it had been to spend all night standing out in the cold but also, he supposed, it had been a nice bonfire and the fireworks display had been better than expected. Sam and Libby and Rebecca went home and wished each other a good night. Sam and Libby went to bed with yawned *happy anniversary*s. Rebecca went to bed relieved the dismal Bonfire Night evening was over.

In her house, with the doors locked and the curtains drawn, Millie curled up in bed alone, but although she was alone, the dread of the loneliness creeping over her had faded. Even in her empty house, the street around her felt cosy and close.

Jasper walked back to his house, through London streets where revelry was gradually fading into the background, and thought how odd it was that he'd happened to be hired by Pen to create a dais for her bed. And look how that had turned out.

'I think,' Pari announced knowingly (but Pari was usually knowing), 'that she's a spy.'

They were sitting on the floor in Teddy's lounge, with Jack settled between them, patiently being groomed, and in the kitchen Dad was pretending to be able to cook.

Teddy wrinkled his nose and said, 'It doesn't seem likely, does it?'

'Spies definitely exist,' Pari said. 'And she didn't have any boxes and she keeps to herself, so she's probably definitely a spy.'

'I just think it's unlikely our street would have so many spies. Considering that it's already got you and me and Jack.'

'Hmm,' said Pari thoughtfully, brushing Jack's fur. And then, 'Why doesn't Jack's fur ever grow long enough for us to plait?'

'I don't know,' said Teddy. 'I think she might be a princess.'

'A princess?' Pari said. 'You think *that* seems more likely than being a spy? Wouldn't princesses have boxes with belongings?'

'No,' said Teddy eagerly, because he'd been giving a lot of thought to this possibility. 'She's, like, an undercover princess. A princess in hiding.'

'Snack?' asked Dad, holding out a plate of sliced-up carrots.

'That's it?' said Teddy. 'You made all that noise in there, and you ended up with carrots?'

'Pari, would you like some carrots?' Dad asked calmly. 'I am no longer providing any to my ungrateful child.'

Teddy stuck his tongue out but then he grinned, and Dad grinned back and ruffled his hair and said, 'What's this we're discussing? Who's a princess?'

'Millie,' said Teddy.

'*Possibly*,' said Pari. 'It doesn't seem likely to me, it seems more likely she's a spy.'

'She could also just be a woman who's moved onto our street from somewhere else, no mysterious backstory required.'

'Dad,' said Teddy in exasperation.

'It's just if she's a spy, it would make sense that she has no belongings and keeps to herself all the time,' Pari explained. 'She's just trying to complete her mission and get out.'

'What's her mission?' Dad asked.

Pari looked thrown off by having to consider this.

'I hope her mission isn't us,' Dad continued lightly.

'But we don't do anything interesting on this street,' Teddy said. 'Pari and I are always saying how difficult it is to be spies on this street because everyone's so boring.'

'Well, actually, nobody is boring on this street,' said Dad. 'Just wait until you grow up and go to live on other streets, and then you'll get to see just how boring the world can be.'

Pari said, 'Okay, so you might be right and she's not a spy, because I can't think what her mission could possibly be. So that leaves us with princess, I suppose.'

'Right,' Teddy agreed. 'A princess *in hiding*. She doesn't want anyone to know she's a princess, so she stays in her house all the time.'

'But how would we know she's a princess?' said Pari. 'She doesn't *look* like a princess.'

'She could! In her country she's probably famous! And probably people are looking for her, so she just stays in her house all the time because she doesn't want them to find her.'

'Why doesn't she want them to find her?' asked Pari with interest.

Teddy thought before saying, 'It's probably a love affair gone wrong. Isn't that what it always is?'

Millie ran into Jasper on her way home after a shift. Really, it was impossible to walk down Christmas Street without running into *someone*, especially Jack, who took it upon himself to greet everyone who arrived, but running into Jasper felt like a special treat.

And then Millie felt ridiculous for thinking it was a special treat, because she was too old and had been through too much for *special treats*; she was being ridiculous.

But Jasper stopped when he saw her and gave her a nice smile and said, 'Hello.'

And Millie felt herself respond, blossoming shyly. She barely remembered how to do this any more, but she suddenly found herself game to give it a try. Maybe there could be such things as a new beginning. 'Hello.'

'I haven't really seen you around much,' said Jasper.

'Oh,' said Millie, and wondered that Jasper had ever thought she was around much at all, because she ... wasn't. She mostly hid in her house. She didn't want to say that, though. 'It's just been ... busy. It's a busy time of year.'

'Yes, especially on this street,' said Jasper, and smiled at the Christmas decorations all around.

'They do take its name rather literally, don't they?' said Millie.

'That's what I said!' said Jasper. 'And it's sweet. I think their goodgymming idea is such a good one.'

'Their what?' said Millie.

'Oh, Pen's cooked up this whole project for Remembrance Sunday. Running to a convalescent home to visit some of the veterans there. It's a nice plan, really.'

'Oh,' said Millie, both surprised and not at all surprised. It seemed like just the sort of thing this street would do. 'That sounds lovely.'

'Doesn't it, though? I'm going to take part. You should, too.' Jasper smiled at her.

Millie wished Jasper would stop smiling at her, because it made her feel foolish and silly and ... *young*. Younger than she had felt in years. How dangerous, to feel like everything could start anew again.

How wondrous, to feel like everything could start anew again, and it could be *better*.

'I'm not much of a runner ... ' Millie said, because she wasn't, and she didn't want to make a fool of herself in front of Jasper.

'Oh, you don't have to run,' said Jasper. 'Everyone's participating in all sorts of ways. Diya's making a load of food, for instance.'

Millie thought of food. Millie thought of the baked goods that she had sold up and down her old street, the baked goods that her neighbours, with knowing looks of pity Millie had tried to ignore, had paid so much money for. Millie hadn't really baked since leaving Daniel, and baking used to be her shelter, the place where she could go and it felt like nothing could hurt her, because butter and sugar and eggs would still reliably come together into something delicious. If you put the right things into baking, you got the right things out of baking, and Millie had loved that steady predictability. She suddenly wanted to rescue it, to not leave it drifting in her memories of life with Daniel but to bring it here, into this new life with her. This new life with this street, and with Jasper who stopped to smile at her and talk with her as if it were a valuable and welcome part of his day.

Jasper made her thoughts feel slightly muddled, and that probably explained how Millie found herself at Pen's door.

Pen looked delighted to see her. 'Oh, wonderful!' she exclaimed. 'I've been working for ten whole minutes and I was in desperate need of a distraction. What can I do for you?'

Millie said, 'I heard you're organising some kind of event for Remembrance Sunday, and I was wondering if you might need a baker?'

Bill woke on Remembrance Day thinking, *Another Remembrance Day*. He got up and got dressed with special care as befit the importance of the day. Jack had stayed at his house the night before, and Jack watched solemnly, clearly knowing what day this was. Even his tail wagging was solemn.

'Well, Jack,' Bill said heavily, giving him a scratch behind his ears. 'Here I go.'

He opened his front door, and Jack went bounding out, and on the street stood all of his neighbours, every single one of them, even Libby's mum.

'Ready to go?' Pen asked, stepping forward to greet him.

He blinked at her, bewildered. 'Are you ... Are you ...?'

'We're going to go to the service with you,' Pen said.

'Of course,' said Diya.

'We'd never leave you do it alone again,' said Sam. 'Not now that we know.'

Teddy sent him a toothy grin and waved at him.

Bill turned away, to make a big show out of locking his door, and it gave him a moment to heave in a breath and compose himself. Not that he needed it, of course. Bill never lost his composure. Never. It was strange weather to be causing his eyes to tear up this way.

They walked together to the church, even the new woman, with their red poppies pinned to their coats. Jack followed along with them for a little way. Everyone was far quieter than they were ordinarily, and Bill appreciated it. Even little Charlie, decked out in a little suit with a red poppy of his own, was on his best behaviour.

They sat together at the service, in a little cluster. Teddy slid in to sit close to Bill, and Max sat on the other side of him. Charlie moved back and forth between Max and Arthur according to his desires, and at one point, unexpectedly, Bill found him thrust onto his own lap, as Max and Arthur rooted around in one of their bags for something. Bill looked at the baby, who looked back at him, and Bill thought of the newness of Charlie's life, on this particular day.

He had never had a Remembrance Sunday like this one.

When the service was over, Pen said, 'Was it okay? That we all did this?'

And Bill said, inadequately, 'Yeah.'

And then Pen said brightly, 'Good! Because we've got more planned!'

Most of the street, Millie was relieved to learn, did not run to the old people's home where Pen had made the arrangements. It was nice not to be completely humiliated by wanting to walk there instead. The walking was a slow, leisurely pace, and it gave Jasper an opportunity to drop behind and talk to her.

Jasper said, 'So what have you made for today?' and gestured to the containers Millie was carrying.

'Biscuits,' answered Millie. 'Lots and lots of biscuits.'

Jasper smiled at her. 'Think I could steal one?'

'I might be persuaded to give you one,' said Millie. 'Free of charge.' It felt coquettish to her, daringly so. She could never have imagined herself *flirting* like this with a man who wasn't Daniel. Honestly, she couldn't even remember ever having flirted with Daniel. This all seemed wholly new, and exciting in a good way, and Millie's heart was pounding with an uncertainty that for once was with tinged with joy rather than dread. Millie felt like she could get used to that.

'So,' said Pari Basak, skipping up to her. 'Where did you get the biscuits?'

'I made the biscuits,' said Millie, bewildered by the question.

'Did you?' said Pari thoughtfully. 'You *made* the biscuits, hmm?'

Millie didn't know what to say in response. 'Yes?' she offered.

'You made them *yourself*?'

'Pari!' Diya shouted. 'Stop bothering other people and come over here.'

'Hmm,' said Pari, one more thoughtful little noise, with a narrow-eyed glance as she moved away.

'What was that all about?' Millie asked, confused.

'Children are mysteries,' said Jasper, sounding indulgent. 'I've often thought, if I were ever going to have any, they'd be tremendously entertaining but also the most confusing possibilities in the universe. Have you ever thought about it?'

'Having kids?' asked Millie, caught off-guard by the question.

Jasper smiled, sunny and open, like this was a normal topic of conversation, and Millie supposed that it was for people who weren't Millie.

Had she ever thought about having children? Yes, she had. In the early days. She had dreamed of babies with Daniel. Gorgeous babies, she'd thought they would have. So many little babies for them to cuddle and shower with love.

And then Millie had begun to learn what Daniel's definition of 'shower with love' was, and that had been the end of any fantasy about children. Millie had grown to be terrified of bringing a child into the cruelty of that life, horrified by the idea of raising a child who would think that life was Daniel was the way life ought to be. Having children had become an impossibility in Millie's imagination, because she would not raise a child in a home without love and safety.

But now, maybe, Millie's imagination was big enough

to include the possibility of a child. Maybe, if Millie let herself think past just making it through the next day, maybe she could think about being in a position to let herself have a child. Maybe she would even start to think of herself as someone capable of being an acceptable mother to someone.

Millie looked at Jasper and found herself matching his smile and said, 'Yes. I have thought about children. I think children could be lovely.'

'You'd be a wonderful mum,' Jasper said.

Millie felt herself blushing, and looked away. 'Stop.'

'No, no,' Jasper protested, laughing. 'I'm allowed to say such things. People are allowed to say nice things about you, you know.'

Millie wanted to say, *Really? Are they?* Because it had been so long since she had lived in a world where that happened, and because Daniel would have said, *Absolutely not, no one should say anything nice about you ever, because you're a dreadful woman.*

Millie swallowed and concentrated on arriving at a normal reaction to Jasper's words. She said, 'I've never changed a single nappy in my life.'

'Oh,' said Jasper dismissively. 'That's the least important thing about being a parent, I think. I mean, you can learn how to change a nappy easily enough. Look at Max – even he manages to change nappies. I thought for sure he'd make the changing of a nappy into some kind of art project, but no, he just changes a nappy, as no-nonsense as can please. If he can learn it, anyone can learn it. That's not the measure of a good parent.'

Millie laughed, because she couldn't help it, and because it felt *good* to laugh, it felt good to let that enter her life routine again. She was baking biscuits, and she was laughing.

Things were going *well*.

And they kept going well all through the Remembrance Sunday at the old people's home. Jasper stayed by her side as they walked up and down the halls and delivered biscuits to everyone they encountered. And Jasper only ate a few dozen for himself.

'What is that?' Millie teased good-naturedly, as Jasper stole another one, 'your fifteenth biscuit? Sixteenth?'

'It's my fourth,' Jasper said.

Millie laughed. Now that she'd started laughing again, she felt like she was getting the hang of it. She might start laughing all the time now. 'I think that's a lie, but I'm going to let it go.'

'It's just that they're so delicious,' Jasper enthused. 'They're the most delicious biscuits I've ever tasted.'

'You haven't had many biscuits then,' Millie rejoined lightly.

Jasper stopped walking, putting a hand lightly on Millie's arm to stop her as well.

Millie stared at the hand on her arm, and must have looked alarmed, because Jasper dropped it away from her. He then said gently, 'Why do you do that?'

'Why do I do what?' asked Millie, a little breathlessly.

'Constantly deflect me when I tell you how lovely you are.'

Millie stared at him, completely and unabashedly breathless now. She wasn't sure she'd ever remember how to breathe again. She heard herself saying, as if from a great distance, 'Jasper. I want to thank you.'

'For what?' asked Jasper quizzically.

'For always wanting to talk to me,' said Millie. 'It means so much to me, how . . . I look forward to you.' It was a stunning admission, a terrifying admission, because Millie wanted to be entirely self-sufficient, she had told herself not to be dependent on anyone, after how helpless Daniel had managed to make her, but she had to admit it. She looked forward to Jasper. She was in danger of looking forward to many, many things about her new life. And that was terrifying, because it meant so much more to lose.

Jasper said, 'Millie,' in a very wonderful, gentle way that made Millie want to proclaim that no one but Jasper should say her name from now on. Then he smiled. 'I would love to pretend it's a kindness, but I talk to you out of very selfish desires.'

Millie had no idea what to say when Jasper was looking at her *like that*. She clung foolishly to her nearly empty tin of biscuits and sought to come up with something to say. *You can do this*, she told herself, by way of pep talk. *You can.*

'Oh, good!' said Pen, coming around the corner, and both Millie and Jasper jumped in startled surprise. 'I've been looking for you two. You're my only two left.'

'Only two for what?' asked Jasper, his voice sounding a little strained.

Pen held up her phone and said, 'Smile!' and then took their photograph.

'We need to go look at venues,' was what Libby had said, and this seemed like the most innocent of occupations. Venues were surely just about looking to see which was the most beautiful, the best located, had the best food.

Except that naturally Rebecca tagged along whilst they went looking at venues. That was, after all, why she was in town. And Sam was unprepared for how fundamentally they disagreed on everything about the wedding.

'Oh,' said Rebecca, when Libby gave the estimate for the guest count at the very first venue. 'That seems like a very low estimate to me.'

'Well,' said Libby, 'Sam and I discussed it, and we wanted to keep it small.'

'Well, yes, I'm sure Sam wants to keep it small,' said Rebecca. 'I'm sure you had a big wedding your first time around.' Rebecca looked at him with even innocence. 'Didn't you?'

Sam wished desperately that he could say no, he'd had a small wedding then, too. But he couldn't just *lie*. 'Yes,' he admitted. 'We had a big wedding.'

'Then I'm sure you understand that Libby is entitled to have her chance at a big wedding, too.'

'Mum,' Libby protested, 'it's not a big deal, I really don't care—'

'Maybe we could see what your options are for big weddings as well as small weddings,' Rebecca requested of the venue employee. 'That would give us options. I mean, Libby, presumably it is going to be your only wedding, so you simply must invite much of the village.'

At the next venue, they not only were shown options for large and small weddings, but there was also a disagreement over whether it would be a religious ceremony.

'Oh,' Sam said innocently, upon being shown a particular vestibule covered with gorgeous art. 'This might be an ideal place for the ceremony.'

'The ceremony?' Rebecca said sharply. 'Won't the ceremony take place in a church?'

'Oh,' Sam said blankly, completely not anticipating this disagreement at all. He looked to Libby for help.

'We'll have to talk about that,' Libby said vaguely which didn't exactly sound like help.

That night, at dinner, Sam chose as his adventure 'wedding venue hunting,' and Libby and Rebecca both agreed, but Sam felt like they were probably choosing it for different reasons.

He chose bedtime to broach the subject, because that was the time when he and Libby were finally alone.

'Okay,' he said. 'I think we should talk about all of that.'

'All of what?' asked Libby, brushing her hair out.

'Do you want a big wedding? You've never said that before.'

'I mean,' said Libby. 'I can see my mother's point, about inviting most of the village. Especially since we're getting married here and not in the village.'

Sam was bewildered. 'We can get married in the village if you like. Really, you never said any of this to me. If you've never said any of this, how am I to know?'

'I thought I was fine with having a small wedding,' Libby said, 'until my mother mentioned how it's going to be my *only* wedding. And then I thought . . . I don't know. If I'm only doing this once, I want to get it *right*. You know?'

'Yes,' said Sam. 'I do know.' He remembered well having similar conversations with Sara. 'It's fine. I don't care either way. I just want to make you happy.'

'Now that's not fair,' Libby said. 'It's your wedding, too. It shouldn't just be mine. Just because you've done this before doesn't mean you shouldn't care.'

'That's not what I mean,' Sam said on a sigh. 'I do care. Of course I care. You're right. It's not because I've already had a wedding. I care about this one, too. I just want it to feel like ours. Because we're the ones getting married. It should feel like us. And I don't know a ton of people who I feel need to share this day with us. That's why I suggested a small wedding. But if you feel differently, well, then, you should tell me. I should know if you don't like the wedding we're planning.'

Libby sat on the bed, looking thoughtful. 'I don't know,' she admitted. 'Is it okay to just not know? Can we just keep an open mind for now?'

'Yes,' Sam agreed soothingly. He sat next to her on the bed and kissed her shoulder. 'We don't have to make any decisions. I don't want to stress you out. I just keep feeling ...' Sam sighed. 'I just keep feeling so off-balance when it comes to your mother.'

'Yes,' Libby said, intertwining their hands. 'I know. I'm sorry. I've been trying to watch out for that for you and I think I'm doing a terrible job.'

'It's okay,' Sam said. 'But I do have to ask: are we getting married in a church now? I had no idea we were religious.'

Libby choked out a laugh. 'Yeah,' she said, 'that one might be tricky.'

'I am begging you,' Sam said to Ellen, 'you *have* to come with me.'

'You don't need to beg me,' Ellen said. 'I am *delighted* to go.

261

Last time you got married a whole ocean away and I didn't get to do any planning at all.'

'"Get to do",' Sam said with elaborate air quotes. 'You act like it's something exciting. It's a disaster.'

'It's not a disaster,' Ellen said.

'I just feel like I can't do anything right in Rebecca's eyes.'

'But Rebecca doesn't matter,' Ellen pointed out. 'It's only Libby who matters.'

'Yes,' agreed Sam, looking glumly at his empty fridge. They really needed to go shopping.

'Uh-oh,' said Ellen. 'You don't sound too confident about that.'

Sam sighed and closed the fridge. 'No, no. I'm confident.'

Ellen lifted her eyebrows.

'No, I am,' Sam said honestly. 'I'm not worried Libby doesn't love me or something ridiculous like that. I know she loves me and I know she wants to marry me and I know we'll be fine. This is just an exhausting time period we're going through right now.'

'I think wedding planning just is that way. It can bring out the worst in your partners. I wanted to murder mine whilst we were wedding planning.'

'Yeah, you frequently wanted to murder him,' Sam pointed out. 'That's not a marriage I'm hoping to emulate.'

Ellen laughed. 'I don't blame you. But it's fine. You and Libby will be together for the long haul.'

On their second day of venue hunting, though, rather than making things better, Ellen made thinks markedly worse.

Sam had wanted Ellen along because he'd felt outnumbered by Libby and Rebecca, and he'd wanted someone on his side. And, anyway, Ellen was his sister and should be involved in the wedding planning process. But he didn't consider how Ellen had no problem being combative.

'A church ceremony?' Ellen said bluntly. 'But neither one of them are church people.'

Rebecca blinked at her.

Sam said, 'Oh, Ellen, I wanted to show you this,' which was hilarious, because they'd never been in this venue before.

'Does she think you're religious?' Ellen asked, confused. '*Are* you religious?'

'No. I don't know. I think she just thinks weddings should happen in churches.'

'Oh. Do you want to get married in a church?'

'I mean, it's fine. I don't care.'

Ellen looked dubious.

'You're supposed to be *getting along*,' Sam hissed at her.

'Okay,' Ellen agreed. 'Fine. I will *get along*.'

Except that at one point Sam said, 'We might be open to the idea of a more informal dinner. Let people mingle. Do away with the old-fashioned idea of seating charts and such.'

'Oh,' Ellen said, 'I love that idea. It can just be a casual, laidback sort of—'

'Absolutely not,' Rebecca cut in furiously, causing everyone to look at her. 'That would just be a . . . a *free-for-all*. Is that what you want your wedding to be?'

'I mean,' said Sam, 'I don't think it would be a *free-for-all*, it would just be people not sitting in formal arrangements.'

'That is hardly the definition of a free-for-all,' remarked Ellen.

'If you want to see a free-for-all, you should have seen this music festival my ex-husband and I went to when we were first—'

'Okay,' Sam said, cutting her off. 'I think maybe we should agree to table the discussion of ... tables. No pun intended.' He smiled brightly at Rebecca.

Rebecca looked distinctly unimpressed and moved frostily away from him.

'I think things are going *so* well,' remarked Ellen.

'Was that "getting along"?' Sam hissed at her.

Chapter 18

> *We want to try it again and invite everyone on the street to another tree-trimming / mock Thanksgiving celebration! Saturday, from four p.m.*

They'd cancelled running because Pen had a deadline she was trying to make, so Libby had been home all night, and everyone was cuddled cosily together in the lounge.

Well. As cosy as they could be with Rebecca radiating disapproval, thought Sam, and wished he didn't have such negative thoughts, but there you were.

'When are you going to put up a Christmas tree?' Rebecca said. 'Or is that something you don't do?'

'Of course we put up a Christmas tree, Mum,' said Libby.

'I didn't know if it was some odd American habit not to do it,' Rebecca said innocently.

'They have Christmas trees in America,' Sam said drily. 'But we don't put one up until after Thanksgiving.'

'Thanksgiving?' echoed Rebecca.

'Yes,' said Sam. 'Another American institution.'

'That isn't celebrated here,' Rebecca pointed out.

'We celebrate it for Teddy,' Sam replied, hoping that he was doing a decent job of not being baited.

'I see,' said Rebecca simply, although she sounded as if she did not see at all.

Millie stepped outside of her house on her way to work and immediately encountered Jasper, who happened to be outside with Max, still dealing with Christmas decorations.

'Hello,' Jasper said cheerfully, sending her a wave.

Millie felt blushy and ridiculous and tried to think of how to behave in a way that wouldn't make her seem ridiculous. She said, 'Hi.'

'Hello,' Max called from where he was twining lights around Diya's hedge in a complicated pattern that looked like lace.

'Hi, little Charlie,' she said to the baby, who was taking toddling steps whilst clinging to Sai's hands.

Sai grinned at her.

She looked back at Jasper, who was still looking steadily at her, and felt herself blush harder and fished for something to say. 'So you two are still dealing with Christmas decorations.'

'Well,' said Jasper, 'they are pretty elaborate Christmas decorations.'

'Elaborate and *gorgeous*,' emphasised Max. 'Speaking of, do you mind if we include your house in the decorating, too?

I didn't want to presume, but it would make the street look more uniform.'

Millie glanced from all the gaily lit houses along the street, to her darkened one. It looked ridiculous. 'I would love you to decorate my house as well,' she said.

Max looked absolutely delighted, and Jasper smiled at her, a wide open smile that made her think of the first time they'd met, of Jasper offering to help her with her light, of all the people on this street offering to help in so many ways, and all she had to do was let herself accept it. *This can be your new life*, Millie thought, and it would be a completely different new life, a wide and varied network of people who would help if she needed it, and who gave every impression of just *wanting* to help, and demanding nothing in return. Millie had thought maybe people like that didn't exist.

But maybe ... maybe they did.

Millie looked at Jasper and smiled back.

Pari and Teddy and Jack had a plan. It involved leaving the house when they saw Millie leave her house, and keeping pace with her as she walked, and then Pari said, according to the plan, 'When you curtsy, does it matter if you put the right foot behind or the left foot?'

Jack wagged his tail to alert Millie to what a good question this was.

'What?' said Millie.

'What did you say your middle name was?' asked Teddy.

'My middle name?' said Millie.

'You have several, don't you?' said Teddy.

'Several middle names?'

'Yeah, lots of middle names,' Pari clarified for her.

'I, er, really don't,' said Millie. 'And I'm sorry, I have to get to work.'

Pari and Teddy stopped walking and let Millie get a few steps ahead, and then Pari suddenly shouted, 'Your Highness!' just to see if Millie would turn around.

Millie did turn around and but she gave Pari a strange look, and maybe she had only turned around because Pari's shout caused Jack to bark in alarm, so Pari decided the results were inconclusive.

'What was that for?' asked Teddy.

'I thought maybe she might respond to it like it was her name, but I couldn't tell.'

'You know,' remarked Teddy, 'she's a really good baker.'

'So?' said Pari hotly, as if Millie being a good baker was personally offensive to her.

'I'm just saying, I don't know if princesses can bake. Why would they have to bake?'

'I bet some princesses bake just for fun,' sniffed Pari, and refused to acknowledge how doubtful Teddy looked.

Millie, walking back from work in the dark, realised that Max and Jasper had begun decorating her house. It twinkled with as many fairy lights as the other houses down the street, and Millie paused in front of it and just admired it.

It looked perfectly ordinary, exactly like it just fit in.

'Hello there,' said Sam from behind her.

Millie whirled to face him, her heart in her throat.

Sam held his hands up placatingly. 'Sorry. I was just taking Jack over to Bill's and I saw you out here and I thought I would stop and say hello.'

'Right,' said Millie, trying to get her heart to start beating again. 'That is a perfectly normal thing to do and I'm sorry I reacted like that.'

Sam smiled and tilted his head quizzically. 'It's fine. I startled you. The house looks beautiful.'

'That was all Max,' said Millie, looking back at the house.

'Oh, it's always all Max,' agreed Sam lightly. 'And Jasper, though, this time around. Jasper took a very particular keen interest in the decoration of this house.'

Millie knew she was blushing again and was glad for the darkness.

'I was wanting to catch you, because I wanted to invite you to Thanksgiving,' continued Sam.

'Thanksgiving?' said Millie.

'Yes,' said Sam. 'Every year I have a Thanksgiving celebration on Teddy's behalf. His mum was American. Well. I say "every year". I tried to do it last year and it was largely a disaster, so we're trying to start fresh this year. Anyway, everyone on the street comes, and we'd love for you to come along, too.'

'Oh,' said Millie, and looked at her gaily decorated house, so beautifully fitting in, and couldn't think of a single reason why she oughtn't go to Sam's Thanksgiving celebration. In fact, she thought maybe she *wanted* to go.

'Jasper's coming, too,' Sam said, with studied nonchalance.

They were an entire street full of matchmakers, Millie

thought, and she should have been horrified by it, she should have been terribly embarrassed, but instead she just felt a little bit giddy.

'What should I bring?' she asked.

On the appointed day, Millie carried her Victoria sponge over to Sam's house and found a boisterous party in full swing. Emilia appeared to be playing – very loudly – recordings that her band had recently made. Apparently this was to prove to the room at large how much they'd improved. Millie couldn't tell if they'd improved or not but they'd certainly got louder.

Which was exactly what Bill said. 'Is it necessary for the music to be played so *loudly*?'

'Oh, Bill,' said Max, grinning. 'What a stereotypical old-person thing to say.'

'But it's *true*,' Bill grumbled. 'It's just *noise*.'

'All music is just noise,' Emilia said wisely.

'Some are definitely noisier than others,' Bill informed her.

Millie left them to the debate and brought the Victoria sponge to the kitchen, where she found Libby.

'Oh, perfect,' Libby said. 'Thank you for this, it looks utterly scrumptious.'

The back door opened and then shut, although it didn't look as if anyone had come in.

Millie tipped her head quizzically. 'Is that ...?'

Libby sighed and shook her head and mouthed, *The kids*, which was exactly when Jack came trotted around the corner of the kitchen island, tail wagging.

Millie could hear furious whispers from Teddy and Pari trying to call Jack back to them, to no avail.

Millie crouched down and said, 'Hello, Jack. Were you just outside? Bit of a nip to the air, wasn't there?'

Jack could not actually answer these questions, but Millie chose to interpret his tail wags appropriately.

And that was when, out of nowhere, a vase that had been sitting on the kitchen countertop went flying off the edge and onto the floor directly next to Millie's foot, whereupon it shattered into a million pieces.

Libby jumped and turned around and everyone else seemed to crowd into the kitchen to see what had happened.

'It's nothing,' Millie said, even though her heart had literally not stopped pounding in her chest. 'I mean, I must have forgotten it was there and nudged it or something and—'

'No,' said Libby grimly. 'I know exactly whose fault it is. Teddy? Pari? Time to 'fess up here, kids.'

Reluctantly, Teddy and Pari poked their heads around the corner of the cabinets.

'Yes?' they asked, with identical innocence.

'Did you just shove this vase off the kitchen counter?' Libby demanded.

There was a moment of silence, and then Pari ventured, 'Yes?'

'Help us sweep it up,' Libby ordered. 'Go and find a broom.'

Sam, jogging down the stairs, came into the kitchen and looked around. 'What's all this? What happened?'

'The kids just dropped a vase,' Libby said. 'That's why they're helping me clean.'

'Oh, dear,' said Sam, regarding Teddy and Pari, who were

now carefully sweeping up pieces. 'I hope that wasn't one of your favourite vases,' he remarked to Libby.

'No,' said Libby. 'It's fine. Except that I don't understand why the kids would deliberately drop a vase.'

Diya, coming in through the back door holding a plate of food, said, 'What's this? What kids dropped a vase? Pari, did you drop a vase?' She fixed Pari with a hard stare.

'I just—'

'Sweep up that vase right now, and then you are to go home for the rest of the party.'

Pari looked alarmed, her eyes welling up with tears. 'But, Mum—'

'You do not go to people's houses and smash their belongings—'

'It was me,' Teddy said hastily. 'It was totally me. I'm the one who smashed it, so Pari shouldn't be punished for it.'

'Can I talk to the kids for a second outside?' Sam said abruptly, and then pushed them outside in front of him.

Diya frowned after them.

Libby said, 'Here, let me take that place,' stepping aside as her mother arrived with a dustpan for the vase pieces.

'This is ridiculous,' Diya said. 'Let me do that.'

'It's quite all right,' said Rebecca.

Millie stood awkwardly, feeling like maybe this was all her fault. This was what happened when she left the house: she arrived at what had been a perfectly lovely party and all hell broke loose.

And then Jasper walked into the kitchen.

'Hello,' he said, and gave her a warm smile. 'This looks like a very busy place. What's all the commotion?'

'I don't know,' Millie said honestly. 'That vase broke, some-how. It was all very confusing.'

She must have sounded a little lost, because Jasper's gaze on her was so unbearably gentle. He said, 'You look like you could use a moment to collect yourself. And I want to show you something. Come with me?' He smiled at her again.

And Millie had just been thinking that she shouldn't have ever left her house. But Jasper, smiling at her with such open warmth and kindness, made her rethink that. She would leave her house a lot, she thought, if the people she met looked at her like that.

'Okay,' she agreed.

Sam marched the children to a corner of the back garden, followed by Jack, who was taking a keen interest in the proceedings.

'Okay,' he said, hands on hips. 'What's going on?'

The children were silent for another few seconds, hanging their heads, before Teddy cracked, because luckily Teddy was still young enough to crack under a stern glare from Sam. Sam was going to cherish that as long as it lasted.

Teddy said, 'Okay, we didn't mean to break the vase.'

'Well, that's a good thing at least,' said Sam. 'I like to hope that my child is not wilfully destructive.'

'It wasn't supposed to break,' Pari said sulkily. 'That was the *plan*.'

'What plan is this now?' asked Sam.

Teddy and Pari exchanged a look.

Sam crossed his arms now and said, 'I can wait out here all day. And, really, you'd rather talk to me about your plan than your mum, wouldn't you?' Sam gave Pari a knowing look.

Pari, after a moment, reluctantly said, 'Okay, yes, I guess so.'

Teddy said, 'We thought she was a ninja.'

'Millie?' Sam guessed.

The kids nodded.

'I mean, she's clearly not a princess,' Pari said miserably. 'None of our tests revealed her secret royalty. So she must be something else.'

'A person,' Sam said. 'She's just a person.'

'So we thought maybe she was a ninja,' Teddy continued, as if Sam hadn't said anything.

'After all, ninjas are pretty sneaky, too. Almost like spies. And then, if she was a ninja, then her ninja skills would kick in and she would definitely not let that vase shatter,' said Pari.

'But the vase shattered,' added Teddy.

'So I guess she's not a ninja.' Pari heaved an enormous sigh.

'Okay,' said Sam, with a sigh of his own, and crouched down to be on eye level with the kids. 'She's just another person on our street. With a thoroughly ordinary life. She's not a puzzle for you to solve. This all started with you wanting to make a difference, remember?'

Pari and Teddy both nodded.

'And this isn't making a difference. Tossing vases at her, or whatever. Why don't we go inside, and decorate the Christmas tree, and think about actually making a difference for Millie? Because we might not know anything about her, really, but I think she might be a bit lonely, and she might want some

274

friends, and we could be those friends for her, and that would make the best difference of all.'

After a moment of silence, the kids nodded again.

Sam had no idea if he'd truly convinced them – after all, Pari especially had proven herself very devoted to a scheme once she'd got it in her head, which, now that Sam thought about it, made her very like her mother – but at least maybe it would be enough to buy them a quiet Thanksgiving Day.

'Let's go back inside,' Sam said, and Jack barked approval of this plan, 'and I'll see what I can do to talk you two down from punishment.'

They both brightened.

'Really?' said Teddy.

'If you are on your best behaviour the rest of the day and help out with every chore requested, uncomplainingly.'

Teddy and Pari both nodded eagerly.

They would forget, Sam thought, and be back to their usual half-hearted whingeing complaints before he knew it, but maybe there would be a little peace and quiet in the meantime, and maybe Diya would be assuaged. They didn't have *bad* kids, they just had *precocious* kids, and Sam couldn't help but think that growing up on Christmas Street was only serving to encourage their precocity.

Chapter 19

Skating boots available from
child's size 7 to adult size 15!

'Okay,' Jasper said, as they stepped out of Sam and Libby's house, 'I didn't want to alarm you, or anything. I mean, I didn't want you to think that I was ... being inappropriate.'

This put Millie a bit on her guard, and she wished Jasper could go back to just being uncomplicatedly lovely again. 'Why?' she asked warily.

'I mean, it's nothing that I think should be alarming, it's just that you're ...'

Jasper trailed off but Millie could finish the sentence well enough. 'I'm difficult.'

'No,' Jasper said hastily. 'That's not what I meant at all.' Jasper stopped walking, and Millie stopped as well. 'Hey,' Jasper said, with a gentleness that was nevertheless urgent, 'you're exceptional.'

Millie's heart stopped, and her breath stopped, and all other vital life processes as well, she was fairly sure. She stared at him and almost thought she must have misheard, because no one had ever called her exceptional in her life. And definitely not exceptional in a *good* way. And Jasper, his brown eyes so warm on her that she felt she could feel them like a physical glowing heat, clearly meant it in a *good* way. 'No, I'm not,' she managed breathlessly.

Jasper chuckled a little. 'Yes, you are. You have this air about you that causes people to want to know more about you. You draw people in. You are effortlessly fascinating. Surely you must have realised this about yourself, this power that you wield. You've enthralled the entire street.'

Millie knew she must be blushing. 'No, I haven't,' she denied. 'I really definitely haven't.'

Jasper lifted his eyebrows. 'You are not privy to all of the many speculative conversations you have provoked. I have basically been going house-to-house working on carpentry projects, so I do know.'

'Oh, no,' Millie said. 'But what are they all saying?'

'How much they want to get to know you better,' Jasper said. 'How much they want to be your friend.'

Millie, caught in Jasper's gaze, didn't think Jasper was talking about the rest of the street any more, or even about friendship. 'I . . . ' she said, and then cleared her throat. 'I'm not that interesting. Everyone will be disappointed.'

Jasper shook his head. 'I don't think so.'

Millie didn't know what else to say, so she decided to change the subject. 'Tell me,' she said, 'about this surprise that you have for me.'

Jasper grinned. 'You are unusual, so I wasn't sure if you

would really appreciate a present out of the blue. But I thought I would give you one anyway. Because you looked like you could use it.'

'Okay,' Millie said slowly, still unsure what to expect.

Jasper led her to her house, and Millie's confusion only grew, until she saw what was perched on the front step. And then she started laughing. 'A stepladder?'

'Well,' said Jasper, looking delighted by her reaction, 'you may recall that we met because you were being precarious. I thought I would get you something more solid to help with things over your head. It's a form of assistance, but I don't think it will sacrifice any of your independence.'

'No,' Millie said, smiling at the stepladder. 'It won't.' And then his words sank in, and she looked up at him. 'Do you think I'm independent?'

'I think you are one of the most independent people I've ever met,' said Jasper, and Millie wasn't sure what her face looked like, but Jasper rushed to explain himself. 'I don't mean that in a bad way. I mean that you are just so self-contained, so sure in your trust of yourself. It's impressive.'

'I am not at all anything you say I am,' Millie said. 'I'm not sure who you've been meeting, but that's not me.' She was the opposite of *independent*. Look how long it had taken her to leave Daniel. She was anything but trusting of herself. And she was definitely not exceptional.

'Maybe,' Jasper said with a smile, 'maybe you need to be introduced to you.'

278

Sam thought his Thanksgiving was going better than last year, in that he managed to get a turkey on the table at one point, and so that was good. Sure, there had been some squabbling over how the Christmas tree was being decorated, because he knew far too many artistic perfectionists, and the kids had quickly forgotten that they were supposed to be on their best behaviour, but overall things were going better than expected.

And the best unexpected thing was how much Bill kept Rebecca occupied. They barely spoke, because Bill under any circumstance was not especially talkative, and yet Rebecca seemed to prefer his company. Sam assumed it was because Bill shared Rebecca's scepticism about virtually everything. And, upon reflection, Sam thought he therefore ought to be used to Rebecca. After all, he was used to Bill, and he was friends with Bill, so why should Rebecca's negativity affect him so much?

Sam looked at Libby on the other side of the room, happily laughing with Pen and Ellen about something, and thought how there was a difference in tolerating constant dubiousness from a neighbour and tolerating it from a mother-in-law. That was the reason he was having difficulty dealing with Rebecca, of course.

But today, he and Rebecca had interacted little, because Rebecca had spent most of her time with Bill and Sam had purposely circulated around talking to everybody else, and for that reason things had been going well.

If only they could have kept that up.

'I want to thank all of you for being so amazing about the goodgymming,' Pen said. 'I placed my article and it's getting tons of attention.'

'What?' said Millie. 'What article?'

'Oh,' said Pen, 'I wrote it up as a piece for an online outlet. No big deal. And I made a little photo album from the day and linked to it.'

'You made a photo album from the day?' said Millie. 'Why would you do that?'

Pen looked caught off-guard, and Sam felt like things were starting to get awkward. 'What?' said Pen. 'Why wouldn't I? We did a good thing.'

'I just wish you'd asked me,' Millie said, sounding unaccountably anguished. 'Before putting pictures up of me online.'

'Libby,' said Anna, 'I haven't had any time to get to talk to you about wedding planning at all. How's it going?'

Anna had clearly decided they needed to change the subject, but Sam wanted to beg her to choose *any other subject* but wedding planning.

But it was too late. Once the wedding planning topic had been broached, everyone rushed in to ask questions about it.

'Yes!' Diya chimed in enthusiastically. 'How is it going? You've told us nothing!'

'Oh,' said Libby, looking uncomfortable about the topic. Wedding planning was not a topic either of them relished these days. 'I mean, it's coming along. We're working on it.'

'It shouldn't be *work*,' Max said. 'It should be *fun*.'

'Ignore Max, he did no useful wedding planning at all,' Arthur said. 'Wedding planning is hell.'

'Well,' said Libby, 'I have to admit I'm relieved to hear you say that, because I have been finding it challenging.'

'There's no need for it to be challenging,' Rebecca said, with a sniff of superiority. 'You simply decide on what you want and then you get it.'

There was a moment of awkward silence.

Max, because Max could always be depended upon to fill in an awkward silence, said gallantly, 'Right, but sometimes the trick is deciding what you want. I mean, if only it were easy like it is with deciding on *who* you want.' And Max winked at Arthur across the table.

Libby managed a smile, plainly appreciating Max's effort. 'Yes,' she said, and shifted her smile to Sam. 'Deciding on *who* you want actually turns out to be the easy part. And who would have thought that?'

'You need to make a list,' Diya said. 'Once you've made a list, it's easy to just cross things off the list.'

'Yes,' Libby said slowly.

'The problem is she can't seem to make any decisions,' Rebecca said. 'We have many discussions about these things, and Libby can't make her mind up about anything.'

There was another moment of awkward silence.

Libby said, 'It's not that I can't—'

'We can help,' Anna interrupted her, and Sam knew that Anna genuinely thought this was going to be helpful, but he wished he could get Anna to *just stop talking*.

'It's okay,' he tried to say.

Anna genuinely didn't even seem to hear him. 'You just need to start with little decisions. Like, when would you like to get married?'

'Yeah, I think in the spring,' Libby said.

'Summer would be better,' said Rebecca, 'to give yourself more time to plan.'

Another pause around the table.

Sam said, 'I think that we should—'

'Well, how much time you need to plan depends on how big the wedding is going to be,' said Diya pragmatically.

'Yes, they can't even decide on that,' said Rebecca.

'Well,' said Ellen, and Sam *knew* Ellen was going to have to speak up, that Ellen wouldn't have stayed silent through this whole thing. Sam loved Ellen for her outspokenness and also her loyalty but he really did wish she would just *stay silent*. 'They have made some decisions, but you disagree with them, so—'

'They haven't made decisions. Your brother has made the decisions based on his expertise in having been through this before,' retorted Rebecca.

Sam winced, because to have his first marriage referred to so scathingly was almost a physical blow.

Which of course made Ellen coil up, ready to spring. 'That's not *expertise*.'

'Okay,' Max said, and Sam adored him for trying this. 'Did I tell all of you how close Charlie is to walking? Any day now, we feel.'

'That's right,' Arthur said gamely, 'he is really quite deter-mined to be mobile and start going places.'

'I wanted to ask,' Emilia said, and Sam couldn't believe her bravery in speaking up at exactly that moment, 'if you'd at least consider the Amazing Spiders to play at your wedding.'

'Oh,' said Libby. 'We'll think about it . . .'

'You are definitely not having a random band of teenagers play at your wedding,' Rebecca told Libby.

'They're very good,' Anna defended her daughter hotly. 'They're not "random".'

'We are good,' Emilia insisted.

'Not judging from what I heard at the engagement party,' said Rebecca.

'Mum!' Libby protested, shocked.

'I'm just saying,' Rebecca said. 'It was a disaster.'

'It wasn't a *disaster*,' Anna snapped. 'Emilia and her band are very talented.'

'Emilia is very dedicated to it,' Diya said.

Anna narrowed her eyes at her. 'And what does that mean?'

'Nothing,' said Diya. 'I didn't mean anything by it.' Diya paused. 'Except that I have noticed that Sai's grades have suffered a little since the Amazing Spiders have come into existence. Have you noticed that with Emilia's grades?'

'No,' said Anna. 'I haven't noticed that. If Sai is having difficulty, it's probably because Emilia doesn't have the time to tutor him any more.'

'Emilia was not *tutoring* him!' Diya exclaimed.

'Mum,' Sai inserted, in a quiet pleading tone.

Emilia said, 'We are right here, and I was never tutoring Sai.'

'If he weren't spending so much time at your rehearsals—' Diya said to her.

'Actually,' Max said hesitantly, 'he's been watching Charlie for us, after school each day. He hasn't been going to the rehearsals.'

'Well, either way, he's distracted, and he really needs to focus,' Diya sniffed.

'Well, it is definitely not my daughter's fault that your son isn't focusing,' said Anna, and stood from the table. 'Come along,' she said to Marcel. 'We're leaving.'

Marcel stood as well and followed Anna out.

'Come along, Emilia!' Anna called back.

Emilia made a sound of pure disgust but did stand and stomp out after her parents.

'Well, if they're going,' announced Diya, 'we're going, too.'

'But—' protested Pari.

'That's fine,' Sai snapped. 'I *want* to go. Because that was embarrassing and completely uncalled for, Mum.'

'Uncalled for?' Diya retorted. 'How dare you—'

Sai stomped out.

Darsh said, 'Don't walk out whilst your mother's talking to you! Sai!' and went after him.

Diya stood and said, 'Come, Pari.'

'But—' Pari started again.

'No,' Diya said. 'You're supposed to be punished anyway for the whole nonsense with the vase. Come.'

Pari reluctantly pushed herself out of her chair and dragged herself over to her impatiently waiting mother.

Libby, after a moment, said, 'Mum, that wasn't necessary.'

Rebecca looked offended. 'You're blaming *me* for that nonsense?'

'Well, if you hadn't needlessly insulted Emilia's band ...'

'I didn't needlessly insult anything. She's a teenager with barely any musical talent.'

'*Mum*,' Libby said again.

'I simply don't understand the lack of logic applied to

anything on this street,' Rebecca continued, clearly hitting a groove now. 'Everyone behaves as if it's normal to be so involved in each other's lives. That you should have a collective Christmas decorating scheme, and find it acceptable to have a stranger stringing lights pell mell all about your house, is incredible to me. That you should care, at all, what the new neighbour next door is like, other than that she's quiet and doesn't bother you. But, in fact, the fact that she's quiet and doesn't bother you is what's so upsetting to all of you, inexplicably. You *share a street carpenter*, as if *that's* something sensible. And you shouldn't even get me started on the fact that this one here' – Rebecca gestured toward Pen – 'thinks that she's a cruise director and this street needs to have a constant itinerary of events and activities. And to top it all off, there's a mangy dog constantly hanging about.'

There was complete and utter silence for a moment after Rebecca's outburst. And then, one by one, all the rest of the guests started getting up from the table.

'Oh,' Libby said, looking crestfallen, but she didn't protest that they stay, because, having been so mortally insulted, Sam couldn't imagine forcing them to stay for more.

'I'll ring you,' Pen said vaguely. 'At some point.'

Ellen said to Sam, 'I love you, but maybe you ought to give up on the idea of having a Thanksgiving celebration. It never seems to turn out that great.'

'Yeah,' Sam agreed, feeling a little dazed by what had just happened.

Ellen fixed him with a look. 'You know how important you are to me. Ring me anytime, yeah?' and then kissed his temple like he was a little boy in need of protection. Which he wasn't, but it was soothing to be reminded of.

Sophie and Evie behind her glared at Rebecca the entirety of their way out of the room.

'Well,' remarked Bill, rising to his feet, 'I think I'll be off, too. That was a bit too much excitement for me.'

And considering that last Thanksgiving Bill had had a serious heart attack, Sam thought that that was really saying something.

Bill gave Rebecca a look, and it was really the only look that seemed to have any effect on Rebecca at all. She looked a little stricken in the face of it.

Jack, tail not wagging at all, followed Bill out, with one disdainful glance back in Rebecca's direction.

Which left Rebecca and Libby and Teddy, and then Millie and Jasper, who looked at each other awkwardly.

Millie said, 'I should go, too.'

'Yeah,' Jasper agreed, and they got to their feet.

'Millie,' Libby said, 'you should take your Victoria sponge with you. We didn't even get to enjoy it.'

Millie shook her head. 'No, no, keep it.'

'Thank you, Millie,' said Sam grimly. 'We need something sweet in the house at the moment.' This caused Rebecca to look over at him, but Sam was over trying to placate her.

Millie hesitated, then Jasper said, 'Come on, I'll walk you home,' and they exited together.

The street, Sam thought, would have loved this evidence of a Millie and Jasper flirtation, under normal circumstances, on a normal night. But instead the street had just been viciously attacked, and so all of their harmless little preoccupations had been smashed underfoot.

Sam stood and said calmly, 'Teddy, let's go on an adventure, what do you say?'

'Sam,' Libby said.

'No,' said Sam. 'Sorry, I'm not going to be able to stay here any longer and be polite while your mother insults everything about me, constantly, and you just stand by and think that's okay. I think I've done this quite long enough now. I think I'm tired of being treated like rubbish. And I'm especially tired of doing it while waiting for you to defend me and never having that defence coming.'

'That's not—' Libby began.

Sam deliberately turned to Teddy and deliberately forced himself to speak as calmly as possible. 'Teddy, would you like to come with me?'

Teddy nodded eagerly and practically flew in search of his jacket.

Sam had no real plan for where they should go or what they ought to do; he just knew that he had to get out of the house before he said something he was going to regret.

Teddy walked silently by his side. Sam understood why he wasn't saying anything, why he was just there offering his support, but still Sam felt guilty that Teddy had had to witness any of that.

Sam said, 'Look . . .'

Teddy startled him by slipping his hand into his, which wasn't something Teddy had willingly done in . . . a while, it seemed to Sam. 'It's okay, Dad,' Teddy said gently. 'We can just walk for a bit.'

Sam took a deep breath, trying not to feel too strangled by all the emotions of everything happening. And had a sudden idea. 'Let's go ice-skating,' he said.

The silence that followed everyone walking out of their house was excruciating. It was so *loud* that Libby actually had to fight a desire to cover her ears against the silence.

'Libby,' her mother started.

Libby shook her head, squeezing her eyes shut. 'No,' she said. 'No. I think Sam's right. I think I've been doing this. I've been letting you be horrible to everything I care about because I didn't want to make a big scene, but now you've gone and . . . Everyone at this table was our friend,' Libby said. 'They're all people whose presence in our lives we love and cherish. We don't insult them for the people they are, for the things that they love and are enthusiastic about. We support them in their endeavours. Because all of these people – every single one of them – mean more than any wedding. A wedding is *one day*. What really matters is the marriage Sam and I have after it. And these people on this street, they are going to be part of that life Sam and I will make for ourselves. And I'm happy that they will be. All of them. Every last one of them. And Sam – I *love* Sam. Sam is amazing, and Sam loves me, and Sam makes me happy, and if you can't be happy for us . . . ' Libby paused and looked at her mother and swallowed thickly, making herself say the words, 'Then I'm not sure what place you have here.'

Sam hadn't been ice-skating in ages, and it turned out he was abysmal at it. He could, at least, keep himself upright, so he supposed that was a good thing, but he could hardly move.

Teddy wasn't much better.

Sam looked at him struggling to keep his feet and said, 'I really think I should have taken you ice-skating more often. When's the last time we went ice-skating?'

Teddy scrunched up his face in thought. 'I don't think we've ever been ice-skating.'

'Yes, we've been ice-skating!' Sam protested, because he was positive he'd taken Teddy before. But when he thought back, he realised that it would have had to have been before Sara got sick, because Sara was in Sam's memories of ice-skating. 'Oh. You must have been a baby. No wonder you don't remember.'

'You took a baby ice-skating?' Teddy frowned at him, disapproving.

'You weren't a baby *really*, you were a toddler. You could walk. You could toddle around.'

'And how did I do skating?' asked Teddy.

'Well,' said Sam, 'better than you're doing now, actually. You were just used to falling down every time you tried to take a step, so you just went with it.'

Eventually, they gained their footing a little better and skated around the rink a few times. It took all of their concentration, so conversation was at a minimum, until they were done, and exchanging their skating boots for their ordinary shoes.

And then Sam ventured, 'Teddy.'

Teddy said, 'It wasn't your fault, Dad.'

'But I feel like I should have—'

'It's not your fault. It's not Libby's fault, either. Sometimes people are just grouchy.'

It was such a mild adjective, and yet strangely apt. 'Yeah,' Sam agreed. 'Sometimes people are just grouchy. But listen.' He finished putting on his shoes and turned to face Teddy most fully. 'I've told you before and I'll tell you again: You're the most important thing. So if Rebecca's upsetting you, then I'll . . .'

'Rebecca's not upsetting me,' Teddy said. 'It makes me sad that she upsets you, though. I wish she didn't. I wish she was nicer to you. That's what I want to talk to Rebecca about. It's not about me, Dad. It's about you. I'm worried about *you*.'

Which was not at all how things were supposed to go, thought Sam. So he said that. 'That's not how these things are supposed to go.'

'Yeah,' Teddy said, with a little shrug. 'But we don't do things the usual way all that often.'

'Fair enough,' said Sam, because he supposed he couldn't argue with that. They stood together, ready to go back to their house and face the lions. He said, as they walked, 'I'm sorry I've been worrying you.'

'Don't be sorry,' said Teddy. 'Libby makes you happy, and that's been nice. This has just been bumpy but I think it's going to get better.'

That made some sense, because Sam didn't think it could get any worse.

Chapter 20

The best kind of Victoria sponge will be moist and
tender, with a buttery flavour and an airy lightness.

Rebecca found herself standing all alone in the middle of
a deserted dining room, with the remains of a half-eaten
Thanksgiving dinner all around her, and didn't know
what to do.

So she started methodically cleaning up, because that was
her first instinct, and the house's disarray was easier to deal
with than her mental and emotional disarray.

But her mental and emotional disarray kept leaking into
her consciousness anyway. The cleaning wasn't an adequate
distraction, and she finished it too quickly, and that left her
with nothing to think about but the anguished, hurt look on
Libby's face when she'd walked out on her.

Rebecca sank to the sofa in the lounge, looking at the half-
decorated Christmas tree in front of her, and said out loud,
'What have I *done*?'

She couldn't just sit here in this empty house ruminating

upon it, she decided. She had to get out of the house, she had to *do* something.

But, having pulled her coat on and stepped outside, she had no idea exactly what she planned to do. The fairy lights were coming on all up and down the street, and it looked its usual cheerful winter wonderland self, but to Rebecca the festive decorations seemed hollow and mocking now. This was a street that loved Christmas and joy and good cheer, and she had smashed all of that.

What sort of person did that? What sort of person was she?

Seeing a movement out of the corner of her eye, she turned her head. It was only Jack, patrolling the street the way he usually did, only now, seeing her, he deliberately crossed to the other side of the street and then kept walking. It was a *dog*, and a dog snubbing her should not have felt like the final straw, but it did.

But she was caught, because she didn't want to go back inside, either. And then Bill's voice called from his door, 'Well. You might as well come in here, then.'

It was a gruff invitation, and Rebecca wasn't even sure if he was serious about it, but she seized upon the opportunity to get off the street and into a house with a *person* in it. It would be a lovely distraction.

Bill's house was decorated in a spare, dated style that Rebecca might have judged in other circumstances, except she thought she'd done enough judging for one evening. So she simply said, 'Thank you so much for inviting me in,' when she stepped through the door, with no other comments on the threadbare carpet or sagging sofa.

Bill grunted something inaudible, then said, 'Can I make you a cuppa?'

'Please,' Rebecca said gratefully, and interpreted Bill's arm waving toward the lounge as an invitation for her to make herself at home.

The room's bookcases were crowded with tiny wooden figurines, exquisitely rendered, and Rebecca leaned over to admire them, enchanted. When she heard Bill return to the room, she said, 'Did you do these? Teddy told me that you did wood carving and made little figures but I didn't realise how beautiful they would be.'

'Seems to me,' Bill rejoined, 'that there's a lot of things you didn't realise.'

Rebecca supposed that was, under the circumstances, fair. She turned to accept her cup of tea, unsure what to say.

Bill said, 'Feel free to add a bit of whiskey, if you like. You probably need one today.'

Rebecca accepted that invitation, too, picking up whiskey from the tray she'd seen and splashing some into her cup. Then she sat on the sofa.

Bill said, 'It's a thing I think you're probably inclined towards.'

'What?'

'Making up your mind about things before knowing the whole story. Thinking something must be terrible when in actuality it might be rather nice.' Bill nodded toward his figurines.

Rebecca took a fortifying sip of her whiskey-laced tea and then said, 'Yes. Maybe.'

Bill snorted into his own tea.

Rebecca frowned. 'It took a lot for me to admit that. You needn't get on a high horse about it.'

Bill, sobering, lowered his teacup. 'No,' he agreed. 'You're right. I needn't. The truth is ... '

Bill was silent for so long that Rebecca didn't think that he was going to continue, and then he started speaking again.

'The truth is that I have the same tendency.'

Rebecca wanted to say something biting, like *People in glass houses shouldn't throw stones*. But she held her tongue, because that probably wouldn't be the most productive thing at the moment. She stayed silent and took another sip of her tea.

Bill, after a moment, went on. 'I might have ... made up my mind, about the people on this street, very quickly, and without ... giving them an opportunity to be who they are. They're all daft. There's no denying that. You're absolutely right to think them daft. But they're good-hearted. And they're loyal. And they've made this street feel like a place where you're never alone. And maybe that sounds like a bad thing to you. I understand. I thought it sounded terrible. But it's actually ... oddly ... nice.' He said it almost doubtfully, as if he still couldn't believe it was true.

It seemed like a personal moment Rebecca had intruded on. She looked down into her teacup, unsure where else to look.

'Anyway,' Bill said, clearing his throat, 'you don't need to understand it, or like it yourself. You just have to respect your daughter's wishes in the matter. Libby's a great girl. She's lovely. And she's happy. And she loves you.'

'Does she?' said Rebecca bitterly, before she could help herself. And then she said, 'Sorry. No. Of course I don't mean that. I know she loves me.'

After a moment of silence, Bill said, 'I'm sure she loves you a great deal. She's just a girl getting married, and sometimes mums can make that hard. Sometimes mums can make it so you barely get to enjoy the wedding at all.'

Rebecca looked at him steadily, and then said, 'Are you speaking from personal experience?'

Bill smiled faintly. 'Maybe.'

Rebecca smiled back. 'I'm sorry.'

'There's nothing to be sorry for. It was a long time ago and we had a wonderful marriage. The wedding isn't really the point of a marriage. But it would be nice if you let Libby enjoy it. She would probably like to enjoy it.'

It was such a simple suggestion. It shouldn't have been radical to Rebecca. It should have been obvious. It should have been how she was doing things all along.

Sam got back to an empty house and a half-decorated Christmas tree, and Jack, who came bounding up the street to greet them as soon as they appeared on it.

'Hi, Jack,' Teddy said, scratching him behind his ears. 'Sorry Rebecca called you mangy. You're not mangy.'

Jack wagged his tail.

'I think everything is forgiven,' said Sam.

'Well, he's at least forgiven us. Thanksgiving is just a stressful holiday,' remarked Teddy.

'Apparently so. Your aunt Ellen thinks we should stop celebrating it. What do you think?'

Teddy considered the question as they walked into the house together, Jack following. 'I think ... I think I wouldn't like to stop it altogether.'

Sam had assumed that would be the case. 'It's okay. We're going to have better Thanksgivings. I promise.'

'We'll just have to keep trying until we get it right,' said Teddy.

Sam smiled at him and then called out, 'Hello?' The house was quiet in response. Sam texted Libby. **We're home.** There was no immediate response. He tucked his phone into his pocket and looked at the half-decorated Christmas tree, then at Teddy, who was also looking at the tree. 'Should we finish it?' Sam asked.

'How about tomorrow?' sighed Teddy. 'It's been a long day.'

'Agreed,' said Sam, and ruffled Teddy's hair.

'I'm going to take a shower,' Teddy announced.

'I don't blame you,' said Sam, and watched him ascend the stairs, and then walked into the dining room to deal with the mess.

Except there wasn't any mess. Someone had cleaned up the remainder of the dinner and put everything away. The only thing left out was the Victoria sponge Millie had brought.

Sam regarded it and then decided he deserved some cake, so he cut himself a slice and sat on the sofa to eat it, flipping through the telly restlessly to try to find something to watch.

He was not successful in finding anything before he heard the front door open and then shut. He muted the television and leaned his head back to try to see who had entered.

It was Rebecca, who stood awkwardly and regarded him for a long moment.

Sam said, 'Don't even say a word about how I should be watching my figure.'

'I owe you an apology,' Rebecca said, and that was a start.

Sam said nothing, waiting for her to continue.

Rebecca did continue, sounding very heartfelt, choosing her words with care. 'I've been … unfair to you. And I have no excuse for it. I don't know why I've behaved so appallingly toward you, when you've done nothing but love my daughter, and clearly cherish her, and want to make her happy. I don't know why I've behaved as if you're sabotaging the wedding because you don't care about it. The thing I have learned about you, mainly, is that you care about everything far more than other people would. And that speaks so well of you, that I don't know why I would ever seek to belittle you for that. I'm so sorry.'

Rebecca looked so anguished that Sam, after a moment, took pity on her. 'Do you want a slice of cake? It's rather delicious.'

Rebecca seemed to recognise that he was making a peace offering, and did indeed slice herself a piece of cake and sit next to him on the sofa.

'Where's Libby?' she ventured.

'I don't know. I texted her but she didn't respond. I thought you liked me, you know, this summer. When we first met. I thought we got along.'

'We did,' said Rebecca. 'We do. I just … ' Rebecca sighed and looked down at her cake. 'I had a vision of my daughter's future, and it wasn't … it wasn't *here*. And I don't mean that there's anything wrong with this street, in fact this street is plainly amazing. I mean here in London, without me. And now she's going to marry you, and your life is very clearly here, you're enmeshed in the life of this street, your roots here are deep and you haven't even been here very long, and you have a son in school here so you won't want to move him, and so … that's it. I've lost.'

Sam said, 'You haven't lost. It hasn't been a competition.'

'I know,' said Rebecca, and ate her cake.

Sam, watching her, said, 'But it feels like one.'

Rebecca said nothing.

'It's not like that. We want you to be part of our lives. And we want to be part of yours. We can find a way to make this work. I know we can.'

Rebecca looked at him. 'You're right, of course. I mean, if everyone can forgive me.'

'We're a fairly forgiving street,' said Sam with a smile. 'We've forgiven a lot in the past. We weren't always … like we are now.'

'I find that difficult to believe,' said Rebecca.

'No, no,' Sam insisted. 'It's true. When I first moved here, it was … just an ordinary street. A street like any other. I mean, it had Jack, so I guess it always had something unusual about it. When you think about it, it's really Jack who we have to thank for all of this. Jack's what makes us unusual. Otherwise we really are just a perfectly ordinary street. We all have our individual dramas and challenges. But we also have Jack. And so we don't just view ourselves as alone, dealing with everything by ourselves. We don't have to think of ourselves that way. Because Jack wanders through connecting all of us and all of a sudden you're not alone.' Sam paused, and then said, 'All of a sudden I wasn't alone in my daily struggles, and that meant a great deal to me. I'd felt very alone for a very long time. I wanted moving to London to change that, and it did. And just because I have Libby in my life now, it doesn't mean I don't still have all these other people in my life. It's a community. We all fit. There's room for all of us.' He looked straight at Rebecca. 'There's room for you, too.'

Rebecca said, sounding genuine about it, 'That would be nice.'

'We forgive a lot on this street,' Sam said. 'It's going to be okay.' He didn't point out that he still hadn't heard anything from Libby. He was confident she'd come back. She just needed time, the way he had.

After a long silence that was surprisingly not uncomfortable, Sam remarked, 'This Victoria sponge is really spectacular.'

'It's lovely,' Rebecca agreed.

Libby walked in to find Sam and her mother in the lounge, watching TV together. It was not at all what she had expected, and it brought her up short.

'Hey,' Sam said, getting to his feet and greeting her with a kiss to her temple.

'Hi,' she responded automatically, looking past him to her mother.

'I was just going to go upstairs and check on Teddy,' said Sam. 'He's been suspiciously quiet.'

It was giving her time and space to talk things through with her mother, and she knew she needed that, but also she was childishly dreading the situation. Sam met her eyes, looking solemn and also encouraging. He wasn't smiling exactly, but there was a lightness to him that she hadn't expected, and it gave her hope.

He gave her a tiny nod and kissed her temple again and then walked up the stairs.

Libby looked at her mother and couldn't think what to say.

Luckily her mother spoke first. 'The cake that Millie brought is outstanding.'

'Oh, did you have some?' asked Libby, striving for the same relaxed ordinariness her mother was trying to achieve.

'Sam and I had some,' replied Rebecca.

Libby walked over to it and sliced some for herself, still thinking about what she was going to say.

But when she turned back to her mother, her mother surprised her by saying, 'I'm so sorry, Libby. I'm so sorry. I was so thoroughly inappropriate. I've been thoroughly inappropriate the entire time, upon first arriving here. I've hurt you, and I've hurt Sam, and I've hurt Teddy, and I've hurt these lives you've built for yourself, and I've hurt this entire street, and I'm sorry. I've even hurt Jack!'

Libby felt torn between laughter and tears. She just said, 'Yes.' And then she took her piece of cake and went to sit on the sofa with her mother.

Her mother said, 'When you left home, to move here ... I just always thought you'd move back home. I thought this was temporary. I thought it was a phase. I thought you'd get tired of it and come back to all the people who know you and love you. But instead, seeing you here, what I've had to realise is ... you're never coming back. You've found people who know you and love you here.'

'That doesn't mean I love you or anyone from the village any less,' Libby said. 'It's not like there's finite love in my heart, and this street has crowded everyone else out. It's just that this street is ...'

'It's *your* village,' her mother finished. 'I can see that now.

You've found this wonderful community of people to support you, and I'm embarrassed by how badly I behaved because of that. My only excuse is ... I've been scared, this whole time, of how unnecessary I am. It's this moment of a mother finally having to accept being superfluous.'

'Oh, Mum,' said Libby, anguished, and put aside her plate of cake so she could catch her mother's hands up in her own. 'That's not true. You're not superfluous. Not at all. You're my mum. You'll never be unnecessary to me. I was so excited about you coming to visit and help with the wedding planning. I wanted your input. I wanted to do this *with* you. I never wanted to do it without you. I'm so happy to have you here because of how much I love you. I just ... I just want us to work together, instead of against each other. I think we can all work together, and that together we would create the most beautiful wedding anyone's ever seen.'

'I think,' said her mother, smiling tremulously, 'that you're right.'

Sam was pretending that he had stuff to do in their bedroom so he didn't go down and interrupt Libby's heart-to-heart with her mum, so he was relieved when Libby came into the room.

'Hi,' he said.

Libby wordlessly walked over to him and tipped her head into his chest.

Sam pulled her closer and kissed the top of her head and said, 'It's okay. We're doing okay.'

'Are we?' Libby asked.

'Well, I think we're getting there. I thought so, at least. I had a good conversation with your mother.'

'Oh, good,' said Libby, looking up at him. 'I did, too.'

Sam smiled widely. 'Good. I was hoping you would. It was a disaster, I'm not going to deny that, but she just loves you a lot. It wasn't the best way of showing it, but that's where it was coming from.'

'I feel like she got here and she just threw me off,' Libby said. 'I wanted to make her happy so much that I forgot about making you happy.'

Sam shook his head. 'It doesn't have to be a choice, first of all. And second of all, I don't want you to feel like you have to think about making me happy as a task on your to-do list or something.'

'No. I don't think of it that way at all. That's what I mean: I completely lost sight of everything about our lives, everything about them that I loved – and love – so much. It turned into, like, this outside thing almost, like I was playing this part and I'd forgotten how to do it, instead of it being *me*, and *my life*. The fact that I couldn't make any decisions on the wedding, it was because I felt like it was happening to someone else, like I was trying to determine what someone else might want out of their wedding, The Perfect Bride, the bride you might want and my mum might want ...'

'No.' Sam shook his head again. 'Don't think that way. I don't want any sort of bride. I just want *you*. Honestly, that's all I—'

'I know. I realise that now. I'm appalled I lost sight of that. But that's what I mean: I think I can't make any decisions about the wedding because I don't want that kind of wedding.'

302

'Okay,' said Sam, tilting his head in confusion. 'So what kind of wedding do you . . . ?'

'What do you think about a Christmas wedding, right here on the street?'

'I think . . . Christmas is only a few weeks away.'

'Yes.' Libby, beaming, nodded.

Sam, after a moment, smiled. 'I think it sounds brilliant.'

The next day, over breakfast, Sam and Libby stood in front of Rebecca and Teddy and announced their plan.

'We've had an idea,' Libby said.

'We want to get married at Christmas,' Sam continued.

'Right here on the street,' Libby finished.

Rebecca blinked. 'Can you even do that?'

'No,' said Libby. 'Not really. Not legally. But we want to do it anyway. We want to have a grand gesture that just . . . *gets us married*, and then we can worry about the rest later.'

Teddy broke out into a wide grin. 'I think this is *fantastic*. Pari and I can help you organise it! It will Make a Difference!'

'Yes,' Sam agreed, 'I think that is a very good outlet for your scheming skills, actually. You can be our wedding planners.'

Libby looked at Rebecca, who had been silent through this exchange. 'Mum?' she said.

'Yes,' Rebecca said. And then she smiled. 'Yes. If this is what you want, if it will make you happy, then yes. I can't believe I'm saying this, but a fake street wedding is a perfect idea.'

Chapter 21

You're invited to the wedding of
Samuel Bishop and Elizabeth Quinn,
on Christmas Street, on Christmas Eve.

They called a street meeting by walking up and down the street and knocking on doors. It was a Sunday morning, so everybody was home to be bothered. Jack clearly thought this was all the most magnificent fun and bounced along with them as they walked up and down.

Bill opened the door and looked at the knot of them and said, 'Oh, good. You're all speaking to each other again. That's wonderful.' He then went to close the door.

Sam laughed and blocked him. 'Not so fast. We're speaking to each other, and we also want to speak to you.'

'About what?' asked Bill suspiciously, narrowing his eyes at Rebecca.

'Street meeting,' Libby said. 'We need to have a meeting to

clear the air about what happened yesterday at Thanksgiving.'

'You lot have had that meeting,' Bill pointed out, grumbly. 'Must the rest of us be involved, too?'

'Yes,' said Libby stubbornly. 'Because we have an amazing surprise for all for you.'

'Amazing, eh?' said Bill sceptically, as he relented and came outside.

Arthur answered the door with Charlie in his arms and said, 'Oh,' when he saw them, and then, 'Hi.'

'Hi,' Libby said. 'Hello, Charlie.'

'Can we ask you to bundle Charlie up and bring him outside for a street meeting?' asked Sam.

'Good idea!' Max shouted from the top of the stairs.

'Apparently yes, we will bundle Charlie up,' Arthur replied.

Emilia answered the door at the Pachuta house, and gave them a glare, and called out, 'Mum! Dad! It's the rude lady from next door! And Libby and Sam and Teddy.'

Sam thought Rebecca deserved that.

Apparently Rebecca did, too, because as Emilia went to walk away from the door, she leaned past Sam and said, 'No, wait, Emilia. I wanted to talk to you.'

Emilia paused and glanced over her shoulder, without fully turning back around.

'I'm sorry,' Rebecca said sincerely, 'for what I said about your band. From what I heard on Halloween, you are enthusiastic and dedicated and there's talent there. You just need to be ... given an opportunity to blossom,' Rebecca concluded, clearly choosing her words carefully, but it was a nice effort, and Sam smiled.

She had apparently convinced Emilia, who turned fully to

face her and nodded earnestly. 'Yes! Exactly! It's just been hard for us to gain the proper amount of experience but we've been practising so hard!'

'And that is why Sam and I formally want to invite you to play at our wedding,' Libby said, slipping her hand into Sam's.

Emilia's face registered amazement. 'What?! Really?!'

'Really,' said Libby, and Sam nodded.

'Mum!' Emilia shouted, turning, but finding her mother standing right behind her.

'I heard,' Anna said, looking teary. And then she walked over to the doorway and said to Rebecca, 'I am not ordinarily a hugger, but let me just . . . ' She leaned forward and embraced Rebecca warmly. 'Thank you.'

Rebecca looked unsure what to do and just said uncertainly, 'You're welcome,' which seemed to be the right thing to do, because Anna moved away, smiling mistily.

And then Libby said, 'We're having a street meeting, come join us outside.'

By this time, Pari had already opened the Basak door, because leave it to Pari to have already witnessed the activity along the street.

'Hi!' she called. 'Are we having a meeting?'

'Yes!' Libby called back. 'Are your parents around?'

'Mum!' Pari called into the house. 'Dad! We're having a meeting!'

They turned their attention to Millie's house next. Sam wasn't sure if Millie would be home, because of all of them Millie's schedule was the most unpredictable, but she opened the door after a short delay.

'Hello,' she said, and she hardly looked surprised to find

all of them on her doorstep. Clearly Millie had grown used to the ways of the street.

'Hello,' Libby said, smiling at her. 'We're having a street meeting. And, as part of the street now, we want you to join us.'

'We promise,' Sam added, 'that it's going to be less eventful than Thanksgiving was.'

'Well,' said Libby, 'it might be eventful in the opposite way. In a *good* way.'

'When is the street meeting?' Millie asked.

'Right now,' said Libby, and gestured behind her, where neighbours had begun to mill about.

'Oh,' said Millie. 'Let me just grab my coat.'

They ended at Pen's house, and when she opened the door and Jack bounded around her she said cheerfully, 'Hiya, Jack.' Then to the rest of them, 'This looks like a very formal little exercise here.'

'We're going to have a street meeting,' Libby said.

'To clear the air?' said Pen. 'That's a good idea. Because last Thanksgiving we all made up with each other in hospital. This is much better. Let me grab my coat.' Pen disappeared back into the house.

'In hospital?' said Rebecca.

'It's a long story,' said Sam, 'with a happy ending.'

All the neighbours had now gathered in a little knot on the pavement. Sam noticed that Anna and Diya were still keeping their distances, even though Sai and Emilia were stubbornly right next to each other. And there had been no real plan for how the street meeting would go, but Sam thought they ought to start with reconciling Anna and Diya.

But then Rebecca surprised him by being the first one to

speak. 'I just wanted to thank all of you for coming to this street meeting, even though I was wretched to all of you yesterday and you've no reason to put yourself in my company again.'

The neighbours were silent, except for Charlie, who babbled in response.

Rebecca said, 'I just want to apologise. It's clear that what you have here is a lovely street – a special street – and everything I said to you was ... inexcusable. I'm sorry.'

There was another moment of silence.

Then Millie said shyly, 'I will say that it took me a little while to get used to this street. To everything that it is. I think it can seem odd, and off-putting, and scary from the outside. But once you get to know everyone ... it's not any of those things.'

'Well,' said Max. 'We still might be a bit odd.'

'We understand,' Pen said to Rebecca. 'And, as the person who was seeking forgiveness last year, I want to be the first one to give my forgiveness to you.'

Rebecca gave her a grateful look, and the rest of the street also murmured words in encouragement of Rebecca and their forgiveness of her.

And then Diya said, 'I suppose I should also apologise to you, Anna. You know I think the world of Emilia and her band.'

'I know,' Anna said. 'And I'm sorry, too. I think a great deal of Sai, who has been so supportive of Emilia through all of this.'

'We're so lucky,' Diya said tearfully.

'We are the *luckiest*,' said Anna.

The two women embraced and their husbands exchanged knowing, fond looks.

Libby said, 'I'm so glad that all of us are getting back to normal with each other. Because Sam and I have rather extraordinary news.'

'Is it that you're getting married?' Max asked. 'Because all of us already knew that.'

'It's that we're getting married on Christmas,' Libby said.

'Christmas Eve, actually, to be exact,' added Sam.

'Right here on the street,' finished Libby.

'On the street?' echoed Bill.

'This is where everything started,' said Libby, 'so this is where we're going to start the next phase of our life together, too.'

'Isn't it great?' said Teddy excitedly, his eyes shining. 'I can't wait! They said we can help with the planning!' he told Pari.

Pari perked up. 'It'll be our next Make a Difference project! Wait until we tell Mrs Dash!'

'Why is everyone standing around outside?' asked Jasper. He was standing on the outside of the crowd, looking at them quizzically.

'Jasper!' exclaimed Pen. 'What are you doing here? Today wasn't a work day on my house, was it?'

'Nor on ours,' said Max.

Pen looked significantly at Millie, who blushed.

Jasper said, 'No, I'm here for the surprise, I thought.' He looked at Marcel. 'Weren't you going to have a big surprise reveal?'

'Yes,' Marcel said. 'It's been a trifle derailed by the events of today. But surprise!' he said to Anna.

'What surprise?' she asked blankly.

'Jasper's going to start the surprise that's going to be your Christmas present. He's going to construct ramps in our house for the cats to play on. You're always saying you worry they're bored, and I thought that—'

Anna cut Marcel off with a kiss.

'Okay,' said Max, amused. 'Successful surprise.'

Darsh said to Diya, 'I feel like I need to surprise you like that.'

Diya said, 'Wait, can we go back to the street wedding? Is that even legal?'

'What's this?' asked Jasper.

'Sam and Libby are getting married right here on the street,' Pen said.

'If it's legal,' said Diya.

'It's not quite legal,' said Libby. 'But it doesn't matter. That's not what we're going for. Everything's got lost in so much nonsense. We want to be two people who pledge to love each other in front of our closest friends and family. So we should just *do* that. The rest is just . . . legalese.'

'Well,' said Max, after a moment of silence, 'if we're having a street wedding, then obviously I'll help decorate.'

'Max,' said Libby, smiling at him. 'That's so nice.'

'I'll help, too,' offered Jasper.

'Aw, Jasper, that's so lovely of you,' Libby said. 'Thank you.'

Jasper shrugged. 'Hey, I'm here so much, I might as well already live on this street.'

'That *is* true,' remarked Arthur.

'Arthur should officiate,' suggested Max.

'What?' said Arthur.

Max winked at him. 'You're so great at giving speeches, you should be the fake minister, or whatever.'

'That would be a great idea,' said Sam. 'If you don't mind.'

'I mean,' said Arthur, 'if it would help you out, then I suppose I can fake-marry you.'

'Excellent.' Libby beamed at him. 'And Emilia's band has already agreed to entertain all of us again.'

Emilia looked pleased to bursting.

'Obviously I have to supervise the food,' said Diya, with the air of suggesting that if she didn't supervise the food, it would be thoroughly hopeless.

Anna said, 'I am happy to leave the food to Diya, but I'd love to help somehow. Maybe with the flowers?'

'Oh,' said Marcel. 'I can help with that. We will teach ourselves the flower language of love.' Marcel looked playfully at Anna, which made everyone laugh.

Pen said, 'Well, I'm the writer of the group. I don't know what skills I have to offer but they're yours to command.'

'You have plenty of skill,' Libby assured her.

'And we think it would be lovely to have a speech,' Sam said. 'The story of our love, which is really the story of the street. So who better to write that up than our very own street scribe?'

'Aw, I like that title,' said Pen, and nodded happily. 'I would love to.'

Millie said, 'Well, I don't know what special talent I have to offer, but I'm happy to help everybody out.'

'You don't have to,' said Libby, 'we don't want to force you to take part in all of this. After all, you just moved onto the

311

street, you didn't know you'd be planning a wedding two months later.'

'No, no,' said Millie. 'I want to help, too.'

'Well,' said Sam slowly. 'If you're serious about that ...'

'What?' asked Millie blankly.

'You're a tremendous baker,' said Sam. 'And we find ourselves in need of a wedding cake.'

Millie looked amazed. 'Really?'

'Yes,' said Sam. 'Our guests are demanding; they'll definitely want us to serve wedding cake.'

There was a little bit of scattered laughter.

Libby watched Millie closely, wanting to make sure that her reaction was pleased. But it did look genuinely pleased. She said, 'You would trust me with your wedding cake? Really?'

'We can't think of anyone else we'd trust more,' said Libby warmly.

'In that case,' said Millie, 'I would love to bake your wedding cake for you.'

'Wonderful,' said Sam, smiling. 'Then that's settled.'

'This is going to be the best wedding ever,' Pari announced, with the air of someone who'd conducted a series of intense mathematical equations and found that to be the only logical conclusion.

'We think so, too,' said Sam. 'And we can talk about it more over some of that delicious Victoria sponge that Millie made.'

The street, chattering happily together, headed off toward Sam and Libby's house, and Libby, as they walked, turned to her mother and said, 'And then there's your job.'

'What's my job?' asked Rebecca.

'Helping me find a wedding dress, of course!'

When Libby and Rebecca went wedding-dress shopping, Sam tracked down Teddy, playing videogames in his room. 'So,' Sam said. 'Can I interrupt this very important videogame to ask a somewhat less important question?'

'One second,' Teddy said, his tongue literally caught between his teeth in concentration.

Sam waited patiently, studying him, his little boy, who had once been so tiny and helpless and now was so much his own person. A person Sam was so proud of. Teddy's life had been full of unexpected moments, and through every single one Teddy had been brave and sweet and steadfast. Teddy had been, for so long, Sam's lifeline in the whole mess, the reason he got himself out of bed in the morning, the reason he'd held things together. He looked at Teddy and felt such an impossible amount of love for him that it was amazing that he could feel so much love and still be standing upright, not have his heart explode out of his chest and topple to the floor.

'Okay.' Teddy set his controller down and gave his attention to Sam, and then lifted his eyebrows. 'You're staring at me. What's that for?'

Sam wondered what his face looked like, for Teddy to seem so alarmed. 'I'm just amazed,' he managed to answer.

'Amazed about what?' asked Teddy quizzically.

'How amazing *you* are,' answered Sam.

Teddy grinned. 'Okay, then.'

'I wanted to talk to you about wedding stuff.'

313

'There's a lot going on,' said Teddy, which was an under-statement in Sam's view.

'Lots,' Sam agreed. 'And in all the commotion, I didn't want to forget to ask you.'

'Ask me what?'

'At weddings, it's traditional for the groom to choose his best friend to stand up with him and provide moral support. Just a friendly face by his side to get him through the day. They call that the "best man."'

'Yeah,' said Teddy. 'I know.'

'I was hoping that you would agree to be my best man,' said Sam.

Teddy's face completely lit up. 'What, *really*?'

'Really,' said Sam. 'I honestly can't imagine a better man, so that means you just have to be best man.'

'Dad!' exclaimed Teddy, and Sam thought he was going to say something else, but instead he just stood and ran over to Sam and hugged him.

Sam hugged him back, fierce and tight, kissing the top of his head. 'Thanks for being my best friend,' he said.

Millie was trying to tell herself not to worry. She'd seen the picture of herself with Jasper up on the photo site Pen used. She'd asked Pen to take it down, and Pen had seemed confused about it, and clearly had wanted to ask questions, and Millie didn't want to answer any of Pen's questions, it was too humil-iating. Millie wanted to be an ordinary person, a person who could have photographs of herself online and not worry, who could just be happy and smiling next to Jasper, doing good for veterans on Remembrance Sunday. Millie wanted that – oh, how Millie wanted that – but that wasn't her life. And it had been dangerous of her to forget that.

And now she was so embroiled in the life of the street that she felt like she couldn't detach from it, even though her instinct was to curl into a ball and not answer the door any more ever again. Millie wanted to retreat.

But that felt like cowardice. She didn't want to be a coward. She'd told herself to be brave when she'd left Daniel, and she was still trying to hold on to that bravery.

All the same, when Jasper tried to say hi to her when she passed him in the street on her way to work, she said, 'Sorry, sorry, I'm so sorry, I'm late,' even though she really wasn't, and basically dashed right by him.

At work, she tried to tell herself that she was panicking over nothing, and she was perfectly safe, and Jasper was perfectly safe, and she should have spoken to him, and now he would never forgive her.

Or maybe Jasper *would* forgive her, which would be even worse, maybe, then she would just keep on going on pretending this was her life, when it was all a lie, when her life was nothing like this, when her life was still – *still* – all caught up in Daniel.

And then there was the fact that she had somehow agreed to bake a wedding cake. A *wedding* cake. Millie loved baking, and she always looked forward to doing it, but baking a *wedding cake*, when Millie really felt so conflicted about weddings. She didn't want to feel conflicted. She wanted Sam and Libby to have the most beautiful wedding ever. She didn't want to be cynical. She wanted to believe in true love and happy endings.

It was the day before Christmas Eve. The shops were bustling and busy.

Millie usually spent all of her time at work hiding in the back, but it was busy enough that Thea asked her to run out front to do some restocking.

Millie said, 'But usually I—'

'It's busy,' Thea said, dismissing her protests.

Millie wanted to protest more, and then thought how once again this set her apart, as someone different, someone who couldn't just go out and be in public like everyone else. She was so tired of being *different*.

So Millie seized hold of her determination and marched out to the supermarket floor, and for a little while it was completely uneventful and she told herself how much she'd been overreacting to everything, and then she heard his voice.

At first, as she froze in panic, she thought maybe she was imagining it. In the early days, she had imagined she had seen Daniel everywhere, lurking in every crowd, around every corner. *It's not him*, she tried to tell her racing heart. *You're imagining this.*

But the rumble of his voice persisted, so recognisable, so unforgettable.

People were giving her odd looks where she was standing, blocking the aisle. She squeezed her eyes shut and tried to take deep breaths to get herself under control, and then his voice solidified into words, and then into the shape of her name.

' ... Millie,' she heard him say. 'Does she happen to be here today?'

And Jenna at the front of the store said, because why wouldn't Jenna say anything, Millie hadn't told anyone how much she was in hiding, how much she was running from, 'Oh, yeah, she's in the back. That way.'

'Thank you so much,' said Daniel, in that cordial tone he had that made women melt, that had made her melt oh-so-long-ago, and had made her excuse so much unacceptable behaviour, had made her stay when she might have left long before that.

She should have fled, but at the same time she felt futility rising inside of her like a tide, choking her. She could flee, but where would she go? Wasn't that what Daniel had said all the time? He would find her, he would just keep finding her.

He came around the corner and caught sight of her, frozen stupidly into place, and their eyes met, and it was like Millie had never left at all, it was like Millie was right back in their house, frozen in whatever room she had tried to escape to, whilst Daniel tracked her down and always managed to corner her and always just began his approach.

He approached her now, whilst she stood still and stared. And then, upon reaching her, he said, 'Millie,' and smiled, and lifted a hand as if to touch her hair.

Millie flinched, with a sound like a small whimper, and managed to take a step away from him.

Daniel lifted his eyebrows at her, looking hurt. 'Now, Millie. Is that any way to greet your husband after all this time? Haven't you missed me? I was just going to say you looked well.'

Millie found the words floating somewhere inside her,

where she'd stashed them in safe keeping for just this moment, and she grabbed them close to her and pushed them out of her. 'You should leave,' she said. They came out small and quiet but they were there.

Daniel ducked his head. 'Sorry? What was that?'

Millie cleared her throat. Now that the words were there in her mouth, they seemed easier to say. 'You should leave.' They were louder now, firmer, more forceful.

Daniel looked shocked. 'What?'

'Leave,' she said, her voice rising in crescendo. Now that she'd started, she wasn't going to stop until he was gone. 'Leave. Go.'

'Millie—' he began.

'Go!' she said, practically shouting now. '*Go!*' People were looking at them, and she knew that they were, but she was glad. She wanted people to look and see this strong confident woman casting this man aside before he could do her any more harm.

'Millie—'

'I said to leave!'

Jenna came running up, looking alarmed, and looked from Millie to Daniel. 'Is there a problem?'

'She just— ' said Daniel.

'I've asked him to go,' Millie said, keeping her voice at calm levels. 'So he should leave.'

Jenna looked at her for a long moment, and then looked at Daniel. 'She says you should go.'

'I don't think—'

'Oi,' interjected one of the customers. 'She asked you to go, mate.'

Strangers, Millie thought. *Strangers* were helping her. Why had she never thought that strangers would help her before? Every stranger she'd met since leaving Daniel had been exquisite.

Daniel gave her a look of cold, concentrated fury, then turned and stalked out of the shop.

Jenna turned to Millie. 'You okay?'

'I'm fine,' Millie said shakily, although now that Daniel had exited, she was trembling all over.

'You don't look okay,' Jenna said with concern. 'What can I do? How can I help?'

Everyone was still looking at her, and Millie had lost control of that feeling of power that had helped before. Now Millie just wanted to get to her house, to lock all the doors, to draw all the blinds, to crawl into her bed, to try to be safe in her house on her street.

Millie looked at Jenna and said, 'I want to go home. Can I leave early?'

'Yeah,' Jenna said. 'Yeah, of course. But I don't want you walking home by yourself with that bloke around. I'll call you a cab.'

The street was a scene of chaos, and Libby was glad they were having a rehearsal. There seemed to be a million people milling around, and luckily everyone seemed to be coordinating what they'd been put in charge of coordinating, but when you had a dog walking down the aisle, a rehearsal was just necessary.

'Where's Teddy and Jack?' Libby said, as they were trying to assemble everyone for the dry run. 'Have you seen them?'

Sam turned to shout for them, but then they came running up, Pari with them.

'Here. We're here,' said Teddy.

'There was a strange man lurking around on the street,' Pari said. 'We had to investigate him.'

'What?' said Sam in alarm. 'Don't be investigating strange men. Come and tell me about the strange men. Where's the strange man?'

'Don't worry,' Teddy said. 'Jack scared him away.'

Jack barked and wagged his tail.

'We're the street spies,' Pari said. 'It's our job to—'

'No,' Sam said sharply. 'Listen seriously to me here. I don't mind you lot running around on this street, with the people we know. I trust them. But when you see strangers on the street, you come and tell one of us. You don't investigate them. Do both of you understand me?'

They hung their heads, looking contrite, and nodded.

Sai came up and said, 'Okay, everyone's in position. Here, Pari.' He handed her a basket, because Pari was going to serve as flower girl.

'Here we go, then,' said Libby, and looked around at everyone, waiting for the rehearsal to start.

And then Pen said, 'Hang on, has anyone seen Millie?'

'I think she had to work,' Jasper said. 'I walked past her leaving the house.'

'Aww,' said Pen, 'that means she's going to have to miss the rehearsal.'

'She'll probably show up later,' Libby said, and they got started.

Jasper stood and watched Max help Charlie toddle down the aisle toward Arthur, followed by Pari, pretending to toss flowers (jasmine, Jasper had been told they would be, which was a symbol of love and paid homage to Pari's culture), followed by Teddy, grinning at his dad, Jack keeping pace beside him. It was a procession full of love and laughter.

And Millie came down the street just as everyone had settled into position.

'Oh, good!' said Pen. 'We were worried you'd miss it!'

'I can't,' Millie said. She looked dazed and panicked and Jasper watched her closely. 'I can't go to the rehearsal.'

'What?' said Pen, bewildered. 'Why not?'

'I can't,' said Millie. 'I just can't.' She looked around the street with an expression of unreality, like she'd never seen it before, like she wasn't even seeing it now.

'Millie,' Jasper said gently, stepping forward. 'Did something happen? What's wrong?'

Millie turned her wide, panicked eyes onto him. 'All this ordinariness is so impossible,' she said.

'What?' he said, confused.

And then she turned and fled into her house.

Chapter 22

A traditional fruitcake
With brandy? Whiskey? Bourbon?
Marzipan? Fondant? Almond paste?

Millie, alone in her house, curled up in bed and just wished that everything would go away for a little while. She could hear the sound of the rehearsal underway outside, and it *hurt* not to be there. But Daniel's appearance had reminded her today of the lie in this life she was living: she wasn't this person who got to have an ordinary life of friends and joy and wedding rehearsals. She'd thought she could run away and start everything anew on Christmas Street, and she had really managed to delude herself that it had worked. And then Daniel had proven – as Daniel always did – that nothing in Millie's life could ever really change, she was always at his mercy.

Millie wanted the world to go away, but it seemed determined not to, as the current persistent knocking on her door indicated. Millie eventually got up and peeked out the window. Libby. Libby whose wedding cake she was supposed to be baking. She'd been practising for it intensely, testing flavour combinations out on Libby and Sam. Sam had said, smiling, that the cake practice was his favourite part of the wedding, and they had laughed together, and all of that felt as if it had belonged to a completely different Millie, a Millie who'd been living in a fairy tale.

But still: she'd promised Libby she'd bake her the wedding cake, and the wedding was the next day, which also happened to be Christmas Eve. Millie was Libby's only choice at this point, and Millie knew it. So even though there was nothing she felt like doing less than making a wedding cake, she knew she had to do it.

She made herself open the door and talk to Libby, plastering a smile on her face, even though it felt demented to her.

It probably looked demented, too, because Libby seemed alarmed. 'Hi,' she said.

'Hi,' Millie replied.

'Is everything okay?'

'Fine,' Millie said. 'Everything is fine. Perfect. Why wouldn't you think so?' What a stupid thing to say. She knew exactly why Libby didn't think everything was fine and perfect.

Libby said, 'It's just . . . the rehearsal . . . '

'I just couldn't today,' Millie said, trying to stay calm. 'I just couldn't.'

Libby was silent for a beat. 'Okay,' she agreed slowly. 'Is this about the wedding cake?'

'What?' said Millie.

'If you're feeling overwhelmed about the wedding cake,' said Libby, 'if you don't want to do it, then you don't have to do it. I don't want to make you feel like—'

'No,' Millie said, feeling terrible. Here was Libby, about to be a bride, and sacrificing her own wedding cake to try to make Millie happy. Daniel was right about her: She brought misery to the people who loved her. 'It's not about the wedding cake. Please don't worry about the wedding cake.'

'Honestly,' Libby said earnestly, 'whatever it is, if for any reason the wedding cake is too much right now, you don't have to—'

'It's not,' Millie insisted. 'I'm excited about making the wedding cake.'

'Okay,' Libby relented after a moment. 'Well, good. I'm glad. We asked you because the Victoria sponge was delicious but also we thought it would make you happy. We don't want you to have to—'

'It's fine,' said Millie. 'I am delighted about everything.'

Nothing could be farther from the truth, which Libby clearly saw. 'You're still coming to the wedding tomorrow, right?' said Libby.

It didn't seem likely to Millie, who felt like the weight of going out and pretending to be the Millie these people thought she was was too much for her to handle. She was about to say something hollow, though, designed to appease Libby, when she noticed movement behind Libby, in the deepening darkness across the street, and realised with horror that it was Daniel. *Daniel! Here!* On her *street*! This precious street with its precious people and this precious life she had made for herself. Daniel had come *here*.

Panic rose inside of her again, in that familiar choking wave. Even though she'd been feeling herself that this life was a lie, it had still been protected from Daniel, but now it wasn't even that. Now Daniel was *here* and could—

'I have to go,' Millie blurted out.

'What?' said Libby, blinking.

'Sorry, I have to go,' said Millie, and slammed the door shut and locked it and stood on the other side of it and tried to breathe.

'Did you get to talk to Millie?' Sam said, when Libby came back inside.

Libby was frowning thoughtfully. 'Yes.'

Sam lifted his eyebrows. 'And?'

'I don't know. It was very strange. She was—'

Jack began barking furiously outside. And it wasn't the sort of bark that was just asking to be let in. It was the sort of bark Sam had heard from Jack once before, when he had come outside to find Bill collapsed and near death. So Sam reacted instinctively, shoving past Libby to dive outside.

There was a man pounding on Millie's front door and shouting for Millie. From within her house, Sam could hear Millie shouting for help. Jack, growling and barking at the man, moved up to him, and the man turned and lifted his leg as if to kick him. Jack scurried away, barking even more furiously.

And Sam sized everything up in a heartbeat. Suddenly everything fell into place: why Millie kept to herself, why she'd been hesitant and cautious, why her doors were always locked and her curtains were always drawn, and, most especially, why she'd withdrawn from them today.

Sam walked over to Millie's house and said sharply, 'Oi.'

The man turned and looked at him dismissively. 'Get lost. This is a private matter.'

'I don't think it is,' said Sam.

'Look,' said the man patiently, 'Millie's my—'

'No,' Sam cut him off. 'Millie's *mine*. So maybe you should back off.'

'Really?' sneered the man. 'I don't think so. That photo online didn't have *my wife* smiling with *you*.'

'Oh, no,' Sam heard Pen murmur behind him.

And then Jasper stepped up beside him. 'No. You're right. It was me.'

The man immediately turned his focus to Jasper. 'There you are. What makes you think you have any right to—'

The man lunged at Jasper but Jasper sidestepped him neatly, leaving him staggering off-balance.

'This violence,' Jasper said mildly, 'is completely inappropriate and of great concern to me.'

'Oh,' said the man, breathing hard with obvious rage. 'You think this is *violent*? I haven't even got started.'

Sam stepped in front of the man and said, 'Mate. Take a second. And look around. Because right now this street is full of people, and I highly doubt that you're going to be able to take on all of us. You seem clever. You should walk away.'

The man looked around at all of the neighbours spilled out onto the street.

'Yeah, okay,' the man said haughtily, as if he were not acquiescing at all. 'Okay, fine. I'll go. It's fine. No need to blow this all out of proportion, eh? It's only natural that a man should get upset when another man moves on his wife, you know?'

'I don't think she's your wife,' said Jasper quietly.

'Shows how much you know,' scoffed the man.

'Shows how much you *don't* know,' Jasper countered, in that same calm, quiet tone of voice.

The man stared at him for a long moment, his eyes glittering with fury, and then he backed away, stepping off the stoop and onto the street. He walked past all of the neighbours, keeping his chin raised belligerently, and they all watched him walk all the way up the street. Jack followed behind him, barking as if to say *Good riddance*.

Although the likelihood of that being the last time they saw this man on this street was slim, thought Sam grimly.

Sam turned to Millie's closed door and said, 'Millie? Please let us in. Please. We want to help.'

There was silence from the other side of the door.

Sam said, 'He's gone, but you and I both know it won't be for good, and you and I both know how hard it's going to be for you to keep picking things up and running, so why don't you let us help?'

Millie's voice was muffled behind the door. 'There's nothing you can do. There's nothing anyone can do.'

'That's not true,' Sam said gently. 'It's not. You can let us help. We can help.' Sam paused for a moment, then said, 'I helped my sister get out. I can help you.'

Millie, after a long moment, opened the door. 'How?' she asked. Her eyes were wide and wet and Sam felt terrible.

'By not letting him isolate you,' Sam said. 'By making sure he doesn't isolate you. We're here, and we're going to stay right here.' It was trite, Sam knew. The truth was there was no real way to keep Millie safe. The truth was this was the most dangerous time in Millie's life. But all Sam could do was

327

what he'd done for Ellen, all those years earlier, and just *try to be there as much as possible.*

Jasper said, 'We're all here,' and stepped forward and, telegraphing his intention carefully, enfolded Millie into a hug.

Millie clung tightly, Sam could tell, and Sam was relieved that Jasper gave her that little moment of comfort.

'You can't possibly sleep in the house on your own,' said Pen.

They were all at Diya's house, because everyone had insisted they go to Diya's house, even though Millie really, really didn't want to be around people.

But she also really, really didn't want to be alone. So, on balance, she relented to going to Diya's house, and Diya thrust a cup of tea at her, and it was nice to have her hands around something warm, she felt very cold.

'I'm fine,' said Millie, even though she obviously wasn't fine, but she didn't like the way everyone was looking at her like she wasn't fine.

'You're perfect,' Jasper said. 'It's him I'm worried about.'

You're perfect. The words echoed in Millie's head, and she looked at him, feeling abruptly teary, which was horrifying, she didn't want to *cry* in front of all of her neighbours, this evening had been humiliating enough without adding that to it.

'I'm sorry,' Millie said, wiping at her tears with a furious fierceness.

'For what?' asked Libby calmly.

'I should have told you,' Millie said. 'You've all been so nice and . . .'

'Millie,' Pen said gently. 'You've done nothing wrong here. You know that, right? Absolutely nothing wrong.'

Which didn't help Millie's tearful state.

'You can stay at our house,' Sam announced.

'No, no.' Millie shook her head, wiping at more tears. 'It's the night before your wedding.'

'You can stay here,' said Diya.

'You can stay at any house on the street,' said Pen staunchly. 'Sure, mine is half a construction zone, but you can stay there.'

'I think she should stay at her own house,' Jasper interjected suddenly. 'I think – I think I don't want her to feel like she has to run again.' Jasper looked straight at Millie, his eyes dark and intent. 'You should get your life on your terms. He's had his terms for too long.'

'She can't stay there alone,' Anna insisted.

'No,' Marcel agreed. 'I'll stay.'

'Me, too,' said Arthur.

'I'll stay, too,' said Jasper.

'We'll all stay,' said Darsh.

'I'll stay, too,' grumbled Bill, and he sounded grudging about it but Millie knew he meant it.

'Not you, though, Sam,' Marcel said. 'It's your wedding eve. You should go home.'

'I don't even know if there's room for everyone,' Millie said. 'I mean, I know there's not, there's no reason—'

'You're not alone,' Jasper said. 'And we're going to make sure you know that.'

'The fact that we need to make sure that he knows it, too, is a bonus,' said Arthur.

Sam and Libby crawled into bed together the night before their wedding.

'Should we be superstitious about this?' Libby asked.

Sam was already yawning into the pillow. 'Do you want me to sleep on the sofa?'

'No, I want you sleep right here with me,' Libby said, curling into him. 'On tonight of all nights, I want you here with me.'

'Yeah,' Sam said. 'Agreed. To hell with superstition. We've done okay without them so far.'

'Yeah,' Libby said. There was a moment of silence, and then Libby ventured, 'We don't have to talk about this if you don't want to, especially not tonight. But how did you know what would make that man walk away?'

Sam was silent for a long time. And then he said, 'Ellen's ex-husband wasn't a great person,' and left it at that.

Millie's house had been empty for so long that it felt odd to have all these people in it. Then again, Millie's *life* had been empty for so long, and now she had all these people in it, and it felt . . . odd. But in a good way.

'I don't even have enough pillows,' said Millie, fretting. 'I think I might have just enough blankets.'

'It's fine,' said Marcel. 'We're fine.'

'Can I get any of you anything to eat? Or drink? Or something?' asked Millie.

'Don't worry about us,' said Darsh. 'Just get some sleep. Or try to, at least. We have a big day tomorrow.'

'Oh,' said Millie. She kept remembering the wedding was tomorrow with a little start. 'You're right. We do.' Instead of going to bed, Millie went into the kitchen and contemplated the ingredients for the cake.

Jasper entered the kitchen with slow deliberateness, watching her warily like she might spook and run away.

'I'm okay,' Millie said, and smiled for his benefit.

'You don't have to smile for my benefit,' Jasper said.

Which made Millie laugh.

Jasper said, smiling but looking bewildered, 'What?'

'Nothing.' Millie shook her head, because it was impossible to explain the maelstrom of emotion running through her.

'It's also okay not to be okay,' Jasper said. 'I just wanted to make sure that you knew that.'

'I know,' said Millie, and felt dangerously close to tears again, and concentrated on looking at her ingredients again. Then she said suddenly, 'His name was Daniel, and I thought I was in love with him.' She looked at Jasper, who was looking at her evenly, without judgement or pity, just like she was ... telling him a story. 'So I married him. I probably should have realised ... but I married him.'

'It wasn't your fault,' Jasper said again. 'It was entirely his fault. You know that, right? It was nothing you did. And I think you're amazing, and extraordinary, to have built this life you've made for yourself here and to have been so fierce and single-minded about it. You're incredible.'

Millie contemplated what to say. She thought of Daniel, over and over telling her the opposite, and thought, *I could get used to being told I'm incredible.*

She smiled at Jasper, and Jasper smiled back, and they just stood there, smiling.

Eventually Millie said, 'I'm supposed to bake Sam and Libby's wedding cake.'

'I'll help you do it in the morning,' Jasper promised.

'Obviously Bill can't sleep on the floor,' Marcel said, once Millie had gone up to bed.

'Why not?' demanded Bill, indignant.

They all looked at him.

Bill relented by waving his hand around.

'You don't need to be here at all,' Darsh said.

'Of course I have to be here. I'm not letting that miscreant think Christmas Street is a place where he can get away with that balderdash.'

'Miscreant,' echoed Arthur. 'Balderdash. Those are great words.' Arthur put a deck of cards out on the coffee table and said, 'And I come with a gift from Max. Who's up for some poker?'

They sat up, by tacit agreement, playing poker, until Arthur looked up suddenly. 'Did you hear something?' he murmured.

The other men all agreed, nodding their heads silently.

'Call the police,' Arthur whispered, and stood to creep into

332

the kitchen, to the back door of the house, which was all locked up but yes, there was definitely a scuffling on the other side of it.

Arthur was going to feel like an idiot if it was nothing but the Pachutas' cats getting out for the night or an intrepid fox or something. He glanced behind him at the rest, who were clearly prepared to serve as his back-up, and then he reached out and opened the door quickly and grabbed.

The man struggled but Arthur kept an iron grip on him and then everyone else descended upon him as well. He threw a couple of punches, one that Marcel dodged and one that Arthur couldn't dodge without letting go of the man, although he tried to duck his head out of the way so that the blow along his cheek was only glancing. He did loosen his grip a bit and the man tried to squirm away but Darsh rugby-tackled him and between them all they managed to drag him into the kitchen, subdued.

'We've already called the police,' remarked Arthur, 'and they're on their way, but we also thought you should know that Millie lives on Christmas Street now, and she's happy here, and we're all going to make sure of it.'

'Consider us,' said Marcel loftily, 'better than a restraining order.'

Even if Millie had been sleeping, she would have been woken by the altercation downstairs, and then woken again when the police arrived. But she wasn't sleeping to begin with. So she was awake to give a statement to the police and she only trembled a little bit during it.

When it was over, she sent all of the men in her house a smiling, tremulous thank-you. With Daniel now in police custody, they were dispersing to their homes, but Jasper stayed. He didn't even say anything. He just sprawled out on the sofa and pulled the blanket up over his head and just ... stayed.

Millie went back to her bedroom and crawled into bed and looked up at the ceiling and thought, *Tomorrow, in the morning, you'll wake up and you'll bake a wedding cake.* And she no longer felt conflicted toward it. She felt like baking a wedding cake for the people on this street was the best thing she would ever do in her life.

And then she finally fell asleep.

Chapter 23

*We are all of us so honoured to share in the
love story of Sam and Libby. In fact, I venture
to say it is also our love story, in that it is part
of the fabric of our street, part of what binds us
together. Sam and Libby love each other, and we
love Sam and Libby.*

Sam and Libby were married under an arch built and decorated by all of their neighbours, and it was the most beautiful
wedding they could have imagined. Pari tossed her jasmine
and Jack walked the rings down the aisle, following Pari
and stopping at Teddy, next to Sam at the front, just as they'd
trained him. Arthur officiated with a beautiful heartfelt paean
to marriage as a wonderful institution, and the fact that he
boasted a bit of a black eye didn't detract from his message of
love at all. Although it was frosty outside, Sam felt warm with
love, which was a ridiculous thing to think but was true. He
and Libby kissed under the arch, and Arthur presented them
to all of their friends and family crowded onto the pavement,
and Sam thought, *Married. We're married.*

The Amazing Spiders had learned Christmas carols for the

occasion, and played a steady stream of them sprinkled with 'old people' love songs, and Sam and Libby and their guests sat under blankets when they weren't dancing and ate Diya's delicious food and read Pen's beautiful write-up tribute to their love.

Rebecca came over to them and said warmly to Sam, 'Welcome to the family,' and kissed his cheek. Then she leaned away and looked him seriously in the eye and said, 'I'm so happy to have you part of it.' Then she turned to Teddy, sitting next to them. 'Same to you,' she said, and kissed his cheek as well.

'Thank you,' Sam replied. 'And we're happy to have you as part of our family, too.'

'Yeah,' Teddy agreed.

Rebecca looked at Jack, who was sitting contentedly next to Teddy, and said, 'How about it, Jack? Are we friends now?'

Jack barked and solemnly offered his paw.

Rebecca laughed and shook it.

Max, with an arm flung over the back of Arthur's chair, pressed his nose behind Arthur's ear and said, 'You were the sexiest officiant to ever officiate a wedding.'

'Oh, stop it,' Arthur said good-naturedly, watching Charlie cling to his chair for balance and look longingly at the dance floor, which was full of teenagers at the moment.

'I'm serious,' said Max.

Arthur glanced at him. 'Yeah, but you always think I'm the sexiest whatever to whatever.'

Max grinned. 'That's true. Look at you, that doesn't even impress you any more. You are unimpressed. You're so spoiled by compliments. I have to come up with something better.'

'Well,' said Arthur, dimpling at him, 'if you want to strive to come up with even more amazing compliments to give me, I won't protest.'

Max laughed. 'I think it was the black eye. It made you look very rakish. Does it hurt?' Max peered closely at it, not touching.

Arthur shook his head.

Max, looking satisfied Arthur wasn't in pain, turned his attention briefly to Charlie.

Arthur said softly, 'Hey,' and reached out to close a hand lightly around Max's tie, just enough to make him pay attention. 'When we got married.'

'Yeah?' said Max.

'I thought it was going to be the happiest day of my life. But it turned out to just be the beginning of them. And I just want to make sure that you know that. And that I hope it's been the same for you.'

Max after a moment leaned forward to kiss him lightly. 'Yes. It has been.'

'We've been dads for a year now,' Arthur remarked.

'We have.'

'I think we're doing a good job,' said Arthur, preening a little.

'Do you?' Max looked openly amused. 'And your standards are so high, so we *must* be doing a good job.'

'Don't you agree?'

'No, I think we're doing a *fantastic* job. Look at him.'

They both turned to admire their son . . . which meant they

got to be watching him when he took his first hesitant step forward. He collapsed to the ground almost immediately afterward, looking affronted at how that had worked out, but it was a start. It was a literal *first step*.

Arthur and Max looked at each other, amazed.

'Did you just see . . . ?' said Arthur.

'Charlie!' Max exclaimed. 'You just took a step!'

Charlie gave him an unimpressed look.

'Unimpressed,' said Max. 'Just like your dad.'

'Hey,' Sai said, coming over to them, slightly breathless from dancing. 'What's up?'

'Charlie just took his first step!' Max enthused.

'Whoa,' said Sai, and leaned down to give Charlie a tiny high-five. 'Well done, Charlie!' Then he straightened and looked back at Max and Arthur. 'I thought I'd offer to watch Charlie for a bit. It's a slow song.' Sai gestured to the dance-floor, where Sam and Libby and Darsh and Diya and Anna and Marcel were all swaying to the beat.

'Thank you for the offer, Sai, we are happily accepting it,' said Max, and dragged Arthur out there with him.

With all of the couples firmly ensconced on the dancefloor, Rebecca sought out Millie and sat beside her.

'I wanted you to know,' she said, 'that your wedding cake was a triumph. You're an excellent baker.'

Millie smiled. 'Thanks. I did a lot of it, at one point in time. And I guess I got good at it.'

'Do you enjoy it?' asked Rebecca.

'Very much,' Millie answered.

'I thought so. You can taste it in the cake. Anyway, you should think about that. It's a talent you have. And talents are made to be shared with the world.'

Millie had literally never thought about that before. She'd never thought of herself having *talent* before. She marvelled for a moment. 'That's so nice,' she said finally. 'That's so incredibly nice of you to say.'

Rebecca said, 'Well, I decided I ought to be incredibly nice to try to make up for how wretched I had been. But I'm also telling you the truth.'

And that was when Bill came over.

'I don't want to make a big production out of it,' he said to Rebecca, sounding miserable about it, 'but would you like to dance?'

A wide smile spread over Rebecca's face. 'Actually, I'd love to.' She glanced at Millie. 'Do you mind?'

'Go right ahead,' Millie smiled, and shooed them away with a gesture, and then watched them settle onto the dancefloor.

And then Jasper said from behind her, 'I've been working up the nerve all night to ask you to dance. I can't believe Bill beat me to it.'

Millie turned and smiled at him and said honestly, 'I'd be delighted.'

It had been a long time since she had danced with a man. It wasn't like she and Daniel had gone dancing much, or even been to many weddings. Millie was realising that her life with Daniel had deliberately isolated her from so many people, probably so she wouldn't see that people were wonderful.

339

Millie knew that it wasn't *all* people who were wonderful – she knew that very, very well – but there was a high percentage of them, and she'd found the best street of them.

Millie said, 'I feel like you've been waiting for me a long time.'

'I'd wait longer,' Jasper said, one corner of his mouth tipped up at her.

'You might have to,' Millie admitted. 'I feel like I'm just starting to determine who I actually am. I feel like maybe I've never really known.'

Jasper said, 'I want to give you all the time and space in the world to find that out. Because I have a rather good impression of the person you are, and she's amazing. You want to get to know that person.'

'I can't believe how much you seem to think that,' Millie said. 'It's incredible to me every time you say it.'

'Then,' replied Jasper, 'I'm going to have to keep saying it, until you believe me.'

'It might take a while,' Millie admitted tremulously, because she still wasn't exactly good at thinking nice things about herself. She'd had too many years of not being allowed to think anything of the sort.

'That's all right,' Jasper said. 'Because that just means I'll have to stay around a while, telling you how amazing you are.' Jasper's smile kept getting wider and wider and sweeter and sweeter and Millie felt that he was so lovely she might not be able to bear it.

Or maybe she could learn how to bear something so wonderful. Maybe she could start learning how to bear it right now.

'This will suit me just fine,' Jasper continued. 'I'm very happy to keep saying you're amazing.'

Millie pondered how to handle something as wonderful as Jasper, and came to only one conclusion:

She kissed him.

'Well,' said Sam, as the night was winding down, as they were all helping to pick up after their wedding party. 'Do you think you Made a Difference?'

Teddy and Pari, stacking paper plates to toss in the bin, both looked thoughtful.

'Well,' Pari said eventually. 'We got you married, so yes, I think that's a Difference.'

'You're right,' Sam agreed, 'I couldn't have done it without your help. And now I think it's bedtime. Father Christmas still comes tomorrow.'

They all wished each other a good night, and Sam walked upstairs to change out of wedding clothes and get Teddy settled.

'Dad,' Teddy said, as he got into bed.

'Yeah,' said Sam, pulling the blanket up over him.

'Is Father Christmas real?'

'What sort of question is that?' asked Sam, and kissed Teddy's forehead. Then he said, 'I'm just making sure, but are you happy?'

'You mean, now that you and Libby are married?' Teddy already sounded sleepy.

'Yeah.'

'Yeah. I'm really happy.' Teddy gave him a lopsided smile.

Sam thought Teddy was sleeping before he even exited his

room, which was good, because there was still much to do that night.

But all of it went out of his head when he saw Libby, curled up on the sofa regarding the soft twinkling lights of their Christmas tree.

'Hey,' Sam said. 'Mind if I join you?'

Libby grinned at him. 'I was hoping you would.'

He sank onto the sofa next to her and she cuddled up against him and they were companionably silent for a long while. 'I'm so happy we did it like this,' said Sam. 'I'm so happy we stayed home, and did it quickly, and just focused on it being about us and the people we love.'

'Yeah,' said Libby. 'And I'm glad we did it on Christmas Eve. Our own little moment of light in the middle of the long, dark winter. We can look forward to it every year.'

'That's lovely,' said Sam. 'That's a lovely way to put it. Happy wedding, happy Christmas.'

'Same to you,' said Libby, and kissed him.

The clocks struck midnight all around them, bells pealing through the air. Midnight on Christmas Eve, and Sam thought he could almost hear sleigh bells in the distance. How silly Teddy's question had been, Sam thought. Obviously the magic of Christmas was real.

Epilogue

On Christmas Street, time keeps passing. Charlie gets better at walking, Libby and Sam plan a honeymoon, and Jasper finds many excellent reasons to spend more time on the street. Emilia's band improves, and so do Sai's grades, and Pen finds even more random new trends to share with her street.

Jack doesn't think about the passage of time, though. Jack just thinks about how every door on the street has a friendly face, ready to greet him with a head scratch and a biscuit if he's really lucky.

And just like that, new relationships become married couples, and babies become toddlers, and children grow older, and new neighbours become old friends. And, on Christmas Street, they throw lots of parties.

Jack remains a very lucky dog.

Acknowledgements

As usual, I have a small army of people to thank, including:

Maddie West, Thalia Proctor, and the entire team at Little, Brown UK, for being so kind and welcoming and nurturing to this little sequel;

My agent Andrea Somberg, for being incredibly supportive throughout;

Sonja L. Cohen, for once again putting up with me writing all over the place instead of hanging out;

Larry Stritof, for all the continued tech support;

Kristin Gillespie, Erin McCormick, Jennifer Roberson, and Noel Wiedner, for witty conversation;

Aja Romano, for cheerleading through lots of whining;

Everyone on the internet who restored my faith in humanity (thanks for existing!);

NBC's Olympics broadcast, for having so many commercials that I was literally able to write an entire novel during them;

And, as ever, Mom, Dad, Ma, Megan, Caitlin, Bobby, Jeff, Jordan, Isabella, Gabriella and Audrey, for being the best family anyone could ever hope for. I love you.

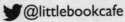